D1233759

Eye of Newt

***Other Five Star Titles
by Denise Dietz:***

Hallie's Comet

Eye of Newt

Denise Dietz

Five Star • Waterville, Maine

First Edition
First Printing: October 2004

Published in 2004 in conjunction with
Tekno Books and Ed Gorman.

Set in 11 pt. Plantin by Al Chase.

Printed in the United States on permanent paper.

Library of Congress Cataloging-in-Publication Data

Dietz, Denise.
  Eye of newt / Denise Dietz—1st ed. Five Star Mystery
  Published: Waterville, Me. : Five Star, 2004.
    p. cm.
  ISBN: 1-59414-096-0 (hc : alk. paper)
  Subjects: 1. Rock musicians—Crimes against—Fiction.
2. Women detectives—Colorado—Fiction.   3. Salem (Mass.)—
Fiction.   4. Herbalists—Fiction.   5. Colorado—Fiction.
6. Witches—Fiction.   7. Amnesia—Fiction.   8. Mystery fiction.
I. Title.
  PS3554.I368E94 2004
  813'.54—dc22   2004053706

Dedication

This book is dedicated to librarians . . .
with affection and gratitude.

2 Witch:
Fillet of fenny snake,
In the cauldron boil and bake
Eye of newt and toe of frog,
Wool of bat and tongue of dog.
Adder's fork and blind-worm's sting,
Lizard's leg and howlet's wing,
For a charm of powerful trouble,
Like a hell-broth boil and bubble.

—Shakespeare, *Macbeth*

Manitou Falls

Sydney St. Charles: a witch who doesn't believe she's a witch
Oliver St. Charles: Sydney's brother, an ex cop and a best-selling author of "cop fiction"
David St. Charles: Sydney's brother, a "Wizard-With-A-Webpage"
Aunt Lillian: Sydney's great-aunt, who has a "checkered past" and a modern outlook on sex that would send the family value people into a tailspin
Xanthia St. Charles: Sydney's niece
Megan, Natasha, Ashley: Xanthia's best friends
Tommy Murphy: Sydney's imaginary chum
Augusta (Gusta) Lowenfeld: a snoopy gossip
Terey Lowenfeld: Gusta's daughter.
"John Elway": an attractive amnesiac
Mary Lou Dinardo: an elderly ogress
Paulie "The Pimple" Dinardo: Mary Lou's son.
Martina Brustein: a romance author; Paulie's fiancé
Lynn Whitacre: Sydney's pretty neighbor
Susan Partridge: a bank teller with an attitude
Jessica Whitney St. Charles: Oliver's wife
Carol Rodrigues St. Charles: Oliver's ex-wife
Veronica Whitney Sanderson: Jessica's sister, manager of The Newts
Yogi Demon (Nee Yogi Berra Brustein): lead singer of The Newts
Tiffany: a magenta-haired yogi demon groupie
Rosie All-Fall-Down: a Vegas chorus girl

Harlan: a chauffeur
Manny Glick: a motel desk clerk and part-time usher
Annie: a cat, supposedly Sydney's "familiar"
Mercy: a parrot, supposedly Sydney's "familiar"
Chasdick: a yellow Labrador retriever, supposedly Sydney's "familiar"

1692 Salem:

Anne Kittridge: a witch who perches on Sydney's family tree
Mercy Birdwell: Anne's sister
Chastity Barker: Anne's sister, author of the 1692 family journal
Obadiah Barker: Chastity's husband
Old Scratch: Obadiah's dog
Yosef Solom: a puritanical puritan
Ketzia Van Rijn: a Salem village spinster
Trump: a servant
Dog: Trump's dog
Sally: a servant
Jack Grayson: Chastity's secret lover
Matthew (Matt) Grayson: Jack's twin brother
Rueben Cavin: Chastity's neighbor
Jonathan Corwin: a magistrate

Salem Village

10 June, 1692

Bridget Bishop danced, though dancing was forbidden. In death she cared naught for the laws of the Church, much less for her neighbours' opinions.

Several people craned their necks, straining to see if Bridget would turn herself into a black pig. But the witch-woman merely flaunted her macabre dance, her sway aided by a whistling wind.

During Bridget's trial, John Gedney had testified that she had no substance. "I endeavored to clap my hands upon her and said, 'You devil, I will kill you,' but could feel no substance," John testified. "Whereupon I struck at her with a stick and broke the stick but felt no substance."

Lies, all lies, thought Anne Kittridge. Because Bridget was unquestionably flesh and blood. If she truly lacked substance, would she not have vanished into thin air before they tied the rope around her neck?

Anne drew her gaze away from Gallows Hill and focused, instead, upon a secluded pasture. Four and a half months with child, she had pleaded a backache, but her ruse proved unsuccessful when the Reverend resolutely insisted that every woman in his congregation attend the hanging. Men burdened with chores had been granted leave, the reason why her beloved John was absent.

Fence shadows had begun to lengthen across a dun-colored road and the setting sun deepened the adjacent hills to amethyst. Somewhere, a shepherd piped a homing tune to his flock. A dog joined in, its condemnatory bark louder than the piper or the bleating sheep.

In close proximity, Anne heard snatches of conversation. Stemming from three or four different directions, the disjointed sentences converged upon her ears like claps of distant thunder.

"Dorcas Good, five years old, has a familiar . . ."

"Isaac Cummings' sick mare was ridden all night by witches . . ."

"A small snake that sucks at her forefinger . . ."

"Isaac lit the mare's fart . . ."

"Reverend Parris preached on John 6, 70 . . ."

"Dorcas Good's finger has a red spot the bigness of a flea bite . . ."

"Reverend Parris had in mind Rebecca Nurse . . ."

"Tituba Indian swore the devil bid her serve him . . ."

"The child's mother, Sarah Good, has a cat and a yellow bird and a thing with wings and two legs and a head like a woman . . ."

"Is it not difficult to catch a witch? Satan is the Prince of Lies . . ."

"Isaac said he'd rather ha' a dead mare than a burnt barn . . ."

"When ye seek a witch, look for evidence of malice . . ."

Anne wished she could stop up her ears, especially when she spied Sally, her sister's sluggish maidservant, with two other girls. Their voices rode the wind.

"Oi seen a werelion last noight," Sally said. "Atop the ridge."

"Ye means a werewolf," said the second girl.

"Nay. Oi seen a werelion."

"Mayhap 'twas a ghost to witch us off the land."

"Forfend 'twasn't ould Satan hisself," said the third girl.

"In the ould country," said the second girl, "oi seen a man

what et children. He'd cotch a poor mite, hang 'im on the wall like a strung-up fowl, an plunge a dagger through 'is heart. The man done it to please the devil."

"After I seen the werelion, me grannie cotched a toad an put 'im in a cage an dragged 'im round the church three toimes an buried 'im near the graves . . ."

Sally's voice trailed off as she drew her companions closer to the gallows.

Anne grimaced. A werelion? What next? A weresheep? A werespider?

"Goody Bishop bewitched her first husband to death."

Anne turned toward Yosef Solom, a stout man whose voice would put a loon to shame. " 'Tis nothing more than a rumour," she said.

" 'The devil did come bodily unto her,' " Yosef shrilled, " 'and she was familiar with the devil, and she sat up all night long with the devil.' So says Bridget Bishop's third husband, Edward Bishop."

A Dutch woman, Ketzia van Rijn, said, "God allemachtig, Bridget oft vears a red stomacher! Does that not prove she's a vitch?"

"Red is not uncommon," Anne said, "and stomachers can be easily dyed."

"The dyer, Samuel Shattuck, says Bridget brought him sundry pieces of lace, so short he could not judge them fit for use. Everyone knows that a vitch doll is oft clothed in the same materials and colors as clothing vorn by her victims."

"Samuel Shattuck carries a grudge," Anne said earnestly. "His son was unaccountably ill of fits. A passing stranger proposed the boy was bewitched and offered to take him to Bridget and scratch her face."

"Aye. Drawing blood from a vitch's face can break a spell."

"Bridget said she was not a witch and chased the stranger off with a spade."

"And ever since, the child hath been followed with grievous fits, his head and eyes drawn aside as if they would ne'er come to rights no more . . ." Yosef paused to sleeve the perspiration from his forehead. "He'll fall into fire and water, if he be not constantly looked to. Bridget Bishop did not have her face scratched, but she scratched the face of Samuel Shattuck's son."

With an effort, Anne kept her hands by her side, sorely tempted to scratch Yosef's face. " 'Twas only Samuel's word that his son was branded."

Beneath the three stiff white caps that concealed her hair, Ketzia's cheeks glistened and her under lip thrust out. "Nay," she said. " 'Tis the judgment of doctors that the boy doth suffer the evil hand of vitchcraft."

Anne heard a disappointed murmur hum through the commons. The mob had honestly believed Bridget Bishop would turn herself into a pig. Or a monkey with cock's feet and claws. Anne's eyes, usually serene, burned with unshed tears.

Looking toward her sisters, she saw that Chastity's eyes were red-streaked and puffy. Mercy had bitten her bottom lip until she drew blood. Capturing their attention, Anne crossed her second finger over her first finger, held up seven fingers, pressed her thumbs together, and waggled her fingers.

Mercy and Chastity nodded. Both understood Anne's silent signal. On the morrow, following cock crow, they would convene alongside the round-tiled roof of the Kittridge dovecote.

Gazing one last time upon the gallows, Anne felt her own throat constrict. Bridget had been brought to trial on June second. At her trial, several girls told how Bridget's specter had tormented them. Several men stated that Bridget's shape had appeared to them in the night and climbed into bed with them.

Bridget had entered a plea of innocence but the Reverend said: "I believe she practiseth Witchcraft in the Congregation," and the court found her guilty.

Guilty. Sinful. Unholy. Anne felt a chill course through her body. Admired for her medicinal skill, she had accrued no malicious gossip. Neither had her sisters, Mercy Birdwell and Chastity Barker. Wed to proud, prosperous, religious men, they had dodged the accusations leveled against less favoured goodwives.

When household chores were completed, or in Chastity's situation bypassed, Anne and her sisters met inside a bell-shaped cave.

There, they practiced witchcraft.

Chapter One

Friday morning

My childhood chum, Tommy Murphy, once said: "Never do anything you wouldn't be caught dead doing."

Friday the thirteenth was a Murphy's Law kind of day.

Invisible to everyone except me, Tommy Murphy is the spittin' image of Gene Kelly. More often than not, I can feel Tommy's presence, or at least hear the echo of his tap shoes. I've never told anybody about Tommy, not even my great-aunt Lillian. She'd say she could materialize a Gene Kelly look-alike, but she tends to screw up incantations. In fact, I'm not sure she's successfully cast a spell since nineteen-sixty-something. So Gene Kelly might very well come out looking like Liberace. Or Kermit the Frog.

Supposedly, I'm descended from a long line of witches, some good, some bad. To my knowledge, none materialized inside a bubble, none ruled Munchkins, none gave orders to flying monkeys, and none polluted the air with smoke or broom straw. The majority of my ancestors traveled from Europe to Massachusetts via conventional means. In other words, they shipped themselves.

Seventeenth-century men and women didn't practice birth control. Therefore, the prolific members of my New World family spawned multiple progeny, the majority of whom were male. Still, the family allegedly birthed at least one witch per generation. I'm the nominee for this generation.

I own Lilly's Apothecary, and witchy gossip is good for business. While I don't believe for one moment that I'm a

17

witch, if people want to pay big bucks for a spell or medicinal herb why argue with them? The IRS allows me to deduct eye of newt, magic potions, and prickly plants steeped in honey, guaranteed to protect against hostility and drive out all diseases. Those are business expenses. I wonder if the IRS would be so compliant if they knew I didn't believe in magic.

I've got to hand it to my great-aunt Lillian, who tried her best to make me a good little witch. While other kids chanted their ABCs, I memorized incantations. While other little girls groomed Barbie and Ken, I stuck pins into nameless rag dolls. I even toted Aunt Lillian's black goat, Tituba, to Show and Tell. As I earnestly explained the history of "familiars," Tituba suffered stage fright, pooped all over the classroom floor, and ate our spelling tests. To this day, I think my teacher's reaction was unwarranted.

Shortly thereafter, my family (minus Tituba) moved to Colorado and I learned to keep my mouth shut. Still, rumors surfaced. "Sydney's ancestors were wiped out, burned at Salem," the kids whispered loudly.

First, if my ancestors had been "wiped out," I wouldn't be here. Second, Salem witches were usually hanged, not burned. Third, it's common knowledge that no witchcraft was practiced in 1692 Massachusetts, that the behavior of the afflicted, including their convulsive fits, was fraudulent, and that the witch accusers were encouraged by the clergy, who used the fear of witchcraft to bolster their power.

My father, Nicholas Nickleby St. Charles III, always said that witchcraft did exist and was widely practiced in seventeenth-century New England. However, it worked then, as it works now, through psychogenic rather than occult means, producing hysterical symptoms. The witch accusers, Nicholas said, were not fraudulent. They were pathological.

I tend to side with my father. Take Elvis. His fanatics

reached a state of mass hysteria, despite dire warnings from parents and clergy. Elvis possessed more power than a dozen priests put together, and his pelvis could generate more hysteria than a whole coven of witches.

Which brings me, in a round-about way, to the murder of Clive Newton.

Chapter Two

Friday morning

Never do anything you wouldn't be caught dead doing.

Ignoring Tommy Murphy's advice, I hurriedly grabbed some rumpled clothes from my hamper, brushed off my hairbrush, and shunned all makeup.

My great-aunt Lillian would never step outside the house unless she was coordinated, and I don't mean to suggest that her pointy hat matched her pointy shoes. Except for Disney films, Casper cartoons, and poorly directed Macbeth productions, witches tend to look like everyone else. *Bewitched* is a good example of a normal, everyday witch, if you exclude the nose-twitching. Witches don't nose-twitch.

I hadn't even bothered to shave my legs, which poked out from a pair of cutoffs that had once been bell-bottoms. Since I'm not real good with scissors, the faded denim molded my right buttock and kitty-cornered my left buttock. My rubber flip-flops flip-flopped through the aisle of a Colorado Springs Safeway. Rapidly stocking my supermarket cart, I spied Augusta Lowenfeld. She swept by me like the prow on a ship, then did an about-face. In a voice that made the fillings in my teeth ache, she said, "Sydney St. Charles, as I live and breathe! Have you heard the latest news about the murder?"

Gusta talks in exclamation points and question marks. Fifty-six, she tries to look forty-six. During a power failure she almost succeeds.

"What murder?" I said, knowing that Gusta writes a gossip column for the *Manitou Falls Monthly* and is usually a month behind.

"Clive Newton, of course! He's a local boy!"

Well . . . not exactly. Before his untimely demise, Clive lived in Colorado Springs, next door to Manitou Springs. Manitou Falls is nestled between Manitou Springs and Green Mountain Falls, so "local" is stretching it.

I had heard about Clive's death. Who hadn't? A young star on the brink of making it Jim-Morrison-big, his body had been found in Black Forest, a residential area that's zoned for horses. In fact, Clive's body and head—minus ears, testicles, fingers, and toes—had been discovered one month ago, immediately following the February issue of the *Manitou Falls Monthly*. So I could be polite and let Gusta ramble on about the murder, or I could be rude and finish my grocery shopping.

"I saw the news on TV," I said, compromising. "All the local channels carried it. Then Denver picked up the story, then CNN, then *Dateline* and—"

"Does your mother know you go out in public like that?" Gusta examined me, her thickly-penciled eyebrows merging, and I made a silent vow to lose the fifteen (or twenty) pounds I'd vowed to lose last New Year's Eve. "You're how old now, Sydney? Forty?"

"Thirty-five," I blurted, stung. Trying to regain my composure, I reminded her that my mother had passed away.

Her thin-lipped smile of satisfaction vanished as she said, "If you've got lemons, make lemonade!"

"Excuse me?"

"Have you heard about the latest body part?"

My mind hop-scotched from lemonade to Clive Newton. The killer had been mailing the missing portions of Clive's body to members of his singing group, The Newts, although no one, including the Colorado Springs Police Department, could fathom why. The last gift, a big toe, had been soaked in formaldehyde.

Gusta's scornful glower had pin-pointed my crotch so my first thought was: *testicles. Someone priority-mailed Clive's testicles.*

My second thought was to wonder if Gusta's glare had merely encompassed my cutoffs. The shorts were skin-tight and I had shunned panties along with my makeup.

"Did they mail Clive's testicles, Mrs. Lowenfeld?"

"Sydney St. Charles! Don't talk dirty!" She smoothed the black lace at her sagging chin line, then tiddly-winked a piece of lint from her black pedal pushers. "They mailed . . ." She paused for effect. "His ring finger!"

"Did it happen to have a ring on it?"

"Yes! Rampart High!"

Ashamed of my sarcasm, I remembered that Clive had graduated from Rampart a mere three years ago. Luckily, Old Ed Vernon turned the corner and propelled his squeaky cart toward us. After lecherously staring at my blouse, missing its top three buttons, he said, "Is it true the killer mailed a finger?"

Gusta's face lit up, and I surmised the frozen chicken in her basket would saturate its Styrofoam with bloody rime before she finished her recitation.

As unobtrusively as possible, I maneuvered my cart around Gusta and Ed, then navigated the rest of the aisle. Parallel to Meat, traveling toward Dairy, I bumped into half a dozen Manitou Falls taxpayers. After appraising my tangled ebony curls, the smudges beneath my blue-black eyes, my uneven cutoffs, and my rubber flip-flops, they all told me about Clive Newton's ring finger.

The unspoken question was: *Can you devise a spell to catch the killer, Sydney?*

The unspoken answer was: *No.*

Soon my cart overflowed with the items I planned to serve at my niece's birthday party. Plus, "impulse groceries." Goodies included pretzels and doodles, various chips and dips, eggs for deviling, and Coke/Pepsi. Also, economy-size Ocean Spray juices. Condiments. Detergent. Furniture polish. Bacon. The latest Dean Koontz bestseller (with Kevin Bacon on the cover). Frozen waffles. Bagels and cream cheese. Three tubs of ice cream. A box of cake batter, a can of white frosting, and a jar of green food coloring.

My niece Xanthia, who will turn thirteen this Sunday, collects frogs. So I thought I'd bake a frog-shaped cake with green frosting and serve it with pistachio ice cream. This morning I had considered hiring a magician, but the supermarket receipt, almost as long as my arm, negated that scheme.

My Honda's trunk was filled with cartons of clay storage pots, ordered from a local pottery. Haphazardly stacking my groceries on the back seat and floorboards, I hoped I wasn't breaking any eggs.

A couple of women, beautifully dressed and rouged and coifed, click-heeled past me. I had met Pam and Deb at a local romance writers' session, after accepting an invitation to give a talk on witches. My great-aunt Lillian, who lives with me, said a Merlinesque dissertation (her words, not mine) would be good for business.

Halting momentarily, the two romance authors surveyed my hairdo, my cosmetic-free face, and my tacky outfit, all the way down to my flip-flops. Then they nodded hello and continued clicking. I smelled Deb's potent perfume, heard the words "a shame," and wished I had taken the time to safety-pin my gaping bodice. Or at least spray myself with cologne.

Never wreck your car unless you're wearing clean underpants. Translation: Never do anything you wouldn't be caught dead doing. So far, I had encountered the town gossip, the town lecher, a slew of chatty acquaintances, and two high-heeled advertisements for a torrid romance novel. Thank God my Murphy's Law day was almost over.

My stressed-out shoulders sought my car's fake-fur seat cover as I buckled my seat belt, turned on the radio, started up the engine, cruised through the parking lot, and just missed the light at the Safeway exit. A watched pot never boils and a watched red light never changes, so my gaze strayed, catching the avid gaze of the homeless man who stood near my car. I wanted to look away but was mesmerized by a pair of intense indigo eyes.

Did Deb's "a shame" refer to the homeless man?

He looked part Irish, part American Indian; Daniel Day Lewis and Tonto. The strap of a shabby guitar case was slung across one shoulder. Clothed in too-short, oversized jeans, held up by a pair of red suspenders, his long russet hair was neatly trapped by a beaded headband and three buttons on his once-white shirt were missing. Although he possessed a furry chest, rather than bra and breasts, his shirt-gaffe duplicated mine, and I experienced a moment of genuine empathy.

Before I could look away, he glimpsed the expression on my face. Thrusting forth his WILL WORK FOR FOOD sign, he smiled.

I had never seen a vagrant with such perfect incisors, not to mention canines and bicuspids. He could star in a toothpaste commercial. Or the late-night infomercial that promises bleached teeth.

Damn. Here I sat, grocery sacks threatening to burst my car at the seams. The Miracles crooned "Get a Job" from my car radio, and I knew my expression had changed from empathy to guilt.

Reluctantly, I beckoned him closer and fumbled for my purse.

"No, ma'am," he said. "I don't take charity."

"Then you meant what you said?"

"Ma'am?"

"Your sign?"

"Yes, ma'am, I'll work for food." He smiled again. "Or, even better, a bath and some fresh clothes."

He didn't sound like a bum. A panhandler, or tramp, or whatever the heck they're called nowadays, wouldn't be concerned with a bath and fresh clothes, at least not as an alternative to cold, hard cash. Had he seen the disdainful glares of the romance writers? If true, we definitely had something in common.

Maybe he was incognito, planning to write a tell-all article. In my mind's eye, I could see the first lines of the last paragraph: *Sydney St. Charles, a good Samaritan, kept me from starving to death. Ms. St. Charles, a local witch who owns an herbal apothecary at 36410 Reverend Hale Avenue, also cast a charming charm . . .*

Aunt Lillian would say it was "good for business."

What charming charm could I cast? The one that helps a person gain favor in the eyes of others? An easy spell, all it requires is sand and a magnet. Plus, an incantation that includes the words: "Metal of strength. Blood of earth. Out of death. I draw thee forth."

It had been a mild winter, an early spring. My grass had begun to grow, along with a few weeds, and my white picket fence needed a new coat of paint. There were heavy boxes in the trunk of my car, not to mention my multiple grocery sacks. Toting them up the steps of my house would justify herbal shampoo and soap.

I even had some Jim clothes and sneakers, stored inside a

guest room closet. My stormy three-year relationship with Jim had ended nine months ago, but I'd kept some of his clothes, tempted to chant a nasty incantation over them. If I were a real witch, I'd have put a curse on Jim without a moment's hesitation.

Suddenly, I heard Tommy Murphy's precautionary *tap-tap-tap* and remembered Clive Newton's big toe and ring finger.

Yeah, sure, but would a vicious killer plead for clean clothes? No. He'd rob a Laundromat.

"Your eyes don't look like a murderer's eyes," I mumbled, unaware that I'd spoken out loud.

Until the man said, "No, ma'am, I'm not a murderer, and you've got very pretty eyes."

He gave me that killer smile again. I'd have to make a decision soon. The light had turned green and several pickup trucks were honking like a flock of angry geese. The truck directly behind me sported a National Rifle Association bumper sticker.

"Get in the car," I said. "Hurry."

Chapter Three
Friday, noon

The handsome drifter climbed inside my car and settled his guitar case on his lap. Using his sign as a floor mat, he rested his bare, dirty feet against WORK and FOOD. I appreciated his thoughtful gesture and told him so. Then, making casual conversation, I asked him what had happened to his shoes.

"Who's on your car radio?" he countered.

"The Miracles. No. Wait. The Drifters. 'Memories Are Made of This.' "

For a moment he looked startled. Then he said, "May I ask your name?"

His "may" hooked me; polite and grammatically correct. I'm a sucker for polite, and good grammar makes my heart beat like a trip-hammer.

"My name is Sydney St. Charles," I said. "Please call me Sydney. And your name is?"

"John."

"Do you have a last name, John?"

"Please call me John," he said with a grin.

If his smile was perfect, his grin was devastating. He even had a couple of deep, devilish dimples. "Where do you hail from, John?"

Procrastinating, he stared at my legs. Finally he said, "The Safeway parking lot."

"I mean, before that?"

"The bus station, I guess."

"You guess?"

"What kind of work do you have for me, Miss Sydney?"

"Neglected yard work, John. Mowing, weeding, and my back fence could probably use a new coat of paint."

"I can do that."

"What else can you do? Maybe I can find you steady employment."

"Yes, ma'am . . . Miss Sydney."

He was getting under my skin, refusing to answer a question with a comprehensive answer. Once again, I remembered Clive Newton. What woman in her right mind picks up a stranger when there's a killer running loose? The solution was to dump him. Now. But how? Stuck in the lefthand lane, I couldn't stop the car and let him out by the side of the road. Furthermore, the NRA truck was glued to my right, speeding up and slowing down whenever I did.

I reassured myself with one indisputable fact. John was weapon-less. Unless he'd hidden a knife in his underwear or a machete inside his guitar case.

"Do you play the guitar, John?" Stupid question. Of course he played the guitar. Unless he'd hidden a machete—

"I don't know."

"You don't know if you play the guitar?" Despite a pothole, I managed to nod toward his guitar case. "Is that yours? Or did you steal it?"

"Pull over and let me out!"

His voice sounded so agitated, I instinctively obeyed, cutting in front of the truck. Then, ignoring the obscenities directed toward my gender in general and my lineage in particular, I wondered if John planned to throw up. Was he ill? Had I encountered an alcoholic? My father had been a "social drinker." Which meant he often slurred when he talked, staggered when he walked, and puked his guts out. Nicholas was also responsible for driving his car into a telephone pole, with my mother sitting beside him. The car was totaled. So were my parents. I can't tolerate drunks, the reason why Jim and I severed our so-called relationship.

But John hadn't slurred or staggered. Watching him grope for the door handle, I said, "Just a minute. You owe me an explanation."

"I don't owe you anything," he stated, his voice neither angry nor petulant.

"Yes, you do. You almost killed my car, making me cut in front of that stupid truck. I want to know who you are and where you come from. I have a cell phone," I fibbed, "and I'll call the police. You won't make it back to the supermarket, much less the bus station."

He stared at my face, as if memorizing every imperfection. Finally, he said, "I can't tell you who I am or where I come from because I don't know."

Stunned, I blurted, "Oh my God, you've lost your memory."

"Yes," he said, and that one word sounded so sad, so lost, I half-expected a full-boogie orchestra to kick in; a movie soundtrack; Simon and Garfunkle; Bridge Over Troubled Colorado Avenue.

Despite Tommy Murphy's *tap-tap-tap,* I believed John. Maybe it was his eyes, maybe his smile and his non-vagrant aura, maybe I simply wanted to believe in something. I didn't believe I was a witch. I hadn't believed my father was a hopeless drunk or that Jim couldn't be rehabilitated.

"I won't call the police," I said. He visibly relaxed, and I wondered if I was making what my great-aunt Lillian would call a humongous boo-boo. Still, I forged ahead. "We'll follow our original game plan. You'll work for me on a temporary basis while I find you steady employment."

"Thanks, Miss Sydney, but without identification I can't find employment." He pounded the dash with his fist. "Don't you understand? I have no last name, no driver's license, no Social Security card, no damn wallet."

At least this time I knew the reason for his anguish. "Do you want to talk about it? Usually I don't pry into other people's—"

"There's not much to talk about. I woke up inside a motel room and couldn't remember anything. I didn't even recognize myself in the mirror."

"Did you check your pockets?"

"No."

"Check them now, John. There might be—"

"I woke up naked, except for my headband and these." He snapped his red suspenders.

"You woke up naked, wearing a pair of suspenders?"

"Not exactly. The suspenders were wrapped around my throat."

"Someone tried to kill you?"

"That would be my guess."

"Who?"

"If I knew who, I'd probably know who I am."

"Sorry. Stupid question." I turned off the ignition and extended my head like a turtle. Sure enough, I saw a suspender-shaped neck bruise.

Score one point for belief.

Unless John had attacked someone and the victim fought back.

But why would a victim steal John's wallet?

And why didn't he, or she, call 911?

What if two people killed Clive? What if John's strangler was his partner in crime? What if the partner had strangled John to shut him up? Last week I'd seen a *Law & Order* rerun with exactly that plot. In fact, if I remembered correctly, the prosecutor lost the original case, then re-prosecuted the perpetrator for the murder of his partner.

Could a person lose his memory through strangulation? Medical doctors didn't tend to endorse my homeopathic cures, but I'd call an M.D. and—

"Never play poker, Miss Sydney."

"Huh?"

"You were wondering where I got my clothes and guitar. Right?"

Thank goodness John couldn't read my mind. Glancing out the window, scrutinizing the exterior of the local Buffalo Bill museum, I said, "Yes."

"I found the guitar case under my bed. Inside the case, along with a guitar, was thirty dollars."

"You bought your shirt and jeans at a thrift shop?"

He looked at me as if I were a Steven Spielberg alien. "Are you kidding? I couldn't stroll down the street naked."

True. John might be able to get away with naked in Manitou Springs. But not Colorado Springs. Or Manitou Falls.

"I watched a man leave his room, get into a car, and drive toward the exit," John continued. "He didn't have luggage."

"So you opted to steal his clothes?"

"I didn't steal anything. I used the thirty dollars to buy his shirt and pants."

"They don't look like they're worth thirty bucks." Instantly ashamed of my sarcasm, I realized that my outfit wasn't worth thirty cents. "Who paid for your motel room, John? I mean, who registered?"

"Mary Smith."

"Mary Smith?"

"That's what the guy behind the desk said."

A new thought occurred. "How'd you get into the room next door?"

"I picked the lock."

31

Once again, the image of a knife blade filtered through my brain. Then, the image of a credit card. But, allegedly, John didn't have a wallet. "With what?" I asked.

"A guitar pick."

He showed me his fingers. Slightly swollen, they looked as if they'd been pierced by splinters. Instinctively, I winced and said, "It couldn't have been easy."

"Especially when you're wearing a wet towel and there's a cold, numbing wind."

I pictured John without his scruffy clothes, a towel wrapped around his waist, and liked what I saw. "Did 'Mary Smith' leave anything behind?" I asked, grasping at straws.

"Yes. Some kind of hairpin."

"Hairpin or bobby pin?"

"Huh?"

"Never mind. Where'd you find it?"

"In the bathroom."

"What color was it?"

"The bathroom?"

"No, John. The hairpin. Light or dark?"

"Um . . . light."

Ms. Smith has blonde hair, I thought, then asked John for the name of the motel. And his room number. He replied without hesitation, and didn't ask why I wanted to know. Frankly, I didn't know why I wanted to know.

Aloud, I said, "Where'd you get your work-for-food sign?"

"I found it behind the Safeway. It's lucky I did. Otherwise, I wouldn't have met you."

He reached out with long, graceful fingers to take my hand and raise it to his lips. I felt my cheeks bake, but couldn't tear my gaze away from the lips that grazed my knuckles. Flustered, I said, "Did you really visit the bus station?"

"Yes," he replied, placing my hand on the steering wheel.
"Why?" I asked.
"To read cities."
"Read cities? Oh. You thought a city might spark your memory. Did one?"
"Yes. Denver. I pictured the blonde girl who rides the white horse around the football field when the Broncos score. I remembered cheering for the Denver Broncos, pictured quarterback John Elway, and chose his name. I'm not sure he'd appreciate the honor . . ." John shrugged.

Score another point for trust. It may sound simplistic, but an amnesiac who loves the Broncos couldn't have serious flaws. I'm a fanatical fan. My father, who never cared for sports, would have said I'm pathological. If I truly practiced witchcraft, the Denver Broncos would have won the Superbowl prior to 1998 and John Elway would still be quarterbacking.

By now the ice cream had surely experienced a meltdown. Or at the very least was engaging in a relationship with the cheese doodles, so I said, "Let's roll."

Fingering my ignition key, I heard Tommy Murphy's *tap-tap-tap*.

Chapter Four
Friday, noon-thirty

Tommy Murphy's *tap-tap-tap* merged with the Beatles' *jude-jude-jude*.

The next song was by The Newts, so I turned my car radio off. I don't care for Newt music. I guess you'd call it folk rock, but it doesn't have the charm and poetry of a Bob Dylan or Paul Simon.

Ever since Clive Newton's well-publicized murder, every radio station plays Newt songs. The group even elevated back-up singer Yogi Demon (*nee* Yogi Berra Brustein) to lead vocalist, and they would appear next week at the Colorado Springs Pikes Peak Center.

Talk about posthumous hype. I wanted to buy concert tickets for my niece Xanthia, but my brother Oliver said they sold out in less than ten minutes. Desperate to surprise Xanthia on her birthday, I ended up purchasing the latest Newts CD, just released. My adorable niece and her friends have this teenage "thing" for Yogi Demon. Frankly, I don't get it. Clive was young, cute, talented. In my opinion, Demon, a tall, white-haired man who always wears black, has no voice, no charisma.

With the radio silenced, I could hear Tommy Murphy's tapping loud and clear. It sounded like "I'm Singin' in the Rain," except Colorado raindrops are the size of marbles and they never fall straight down.

Peering through my windshield, I saw that dark clouds had gathered and I knew the sky would soon spew its wrath. Gene Kelly would run for cover, just like everyone else, despite his euphoric reaction to Debbie Reynolds' chaste kiss.

Speaking of euphoria . . .

While reaching for the radio's knob, my hand had brushed against John's hard-muscled thigh. He either worked at a physical trade or worked out. One brief touch had nearly jolted me backwards, and I wondered how the romance writers, Pam and Deb, would have described my thigh-touch. A stab of desire coursed through Sydney St. Charles? Sydney's heart pounded like a drum? Sydney's legs turned to jelly? An electrical shock jolted Sydney backward?

John might be a vagrant, but he possessed an attractive, albeit grungy, charisma, and I hadn't shared one shred of intimacy with a man in nine months. To put it nicely, Tommy Murphy would have said I craved tongue, but was John the right candidate? He might be a murderer. Or, even worse, married. I don't mess around with married men.

Jim was legally separated when we met. We celebrated his divorce with a bang, then clashed like cymbals for three years. To Aunt Lillian's credit, she didn't say, "I told you so" when I kicked Jim's butt—

Oh my God! Aunt Lillian!

Lillian Levana, seventy-ish, doesn't fancy strangers. Paying customers, and believe me some are strange, don't count. My aunt and I live above the apothecary. Jim was the only man who'd ever invaded our domain, and Aunt Lillian didn't exactly jump for joy when he set up his tape deck and his collection of Golden Oldies inside my bedroom. Not that she's a prude. On the contrary, she's led what she calls a "checkered past" and her modern outlook on sex would send the family-value people into a tailspin.

Assuming Aunt Lillian accepted John's presence, my menagerie would not. Mercy the Parrot doesn't like men. Annie the Cat . . . well, she's a cat. Smart, independent, she shuns affection, unless *she* wants strokes. Chasdick the Dog, fat and lazy, might growl every now and then, but mostly he chases rabbits in his sleep. I had adopted Chasdick, a yellow Labrador retriever, during a rash of robberies, thinking a guard dog would be a worthy investment. Unfortunately, my fearless watchdog fears his own shadow.

Aunt Lillian, bless her heart, believes that my beloved pets possess the souls of three Salem sisters—Mercy Birdwell, Anne Kittridge, and Chastity Barker. The Salem sisters crown my family tree, and family journals, handed down from generation to generation, clearly state that the original Mercy, Anne, and Chastity learned an incantation that would allow them to re-emerge in other forms.

Yeah, right.

Cresting a hill, I decided to forewarn John, who stared at the scenery like a Columbus sailor, as if he couldn't quite believe the earth was round rather than flat. After I cautioned him about my pets and my aunt, maybe I'd off-handedly mention my witch pedigree.

Chickening out, I said, "We're now entering Manitou Falls."

"It's . . . quaint," John said.

Quaint was an understatement. Small townish, picturesque, even gothic would be relevant.

Except for Arthur Miller High School, all structures are at least one hundred years old. Satellite dishes, hot tubs, and pink flamingos decorate yards, but no golden arches pierce our vista, and the local K-Mart is Kendra's Consignment Shoppe, pronounced shop-ee. We have an upscale Italian restaurant, a pizza parlor, and a Chinese restaurant (that does mostly take-out), but our breakfast-lunch-dinner eatery is Nina's, open twenty-four hours unless Nina decides to close. Then she puts a GONE FISHING sign in the window.

Years ago, Nina crossed out FISHING and scribbled in SLEEPING.

Manitou Falls' professional establishments include a "quaint" bank, a cleaners, Bess Wyndham's Bed and Breakfast, a real estate office, two lawyers (one older than God), a chiropractor, a veterinarian, a podiatrist who shares his home and office with a dermatologist, a dentist, a consignment store called Merry-Go-Round-Round-Round, and Gusta Lowenfeld's monthly "newspaper," filled with gossipy chit-chat and discount coupons. The tourist trade is Manitou Falls' bread and butter, but many shops, including mine, also draw patrons from the surrounding areas.

I could tell by his knee-jerk reaction that John had seen the high school. Streamlined, rectilinear, it sticks out like a sore thumb. As we school-zoned past a GO MINERS football banner, he said, "Arthur Miller?"

"A famous playwright, Miller wrote a drama called *The Crucible*. It's about people who were hanged as witches." Now would be the perfect opportunity to mention my background. Instead, I opted for some local background. "There was an argument over the high school's name. A Manitou Falls contingency, led by town matriarch Augusta Lowenfeld, wanted to call our school John Winthrop High, after the first governor of Massachusetts. Winthrop was stern, super-critical, a very moral man. Nicholas, my father, headed up the Miller faction. Arthur Miller married a sexy actress named Marilyn Monroe. Does that name sound familiar?"

John's expression clouded and something flickered in his eyes. "Yes. She has a spot . . . a mole? On her face, next to her mouth."

Had! Marilyn's death wasn't relevant, but John's response was intriguing. He'd remembered a beauty mark, not platinum hair or MM's bodacious body.

I've got a soft spot for Marilyn Monroe, who by today's standards would be considered a tad hefty. My mother once told me that when Marilyn died, my great-aunt Lillian wanted to bring her back to life. There's a family spell that can do that. But, unfortunately, the body has to be close at hand, out of its casket. I think Aunt Lillian wrote a letter to Joe DiMaggio. I don't think he responded.

Returning to the subject at hand, I said, "My father insisted on a vote. At a town meeting. That night there was a blizzard. Gusta Lowenfeld's station wagon, overloaded with members of the Winthrop clique, got stuck in a snowbank. The townies voted and Miller passed by a narrow margin, so I guess God smiled."

Actually, my mother had smiled. Only nine at the time, I can still picture Nicholas begging my mother, a weather witch, to perform her magic. If I truly believed in witchcraft, I'd swear on a stack of Bibles that my mother conjured up the snowstorm.

John said, "How did Manitou Falls get its name?"

"Manitou means Great Spirit, and there's a small waterfall, smack-dab in the middle of a lush forest. Legend has it that a Manitou Springs witch married a Cripple Creek prospector. The prospector had discovered a small vein of ore . . . this was back in 1895 . . . so the happy couple established Manitou Falls. It's laid out like a six-fingered hand and the streets are named for Salem Reverends. Witches were hanged in Salem, Massachusetts. Does Massachusetts ring a bell?"

"Yes. Football. The New England Patriots."

I gave him a quick smile, even though it wasn't perfect. My irregular front teeth have never been braced, because, my father said, what's the point? Until I grew breasts, Nicholas thought his only daughter looked like Ronald Coleman, the

Tale of Two Cities film star. My hair had even been styled in a French peasant's queue. I developed late, too late for braces. By then Father had left what he called the bullshit world of commerce and we couldn't afford an orthodontist.

"Some people blame the 1692 witchcraft hysteria on a black slave named Tituba," I said. "Some blame it on the clergy. Some people even think that I'm descended from a long line of—"

"What's a crippled creek?"

"Excuse me?"

"You said the Manitou witch married a crippled-creek prospector."

"Cripple, not crippled. Cripple Creek isn't far from Manitou Falls. The town was named for a cow who broke her leg crossing the creek."

He flashed his devastating grin. Maybe now was a good time to mention the family journals. "I was named for Sidney Carton, the protagonist in a book called *A Tale of Two Cities*," I said, chickening out again. "My big brother was christened Oliver."

"Oliver." John tasted the name.

"*Oliver Twist*. It's the title of another book. By Charles Dickens. My father was a Dickens fan, as was his father, grandfather, and great-grandfather. Before my father renounced all religions, my little brother was baptized David Copperfield St. Charles. Do you have any family, John? I mean, can you remember a brother or sister? Or a wife?"

"No. I've been trying, but it makes my head ache. Maybe you should pull over and let me out, Sydney, before I mess up your life."

"You won't mess up anything, John. I'm good with brooms." My sarcasm was instinctive, even though he couldn't understand the witch reference. "I own an apothecary, herbal medicines, so I'm fairly certain I can cure your headache."

"Nothing will cure my headache until I know who I am." His mouth contorted. I desperately wanted to comfort him, but didn't know how. I only knew that if John was faking his amnesia, he was one hell of an actor.

Chapter Five

Friday afternoon

Manitou Falls' main thoroughfare, Salem Street, has pedestrian crosswalks. One is required to stop for foot traffic, and one merits a stiff fine if one breaks the law. Braking my Honda, I drummed my fingernails against the steering wheel.

An ogress walked her bike across the street. She looked like Margaret Hamilton on steroids. Her face even had a greenish tinge, as if she celebrated St. Patrick's Day twenty-four/seven.

Usually ogresses don't bother me, but today's ogress was Mary Lou DiNardo, mother of Paulie the Pimple DiNardo, whom I'd edged out for high school valedictorian. Everyone knew that Paulie, who reeked of Clearasil, cheated on exams and plagiarized Williams and William; Tennessee and Shakespeare. Everyone, that is, except Paulie's teachers.

When Mary Lou learned that valedictorian meant smart (rather than having a big dick), she never forgave me. Birthing Paulie late in life, naming him after her favorite Beatle, Mary Lou's runt of the litter gave "spoiled rotten" a whole new meaning. Other DiNardo offspring entered politics . . . or prison . . . but Paulie was destined to become a rock maven, and I'm not talking diamonds.

Come to think of it, Paulie would have the perfect motive for rubbing out Clive Newton. According to Gusta Lowenfeld's monthly gossip column, Mary Lou's brat had been hired and then "downsized" by Clive.

"Have you ever heard the name Paulie the Pimple?" I asked John.

"Doesn't sound familiar. How about Zach the Zit?"

"You know someone named Zach the Zit?"

"Not really. It just popped out."

We both laughed. Mary Lou stopped in the middle of the crosswalk and began to serenade me with cuss words, half English, half Italian, one of her more endearing qualities. She even cussed at movies. No one has ever had the nerve to say: "Turn off your cell phones and Mrs. DiNardo," but it's just a matter of time.

Leaning out my car window, I yelled, "Grimalkin, grimalkin, feasted in my kitchen; there shalt thou stay; nor from it care to stray."

Mary Lou made the sign of the cross as she and her bike quickly crept toward the curb.

John stared at me. "What did you say?"

"It's a charm to keep a cat from straying. But the woman who cursed me doesn't know that. She thinks I'm cursing her back. Works every time."

"You're very weird," John said.

I turned right onto Reverend Hale Avenue, drove half a block, then idled in front of my shop's sign, located just behind the waist-high shrubbery that encompasses my front yard. Mounted on a post atop a sturdy wooden scaffold, my sign is simple; black letters across a white background. Aunt Lillian wanted to add a witch logo, but for once I put my foot down.

"*Lilly's* Apothecary?" John leaned forward in his seat.

"I could say my shop was named for my great-aunt Lillian." Shifting into reverse, narrowly avoiding a huge oak entangled with ivy, I pulled, taillights first, into my driveway. "But the truth is, I bought it from a witch named Lilly."

"A real witch?"

"She sold notions and potions."

The perfect cue line. I probably wouldn't get another before we entered my shop and John saw my notions, potions, and hand-printed spells.

He said, "Why didn't you change the name to Sydney's Apothecary?"

"Because Lilly's Apothecary tickled my funny bone. You see, my great-aunt Lillian believes she's a—"

"Sydney, your house! It's—"

"Quaint?"

"No. Beautiful."

I felt my delicate ego expand. When I signed the deed, my house was an eyesore, run-down, surrounded by foliage. Aunt Lillian helped me weed, patch, and repair. Frankly, I feared for her life when she tucked her petticoats inside the waistband of her bloomers and climbed a tall ladder. Singing her favorite song, "Moon River," she'd brandished a brush, sprinkling white paint on anyone who ventured near her ladder. Soon my house, two stories high, shone with white, dark blue, and light blue paint. The gingerbread trim is lavender, and my front door sports a big brass toad knocker.

During the reconstruction, my whole family pitched in, harmonizing for the first time in their lives. Oliver's ex-wife, Carol, sewed window curtains. Oliver's young bride, Bambi, set up Annie's new litter box and lined Mercy's old parrot cage with some kind of scrap paper. My brother, Davy, planted an herb garden. Jim said he'd clean the upstairs, but I found him later, passed out in a bedroom, an empty bottle of Jack Daniels by his side. Jim had managed to turn his portable tape deck on before he reached a state of blissful oblivion, so my niece Xanthia and her friends scrubbed and polished to Archie Bell and The Drells.

My neighbors begged to join us, drawn by our laughter.

Watching them paint my backyard's picket fence, I felt very Mark Twain-ish. Then, while clipping my six-foot-high hedges, I bonded with six-foot-two Nina, the woman who owns Nina's Diner. She cropped the hedges and contributed tons of food and we've been best friends ever since.

Jolted from my reverie by the rain that snapped against my windshield, I heard John say, "Let's get these groceries inside."

The rapidly-falling drops drowned out Tommy Murphy's *tap-tap-tap* as I grabbed three sacks, navigated porch steps, and reached for the doorknob.

"Nice knocker," John said, struggling under the weight of his guitar and four grocery sacks.

I glanced down at my breasts before I realized he meant the brass toad. Jim had called my breasts knockers, which should have warned me from the get-go. I shook my head to banish Jim-memories, then opened the door.

"Aunt Lillian, I'm home," I yelled, "and I've brought a . . ." Turning, I surveyed John, wondering how I'd describe his status.

Homeless man?

Amnesiac?

Attractive panhandler?

"A guest," I finished lamely.

Aunt Lillian bounded down the steps so quickly, I knew she'd been peering through her bedroom curtains, previewing John. Spry for her age, spry for any age, her dress swirled and her bloomers teased. No gent over sixty, unless he'd been eunuch-ed, could possibly resist her charms.

Correction: John, guestimate late thirties, wasn't immune. "Howdy, ma'am," he said, giving her his best smile yet.

"You'd better get rid of those groceries," she said, making

an about-face. "Upstairs. March."

Like good little soldiers, we followed. Stumbling up the steps, I managed to hide my stupefaction. Aunt Lillian had invited a man, a stranger no less, into our sanctuary. Had she succumbed to John's charisma? Or had she determined that our cobwebs would be sufficient to bind an enemy? The cobweb charm requires a recently dead fly, a black cloth, and an incantation: "East, west, north, south, hold his limbs and stop his mouth. Seal his eyes and choke his breath, wrap him round with ropes of death."

I've never had to bind an enemy, but Aunt Lillian swears the spell works. As luck would have it, dozens of cobwebs graced the apothecary when we first moved in, and the mass of icky, sticky webs is stored in the attic.

"Aunt Lillian, this is John Elway," I said, easing my sacks onto the kitchen table.

"Ma'am, my name isn't John Elway, even though it could be John. My wallet was stolen, I've lost my memory, and Miss Sydney was kind enough to offer me temporary employment."

Silver ringlets frame Aunt Lillian's face, but I could see her ears perk. She loves a good mystery and John's I've-lost-my-memory would shiver her timbers. In this case, her timbers were her arms. They quivered with excitement as she patted the table top.

"Put the groceries here, young man," she said. "Sydney, your friend has a headache. Go down to the shop. Fetch some Anise and Windflower Wort."

Windflowers heal. An anise-filled pillow keeps away nightmares, and the seeds are especially effective if you've accidentally (or intentionally) killed someone. Staring at my aunt's face, I couldn't detect her expression.

"How'd you know I had a headache, ma'am?" John removed his beaded headband, revealing a nasty bruise.

It looked as if someone had hit his forehead with a fist that included a sharp ring. Maybe that, rather than strangulation, had caused his amnesia. And while Windflower Wort might cure his headache, he really needed a medical doc—

"Reeky ratsbane."

I shifted my gaze to Mercy, who makes her home inside my cozy kitchen. The cage door was open. However, my contrary parrot perched on her swing.

"John, meet Mercy," I said. "Mercy, John."

"Beef-witted barnacle."

"Howdy, Mercy." John tried a smile.

Mercy couldn't care less. *"Suck-egg weasel,"* she spat through her beak. *"Maggot-pie."*

"Sydney dear, the medicinal herb."

"Yes, Aunt Lillian."

When I returned, John was seated at the table, a mug of coffee in his hand. His guitar case decorated the wall near Mercy's cage. Mercy's cage was covered, her blasphemies silenced by a piece of cloth.

"That's mighty interesting, ma'am," John said.

"What's interesting?" I asked Aunt Lillian, who was shelving the groceries.

"I was telling your young man about how the souls of our Salem ancestors inhabit Mercy, Annie, and Chastity."

"Chasdick. He's a male dog," I explained to John, who was laughing.

If John's smile was perfect and his grin devastating, his laugh was contagious. I, who rarely giggle, giggled. When I caught my breath, I said, "Where are Annie and Chasdick, Aunt Lillian?"

"I don't know about Annie, but I locked Chastity—"

"Chasdick."

"Inside your bedroom. She—"

"He."

"Was frightened. When Chastity's frightened, she pees."

"And when *she* pees, *she* lifts *her* leg."

John's laughter reverberated off the kitchen walls. "Chasdick," he managed. "For Charles Dickens?"

"Yes. Part Dickens, part Chastity." John might have lost his memory, but he was sharp as a tack. I wondered if he'd known a Charles, nicknamed Chas. Glaring at Aunt Lillian, now popping party popcorn into her mouth, I said, "Then there's his big . . . uh, thing."

She slanted a glance toward John, but couldn't curb a vinegary response. "I don't think Charles Dickens had a big . . . thing, Sydney."

Afraid she'd go into a lengthy spiel about a nineteenth-century family member who'd met up with Dickens personally, and intimately, I said, "You know very well I meant Chasdick. Stop chortling, John."

"Yes, Miss Sydney. I'm not sure I need your medicinal herbs anymore."

"Laughter is the best medicine," Aunt Lillian said. "But I'll give you some Windflower Wort, just in case." She waggled her finger. "A Pigeon's Grass bath should spruce you up nicely."

Pigeon's Grass. Vervain. Another remedy for nightmares, it helps soldiers escape their enemies. I suddenly recalled that Vervain, or Juno's Tears, can be used in love potions, but I still couldn't decipher my aunt's expression.

"Then you'll nap, young man," she continued. "Supper is served at seven."

She was issuing orders again. I waited for John to acquiesce, but he shook his head.

"Chores first, bath later," he said.

"What chores?" Stirring Windflower into a glass of orange juice, she placed the glass near John's coffee mug.

"Mowing, weeding, fence-painting."

"The house should be 'spruced up' for Xanthia's birthday party," I said, my cheeks inexplicably flaming. Because it wasn't true, not anymore. Bells and sirens were still ringing inside my head, along with Tommy Murphy's *tap-tap-tap,* and yet I wanted John to stay. If necessary, I'd invent chores.

Aunt Lillian caught my vibes; she always does. "You'll sleep in the guest bedroom, young man. Meanwhile . . ." She nodded toward the window, where raindrops pelted the pane. "I'm afraid you can't mow, weed, or paint. That gullywasher could last for hours, so you might as well bathe and nap. Sydney, change your clothes and tend to the shop."

"Yes, ma'am," John and I said together.

"Hook your pinkies and make a wish," said Aunt Lillian.

John blinked. "Why?"

"Because you both said the same thing at the same time."

We hooked, and the romance writers would say a spidery tingle traveled up and down my spine.

John was probably wishing he'd recover his memory.

My wish made my cheeks flame again.

Chapter Six

Friday evening

While John bathed, I changed my clothes and rearranged the apothecary. I might be negligent about making my bed, washing dishes, dusting picture frames, and doing the laundry, but my shop is as neat as the proverbial pin. Aunt Lillian's sixth beau, a sailing enthusiast, would have called it shipshape.

However, I needed to create chores. That meant my books and pamphlets, arranged alphabetically by author, would have to be un-alphabetized. Perhaps I'd shelve a few jars of yam estrogen cream with the self-healing crystals. I couldn't make my "mess" too obvious. John had lost his memory, not his brain-power.

John. He'd obviously won Aunt Lillian's regard, which was a minor miracle. How come? My big brother Oliver, a walking thesaurus, might say that John was "physically combustible." In other words, he had a hot body. But John possessed more than good looks. Despite his grungy exterior, he had an innate politeness. Not to mention a substantial amount of self-assurance, as if he stood before a crowd, graciously accepting their accolades.

For what it's worth, Aunt Lillian's opinion isn't swayed by handsome. She once said that her fifth lover was "ugly as sin."

Before I could ponder any further, my toad knocker *thwacked*.

I opened the door and greeted Terey Lowenfeld, Gusta's daughter. Her hands clutched a shabby briefcase. Rain dripped from her yellow slicker as she said, "Hi, Sydney. My mother sent me to pick up your ad."

I advertise in Gusta's *Manitou Falls Monthly*. Sometimes, just like my spells, the ads even work. Walking behind the counter, I retrieved the half-page layout and handed it to Terey, who immediately stuck it inside her briefcase.

"It's raining pitchforks," I said. "How about something to drink? Coffee? Tea? Hot chocolate?"

"Thanks, Sydney. Maybe another time. Ma wants me home by five so I can help her cook. We're having Paulie DiNardo for dinner."

I wondered what Paulie the Pimple would taste like, then shrugged off the distasteful image.

Twenty-eight-year-old Terey lives with her mother; has, in fact, never been on her own. Her whole demeanor practically shouts: *virgin,* although she once had a crush on my little brother Davy, her classmate at Arthur Miller High. She used to lurk behind trees and hedges, "scoping him out." My soft-hearted brother took her to the movies. *Fatal Attraction,* starring Glenn Close, whom Terey somewhat resembles. Except Terey's lanky body has no discernable bosom.

What had I been doing before she interrupted me?

Oh, yes, creating chores.

I had barely reached my yam estrogen shelf when the toad *thwacked* again. Whereupon, the door opened and a woman entered.

She looked like a drowned rat until she took off her rain hat and London Fog. Platinum hair fell to her shoulders. A peek-a-boo bang shaded her left eye. To the left of her glossy red lips was a black beauty mark. A white evening gown sheathed her willowy body, and I took a moment to envy her curves, then another moment to wonder why she wore an evening gown.

It was Friday evening. Perhaps she had a hot date. Come

to think of it, she looked familiar. Could she have been one of the romance writers I'd entertained with witch anecdotes?

Pasting an entrepreneurial smile on my face, I said, "May I help you?"

"I need ze love potion, pleece."

She sounded like the Gabor sisters. Maybe she looked so familiar because she resembled Marilyn Monroe. Or Cool Hand Luke. Cool Hand, a former Denver drag queen, was a local celeb. Years ago, he headlined a popular nightclub act. As Marilyn, he sang "Diamonds Are a Girl's Best Friend" and always brought the house down. He and my brother Davy were drinking buds—at least they were until Cool Hand joined Overeaters Anonymous.

Once upon a time Cool Hand had played for the New York Knicks, and Ms. Gabor Sisters couldn't have been much taller than five-three, so I said, "What love potion is that, ma'am? I have many. They start at nineteen ninety-five."

"He's a devil," Eva or Zsa Zsa said. "I need ze potion for ze devil."

"You need a charm to make a devil fall in love with you?"

As she nodded, my mind raced. I had spells to keep the devil at bay, but none to entice one. Ms. Gabor Sisters needed a black witch.

Her hand rose to her jaw and she groaned.

"Do you have a toothache?" Now we were in my ballpark. I have a very nice charm for toothaches, short and sweet. It's expensive, but most people swear it works. Except, of course, dentists.

Tears flooded her eyes. I led her to a comfy chair, a superfluous gesture. Her gown was so tight she couldn't sit. Damn. Tears unnerve me. I never cry and I've rarely, if ever, seen Aunt Lillian cry, so I don't know how to deal with a weeping willowy blonde. "There, there, everything'll be all right," I said inadequately.

"I need ze love po-potion," she sobbed.

"If your husband is a devil, you don't need a potion. You need a divorce."

"I'll pay."

Those two words were magic, to me. "I don't have a spell for a devil, ma'am, but I do have one that will help you gain a man's love."

"Yes. Puh-puh-pleece."

While she continued sobbing, I searched through my hand-printed spells. Some adorned my walls, but not the one that would gain a man's love. Finally, I found it, sandwiched between the spell that would gain a woman's love and the spell that would arouse a woman's passion. Afraid she'd mangle the words with her Gabor-speak, I read the charm out loud. "I invoke the burning force of love, in thee, for thee. The desire, the potent love-spirit which all the gods have created in the waters, this I invoke, this I employ, to secure thy love for me. Thou wilt love me with a burning desire."

"Yes," she breathed.

I fished out a Jasmine-filled sachet from my under-the-counter collection. Jasmine, or Moonlight on the Grove, attracts spiritual love. "You'll need this when you chant the charm, ma'am. Place it in your bodice or beneath your pillow."

"Ze pillow," she echoed.

"Do you want the toothache charm, ma'am? It's verbal."

"Yes, pleece."

I gently palmed her flushed face and chanted, "Galbas, galbat, galdes, galdat."

"Ze toof, it feels better already," she said, slithering toward her raincoat. "Do you take checks, Ms. St. Charles?"

"Yes. Local checks. But the charms won't work if your check bounces."

She dug through her coat pocket, then whipped out a checkbook and pen. I had a sneaky suspicion she wasn't a Gabor anymore, but as long as her check was good I didn't care.

After she had exited the shop, sachet and spell in hand, I looked down at the check. The heading read: CHICKEN FEED PRODUCTIONS. The signature was scribbled, yet I managed to piece together "Veronica Whitney."

Now I understood why the willowy blonde had looked so familiar.

Veronica was the sister of Jessica Whitney St. Charles, my brother Oliver's third bride.

Didn't Chicken Feed Productions handle The Newts? Could Veronica's devil be Yogi Demon? If so, from what I've heard, she has lots of competition. Why had she used Gaborism?

Simple answer. When people purchase my spells, they often hide their true identities. For example, impotence. My spells, along with herbs like Cedar, Mugwort, Saffron, and Myrrh, are as effective as Viagra. Plain old Garlic works well, too. I can understand why most men (and quite a few women) buy my spells for "a friend," but Veronica had to know I'd catch the Whitney in her signature. If she didn't want me to finger her, why hadn't she stopped at an ATM and withdrawn cash? I accepted cash.

Surfing my files for a duplicate hand-printed gain-a-man's-love spell, I sensed an unseen presence, turned around, and saw "John Elway."

What a transformation. His face was clean-shaven. His headband hid his forehead bruise and he'd fashioned his hair in a queue, not unlike the queue I wore as a kid. Without the

53

street grime, John's hair was mink-brown and his sun-streaked strands looked as soft as a mink's fur. He had found the Jim clothes, jeans that fit and a Ray Charles STICKS AND STONES polo shirt that didn't. I knew it was only a matter of time before John's chest burst the shirt seams.

"I borrowed your razor," he said, giving me a smile to die for.

Hadn't I just recited a love spell that Aunt Lillian swore worked like a charm? If our spell achieved the desired results, wouldn't John be tempted to ravage my body? Razor-speak wasn't very romantic.

With guilt, I looked down at my legs, now hidden by a long gingham skirt. I'd have to buy another razor.

He followed my gaze. "I like your shorts better, Sydney."

"When I play shop proprietor I need to look . . ." *witchy* ". . . professional."

I had a sudden thought. John didn't seem the least bit sur-prised by my popular toys: stuffed bats, vultures, toads, and dragons. He hadn't blinked twice at my kitchen witches, cookie jars, wall spells, Aunt Lillian's decorative cauldron, or my colorful Eye of Newt and Root of Hemlock storage pots. Maybe his lost memory bank had conjured up Halloween.

"John," I said. "I'm a . . . some people think I'm a . . ."

"Witch. Yes, I know. Your aunt told me while I was bathing."

"She shouted, 'Sydney's a witch' through the bathroom door?"

"No. She sat on the edge of the tub, along with Annie the cat, and told me all about it."

"Annie sat on the tub? That's incredible. Did she wash your back?"

"Who? Annie?"

"No. Aunt Lillian."

"As a matter of fact, she did."

"Weren't you embarrassed?"

"By your aunt or Annie?"

"Aunt Lillian, damn it!"

"You're cute when you're flustered," he said, stepping closer.

"I'm not flustered. Aunt Lillian has an unorthodox lifestyle. She'd want to wash your back because you can't reach it."

"That's exactly what she said, just before she told me about your family."

"Do you believe I'm a witch, John?"

"You've bewitched me," he said, his eyes warm.

I felt an unbidden blush stain my cheekbones. Flustered, I began to babble. "I need to clean my shop, stockpile some items before my niece Xanthia's birthday party. The kids have a habit of pawing through my stuff. Today's Friday and the party's Sunday, so maybe you can help. I just sold some spells, so I can pay you something, and there should be lots of food at the party. You work for food, right? Xanthia's father, my brother Oliver, will be there—here—at the party. He's a cop, an ex-cop, so maybe he can . . . what's the matter? Why are you looking at me like that?"

"I can't attend your niece's birthday party, Sydney. I'm leaving tomorrow, after I finish the yard work. I'll help you clean the shop, but I can't stay."

The way he said my name was a sigh, a soft wind against my cheek that flowed in an eddy down the hollow of my throat to lodge in the hollow of my breasts, and wouldn't the romance authors have fun with that thought?

"Sure you can," I said, stumbling backwards. "I'll bet my friend Nina would hire you without I.D. She owns a diner and always needs waiters, not to mention dishwash—"

"Let me think about it, okay?"

"You remembered something, didn't you?"

"No."

John was lying through his perfect teeth. His mood had changed when I mentioned Oliver. Why?

I pictured John in the tub. Relaxed, headache gone, he might have had another memory flash, not unlike his Denver Broncos memory flash. What had he remembered this time? Blood? Bloody clothes? A ring finger? Until he pieced it all together, John wouldn't want a cop snooping.

Not that Oliver snoops much anymore. No longer a member of the Manitou Falls police department, my brother writes cop books, fiction, and he's right up there with the lawyers who write lawyer fiction, a best-selling author.

"Never play poker, Sydney."

"What was I thinking, John?"

"I saw your eyes narrow. You're thinking you don't know anything about me, that I might be a con man or an ax murderer."

Ax murderer hadn't occurred to me, but con man had.

And it wasn't just low self-esteem. John seemed too good to be true. Polite. Grammatical. Attractive. He *had* to have a major flaw. Flaws. Maybe he picked his nose. Maybe he picked his teeth. Maybe he never cleaned the wax from his ears. Maybe he had a knife. Maybe he had a wife.

Clive Newton's body parts had been severed. Could a knife's blade hack off fingers and toes? Wouldn't it be less difficult with a machete? Or a hatchet? Or a chainsaw?

My severed-body-parts knowledge was restricted to horror films and Stephen King novels, my sleuth skills negligible, yet somehow I'd have to surreptitiously pry open John's guitar case, just in case he'd hidden a machete-hatchet-chainsaw inside.

Or a knife sharpener.

Chapter Seven

Saturday morning

Just inside Lilly's Apothecary is a New Hampshire grandmother clock. Its hands arrowed eight a.m. as I snapped a fake-diamond-studded lead to Chasdick's fake-diamond-studded collar and dragged him from the house.

Afraid of other dogs, other dog walkers, fire hydrants, strange cats, even *The Denver Post* (which usually lands in our shrubbery), Chasdick has to be cajoled, rewarded, or trawled before he'll function. Sometimes Aunt Lillian walks our yellow Lab. When she does, Chasdick squats to pee, as if he really did possess Chastity Barker's spirit.

I spied Lynn Whitacre sweeping the rain from her sidewalk. Lynn has curly red hair, a curvaceous body, and a porcelain complexion. Twenty-six, she collects glass unicorns and stray cats; totes her brindled Boxer, Baron, to dog shows; attends community college; and waits tables at a Manitou Springs restaurant called Loop-de-Loop.

"Did you hear the latest news, Sydney?" she shouted from across the street.

"Yes," I shouted back, thinking: *Clive Newton's ring finger.*

Baron's corrugated snout elevated. He let out an unbroken succession of Germanic barks. Chasdick cowered, and I missed Lynn's next shout. I didn't want to be rude, but I was in a hurry, hoping to join John for breakfast, so I dragged Chasdick to the corner mailbox, where he likes to lift his leg. Then I towed him toward our quaint bank, open on Saturdays from eight till noon. After stashing my pooper scooper behind a bush and tying Chasdick's leash-reins to a fencepost, I entered the bank . . . and waited in line. Sometimes people cancel their checks when spells fizzle, so I wanted to deposit Veronica Whitney's check ASAP.

Manitou Falls' quaint bank had opted for a western motif; had, in fact, won Gusta Lowenfeld's annual *Manitou Falls Monthly* "John Wayne Award" (the Chinese restaurant came in second). Authentic reproductions dominated the bank's off-white walls; a Seth Thomas look-alike clock; several lithographs of hunky cowboys herding hunky cattle; memorabilia that included old boots, old spurs, old bullwhips, and old money. The décor made me antsy. I'm always expecting an authentically-reproduced Robert Redford and Paul Newman to come bursting inside. Suppose, after robbing the bank, they used me as a human shield and took me with them?

As I gleefully contemplated both Butch and Sundance ravaging my poor, defenseless body, a man accidentally nudged me from behind. Like a car pileup, I lost my balance and nudged the woman in front of me.

Terey Lowenfeld made an about-face. Her hair, twisted into a topknot, looked as if a drunken bird had fashioned a nest with straw and bobby pins. Her eyes blinked like a freaked-out rabbit, and I realized that she was only half awake.

"Good morning," I said with a smile. "Long night?"

"Sydney. Hi. Sleepless night. Bad dreams."

"Why don't you stop by the shop, sweetie? We have a special talisman for stability . . . a small, simplified skull at the center of a spider's web. The skull has eight spider legs and the back of the talisman says: 'My threads bind the restless mind.' Most people swear it works like a charm."

"Thanks, Sydney, but I simply ate too much. At dinner."

Her hand patted her belly. The shabby briefcase that dangled from her other hand gaped open. I saw a scarf, a padded mailing envelope, a pair of gloves, and a book—*Bones* by Jan Burke.

"You'll love that book," I said, pointing at the paperback. "But catch up on your sleep before you read it. I couldn't put it down."

Her cheeks reddened. "I bought it for my mother," she said. "It's about an investigative reporter. Ma wants to be an investigative reporter. She took a correspondence course, hoping to get a journalism degree, but quit halfway through the course."

While we'd been talking, the line had moved forward. Terey reached inside her shabby briefcase, withdrew a withdrawal slip, shut the case, then thrust the slip at the teller. I thought I heard her whisper, "Please let there be enough money."

Apparently, there was. A look of relief washed over her face. Heading for the exit, her shabby briefcase slapped against her leg, punctuating every step. As if she'd suddenly remembered her manners, she turned and waved goodbye.

"Whatever happened to bankers' hours?" Without even glancing down at the check, Susan Partridge stamped my deposit slip so viciously she might have taken tae kwon do lessons. Then, in the hushed tones reserved for a church or funeral parlor, she said, "Have you heard the latest news, Sydney?"

"Yes." Damn, I was sick of hearing about Clive Newton's ring finger. "And no, I don't have any catch-a-killer spells available."

"Maybe your great-aunt Lil—"

"She doesn't have time, Susan. Aunt Lillian's busy cooking for the party. You'll be there, won't you?"

"Absolutely. I'm donating coleslaw. But I haven't bought

Xanthia's birthday present yet. Do you have any suggestions?"

"Frogs. There's a stuffed frog in my shop. It's only . . ." I hesitated, calculating her budget. "I'll sell it to you at cost, Susan, fifteen bucks."

At fifteen dollars, I'll still make a profit. Tommy Murphy always says: "Money may not be everything, but it's a pretty good cure for poverty." Aunt Lillian says: "If the dollar keeps shrinking, George Washington'll have to get a haircut." For the record, she believes Martha Washington might be kin. Aunt Lillian even sketched our family tree and perched Martha on a branch.

"Okay," Susan said. "Gift-wrap the frog for me, please."

She handed over a crumpled five and ten. I thrust the bills inside my jacket pocket, planning to hand them over to John. He might work for food, but I knew from experience that a man needed pocket money to feel like a man.

Walking backwards, towing Chasdick, I returned home. Lynn had disappeared and so had her car. I'd have to apologize for my rudeness tomorrow, during the party. Lynn had promised to contribute Loop-de-Loop enchiladas.

I wondered if John liked Mexican food. There were so many things I didn't know about him, so many things he didn't know about himself. I'd have to convince him that Xanthia's party was a necessity, especially since I anticipated a crowd. People rarely turn down one of my party invitations, motivated by curiosity as well as free eats. Maybe someone would recognize John. "As I live and breathe, blah-blah-blah!" Gusta Lowenfeld might very well screech, providing a first and last name.

Wasn't the chance of recognition worth the danger of recognition?

John had remembered the Denver Broncos. More importantly, he'd remembered the cowgirl who rides the white stallion around the football field every time the Broncos scored, not always shown on NFL broadcasts. So John could very well be a "local boy."

Maybe he'd let me snap his picture.

I had film in my camera, left over from Christmas. What a great idea. I could show the picture around, starting with Gusta Lowenfeld.

Except, my gut told me John wouldn't let me snap his picture.

Reaching into the shrubbery, I retrieved the *Post*. Then I entered the house, unsnapped Chasdick's lead, and followed him upstairs.

He headed for my bedroom, where I keep his Linus-blanket; a soft baby blanket with a faded-from-washing Mickey, Goofy, and Pluto.

I glanced at the guest room door. Shut. I traveled down the hall and pressed my ear against the door. No snores. No sounds of breathing, either.

For some ungodly reason, I remembered one of my father's favorite quotes. Charles Dickens, of course. *Marley was dead to begin with . . . Old Marley was as dead as a door-nail.*

"Dinggg, donggg, the wicked witch is dead . . ."

Aunt Lillian sang at the top of her lungs while our poached eggs fossilized, our pop-up waffles scorched, and our bacon burned. Despite the lucky kitchen witch that hangs from our curtain rod, neither one of us can cook.

My aunt had promised she'd decipher the instructions on the cake batter box and "concoct" Xanthia's birthday-frog-cake while I worked the shop. Until the tourist trade arrives we employ a flexible schedule, but every Saturday we open at ten and close at six. Aunt Lillian also said she'd follow the directions on a can of tomato sauce and bake the party lasagna.

Aware of my kitchen skills, several friends, including Nina, had promised they'd bring food, so I figured we'd be okay if/when Aunt Lillian screwed up the pasta.

"Sing it hiiigh, sing it looow, let them know the wicked witch is . . . shit." Hands mittened by pot holders, Aunt Lillian dumped the skillet into the sink, turned on the faucet, and watched our bacon go up in smoke.

"I should have learned from osmosis," she muttered, shedding her mittens.

I knew she was referring to her favorite lover, who had been a chef at the Broadmoor Hotel. "Don't sweat, sweetie," I said. "I'm not hungry."

"Don't sweat sweetie," Mercy parroted from her cage.

Annie sprang into my lap and began to purr.

Aunt Lillian placed a couple of bagels on the table. "Here, Sydney, I didn't burn the cream cheese."

"No, thanks. 'Destiny shapes our ends but calories shape our middles.' "

"Who said that?"

"Oprah," squawked Mercy. She preened in front of her miniature mirror, and I could have sworn her beak creased into a smirk.

Mercy was wrong. Tommy Murphy had said it. But while Aunt Lillian believes in the rebirth of new bodies and forms, she tends to scoff at imaginary chums.

"Veronica Whitney," I fibbed. Picturing the slinky white evening gown, I figured Veronica could have said it. "Oliver's sister-in-law. She bought one of our love spells. And here's the funny part. She wanted to entice a devil."

"Then she should have gone to a black witch."

"That's what I thought, but a sale is a sale."

With a shrug, I glanced toward the open window. The

kitchen witch aviated and the window curtains fluttered, generated by a lilac-scented breeze.

"Maybe we should wake our house guest," I said, stroking Annie's cocoa-colored fur and tickling the chin beneath her white, freckly muzzle. "I know he's exhausted, he barely managed to keep his eyes open during supper last night, but he might like some bagels and cream chee—"

"John's gone, Sydney."

"Gone? That's impossible." My elbow knocked the newspaper from the table to the floor, and I heard the rubber band snap open. "He promised to mow, weed, help me rearrange the shop. Yesterday he didn't even want to eat or bathe . . . until he'd finished . . . how the bloody hell can he be gone?"

"Take it easy, girl." Aunt Lillian scooped up the newspaper and tossed it onto the counter. "John's not gone for good. He left around seven. He rose at cock crow, we shared some coffee, and he said you invited him to Xanthia's party."

Aunt Lillian likes to say she rises at cock crow, except we don't have any domestic fowl and our weathercock is mute. "I did invite John, but he said no."

"Obviously, the anise-seed pillow changed his mind. He wants to buy Xanthia a birthday present."

"At seven in the morning? The stores aren't even open yet."

"I imagine John needs to acclimate, drive around a bit."

"In what?"

"My car."

"You gave him the keys to your car?"

"Of course."

"Are you crazy?"

"*Are you crazy?*" Mercy parroted. Annie gave her a green-eyed glare, the kind of glare only a cat can give, and I could have sworn Mercy looked contrite.

63

"Where," I asked, "did John get the money for Xanthia's present?"

"I loaned him a few dollars."

Susan's fifteen bucks was burning a hole in my jacket pocket. Still, I said, "Don't you think it's strange that he accepted your loan?"

"Why?"

"Because yesterday he was adamant about not taking charity."

"I insisted, Sydney, and John said you said he should work for Nina."

"I did, but—"

"He looked through the phone book, jotted down some addresses, and said he'd be back around noon."

"But we don't know anything about him, Aunt Lillian. He could have driven off into the sunset."

"Sunrise, Sydney."

"He has no driver's license. He might lose his memory again, or get lost and forget where we live."

"He promised he'd drive carefully, my registration is in the glove box, and he can always ask for directions."

"Men never ask for directions. I wonder if we should call the police."

She shook her head so emphatically, her ringlets spread out like a curly fan. At the same time, her face looked . . . smug.

"What did you do?" I said. "Put a spell on the car?"

"Yes. Gretel will find her way home, even if John gets lost."

Aunt Lillian believes her nineteen-seventy-something Volkswagen possesses the soul of a dead German relative, a witch named Gretel who settled in Green Bay, Wisconsin. Gretel the Beetle has been driven approximately 20,000 miles and will live forever.

I didn't bother to mention that Aunt Lillian's spells haven't worked since the Beatles invaded the USA. "John should pay the police a visit," I said. "They'd have his fingerprints on file, assuming he's ever applied for a Colorado driver's license."

"That's what I told him." Aunt Lillian beamed.

"Dollars to doughnuts he won't set one foot inside the precinct."

"Maybe he doesn't want to remember, Sydney. Maybe something god-awful happened to him, aside from a head bruise and strangulation. Give him time, and try not to be so harsh."

"I'm not being harsh. I'm being pragmatic. Handing over the keys to your car isn't smart. It's—"

"My car."

Aunt Lillian rarely gets angry. When she does, she sounds . . . pragmatic.

"I guess the milk's already been spilled," I said, backtracking. "The barn door locked after the horse—"

"We don't have a barn and we don't have a horse. Here's a mug of coffee, just the way you like it. With milk. It's ten o'clock. Please open the shop."

"Yes, ma'am."

At the same time, Mercy squawked, *"Yes, ma'am."*

Too bad John, rather than my parrot, wasn't nearby. We could have hooked our pinkies again.

Except I felt certain he'd flown the coop, even though we don't have a coop.

Chapter Eight
Saturday, noon-thirty

Lilly's Apothecary is busy on Saturdays, when doctors and dentists shut down for the weekend and head for the golf course or the mountains. I had planned to call an M.D. about John's memory loss. But, along with everyone else, I'd have to wait until Monday . . . assuming John returned, stayed for Xanthia's birthday party, and stuck around long enough to pay Aunt Lillian back.

Yeah, right. That supposition was as believable as my being a witch. Or Aunt Lillian's Gretel-spell. Or Veronica Whitney's love charm.

In any case, people tend to buy medicinal herbs for weekend emergencies, and twice I chanted my toothache cure.

We were fast approaching Easter, which made my stuffed animals very popular. I carry magic rabbits, along with my dragons and bats and frogs. Aunt Lillian sews them all, and she puts a hand-written "happy spell" into the stuffing before she completes the last few stitches. Aside from the cost of materials, our animals are pure profit, and yet Susan Partridge had gotten a real bargain since, depending on size, my prices range from twenty-five to seventy-five dollars.

There's even an enormous lizard, "on sale" for three hundred dollars. It takes up too much space, but Aunt Lillian hopes we'll never sell it. She claims "Lucinda Lizard" possesses the soul of a dead Arizona ancestor. If she/it does, I've never seen any evidence of revival. Furthermore, dusting Lucinda is a pain in the neck. Sometimes I wonder what kind of spell Aunt Lillian stuffed inside, or what she says when people express a desire to purchase our reincarnated reptile.

Aunt Lillian puts a percentage of what she calls our stuffed critter profits into an enormous piggy bank. The pink porcine pig has a dopey smile. Across its behind, beneath its squiggly tail, Aunt Lillian printed: NOAH.

Knock on wood, we haven't had a day rainy enough to break the bank.

I placed Susan's frog and my Newts CD in white boxes, planning to wrap them later. My gift-wrap, designed by Aunt Lillian, has cute little witches boiling stuff in cute little cauldrons. The witches are surrounded by repetitive print that says: DOUBLE DOUBLE TOIL AND TROUBLE . . . HAPPY BIRTHDAY.

Then I sold a couple of talismans, round chips of polished wood with symbols on one side, invocations on the other. I'll never figure people out. If the talisman for wealth worked, wouldn't I be sunning myself on the deck of a cruise ship? And if the talisman for beauty worked, wouldn't I look like Miss Universe? Or Veronica Whitney?

Business had slacked off by lunchtime, when shoppers usually head for the pizza joint or Loop-de-Loop or Nina's. John hadn't returned. Big surprise.

Aunt Lillian bounded down the stairs, her skirts swirling, her bloomers flashing. She carried a plate, heaped high with peanut butter and jelly sandwiches, only she calls them "sandwitches." Her armpits anchored a thermos and *The Denver Post*, and she was followed by Mercy, Annie, and Chasdick.

I let Chasdick out into the backyard, where the only things that'll frighten him are my gazebo, my herb garden, and a bed sheet flapping from my clothesline.

Annie curled up on Lucinda Lizard and Mercy perched atop my counter.

"If you open that potty-mouth," I told my parrot, "you go back upstairs."

Aunt Lillian placed the newspaper on the counter, the thermos on top of a small table. Then, with a shaky hand, she offered me a P&J sandwich . Her blue-black eyes looked enormous, so I said, "What's up?"

"Didn't you say something about Oliver's sister-in-law buying a love spell?"

"Yup. Veronica Whitney, Jessica's sister. She bought the spell yesterday. Why?"

Aunt Lillian pointed to the newspaper. Ignoring Mercy, who was beak-kissing my ear, I glanced down at the headlines.

DENVER HEIRESS DIES IN FIRE practically leaped from the page. Next to the capitalized typeface was a photo of Veronica Whitney. Directly underneath the photo, a smaller font stated that she was Veronica Whitney Sanderson. Now I knew why Lynn and Susan had asked if I'd heard the latest news. Too bad Gusta Lowenfeld hadn't asked me. She wouldn't have taken yes for an answer.

Stunned, I said the first thing that came into my mind. "I didn't know Veronica was an heiress."

"The *Post* says she's Denver born and bred, but she married an Arkansas chicken rancher. He died a few years ago and left her a fortune. She invested in real estate and politics, then bought some sort of theatrical agency."

"Chicken Feed Productions. They handle The Newts."

"The Newts?" Aunt Lillian placed the P&J sandwich plate on the table.

"Clive Newton's rock group, now Yogi Demon's rock group. Holy shit!"

"*Holy shit.*"

"Hush, Mercy, or I'll serve Colorado Fried Parrot at Xanthia's party."

"What's the matter, Sydney?"

"Veronica wanted to entice a devil, remember? I had a sneaky suspicion her devil might be Yogi Demon. How did the fire start?"

"She was smoking in bed and fell asleep."

"Oh, my God!" My mind tried to erase the image; hopefully, she'd passed out from smoke inhalation first.

"Did she pass out from smoke inhalation first?" I asked, hopefully.

"The newspaper didn't say. Sit down, Sydney. You look as if you're about to swoon."

"No. I'm okay. It's just that I knew her. Well, I didn't *know her* know her. She pretended to be somebody else, a Gabor sister. She bought a love spell, wore a slinky white dress, asked if I took checks. And a toothache spell. I almost forgot about the toothache spell. She bought a toothache spell . . ." Aware that I was babbling, I swallowed my next words, which probably would have been something about a toothache spell. "Did this happen in Denver? The fire, I mean?"

Aunt Lillian shook her head. "Veronica owned a 'rustic retreat' in Black Forest."

"That's where Clive Newton's body was found. Define rustic."

"Three acres, a stable and horses, swimming pool, and tennis court. Do you think the police will question us, Sydney?"

"Why would they?"

"Her stable hand called the fire department. The house was badly damaged, but it didn't burn to the ground. If our love spell didn't burn, it has our stamp in the corner. Lilly's

Apothecary, followed by our address and phone number."

Abandoning the stuffed lizard, Annie sinuously strolled toward the counter, leaped up onto its surface, and sat next to Mercy. I sometimes wonder how come my bird and parrot get along so well, considering that cats are natural predators and birds are their fundamental prey. Maybe Annie, who is not a large cat, signed a mental truce with Mercy, who boasts a sharp, stout, curved, hooked bill.

I had squeezed my bread so hard while reading the *Post* headlines, peanut butter and jelly had squirted onto my palm. Trashing the bread, I let Annie's sandpaper tongue cleanse my hand.

"Don't fret, our spell had nothing whatsoever to do with the fire," I told Aunt Lillian. "Or Veronica's murder."

"Who says it's murder?"

"I meant death. We don't even know if the spell worked."

"Of course it worked. Veronica lit her cigarette after screwing her devil."

"Screw the devil."

"Hush, Mercy. Not everyone smokes after making love, Aunt Lillian. And assuming Veronica made love and smoked, where the devil was her devil? Why didn't he burn in the fire?"

"Slam, bam, thank you ma'am?"

"Slam, bam, thank you ma'am."

"Aunt Lillian! Mercy!"

"Sorry."

"Sorry."

"When a man slam-bams in bed," I said, "he falls asleep immediately if not sooner. Let's suppose Veronica's lover, if she even had a lover, didn't fall asleep. He'd get out of bed, throw his clothes on . . . or at least pull his pants up and zip his fly . . . maybe say a few farewell words. By then, she would have puffed her post-intercourse cigarette. So I repeat. Our love spell had nothing to do with the fire."

Before Aunt Lillian could reply, my brother Oliver walked into the shop.

Correction: According to Oliver, he never walks. He saunters, stomps, treads, sometimes slithers-like-a-snake, but mere walking would be too mundane. The only thing I don't like about my brother's books is that he never uses run-of-the-mill words. He even tries to find synonyms for "room" and "door" . . . virtually impossible.

At six feet, four inches tall, Oliver is hard to hug, but I tried, my feet arching like a ballerina's. "I'm so sorry," I said into his neck.

"For what?" He tolerated my hug, then pecked Aunt Lillian's cheek.

"Veronica. Jessica's sister," I reminded him, just in case he'd forgotten the family connection. "I assume Jessica won't be partying tomorrow."

"Of course she will. Why wouldn't she?"

Normally my big brother hides his emotions, but right now he sounded too shrill. "Isn't Jessica in mourning?" I asked.

"Not really." As he glanced toward the *Post* headlines, his dexterous fingers twisted the ponytail that compensates for his balding forehead. Only he'd say he's in follicle regression. "Jess hasn't spoken to her sister in ten years."

"They didn't get along?"

"That's an understatement." He sniffed. "Something's burning."

"Damn! The lasagna." Aunt Lillian turned toward the stairs.

"Damn the lasagna."

"Auntie, take that foul-mouthed parrot with you," Oliver said.

But Mercy wanted to stay. Fluttering her wings, she rose to the light fixture, a revolving fan that won't revolve. If I didn't know better, I could almost swear she fragmented the mechanism with her beak.

Perched on a fan-blade, she screeched, *"Ollie, Ollie, oxen-free."*

"Syd, you really must do something about that bird."

"Snail-skulled half-wit."

"Hush, Mercy." Watching Aunt Lillian bound up the stairs, I heard my toad knocker thwack. But curiosity overwhelmed courtesy; besides, there's an OPEN sign in my window. "Why hasn't Jessica talked to her sister in ten years, Oliver?"

"Because Jess was once engaged to Sandy."

"Sandy?" The toad thwacked again.

"Major Cary Sanderson, the Chicken King."

"Oh. Veronica's husband. What did *he* die of?"

"Old age and too much sex. Ronnie was his seventh wife."

If our town matriarch, Gusta Lowenfeld, talks in exclamation points and question marks, my brother nicknames everybody—except his ex-wife, Carol, and our brother, David. I didn't bother to mention that "Sandy" and Oliver had a lot in common. For instance, Oliver is a sex machine, what he'd call "romantically automated." He's also been multi-married, multi-divorced, and he's filthy rich.

I wondered how long *Jess* would last. Oliver was already lusting after my pretty neighbor, Lynn Whitacre, and at this very moment he was sizing up a young redhead—make that magenta-head—who wore one of those lacy bras beneath her open blouse. With her kohl-darkened eyes, she could have starred in something called *Zombie Sluts*, and she stood just inside the shop entrance.

Sucking in his gut, Oliver said, "May I help you, darlin'?"

"I knocked the frog but no one came." Ms. Darlin' sneezed and her breasts bounced. "A friend said I should talk to a, you know, witch. A Miss St. Charles. About a, you know, love potion."

"*You* need a love potion?" Sauntering forth, Oliver arched an eyebrow.

"Not me," she protested. "It's for my, you know, friend."

Pale-complexioned people should never lie; their cheeks flush. This one carried a denim purse and a copy of *Rolling Stone* magazine with Yogi Demon on the cover. I could see half a face, white hair, and a black shirt.

"Miss St. Charles will need your name and age, sweetheart," Oliver said, propelling the busty magenta-head toward me, his arm casually draped across her shoulders.

"Tiffany. My name's Tiffany. I'm seventeen, but I'll be eighteen in a couple of days. That's why I need a, you know, love potion." She shrugged, giving up all pretense. "He said I was too young, but I figured I could start now, put the stuff in his drink or something. Then, by next week he'll be, you know, ready."

Yup, I knew. Another damn devil worshiper; another Demon worshiper.

I almost smiled when my brother removed his arm. Seventeen is young, even for Oliver. He hadn't given up, though. "Where do you live, Tiff?" he asked, and I could see his brain calculating how many hours would pass before she'd celebrate her, you know, eighteenth birthday.

"Why do you need my address for a love potion?"

I finally spoke. "An address won't be necessary, dear. Lilly's Apothecary doesn't sell love potions to minors."

Her face turned ugly. "Look, I don't want a friggin pack of cigarettes and I don't think there's any law that says you can't sell me a friggin love potion."

I can tolerate potty-mouthed parrots, but not potty-mouthed teens. "Okay, Tiffany, I'll sell you a potion. Except you can't pour it into his drink. It's for you."

"If I take it, he'll love me?"

With a curt nod, I marched over to my medicine shelf and pried open a jar of herbal suppositories. Then I reached beneath my counter for a Eucalyptus sachet. Placing both the suppository and sachet inside a small box, I returned to Tiffany.

"You insert that . . ." I indicated the suppository ". . . up your behind. Chant 'Jembalang, Jembali, Demon of the Earth, accept this portion as your payment.' I'll write it down for you. After you say the words three times, burn . . ." I hesitated, remembering Veronica's fire. "Flush the piece of paper down the toilet."

She fumbled inside her denim purse, pulled out a wallet, then counted her money. "I have ten bucks, Miss St. Charles. How much is the love potion?"

"Ten bucks."

After Tiffany had exited the shop, Oliver said, "Jembalang, Jembali, Demon of the Earth?"

"It's a charm, part of a charm, for curing a fever, and Eucalyptus leaves help heal illnesses. The child sneezed, so I figured it couldn't hurt."

"My God, you ripped her off for ten bucks," Oliver said, his voice chock-full of admiration.

"She wanted the love potion for Yogi Demon," I countered. "She didn't even realize you were hustling her. She has this thing for Yogi Demon."

"Who doesn't? You can't imagine how difficult it was to get tick . . ." He halted mid-sentence, mid-word.

"Damn it, Oliver, you said they were sold out."

"They were. Jess bought the same CD you did, Syd. When

I told her you'd already bought it, she exchanged it for Manilow." He winced. "I managed to wheedle six tickets from Ronnie. She is . . . was affiliated with an agency—"

"That handles The Newts. Why does Xanthia need six tickets?"

"I figured she'd use five for her friends, which would make her very popular. I'm sorry, Syd, but ever since I married Jess, Xanthie spends most of her time with her mom, so I thought the tickets would make *me* popular."

"They will. She'll be thrilled."

If Oliver has one redeeming quality, it's his love for his daughter. I guess his second redeeming quality would be his loving tolerance for Aunt Lillian and me. My big brother, who doesn't believe in charms or spells, is arrogant and stingy, yet he always comes through in an emergency. It was Oliver who made the arrangements for my parents' cremation and memorial service. Davy and I were paralyzed with grief.

"Why doesn't Xanthia like Jessica?" I heard the sound of a car pulling into my driveway. Most people park on the street, so I hoped it was "John Elway."

"Jess tries, Syd," Oliver said, "but she's not good with kids. She simply can't get along with Xanthie, always says the wrong thing."

"Wait a sec. You said Jessica didn't get along with Veronica, either. How on earth did you 'wheedle' six Newt tickets?" I stared at his face. "Oliver, you didn't!" At his nod, I said, "Your wife's *sister*, Oliver. Have you no shame?"

He shrugged. Correction: his shoulders humped like a camel's. "Ronnie had an itch and I scratched," he said.

"She had an itch for Yogi Demon."

"I was a substitute scratch. It's all your fault, Syd. Ronnie said she bought a love charm from you. I drove to her house, figuring she'd have concert tickets. I said I'd pay anything, do anything. She was all hot and bothered, smoldering . . . sorry, bad word . . . oozing with passion."

"Was last night the first time you scratched?"

"Your parrot has been awfully quiet, Syd. I think she's listening to every word."

"Answer me!"

"No, it wasn't the first time. And yes, Ronnie was alive when I left her."

"You've got to tell the police."

"Why? It was an accident. She set her bed on fire with a damn cigarette."

"*Damn cigarette,*" Mercy parroted.

"Who's got a cigarette? I'm out," said a new voice.

Chapter Nine

Saturday afternoon

Oliver and I swiveled together. Oliver just stood there, but I raced toward my younger brother.

"Davy, oh Davy." I hugged his lean body. Since he's five inches shorter than Oliver, I even managed to plaster Davy's face with kisses.

"Where's your hidden stash, Syd?" he said, after hugging and kissing me back.

I shot a glance toward Oliver, who doesn't approve of my occasional cigarette. Neither does Mercy, the reason why I hide my pack. I can't even begin to count the number of ciggies my parrot has shredded with her beak. Aunt Lillian says Mercy doesn't try to shred my cigarettes. Aunt Lillian says Mercy tries to smoke my cigarettes, defiantly flouting Salem convention.

This time Oliver had more secrets than I did, so I kneeled, reached beneath Lucinda Lizard, and pulled out my Camels. Then I put a CLOSED sign in the window. To heck with Saturday. It isn't every day that David Copperfield St. Charles rides into town. In fact, I probably hadn't seen him in nine months because he said, "How's Jim?"

"By now I imagine his liver is shot."

"Not to mention his lungs," Oliver said, referring to the fact that Jim was a chain smoker. "To what do we owe the honor of your presence, David?"

"Jess" and "Ronnie" may not have gotten along, but Oliver and Davy have a sibling rivalry that makes the Civil

War look like a Pennsylvania picnic.

"I came home for Xanthia's birthday," Davy said. "She's my favorite niece."

To my knowledge, Davy has never forgotten a birthday. Even as a little kid, he'd always place a bouquet of wildflowers on our mother's pillow or an elaborate, hand-made birthday card between my father's gin and vermouth bottles. Luckily, he'd pretend the flowers and cards were from all three of us since most little kids (Oliver and me included) fail to remember adult rituals.

Oliver doesn't have a sense of humor. "Xanthie's your only niece," he said.

Davy stared up at his brother. "I see you've lost more hair." Turning to me, he said, "How's the witch biz?"

"Not bad. How's the wizard business?"

"It was booming until I hit Vegas. For some reason, spells don't work on blackjack dealers."

"If you worked for the house," said Oliver, "rather than trying to beat the house, you might be solvent."

"I can always count on sage advice from you, Ollie, but I'm solvent. In Vegas I met a wealthy man who needed a chastity test."

"Oh, lord," I said. "Not the chastity test."

Davy grinned. "The wealthy man's name was Maurice, and he decided, spur of the moment, to marry this virgin. I guess she wouldn't put out until she sported a wedding band. They were very drunk, Maurice and the woman, so I sold him the chastity spell for a couple of thou."

"You had a lodestone?"

"Sure," Davy said. "Don't you?"

"Sure. But I don't travel all over the country with inventory."

"I sold Maurice the stone and chanted—"

"Spare me," said Oliver, his fingers combing back his regressive follicles.

" 'Lay this stone under the head of a wife,' " Davy and I said together. " 'And if she be chaste, she will embrace her husband. If she be not chaste, she will fall forth of her bed.' "

"I'm going upstairs," Oliver said.

"What happened?" I asked Davy, handing him a cigarette, then glancing up at Mercy. "Smoke outside, please, but finish your story first."

"Maurice booked one of those Love R Us chapels and paid me five hundred to impersonate Elvis. Then he put the lodestone under his new wife's head."

"And?"

"Forgetting all about the lodestone, Maurice maneuvered his blushing bride's body on top of his. Consumed by motion sickness and vodka, she upchucked. Then she passed out cold and the disgruntled groom left the room."

"How do you know all this?"

"The virgin's name is Rose. When she awoke the next morning, alone and lonely, she brushed her teeth, gargled with vodka, and knocked on my door."

Weaving his fingers through his thick dark hair, Davy gave me an Elvis grin. "I'd slipped her my room number," he said in a stage-whisper.

"Hell, Davy, you're not all that different from Oliver, even if you like to think you are. Rose is drop-dead gorgeous, of course. Was she a virgin?"

"You've got to be kidding. We 'consummated' her marriage, then seeing as how she had a hundred-dollar bill tucked inside her garter belt, I sold her a plastic container filled with blood."

"Where'd you get the blood?"

"The same place I got the lodestone. Vegas has witches."

"I give up. You're incorrigible."

"Don't you want to know how it all turned out? Why I'm solvent?"

"Well, so far you've amassed two-thousand-six-hundred dollars and a free piece of . . ." I glanced toward Mercy. "Rump."

"It gets better. I bumped into Maurice that afternoon. He told me Rose had puked on the stone. I said it wasn't good anymore and sold him a second stone. The last time I saw him, he was all smiles, so grateful he handed me another thou. He said she'd fallen from the bed, which made him wonder if she was a virgin."

" 'If she be not chaste, she will fall forth of her bed.' "

"Yeah, but they did it on the floor and she bled, so she was obviously chaste."

"And you are an obvious fake."

"But you aren't. What new spells have you conjured up?"

"A suppository love potion. And I made Jim disappear."

"Good. Jim wasn't worthy of you, Syd. He didn't possess one ounce of horse sense, much less human sense. Heck, darn, no more Little Stevie Wonder, no more Jackson Five, no more Marvelettes. I presume Jim packed up his Golden Oldies."

"Yup, but he left some clothes and . . . oh, lord, I just thought of something."

Grabbing Davy by the hand, I led him upstairs, into the kitchen. I allowed him to kiss Aunt Lillian's cheek before I said, "John hasn't come back yet."

"Who's John?" Oliver, seated at the table, looked up from his coffee mug.

"Sydney's new friend," Aunt Lillian said, as if I'd just started kindergarten and discovered a new playmate. "He's our house guest and he borrowed my car to buy Xanthia a birthday present. Sydney thinks he might get lost. But I put a spell on Gretel," she told Davy, "so I'm sure John'll be home soon."

"When did you give him your car keys, Aunt Lillian? This morning?"

"No, Sydney. Yesterday."

"He asked for the keys?"

"Of course not. I suggested he might take a spin, after his bath and nap. Doubtless, he was too tired. He could barely keep his eyes open through sup—"

"Did you hear him leave? I mean, during the night?"

Oliver and Davy were staring at me as if I'd lost my mind. I sleep like the proverbial log. Aunt Lillian sleeps like the proverbial pea-princess.

"No, I didn't hear him leave," she said. "But I was engrossed in a new book by O. T. St. Charles." She smiled fondly at my brother. "Then I put a videotape on the machine, *The Wizard of Oz*. I love the music, but the director should be shot, the way he portrays witches. I've never met a witch like Billie Burke. I'll buy the bubble, but a wand and ball gown? Margaret Hamilton's worse, with her green face and pointy hat. And you can't melt a witch. That was a cop-out."

Aunt Lillian likes her TV loud, very loud. "Then John could have left the house while you were watching the video?"

"I suppose, Sydney. Why?"

As an author, Oliver makes assumptions then jockeys his conclusions to match his suppositions. As a cop, he'd do the same thing. So I didn't want to articulate my embryonic suspicions. The fact is, when Davy mentioned Jim's lack of horse sense, I suddenly remembered what Aunt Lillian had said earlier about Veronica's retreat including a stable and horses. Was one of the horses a white stallion? Who was the blonde

woman John had pictured galloping round the football field?
A cheerleader? Or Veronica Whitney Sanderson?

"Cop-out. Cop-out. Milk-livered maggot-pie. "

Mercy's derisive squawks sounded from outside the
kitchen. Evidently, she'd flown from overhead fan to staircase banister. If we could hear her, she could hear us, and in
her own inimitable way she was welcoming her favorite
maggot pie. With relief and enthusiasm, my sandals sped
toward the hallway.

John plowed into me at the kitchen entrance. "I didn't
leave the house last night," he said, while a purring Annie undulated around our entangled ankles.

Somehow, I managed to make an about-face. "John, meet
my brother Oliver and my brother Davy. Oliver's the ex-cop
and mystery author I told you about. Davy's here for
Xanthia's birthday."

As John walked inside, he palmed both hands across his
face and captured a sneeze.

"God bless," Aunt Lillian said. "Sydney, do you have a
hanky handy?"

I haven't safety-pinned a handkerchief to my bodice in
twenty-plus years. Heading toward a tissue box, cleverly
hidden beneath a Casper-and-Wendy tea cozy, I heard John
sneeze again and Aunt Lillian say "God bless" again.

"Thank you, Aunt Lillian," John said, his voice tunneled
by his hands.

Aunt Lillian? Aunt? Abandoning my tissue quest, I turned
toward my brothers. Oliver's eyes had narrowed, but Davy
sensed a kindred spirit.

"Prove it," Davy said with a grin. "Prove you didn't leave
the house last night."

John tore off a piece of paper towel, blew his nose, trashed
the scrunched-up paper underneath the sink, and opened the

refrigerator. "After the witch melts," he said, poking his face into the fridge, "Dorothy's friends get a brain, heart, and courage. Then Dorothy misses the boat or something."

"Hot air balloon," said Aunt Lillian.

"Right. The last line of the movie is, 'There's no place like home.' "

"I guess the volume was a bit loud," Aunt Lillian understated. "I'm used to Sydney. She sleeps through everything."

Oliver said, "Who on earth doesn't know how that movie ends?"

"John doesn't," I said, "and I don't sleep through *everything*."

Glancing over my shoulder, I saw Aunt Lillian fetch the coffee pot. Oliver crossed his long legs. Davy stared at the lasagna, burned to a crisp.

However, my sleep-through-everything innuendo wasn't lost on John.

"Prove it," he whispered, pocketing an apple.

Then, like a blind person in an unfamiliar room, his fingers caressed the butcher block counters as he made his way toward the kitchen exit.

"Excuse me, I'll be right back," he said.

My cheeks baked as I wondered how it would feel to have him use my body as a kitchen counter, so it took a while to realize that Oliver Twist St. Charles had never actually seen my handsome amnesiac's face.

Chapter Ten

Sunday afternoon

Feeling depressed, dehydrated, and devalued, I fetched food-donation platters. As I ran up and down the stairs, I remembered a scene from the movie *Spartacus*, where thousands upon thousands of Roman soldiers march toward a large but non-specific gathering of rebellious slaves.

Except Colorado doesn't generally indulge in land warfare, John (who supposedly worked for food) hadn't joined the party, and there was only one sweaty slave. Me.

Oliver kept darting greedy glances toward my pretty neighbor, Lynn Whitacre, whose provocative shorts clung to her shapely rump. But he couldn't stray from Jessica, who used his arm as an appendage while accepting "Veronica condolences."

What an actress. Thanks to Oliver, I knew how she really felt.

I've often wondered why Oliver married Jessica, whom he met in a mystery bookstore called *The Poisoned Pen*. Almost immediately, they found they had a lot in common, for instance the bookstore was in Arizona and they both lived in Colorado. Davy says they fell in love because he mixed Annie's catnip with rose petals, then sprinkled the concoction over a meatloaf. Oliver had invited Jessica to our family dinner that night, and Davy *can* cook, so Oliver scarfed down—or in his words "eagerly masticated"—the meatloaf. For what it's worth, Aunt Lillian says Cat's Wort and rose petals make a potent love potion.

While I don't believe for one moment that catnip generates love, I once wore a coriander charm, hoping to lure a suitor. The sachet swung between my breasts and "attracted" one of the personal trainers at a Colorado Springs health club. That was before Jim, and let's just say it didn't work out.

Jessica, who bears a slight resemblance to her dead sister, is not Oliver's usual pick of the litter. For one thing, she didn't play hard to get. For another, she hides her assets under long, matronly dresses or severe pantsuits. She might be wearing crotchless panties for all I know, but I doubt it. Unlike Veronica, Jessica's dishwater-blonde hair, complete with peek-a-boo bang, is kind of wimpy, or limpy, and she uses a black mascara that isn't exactly waterproof.

Maybe, in private, she dotes on Oliver and tells him how great he is. Maybe he was on the rebound from bubbly, bubble-headed Bambi. Maybe the catnip really worked. Maybe I should give John a few sprinkles.

Following yesterday's *Wizard of Oz* discussion, Oliver took off for home and John reappeared. He had changed into a Roy Orbison OOBY DOOBY tee and a pair of faded jeans. The hand-me-down denim molded a butt that was almost as incredible as his smile. Then, with Davy, John weeded the herb garden, mowed the grass, even mixed the paint for the back fence. They bonded, John and Davy, and I could tell during our Chinese take-out dinner that John wasn't about to play footsie with the sister of his new best bud, at least not in front of his new best bud. We all went to bed early and—

"Did you wrap the frog, Sydney?" Susan Partridge asked, interrupting my train of thought.

Startled, I stared at her in her non-bank outfit; white shorts and a blue T-shirt whose white felt letters proclaimed: A DIME MAKES A GOOD SCREWDRIVER.

"Yes," I said, gesturing toward the birthday presents that

enveloped Lucinda Lizard.

"Did you include a card?"

"Good grief, no. Grab a card from the counter, Susan. It matches the store-wrap and I only store-wrapped two presents, yours and mine. Yours is bigger."

"Okay. Thanks."

"You're welcome. I'm not real good with scissors or tape, so you can put the card inside the box and press the tape down again. Or I can rewrap."

She shook her head. "You've got enough to do."

What an understatement. More and more "Romans" were arriving every minute, and Xanthia, seated in the gazebo, chatted with her friends. Too late, I realized that, except for cake-candle-wishes and birthday presents, teens tend to shun parties that include adults.

"How can I help, Syd?"

Davy stood at my side. "There's some picnic tables on the front lawn," I said, "for the food. Round up everybody and 'rawhide' them in that direction. Thank goodness it didn't rain. Where's Aunt Lillian? I don't know half these people. Where did they all come from?"

"Easy, sweetheart. Take a deep breath and a nice hot bath. That'll calm you down. Meanwhile, I'll supervise—"

"A bath? You've got to be kidding."

"Okay. Wash your face. Brush your hair."

"I look like a total grot, right?"

"No." He grinned his Davy grin. "But you might dig out a blouse that has all its buttons."

"Damn." In my haste to greet the first guest, I'd grabbed the blouse that gapes at my bodice. "I forgot to do the laundry, Davy, and I don't have any clean clothes."

"Raid my suitcase."

"What about John?" Davy and John now shared the guest

bedroom. "I mean, what if he's in his underwear or something?"

"So what? You've seen boxers before."

The din around me receded. "John wears boxers?"

Underwear reveals a lot about a man. Oliver wears bikini briefs and Davy wears boxers. Jim wore white jocks with saggy elastic. The health club trainer sported a jockstrap.

"Scoot, Syd." Davy rotated my body toward the stairs. "Gusta and Terey Lowenfeld are standing next to Lucinda Lizard. I'll let Miss Gusta direct traffic. I'll even sell her an eternal youth talisman. 'Who bear my gold, ne're grows old.' "

"She already has that one."

I felt my cheeks flush, and was glad Davy couldn't see into my pocket. Just for grins, I'd scooped up a love talisman and stuffed it into my right front pocket. While I don't believe for one moment that it works, the inscription reads: *Thy fire thine, thy heart mine.*

If Davy hadn't been standing next to me, I would have put it back. John's absence was beginning to piss me off.

This morning, over my scorched toast and Davy's exquisite Eggs Benedict, he had sounded genuinely enthusiastic. He couldn't wait, he said, to meet Xanthia and give her his special birthday present.

"I think . . ." he began, then paused. "I think I had a kid sister."

"Had?" Davy, who knew about John's memory glitch, had stolen the question from my mouth.

"Did I say had? I meant have. I'm sure I meant have."

He appeared stunned, as if he'd suddenly stumbled into a maze of hedges, and the look in his eyes seemed to imply that a rabid Jack Nicholson would materialize round the next bend.

"Sisters are a pain in the butt," Davy said, his voice a mock growl. Not surprisingly, my soft-hearted brother was trying to alleviate John's anguish.

"Watch your mouth, Davy," I taunted, playing along, "or *you'll* drive to the bakery."

An order for a new frog birthday cake had been called in Friday, after Aunt Lillian's attempt went down the drain, despite her incantation while breaking an egg into the batter: *Earth and flesh now one, in this egg the sun.*

I didn't tell Aunt Lillian that her incantation was for fertility.

Chapter Eleven

Sunday afternoon

I climbed the stairs for the umpteenth time.

Tommy Murphy would say that John bought his boxer shorts with Aunt Lillian's money. Tommy would say I was a fool, trusting John and pocketing a love talisman. Tommy would say that Aunt Lillian and Davy had been charmed by John's charisma. Tommy would say—

"Slapsauce lout. Maggot-pie."

Mercy! Was John in the kitchen?

"Dankish, hedge-born whey-face."

John's coffee mug decorated the table, and Mercy's surplus smut gave credence to his recent occupancy. Maybe he was in the guest bedroom, but did I really want a confrontation when my sentiments had begun to echo Mercy's?

"Ta-ta, Sydney."

Did I mention that Mercy has a British accent? I've always thought the people who owned her before I did were U.K. transplants. Or Mercy watched too much PBS. However, she's one smart bird, and although she prefers to spout Shakespearean-style profanity, she's learned just about every nursery rhyme I've ever taught Xanthia.

"Where's John?" I asked, a silly question. Parrots parrot.

"Paunchy boil-brained foot-licker."

"Hush. John isn't paunchy."

"Boil-brained foot-licker."

Sometimes I could almost swear Aunt Lillian's right, that Mercy does possess the soul of our Salem ancestor.

"I need ze love potion, pleece."

Good grief, Gabor-speak. Where was my parrot when the late Veronica Whitney Sanderson bought her love charm? Perched on the staircase banister?

"Mercy, did the lady, the blonde lady who wore a raincoat, say anything when she left the house?"

"Screw the devil."

"No. Aunt Lillian said that. Silly parrot."

Silly me. Conversing with a bird. Heck, I might as well summon Annie and Chasdick, ask them to contribute.

Exiting the kitchen, I felt a derisive grin stretch my lips.

"Screw the devil. Screw Yogi Demon. Snail-skulled, bleating foal."

Mercy's war-whoops echoed through the hall. Yogi Demon? Where did "Screw Yogi Demon" come from?

Xanthia, of course. How many times had she talked about The Newts? That explained it. No, it didn't. Xanthia wouldn't say, "Screw Yogi Demon."

Mercy had simply put the words *screw* and *devil* and *Yogi Demon* together. All four words had been said at one time or another.

My little brother was spot-on. A verbain bath would alleviate stress and clear my mind. Even better, carnation oils. Aunt Lillian says that carnations, or gillyflowers, were once worn by witches to prevent untimely death on the scaffold. We don't have a scaffold, although at one time we carried miniature scaffolds with miniature nooses, souvenir items from Lilly the Witch's inventory. Aunt Lillian hated them, while Annie considered them cat toys. Annie even knocked them off the shelf and "killed" them with her claws.

However, gillyflowers produce added energy, and I could sure use some added energy.

Deep in thought, I didn't knock on the bathroom door.

Just opened it and walked right in.

Saw the bathtub.

And John.

And Aunt Lillian's rubber ducky, decorated with a hand-painted sun in flames. The sun encloses a heart. On the duck's butt, penned with black Magic Marker, it says:

True love doesn't have a happy ending;
True love doesn't have an ending
Umu zuab
Adda pirig
Ag ag ag

The last seven words are an incantation—Protection from Fire and Water—so I'm fairly certain no one will drown in our bathtub while the house is on fire.

"My brother Davy told me to take a b-b-bath," I stammered.

"Join me, Sydney," John said. "There's plenty of room. I'll even wash your back."

"No, thanks. I'm supposed to relax and I couldn't relax with you in there."

"You find me stressful?"

"Not exactly stressful. Disturbing." My gaze darted left and right, as I tried not to look in the antique tub.

Annie and Chasdick entered. Chasdick plopped himself down on the bathroom rug while Annie leaped up onto the tub's rim. I knew I had to retreat quickly, but my sandals seemed nailed to the floor.

"Hand me a towel, please, Sydney."

"That's okay, John. Finish your bath."

"I'm finished."

As Annie sprang to the floor, John began to rise. I tossed

him a towel, then performed a semi *The Exorcist* head turn, my feet still pointed toward the tub.

His hands palmed my hot cheeks as he turned my face back to its proper position.

The tempting portion of his body was draped by a towel.

Correction: every portion of his body tempted.

I fingered the love charm, burning a hole in my pocket.

Anticipating John's kiss, I shut my eyes.

Annie rubbed hard against the back of my legs, pushing me closer, and I snapped my eyes open.

Just in time to see Chasdick's teeth remove John's towel.

Fleeing into the hall, I could hear Mercy, still squawking her Shakespearean maledictions.

Chapter Twelve

Sunday afternoon

Although I usually shun intoxicants—what Aunt Lillian calls "spirits"—a Grasshopper seemed appropriate. Scrounging crème de menthe and crème de cacao, I filled a tumbler, added a dash of two-percent milk, descended the staircase, entered the shop, and leaned against the counter that shields my cash register. I fingered the love talisman, now burning a hole in the pocket of the clean Davy-jeans I'd borrowed. "Draw to me my perfect mate," I chanted under my breath. "That I may love dear and true. Let him my twin soul be, and let our union bring infinite blessings on all we do and on all we meet. So mote it be."

So-mote-it-be is the witch's equivalent of Amen.

"So mote it be," I repeated, hefting my tumbler.

The Grasshopper tasted pretty good; good to the last drop.

A second Grasshopper would taste even better.

Before I could leave the room, Oliver had shed Jessica, pried the tumbler from my fingers, and sniffed.

"Are you nuts, Syd?" His jade eyes blazed. "You can't hold your liquor and I need you to control this damnfool party."

"This damnfool party is for your daughter, Oliver."

"It was *your* idea." He placed the tumbler on a bookshelf, in between Dean James and Anne Rice. "Where'd you get those clothes?" He scrutinized my white tee, borrowed from the same stash as Davy's jeans. "You look like a teenager."

Oliver hadn't meant his remark as a compliment. "Thank you," I said.

"And you've got a green mustache."

As I licked away my mustache, Jessica grabbed Oliver's arm again. "I'm so sorry about your sister," I told her.

"Thanks." Jessica quivered like a squirrel. "I wouldn't be here, except it's Xanthia's big day." She sighed theatrically. "I should be at home with Yogi, but Oliver insisted I come. I'm glad he did. People have been so kind."

"With Yogi? Yogi Demon?"

"Yes. How many people named Yogi do you know? He drove to our house early this morning, grief-stricken over Veronica. They were very close."

Close enough to share Veronica's post-intercourse cigarette? Oliver swore she was alive when he left, so maybe Yogi entered at the same time Oliver exited, like a slapstick comedy where everyone enters and exits through different doors. The cops can judge if Veronica died before she combusted, can't they?

But why would Yogi kill Veronica? Why would anyone kill Veronica?

I heard the echo of Aunt Lillian's voice: *Who says it's murder?*

"Why did he drive to your house?" I asked Jessica.

"Because he and Oliver are friends. Sometimes they party together, men only, no girls allowed. He's stayed with us before, after a night on the town."

I sneaked a peek at my brother. His neck was ruddy and I figured "party together" meant "cat around." Could Jessica really be so naïve?

"Yogi took some sedatives and passed out," she continued. "When he woke up, he wasn't much better. Sick to his stomach and crying. I felt so sorry for him."

My humorless brother tried humor. "Jess feels sorry for that TV actor who plays the acid indigestion man."

"I do not! Oliver gave Yogi your address, Sydney, asked him to stop by and sing 'Happy Birthday' to Xanthia. Yogi said he didn't want to be seen in public, looking red-eyed and weepy and—"

"Old," Oliver interjected.

If looks could kill, my big brother would win the Pulitzer posthumously.

"My guess is," Jessica said, focusing on me again, "Yogi didn't want to spoil the party, him being so sick and all."

But Veronica's death didn't keep you away, I thought. *What's wrong with this picture?*

"Here's what you should do, Jessica," I said, striving for sincerity. "Take a lump of beeswax as big as your thumb, warm it until it softens, then fashion it into a human figure. Light a white candle, hold the figure in your left hand, and anoint it with a tincture of aloes. Then dip it into a small bowl of honey, sprinkle it with ground white pepper and powdered turmeric, and wind a ribbon of white silk around it. Wrap it quickly in a piece of white cloth and—"

"Sydney!"

Oliver's lack of nickname should have warned me, but I plunged recklessly ahead. "Leave the figure before the burning candle for a full hour." I spied my little brother. "Davy, please get over here." When he reached my side, I said, "Tell Jessica the words to the charm that cures the body of sundry ailments. I'm not sure I remember all the—"

"She drank something green," Oliver said. "Something potent."

"You look cute, Syd." Davy grinned elfishly.

"Yeah, right," I said, hoping I wouldn't urp crème de menthe all over his Flip Wilson THE DEVIL MADE ME DO IT tee. Thanks to the lightning-quick consumption of two potent crèmes, my stomach had decided to hold a gymnastics event for grasshoppers.

"Oliver says your magic charms don't work." Jessica's free

hand rose to cover her mouth. "Oh, dear, that was tactless."

Davy said, "Why do you need a charm to cure sundry ailments, Syd?"

"Yogi Demon." One grasshopper attempted a triple somersault, using my esophagus as a springboard. "He's encased inside Oliver's house, and he has a virtual plethora of miscellaneous ailments. Maybe even a guilty conscience."

Davy said, "Who the devil is Yogi Demon?"

"Why would Yogi have a guilty conscience?" Jessica said at the same time.

"Yogi Demon's a rock star, and I should be grateful. Business is booming. Love charms and potions. The charms might not work, Jessica, but people believe they do." I turned toward Oliver. "Do people believe everything you write?"

"Don't be absurd. I write fiction. You sell imaginary cures."

"My cures aren't imaginary and my spells are authentic." I almost choked on the last five words.

"Who says?" Oliver thrust out his lower lip.

"Aunt Lillian, and she's got the journals to prove it." A family storm was brewing. I could feel it, taste it on the tip of my tongue. The impending tempest tempered my belly-grasshoppers. "The earliest journal has a bunch of pages missing, but the first two entries are dated June and September, 1692."

"Wow," Davy said. "Who's the author?"

"Chastity Barker, a Puritan. She lived in Salem, along with her sisters, Anne Kittridge and Mercy Birdwell. Chastity married a man named Obadiah Barker. That's all I know. I didn't read very much, Davy. It's hard to read. Too many squiggly letters. Maybe, together, we could decipher the journal."

"What a great idea, Syd. You decipher while I type, and I'll help if you get stuck on a word. I'll bet we could sell the finished product to Oliver's publisher. How much money did you make on your last bestseller, Ollie?"

"That's none of your business, David!"

Jessica said, "Who'd want to read an old journal?"

I said, "Chastity Barker was a witch."

Jessica said, "Oooooh."

"Doesn't your wife know about our closet skeletons, Oliver?" Splaying my right hand, I began to name my fingers. As I did, each finger bent at its joint and took a little bow. "The Ashe sisters, Fancy Kendal—"

"Enough, Syd!" Oliver's eyes blazed again. Correction: His jade eyes shot daggers at me. Then he glanced toward the staircase landing and gasped.

Following Oliver's gaze, Davy grinned.

Oliver said, "Jess and I will fetch Xanthie and her friends."

"I'll improvise some sort of stage. Near the pine tree." Still grinning, Davy headed for the door.

I'm sure I made an about-face quickly, but it felt like slow motion. Maybe I expected to see demons, or gargoyles, or those busybody TV angels. Maybe I thought I'd encounter a Steven Spielberg third kind.

Instead, I saw a clown.

There he stood, shop interior facing him, staircase in back of him, framed by my arched entranceway.

Clowns frighten me. As a child, watching *Captain Kangaroo*, I used to scream bloody murder when the Town Clown appeared on my TV screen. Other kids hid their eyes as soon as the Oz witch uttered her first cackle. Not me. You could say I was immune, conditioned by the pins stuck in Barbie. Not to mention Aunt Lillian's black goat, Tituba, and my mother's predilection to control the weather. The Wicked Witch of the West didn't bother me. Only the Town Clown.

However, one mystery was solved. I now knew how John had spent at least some of my aunt's money.

as disguised by mime-white makeup. He'd lost his
red bulb decorated his nose and a black derby hid
. Suspenders that had once been wrapped around
cured baggy pants. A tuxedo shirt, oversized bow-
tie, and nuppy brown clown-shoes completed his outfit.

If I met him on the street, I'd never recognize the man who
occupied my guest bedroom, not to mention my ducky-
infested bathtub.

John withdrew a bouquet of paper flowers from the cuff of
his shirt. His oversized shoes flopped toward me. Following
in his wake was Chasdick. I couldn't believe it. My yellow
Lab, afraid of things that go bump in the day, had entered a
crowded room.

Accepting the bouquet, I said, "Please tell me you're not a
mime." Then, "Do you know what a mime is?"

"Yes." He appeared surprised. "Yes, I do."

"Maybe you're from L.A."

"Sydney St. Charles, as I live and breathe! What a nice
surprise! A mime!"

Gusta Lowenfeld's perfume of choice, something sweet
and cloying, invaded my nostrils.

"This is, um, Bozo," I told Gusta, nodding toward John,
watching a grateful expression shade his blue eyes. "He's
from Clowns R Us. If you help me collect the guests, Mrs.
Lowenfeld, Bozo will perform on the front lawn."

Pulling a second bouquet from his cuff, John handed it to
Gusta, who beamed and batted her fake eyelashes.

Another conquest, I thought morosely, even though I
couldn't understand why I felt so dour. Maybe it was
Chasdick, aggressively shadowing John's floppy shoes.
Maybe it was my old fear of Captain Kangaroo.

Or maybe it was because I had just played John's accomplice and now there'd be no turning back.

Chapter Thirteen

Sunday afternoon

John executed some magic tricks, flubbed others, and joked about the flubs. Xanthia and her friends giggled, I chortled, Davy laughed with gusto, Gusta split her sides; even stolid, stony Oliver lost his cool.

Then, to my surprise, unresponsive Chasdick enacted a story.

"Once upon a time there was a yellow dog who wanted to be a rabbit," John told his rapt audience, and I could have sworn Chasdick's ears stood straight up, as if controlled by a puppeteer. I blinked twice, and saw that his ears were normal again. Droopy.

"The white rabbits," John continued, "didn't trust anybody who wasn't a white rabbit (Chasdick's face assumed a hangdog expression), so they posted a couple of rent-a-cops at the burrow's entrance (Chasdick barked twice). Actions speak louder than words, especially when it comes to rabbits (Chasdick momentarily sat up on his haunches and covered his muzzle with his paws), but one of the rabbits somehow managed to sing, 'You ain't nothin' but a hound dog' (Chasdick howled). The yellow dog decided he didn't want to join a society that banned other animals because of their racial and linguistic origins (Chasdick growled). So, do you know what that yellow dog did?"

"He ate the rabbits," Jessica said, then blushed furiously.

"Nope."

"He bombed the burrow," Susan Partridge said.

"Nope."

"He bought a spell from my sister," Davy said with a grin,

"and turned all the rabbits into newts."

John shook his head, and Chasdick seemed to mimic the gesture.

"He decided he'd stay a dog," Xanthia guessed, "and went back to his mother and father."

"Close, honey. He was already weaned, so he didn't go back to his parents. Instead, he wended his way to the Disney studios (Chasdick walked to the pine, lifted his leg, circled the tree, then returned to John), where he joined an integrated group of animals that included a bear, a tiger, a blue . . . donkey, I think . . . a piglet, and a rabbit who *wasn't* a bigot. And they all . . ." John paused.

"Lived happily ever after," the audience shouted, as Chasdick, panting gleefully, plopped himself down near John's feet.

"Until the dog starred in a re-make of *Old Yeller* and died of rabies," Oliver muttered.

"Hush," I said. "Don't spoil it. Look at your daughter, Oliver. She's having a wonderful time."

"Yes, she is. I'll pay you back for the clown, Syd. How about fifty bucks?"

"Okay," I said, thinking I'd give the money to John.

Aunt Lillian handed John his guitar. Some sort of look passed between them, then "Bozo" tuned his instrument.

Forget about checking John's guitar case, I told myself. Chasdick's muzzle now rested on the shabby case. Obviously, Aunt Lillian had removed the guitar without encountering a machete and/or chainsaw.

John started with Aunt Lillian's favorite, "Moon River." Tentative at first, his voice gained resonance as he reached the second chorus. Johnny Mercer, himself, would have lauded John's rendition.

Next, "Somewhere Over the Rainbow." John's fingers caressed the frets and his voice, dreamy and seductive, mesmerized the crowd.

When he tried to leave the improvised stage, Xanthia said, "One more, just for me? For my birthday, Bozo, please? Pretty please?"

He nodded, then sang a song I'd never heard before. If I had to compare it to something, I'd choose Bob Dylan's "Subterranean Homesick Blues" . . . or maybe Ike and Tina Turner's "Funkier Than a Mosquita's Tweeter." John's ballad had a folk rock, rhythm and blues quality; original and highly entertaining.

Naturally, I wondered if there was a correlation to Clive Newton's murder. Not that there aren't any number of talented singers (and songwriters) hanging around Colorado. And yet . . .

One, somebody tried to strangle John. Two, he remembered a blonde woman riding a white stallion. Three, he performed like a pro. Four, he had donned clown gear, hoping to avoid recognition.

Which, when added together, equaled zero.

I saw Oliver's ex-wife, Carol, surreptitiously readjusting her pantyhose.

"Oliver wants Xanthia to open her presents," she said, striding toward the front door. "Meet you inside, Sydney."

Eight years older than Oliver, Carol Rodriguez St. Charles is tall and well-proportioned, with short, blonde-streaked hair and pink-pedicured toes. Impeccably groomed, all her clothes carry the Delta Burke label, and you'd never guess she's what Oliver fondly calls a "Maggotologist."

Fortunately, she isn't squeamish about death and finds beauty in blow flies. Because, when she isn't playing Maggotologist, she's a medical examiner.

That's how she and Oliver found each other. Oliver, intrepid cop, was evaluating a suicide. Carol says their eyes met over the fresh corpse, but I believe my brother's gaze strayed toward the breasts that threatened to burst the buttons of her blood-spattered, white medical jacket.

If you have nothing else to do, except maybe watch grass grow, Carol can entertain you for hours with her forensic entomologist anecdotes.

Especially when it comes to maggots.

"Earth to Aunt Syd."

Xanthia was tugging at my arm. Deep in thought, I hadn't felt her yank until she spoke, so I said the first thing that popped into my head. "Damn, you look so grown up."

"I do not," she said through her braces.

"And so beautiful."

"Yeah, right, I'm too fat. Jessica says I eat like a pig. Daddy says I suffer from reverse bulimia."

"Xanthia, he was joking."

"Daddy doesn't joke." She nudged the lawn with her sneaker. "Aunt Syd, would you chant a spell that'll make me thinner?"

"I'm not a real witch, sweetie."

If I were, I thought, I'd chant something that would give Jessica and Oliver reverse bulimia. Borrowing a page from Oliver's book, they both suffered from rectal-cranial inversion.

Xanthia might be a tad pudgy, but she possessed a wealth of long, curly, chestnut-colored hair, a pair of cat-green eyes, and a Sandra Bullock chin-dimple. Right now, her body, clothed in baggy khakis and a THE NEWTS tee, sagged with obvious disappointment.

"However," I said with a wink, "there's a talisman—"

"For losing weight?"

"Absolutely."

"What does it say?"

"On one side there's a full moon, flanked by two crescent moons. On the other side it says 'Wax thou moon. That I may wane. What I lose, then shall thou gain.' " I didn't tell her that the charm hadn't worked when I tried it on me. Twice.

"Cool," Xanthia said.

I had snapped some pictures of John, two yesterday, two this morning, and planned to shoot Xanthia opening her presents; finish the roll. But now I couldn't find my camera, deposited near John's guitar case. Maybe Aunt Lill—

"Aunt Sydney, come on," Xanthia said.

Hand in hand, we entered the apothecary.

The majority of guests sat on the floor.

Xanthia's three best friends, Megan, Ashley, and Natasha, stood near a window.

"Bozo" sat on top of the counter, semi-circled by six-foot-two Nina, Gusta Lowenfeld, and Susan Partridge.

Perched on the broken ceiling fan blade, Mercy squawked, *"Ollie, Ollie, oxen free. John-John-bo-bon, banana-fanna-fo-fon."* When she spied me, she said, *"Ta-ta, Sydney,"* and shut her beak.

My gaze touched upon Lucinda Lizard. Hidden by gift-wrapped boxes, all I could see was one external, half-lidded eye.

Oliver towered above Lucinda. Dropping my hand, Xanthia walked over to him and said something. Then, approaching the counter, she said something to John. I sat on the floor, in the first row, Davy on my right, Aunt Lillian on his right. Xanthia sank down next to me, on my left, and Oliver sat close to Xanthia's left leg. Completing the first row were Jessica, Carol, Lynn Whitacre, and Terey Lowenfeld. Terey had cut her long blonde hair Joan-of-Arc short.

John navigated his way across the crowded floor until he reached Lucinda. Holding up his hands for silence, he said,

"Xanthia asked me to be Master of Ceremonies. So, without further ado, here's the first present." He lofted a package toward Xanthia's lap.

"This one's from Daddy," she said, then stared, thunderstruck, at the concert tickets. "Oh . . . oh . . . ohmygosh. I can't *believe* it. Thank you, Daddy, thank you." Xanthia looked toward her friends. "Ashley, Megan, Natasha, tickets to The Newts. One, two, three . . . six tickets. We can all go."

The three teens screamed and contorted their bodies, as if they were cheerleaders who had no space to cheer.

Oliver said, "The tickets are from Jess, too. Jess, take a bow."

Jessica scrambled to her feet.

"Thanks, Jessica." Xanthia smiled at her stepmother.

"You're very welcome, Xanthia. Oliver . . . your father . . . got the tickets from my . . .my . . . sis . . . sister."

A sob followed her last word, but before she palmed her face, I saw her eyes spark with . . . resentment? Contempt? Bitterness? Hatred?

She sank down, rump on heels, and listed toward Oliver.

The next present, Carol's, was a gold piano charm for bracelet or necklace. Xanthia, a superb pianist, could (in my unbiased opinion) outplay Billy Joel.

"Mine, mine," Aunt Lillian said with barely suppressed excitement. "It's the box with the holes. The first one on your right."

"It's heavy," John said, placing the box in Xanthia's lap.

"Don't shake it," Aunt Lillian warned.

I wondered why she hadn't used store wrap, but when Xanthia opened the lid, I saw why. Inside the box was a young cat.

"She's a stray," Aunt Lillian said. "Lynn's been keeping her for me. I named her Hamilton. A veterinarian pronounced her healthy and gave her all her shots."

Xanthia, her face pure bliss, said, "May I keep her, Mom?"

"Of course. Do you think Lillian would give you a cat without asking my permission first?"

Carol's expression suggested that no permission had been asked, or granted, but she didn't want to spoil the party. Aunt Lillian looked smug.

Oliver said, "Who'd you name the cat for, Auntie? We have dead relatives all over the country. Isn't there a Hamilton branch in Richmond, Virginia?"

"Mind your manners, young man! The branch in Richmond is Taylor, and I named Xanthia's cat for Margaret Hamilton."

"And your little dog too," Mercy squawked from the ceiling fan.

Xanthia laughed and said, "I like the name Hamilton. Thanks, Aunt Lillian."

Davy scooped up the box. "I'll put Hamilton in the kitchen, honey."

John tossed Xanthia a fourth present.

"There's no card," she said, and began tearing paper.

"It's from your Aunt Syd," Oliver said. "You can tell by the wrapping paper."

Oliver doesn't like my wrapping paper. Oliver doesn't like anything that has witches on it. Or cauldrons.

Mercy fluttered from the ceiling fan and perched on Xanthia's shoulder. *"Rump-fed ratsbane,"* she squawked, her crest quivering.

Cocking her head, she stared evilly down at the present.

Just in time, I snatched the present away from Xanthia. And opened it, planning to pluck out The Newts CD and hand it to my flush-faced niece.

There was no CD in the box.

Hidden within crumples of white tissue paper was . . . a dried apricot.

"Why, Sydney St. Charles!" Gusta Lowenfeld said, her mouth six inches from my face. "How cute! A Mr. Potato Head!"

Her perfume whiffed around me . . . along with something else.

"But where's the rest of him?" she said. "That's just an ear!"

Chapter Fourteen

Sunday afternoon

I heard the soft strum of a guitar.

A cold, damp washcloth anchored my head to a pillow.

As I struggled to a sitting position, the bedroom tilted, and I knew how Judy Garland felt, spinning her way toward Oz, transported by a Kansas tornado.

Why hadn't Judy puked?

I tried to alleviate *my* nausea by focusing on one thing, and one thing only. John. He sat on the edge of an armchair, his guitar in his lap. He still wore his clown clothes and makeup (except for the red nose), but his feet were bare and his hair fell free, below his shoulders. His black derby embellished my bureau.

Or was that Mr. Potato Head's derby?

"Xanthia's too old for Mr. Potato Head," I said, waving the white washcloth like a bon-voyage handkerchief.

At the sound of my voice, John stood and placed his guitar against the wall, next to an orange and blue Denver Broncos wastebasket.

He pointed to the wastebasket. "Do you want to throw up, Sydney?"

"No, thank you. What happened?"

"You fainted."

"Don't be silly. I never faint."

"Okay. You blacked out."

"And?"

"Aunt Lillian told the guests you were stressed out. She said you'd been working non-stop on the party and that you

107

needed to rest for a while."

"How long is a while? I mean, how long have I been here?"

"Ten, maybe fifteen minutes. Oliver took your pulse. He said you had a strong pulse and David shouldn't try to rouse you."

"David?"

"Davy stayed with you, at first, but he had to meet someone at the airport, a friend . . . he got a phone call earlier . . . so I took over."

"Who carried me upstairs?"

"Oliver."

There went my Rhett Butler/Scarlett O'Hara fantasy. Having one's brother carry one up the stairs is like drinking decaf espresso.

Not that I would have noticed, being out cold and all.

Why had I blacked out?

The ear.

I remembered the ear.

"It was an ear," I said. "In the box. An ear. Not an apricot. Not a Potato Head appendage. A freaking ear!"

"Easy, Sydney." John knelt at the side of the bed and removed the washcloth from my compulsive grip. "Easy, honey."

"Oh, God, I've got grasshoppers again."

"Right." He stroked my hair. "Take it easy."

"No. You don't understand."

"Yes, I do. Oliver said you might be . . . distraught."

"Oliver doesn't know squat. Oh, God," I groaned. "The wastebasket. Quick!"

John retrieved the wastebasket, then held the washcloth to my forehead as crème de menthe and crème de cacao topped used tissues, a deformed wire hanger, the wrapper from a Snickers bar, and a Granny Smith apple core. Every time I pictured the ear, in all likelihood Clive Newton's ear, another grasshopper skittered up my throat. Oh, God, the smell inside the gift-box. Formaldehyde.

I pictured my high school chemistry lab. I wouldn't dissect a frog, even if it meant a lower grade, but I've never forgotten the smell of formaldehyde.

"What kind of perverted sickie puts a dead musician's ear inside a young girl's birthday present?" I said, and was sick all over again.

When I finished, John opened a pair of French doors and placed the wastebasket on a small, railed balcony. Then he said, "Feel better?"

"Yes. A little. Did Xanthia see the ear?"

"No. Oliver and Davy and you and I were the only—"

"Where is it now?"

"Oliver took it to the cop shop, his old precinct . . . what's the matter?"

"I've got the shakes and you've got white and yellow dog hairs all over your pants. Chasdick sheds."

John unsnapped his suspenders and let his baggy pants drop to the floor. Then, shedding his suspenders, he scooped me up off the bed, carried me to the chair, sat with me in his lap, and began rubbing my goosebumpy arms.

"Do you want to cry, Sydney?"

"No, thank you."

God, how I wished I could cry. Sometimes my eyes will tear up, but I've never bawled like a baby—not even when I *was* a baby. Aunt Lillian says it's because witches can't weep.

I think I can't cry because Nicholas hated the fact that I never cried. He always tried to make me cry. In a fatherly guise, he'd play games. Rope-Burn (where his hand would chafe my wrist until it turned red) and Slap-Palms.

Slap-Palms was his favorite game. It's a little like drawing two guns from a couple of holsters. You try to slap someone's palms, but if the "someone" pulls his hands away in time, you have to hold your hands steady and get slapped. Nicholas slapped hard. Very hard. Tears would squirt from my eyes, but I never, ever cried.

And I never, ever won.

That thought opened the floodgates. I didn't weep, not even close, but tears squirted.

John pressed my face against his starched tuxedo shirt. Despite a few murmured endearments, I thought I heard his heart beat.

Maybe it was my own heart.

The love talisman still burned a hole in my pocket, along with a roll of Certs. I managed to extract the last three before I re-nestled my head against John's shirt. The shirt scratched my face, so I unbuttoned it, then unsnapped his bow-tie. His chest felt furry-soft and, just for the record, he did wear boxers.

As I sucked Davy's breath mints, John reached beneath my tee and rubbed my back. But my bra straps got in the way, so he unhooked my bra.

Returning the favor, I helped him take off his shirt. Then, with Certs-baited breath, I waited for his kiss. My eyes felt heavy, somnolent. John's hand rubbed my ribcage, and my breasts, now unfettered, strained toward his sensitive fingers.

On their own accord, my legs spread. John unzipped my fly, inserted three fingers through the gap, and rubbed the cotton crotch of my panties.

As I began to moan, I heard Tommy Murphy's *tap-tap-tap*.

But Tommy wouldn't dare interrupt me. He knew full well he'd vanish. Forever. In 1989 I issued an ultimatum. Butt in on my necking and join the *Field of Dreams* baseball team. Tommy wouldn't relish setting up shop in an Iowa cornfield. He's too blasé, too cosmopolitan. At least once a month he tells me to leave Manitou Falls and live in Denver. Or Los Angeles. He says L.A. has witches galore and—

Tap-tap-tap.

What the hell?

The tapping sound came from my bedroom door.

"Are you awake, Sydney?" The voice on the other side of the door belonged to Aunt Lillian. "I've got some garlic. And an onion."

The onion is one of the most widely-used anti-sickness amulets. Rubbed on the soles of the feet or the afflicted part of the body, it absorbs diseases. Another magical cure-all is garlic. Both herbs are attributed to Mars, the planet of war, and both wage battles against any kind of illness.

I didn't want Aunt Lillian to rub my feet with an onion.

Maybe, if I didn't respond, she'd go away.

"Sydney, I heard you moan," she said. "My hands are full. Please open the door."

Somehow, I managed to find the floor with my feet. "Just a sec," I said. Then, whispering, "John, hide in the closet."

"Why?"

My index finger gestured, and he looked down at the slit in his boxers.

"Right," he said, heading for the closet.

I opened the bedroom door.

As Aunt Lillian entered, I heard party noises and a Mercy-squawk that sounded like *"membretoon gipsyfilly."* Then, the slam of the front door.

Aunt Lillian nudged my door shut with her behind. "John, come out of the closet," she said, placing the onion, garlic, and a glass of Windflower orange juice on top of a covered copper cauldron that stands on iron legs. Used to steep hops to make wort, I had unearthed my antique hops cauldron at a flea market.

Apparently, John wasn't into women's clothes. A few brief moments with my shoes, sweaters, skirts, high school prom dress, and one good wool suit had un-erected his erection.

"Who's watching the kids?" I asked Aunt Lillian.

"Nina," she replied, summing up John's boxer shorts with an eyebrow-arch.

"Nina? Where's Carol and Jessica?" From the corner of my eye, I saw John pull up his clown pants.

"Carol's beeper beeped," Aunt Lillian said. "An emergency at the morgue. Jessica, suddenly overcome with grief, wanted to go home. Terey Lowenfeld offered to drive her."

"Why didn't Jessica drive herself?"

"She and Oliver came in one car. Oliver carried you upstairs. Then he took off like a bat out of hell. All he said was, 'I'll be back.' He sounded like Arnold in one of those Dirty Harry movies."

"That was Clint," I mumbled. "Arnold was the Terminator."

"Right. Clint has an Adam's apple. Arnold has . . ." She paused to shiver with delight, then lifted her skirts and retrieved a pocket knife from the waistband of her bloomers. "What happened downstairs, Sydney? Why did you swoon?"

"It's really quite simple," I said, stalling. If Oliver didn't tell her about the ear, I wouldn't either. Hush-hush, sweet Sydney. For your ears only.

I subdued a small bubble of hysterical laughter at the last thought.

"It's really quite simple," I repeated. "After swallowing a love potion, I suffered side effects. All of a sudden, I felt nauseous and dizzy."

"What love potion did you take?"

Good question. Aunt Lillian knows I've tried them all. "Something new," I said, my brain convoking ingredients. "I mixed old man's oatmeal with bloody fingers, then added eye of newt and tongue of dog."

"Bloody fingers? Tongue of dog?" John looked as if he didn't know whether to be frightened or amused.

"Herbal plants, John. Some are mentioned in Shakespeare's *Macbeth*, but the witches in that play aren't boiling a grisly substance. 'Eyes' mean any one of a group of plants resembling the eye. For example, daisies. 'Bloody fingers' is another name for foxglove. 'Tongue of dog' is hound's tongue, a common herb."

"So far, nothing in your mixture is harmful," Aunt Lillian said, fingering the pocket knife, extracting its blade.

"What if I added a goodly portion of crème de menthe and crème de cacao?"

She stared at the bra dangling beneath my breasts, under my tee. "Side effects, indeed," she said with a sniff. "Sit on the chair, Sydney."

"Yes, ma'am."

John headed for the door, taking his guitar and his splendid chest with him. "Almost forgot," he called over his shoulder. "Davy said to tell you that tomorrow morning he'll help you decipher Chastity Barker's journal. I'd help, too, but I've got a job."

"Working for Nina?"

"No. Driving Aunt Lillian."

After John had shut the door, I said, "When did you put Xanthia's cat on the Lucinda Lizard gift pile?"

"Shortly before she opened her presents. You can't keep a cat in a box very long. Might as well try and give it a pedicure. Lynn went home and boxed Hamilton while Oliver rounded up the guests. Why?"

"Did you see anyone lurking? Around the gifts, I mean."

"Everyone lurked."

"Did anybody look . . . furtive?"

"Let me think. Terey looked furtive, but she always looks furtive. Remember how she used to stalk Davy?"

"Anyone else?"

"Susan Partridge. She was fiddling around with the gifts. Frankly, I wouldn't trust her in *my* bank, assuming I owned a bank. I wouldn't even trust her near Noah the Pig. Susan has sticky fingers."

"Susan wasn't fiddling, Aunt Lillian. I forgot to put a card in her present. She said she'd take care of it."

"Is something missing, Sydney?"

Yes. A Newts CD. "I won't know until I do inventory," I fibbed.

Damn, I made a lousy detective. Maybe I should stick to witchcraft, even though I made a worse witch. Remembering John's exit line, I said, "What's with the driving-Miss-Daisy bit?"

"I hate to drive." Having pared the onion, Aunt Lillian pressed a slice against the sole of my foot. "And I have some errands to run."

"But John has no license."

"Of course he does. Would I break the law? One of my beaus left a driver's license behind. On his way to the airport, Davy will leave the license with a friend who will alter the birth and expiration dates. Then Davy will pick up the license on his way home."

"A friend? Man or woman?"

"Both."

"Cool Hand Luke!"

"Hush, Sidney. Luke prefers to remain anonymous."

"Drag queen, basketball player, chanteuse, and *forger.*

114

Gee, there's no end to his talents. Cool Hand might want to remain anonymous, Aunt Lillian, but he has a Marlon-Brando-Godfather complex. He does free favors, then you owe him. He used to write essays for Paulie the Pimple and some say he was responsible for Clive Newton's success."

"Luke owed *Davy* a favor, Sydney."

"What kind of favor?"

As she shrugged her shoulders, I remembered the name of the beau who'd left his driver's license behind.

John Elway would soon be Henry Kissinger.

Chastity Barker's Journal

11 June, 1692

My heart aches and my hand feels unsteady, but the events of today are still clear in my mind. Thus, I must try and pen a well-reasoned, accurate account.

Outside, thunder drums and rain snaps against the leaves. I sit at my table, cold tea pushed aside, the light from a candle my only warmth. Inside the bedroom, my husband snores. He'll not stir, even if I should rend the air with loud, inarticulate howls.

I now know how a wolf feels when she has lost her mate.

My sister Mercy says I must recount every occurrence, no matter how inconsequential, no matter how insignificant. Every footstep. Every observation. Every declaration. Then, of course, I must cache my daybook, conceal my disquisition—hide my life.

For my sister Anne's life is at stake.

This morning, following cock crow, Anne met Mercy and me at the Kittridge dovecote. Whereupon, Mercy uttered a strange remark. "I'll burn ferns," she said. "Ferns will send up an aura of protection."

Later she did not know why she said it.

As we treaded a lichen-mottled path, I saw Anne rub her eyes. In the aftermath of Bridget Bishop's hanging, whilst the sky changed to owllight, my sister did prepare a medicinal potion for Isaac Cummings' mare. And when at long last Anne lay abed, her dreams were haunted by evil spirits. Or so she stated amidst the cooing of the pigeons.

We had walked but a short distance when I heard a twig snap.

Anne halted mid-stride. "Did ye hear that?"

" 'Tis a small animal," Mercy said, peering into the foliage. "A fawn or a rabbit."

"A fawn would stomp more lightly," Anne said, "but it could be a rabbit."

"Let us return to our homes and bolt our doors," I pleaded. Even to my own ears, I sounded like a bleating sheep.

"I cannot, poppet." Anne fingered a necklace of cloves, worn to drive away hostile forces. "Goodwife Carl's foot has begun to fester and I promised her a remedy."

Lifting my chin, I said, "Then I shall accompany you, mayhap amuse you with one of Mr. Shakespeare's sonnets."

"Lud, Chastity," Mercy said, her voice a fond tease. "Should ye do that, our sister shall surely nod off whilst chanting her charm."

"Let us not dawdle," Anne warned. She smiled to mitigate her admonition, but her brow crimped.

Shrouded by trees that looked as if they belonged in a John Milton poem, we hastened toward our secret cave.

" 'Tis Tituba Indian's fault," Anne said, as she ushered us through the cave's narrow entrance then brushed away our footprints with a leafy branch.

"What is Tituba's fault, Anne?" Sinking to the ground, I began to twirl one of my long yellow braids with my finger.

"Bridget Bishop," she replied. "Did ye think I meant my neglected mending?"

"You oft neglected your mending," I said, "to meet with Tituba."

"After the first few visits I stayed away from the parsonage." Anne lit a candle, dripped some tallow onto a rock, and placed the candle in the melted tallow. "I took heed of what was happening. Betty Parris is nine years of age, Abigail

Williams, eleven. Betty, Abigail, and the other girls could not listen to Reverend Parris preach fire and brimstone on Sunday then watch Tituba perform her black magic on Monday, at least not without suffering dire consequences. I was absent when Betty began uttering strange sounds and crawling under chairs, but I saw a dark shadow descend on the Village."

"A dark shadow," Mercy parroted. Tossing her white cap toward a pile of mandrake roots, she wove crimson ribbons through her red braids. Then she preened in front of the reflective piece of glass she had propped against one honeycombed wall. "Greensleeves is all my joy," she sang, "Greensleeves is my delight, Greensleeves is my heart of flame, and who but my Lady Greensleeves?"

"Reverend Parris would not approve," Anne teased.

"Devil take the Reverend," Mercy said. "He is nothing more than a plume-plucked, beslubbering, milk-livered maggot-pie."

"Mercy, you blaspheme." My gaze touched upon Anne, only to find that she had collapsed in a heap, overcome with the giggles. Anxious to change the subject, I said, "Is Tituba a witch?"

Anne's laughter subsided. "Most people believe she is, poppet, just like most people believe Greensleeves was a whore."

"But," I said, "Greensleeves was a whore."

While Anne and Mercy possess dulcet speech inflections, my voice is low-pitched. In total darkness, offering up a hello, I could easily be mistaken for a man. Not that I venture out into the night anymore. 'Tis too dangerous. Suppose milk curdled? Supposed a cow birthed a dead calf? Suppose a barn burned? Suppose someone fell from a loft or roof and broke an arm or leg?

All those things had happened, without repercussions, before Tituba Indian, reared in Barbados, whiled away the tedium of winter chores by regaling her charges, Betty and Abigail, with the mythical deeds she had witnessed. Soon other girls and young women were initiated into Tituba's story-telling circle. I had been invited but said no.

"Tituba baked a witch cake made from rye meal and the urine of the afflicted girls," I said. "She then fed the cake to the household dogs, hoping to ferret out witches. Was the cake a ploy? Would you say she's a witch, Anne?"

"Nay, poppet," my sister replied. "Had Tituba told the magistrates of her parsonage games, all suspicion of witch-craft would have ended and the girls would have been cen-sured. Instead, she told of a red dog that ordered her to hurt the girls, of two large black cats that bid her serve them, and of rides through the air on a pole. She even conjured up a tall, white-haired man dressed in black."

"Why," I asked, "did you not tell the magistrates about Tituba's parsonage stories?"

Anne hesitated. Then she said, "Remember what hap-pened to John Proctor? He could not keep his outraged si-lence, thus became engulfed by the whirlwind of accusations, along with his wife Elizabeth. I had no desire to suffer the same fate, nor did I want you and Mercy persecuted."

Perched on a log, Mercy's long fingernails, shaped by a pumice stone, feathered the auburn tendrils that frame her ears. "I was at the First Church," she said, "when Deputy Governor Thomas Danforth did question Mary Warren, who defected from the group when her master, John Proctor, was denounced."

"Mary has little regard for Elizabeth Proctor." Rising to her feet, Anne stretched like a cat. "But she has a great deal of respect and affection for John."

"The girls then accused Mary," Mercy continued. "Abigail Williams swore that Mary's apparition had appeared to them, offering the devil's book and choking those who refused to sign. When Mary bit her lip, the girls shrieked of being bitten. When Mary clasped her hands, the girls screamed that Mary pinched them. When Mary stirred her feet, the girls stamped their own so forcefully the building quaked. Soon Mary said she had lied and the girls came out of their fits. Then Mary went into a fit. She was removed from the room, replaced by Bridget Bishop."

Anne stared into my face. "Do you understand why I dared not face the magistrates, Chastity?"

"Aye, Anne."

"But one cannot live a lie for long without believing its truth," said Mercy, her cheeks blazing like poppies. "What began as mere mischief has become a web of lies and Abigail doth play the spider with devotion."

"I might have been able to stop the accusations last February," Anne said, "had I told Reverend Parris of Tituba's games."

"Dearest sister," Mercy cried, "you cannot know for certain that your divulgence would have stopped the madness."

"Nonetheless," Anne said, "I've informed Abigail Williams that should her denunciations continue, I shall consult with the magistrates. I believe the court would give credence to my account since it would echo Mary Warren's."

At age seventeen, I am the youngest of my sisters. Plump and of a dreamy nature, I doubt the veracity of my own curative skills and prefer to record my sentiments inside a daybook. That way, I told Anne and Mercy, our father's tutelage would not be in vain.

"Do your incantations warrant eternal damnation, Anne?" I asked, my voice little more than a whisper.

"Nay," she replied, "for I have the good of the Village at heart."

"The good of the Village," Mercy parroted. "And the good of our husbands. Toby doth prosper, though he knows not why, the clotpole."

Mercy has no regard for men, especially her husband Tobias, whom she oft calls a suck-egg weasel, a snail-skulled half-wit, or a bleating foal. Not to his face, of course, though Toby adores his wife and tolerates her frequent outbursts with a bemused smile.

"Do not forget that we practice our skills for the good of our children," Anne said, patting her belly.

I glanced widdershins, as if the bats that inhabit the cave's passages might tattle. Then I said, "Do you think they will hang us?"

Mercy arose from the log and tweaked my nose. "The girls dare not denounce us," she said. "Be thankful for Tituba's tales, Chastity, since the girls believe we might avenge our deaths by reappearing in other forms."

"What forms?" I felt my eyes widen until they surely looked like the eyes of Old Scratch, my husband's favourite hound.

"Cats, dogs, birds." Mercy smiled. "In truth, I'd fancy wings."

"Oh, no," I cried. "Birds are eaten. Birds can be shot and fall from the sky."

"But imagine the freedom of flight, Chastity," Mercy said. "Do you not wonder how a rainbow would feel against your face? Or clouds?"

"Not at all," I said. " 'Tis a fat pillow, stuffed with feathers, that oft lures my face. And, I've no mind to leave God's soil." With a smile, I turned to Anne. "What animal would you choose? A doe? Owl? Cat?"

Before she could answer, the illumination at the cave's entrance was blotted out by three men. "Last night a boat sank," William Bly said, "and all those aboard perished. Abigail Williams saw Anne Kittridge atop a meeting house beam."

"Last night I was at home," Anne said, and I knew she was striving to remain calm, for Yosef Solom, the stout man she had quarreled with yesterday, stood by William Bly's side. "Abigail Williams doth utter false testimony, inasmuch as I threatened—"

"Nay, dearest Anne," I blurted, interrupting. "Last night you prepared a medicinal potion for Isaac Cummings' mare."

Despite Mercy's aggrieved expression, I gestured toward a flat rock topped with dried herbs, a flask, an earthenware bowl of honey, and four candles. "If my sister was here at the cave," I said earnestly, "how could she be atop a meeting house beam?"

Ignoring me, William Bly turned to Rueben Cavin and Yosef Solom. "There's naught inside the cave," William Bly said. "Candles, weeds, cloth, some pottery. Did ye hear enough to damn her, Rueben?"

"Nay," he said. "She and her sisters talked of birds and animals. In truth, 'twas time trifled away."

"Yosef?"

I watched the stout man's eyes glint with vengeful satisfaction as he said, "It matters not what we heard or did not hear. Abigail Williams swore Anne Kittridge flew through the air on a pole, but first she played the whore with Tituba's white-haired man."

I heard Anne whisper, "Lord give me strength," as she fingered her clove necklace.

God help me, I can write no more. The quill of my pen looks like the spine on a hedgehog and tears blur my day-book's ink.

Chastity Barker's Journal

September, 1692

I am situated in the hayloft, hidden from sight. I should not be writing in my daybook, for my scribbles include formulae, rituals, and incantations. But Mercy said, "Chastity, you must pen our family history for posterity," and Anne, bless her heart, concurred. Mercy told me not to pen the account our parents, Samuel and Rebecca Ashe, expound, but the true reason why we emigrated to the New World.

Born in Bury St. Edmonds, my sisters and I spent a happy childhood there. Then, four years ago, shortly before I turned thirteen, Mercy sixteen, and Anne seventeen, our mum was accosted by a Mr. Ratcliffe. As he rent her bodice, Mum stopped struggling, lifted her skirts, and used her knee to great advantage. Doubled over, vomiting upon the paving stones, Mr. Ratcliffe nevertheless managed to threaten Mum—and our family—with bodily harm.

The next day, a host of reddish brown spiders crept up Broad street toward Mr. Ratcliffe's house. The spiders were orderly, without stragglers. All attempts to stop them were ineffectual and they continued on their way until they reached Mr. Ratcliffe's door. Some inched through the cracks into his house while the rest swarmed up two posts and spun an enormous web across the door, from which they hung down in living bundles. Mr. Ratcliffe's servants finally destroyed the spiders by lighting straws under them. But in view of their purposeful march and the knowledge that witches could send such plagues, sorcery was suspected.

Mr. Ratcliffe, now of unsound mind, drooled, wrung his

hands, pissed his breeches, and denounced Mum.

Our family fled in the dead of night, with only the clothes on our backs, three horses, and a small pouch of precious gems. Reaching Sandwich in Kent, we boarded a ship bound for Massachusetts.

Anne met her husband during the voyage and Mercy met hers directly after landing. Alone and lonely, I accepted the first proposal that came my way. Obadiah Barker, stout as a Punchinello and seventeen years my senior, wooed me with pink pigs made from marzipan. I did not love him the way Mum loves Papa and Anne loves her John, but no one else had caught my fancy or given me almond-scented pigs.

Little did I realize that my first wifely duty would commence in the dark, that love-making was not only dull but painful. When I found myself with child, Obadiah got drunk as a lord. When I miscarried, he drowned his sorrows for weeks on end. Then he chased me from room to room, threw me on the bed, lanced my membretoon, and impregnated me again. Three and a half months later, despite Anne and Mercy's charms and potions, I miscarried.

Anne has a son, Johnny, and hopes her new babe will be a girl. Mercy has a son, Tobias Samuel. Even Mum, who lives in Connecticut, gave birth to a fourth daughter, whom she christened Tempest. I smile every time I think about the violent storm we encountered at sea.

I miss Anne terribly. A woman who is with child cannot be hanged. Thus, the ministers and magistrates have put off Anne's trial until they arrive at "a consensus through discussion."

Guilt consumes me. Had I not spoken of Anne's presence at the cave, she might have escaped persecution. Mercy says that when Anne threatened Abigail Williams, her fate was sealed. Mercy says to stop blaming myself. Mercy says the ministers and magistrates are nothing more than sheep-biting, swag-bellied, maggot-pies.

Oh lud, I hear footsteps on the loft ladder. Pray God, 'tis Jack Grayson.

'Tis an hour later and I am distraught. 'Twas not Jack, but Matthew Grayson, Jack's twin brother, who climbed the loft ladder. They look identical, Matthew and Jack, except jagged scars split Jack's chin, cheek, and eyebrow whilst Matt's countenance is unmarred.

Rising to my feet, I faced Matt square. "Obadiah is abed with an attack of rheumatics," I said. "He is in great pain and cannot endure visitors."

" 'Tis cold," Matt replied. "Water's near froze in the conduit."

"Did you not hear me? Obadiah's abed, and I must tend to him," I said, wishing I could retrieve my hidden daybook, ink pot, and pen. "I give you good day, Matt. God keep you in health."

"I've a message from Jack," he said. When I hesitated, he laughed. " 'Tis a dry tale," he said, "so let us wet our whistles and set there for the telling of it." Whereupon, he pulled a flask from the pocket of his coat.

I said, "Spirits? Have you lost your mind, sir?"

"Nay," he said. " 'Tis my heart that is lost, and I wish to take you as my lover."

"You must search for your heart, sir," I said, accustomed to his baiting. " 'Tis my understanding that Ketzia Van Rijn collects hearts."

Ketzia Van Rijn, a too-tall spinster who reminds me of a crane, has collected nary a marriage offer and is getting desperate.

I said, "What is Jack's message, please?"

"The message is mine," Matt said. "Meet me tonight, Chastity, in the field where the dead lady moans on nights o' the full moon."

With a shiver, I said, "The Lady in Red?"

"Or I'll tell Obadiah my tale," Matt said. "Nay. On second thought, I'll tell the congregation. There's a mort o' them canting, psalm-whining Puritans who'd like to hear my tale."

"What tale?" I asked, knowing full well what Matt meant.

"Tonight," he said as he began to descend the ladder. "When the moon is full."

Holding back tears, I watched the top of his head disappear.

Matt is a worm. Save for my neighbour, Rueben Cavin, Matt is the most comely man in Salem, but only on the outside. Inside, he is as scarred as his brother Jack's face.

My first thought was to find Jack, but that would only make matters worse. Jack has a frightful temper. So I shall seek out Mercy, in Jack's stead. She can chant an incantation, mayhap the same spider curse Mum put on Mr. Ratcliffe.

Chapter Fifteen

Monday morning

Shifting in my chair, I looked up from the journal. "Chastity Barker was an adulteress?"

Davy grinned. "That would be my guess."

"No. Impossible. I must have misread it."

"Don't be silly, Syd. Chastity had a fling with Jack Grayson."

"I don't like that word, 'fling.' "

"Would you prefer *affaire d'amour?*"

"Yes. Your accent is flawless, Davy. Where did you learn to speak French?"

"You forget. Our mother spoke French when provoked. Her favorite was *'belle sainte vierge.'* " He grinned again. "If only Nicholas had known that one of Mom's ancestors was a whore. Too bad he didn't decipher the journal."

"Too bad we're missing the pages between June and September, and I wouldn't call Chastity a whore."

"What would you call her?"

"We don't even know if she slept with Jack."

"Let's find out." Davy flexed his fingers. "Keep reading."

My brother sat in front of Oliver's old computer, facing a wall of windows. Beneath the windows were mahogany-stained boards; plywood playing dress-up.

Oliver had lavishly given me the secondhand computer and hand-me-down printer, last year's Christmas present. His gift-tag read: "Books don't change tastes. They reflect taste. Merry Christmas."

He'd also given me a gift certificate to Weight Winners, a

diet club. The certificate lay in my jewelry box, underneath a vial of New Mown Hay oil. A few dabs of the fragrant oil, behind the ears or on the neck pulse, helps one make a transformation in one's life; turn over a new leaf or start a new project.

Aunt Lillian's sewing machine dominated one corner of the long, narrow, closed-in porch, while my potter's wheel filled another corner. Since the room flanks the apothecary, you can hear customers. Lilly the Witch, who'd installed heat, electricity, and a phone jack, had used the sun porch to pot plants. An earth-soil-guano smell still lingered.

Chasdick sprawled near the sewing machine, Annie between his paws. Mercy perched on top of the sewing machine. When I paused to decipher an obscure word, she'd flap her wings, as if ruffled by the delay.

"Maybe we should rest first," I told Davy. "Or eat. We've got party leftovers galore and—"

"What's wrong, Syd?"

"The shop needs a thorough cleaning before we can reopen." I glanced down at my legs, sheathed by Davy's jeans, then the white T-shirt that sheathed my black bra. "My dirty clothes are still in the hamper and I'm on my last pair of undies. If I don't do a wash soon, I'll have to wear the thong panties Jim gave me, and a piece of dental floss breaching my butt might distract me from journal interpretation."

"That's what I like about you, Syd. You're so poetic. And you smell terrific. New Mown Hay?" When I nodded, he said, "If push comes to shove, you can borrow a pair of my boxers. Now, tell me what's really wrong."

"Damn it, Davy, I feel like a voyeur. I'm no better than Gusta Lowenfeld."

"But we're not peeking through bedroom windows, Syd. Chastity Barker lived three hundred years ago, and she's dead."

Chasdick gave a *woof*. It sounded indignant.

Annie *mewed* and Mercy squawked, *"The piper he piped on a hilltop high, butter and eggs and a pound of cheese."*

"Maybe they're hungry, too," I said, pointing toward my livestock.

"Are you really hungry, Syd?"

"No, not really." I heaved a deep sigh. "Okay, Davy, you win." My finger found a journal entry. "Let's decipher."

This time I thought I heard a euphoric *woof.*

Chastity Barker's Journal

September, 1692

I believed things could not get worse, but I was mistaken. Matt must be dissuaded somehow, and Obadiah lies abed, puling and puking. 'Tis a chore to keep visitors at a distance. And yet, if my husband were discovered in his present state, he would be severely chidden by our congregation. Obadiah steadfastly acquires more and more grog, I know not how. Mayhap he bribes a servant.

Even abed, he attacks my sensibilities. He flings lewd threats and bedpans at my head. Anne and Mercy believe I fear for my health. In truth, I fear for my life. And for the new life inside me. Jack's child.

I take full responsibility for the corruption of my morality. Jack tried to stay me from my course. Aware that I live in bedlam and my husband is a lunatic, he merely sought to comfort me.

Jack's wife and unborn babe perished when his wagon hit a rut and overturned. He sustained several disfigurements and a guilt-ridden anguish that will ne'er go away. Part of his guilt, he says, comes from the fact that he experienced a profound fondness for me on the day I first set foot in Salem Village.

Jack ne'er talks of love. That would besmirch the memory of his wife. Nonetheless, he expresses his love by deed, rather than word, whensoever we are cloistered in the hayloft. Jack does not know I am with child, but I must tell him and trust he will have a solution to my quandary. For I can find no remedy, unless God sees fit to make me a widow.

★ ★ ★ ★ ★

Having heard footsteps on the loft ladder, I hid my day-book. Now, as I write once again, my hand shakes. Not from fear but from joy, for this time 'twas Jack Grayson who ascended the ladder.

There are those who find Jack's scars repugnant. I think they make him more comely, even though Mercy has oft suggested that she secure the bandages used on his wounds, sprinkle them with rue oil, and place them inside a hollow-oak hole. If enacted during the waning moon, Jack's scars would be transferred to the tree and dispersed into the earth.

"God bless you, Jack," I said with a smile. Rising, I untied my apron, pulled my somber black gown over my head, then tossed both garments toward a bale of hay.

Jack said, "Are you mad, Chastity?"

'Twas not the reaction I'd hoped for.

Jack was staring at my red velvet gown, worn under my black gown. Mercy had stitched the red gown when I told her I wanted to play-act a scene from one of Mr. Shakespeare's dramas, mayhap Romeo and Juliet.

"You presume too much," Jack said.

Annoyed, I said, "Does my décolletage offend you?"

"Nay," he replied, "but 'twould offend the congregation."

"Oh fiddle, Jack," I said. "Do you not find it puzzling that the ministers and magistrates discipline all who do not see things from their light? Was that not why Puritans shunned the Church of England? If a man dared criticize, 'twas the Star Chamber that chopped off his ears. And now there is talk of a man in Boston who had his ears chopped off."

"I did not ride here to talk about ears," Jack said, "and where did you get that gown?"

"My sister, Mercy. She lauds bright colours. And despite your displeasure, you do too, for you cannot take your eyes off my gown."

"Nay, dearest," Jack said. "I cannot take my eyes off your décolletage."

Surprising myself, I burst into tears.

Alarmed, Jack said, "Why do you weep? 'Twas a tease."

"Obadiah's debauchery grows harsher," I cried, sinking to my knees and covering my face with my hands.

Jack knelt and pried my fingers loose. "Mayhap we should leave Salem," he said.

"We cannot leave. You have worked so hard, even managed to accrue three more acres."

"What good is land," Jack said, "when one has no helpmate, no bedmate, no heir?"

I stroked his face, lingering at his scars. "Ketzia Van Rijn is there for the asking," I said, meaning it as a chaff, knowing I'd die a thousand deaths should Jack take my notion seriously.

His smile was bitter, just before he said, "Have you not heard? Ketzia is gotten, Chastity."

"By whom?"

"My brother, Matt."

"He proposed wedlock?"

"Aye," Jack said. "Ketzia Van Rijn is well dowered, more so since her uncle set sail from Essex to channel her family assets."

"But she is judgmental and shrill," I said. "And she looks like a heron."

Jack laughed. " 'Tis true she resembles a heron. However, Ketzia abhors spinsterhood and desires a child."

"Nay, Jack. She is too old."

"She is eight and twenty," he said. "Matt had no choice,

132

Chastity, for he has been ordered off my land and he is destitute."

I breathed a sigh of relief. "Then you know of the threats."

"What threats?"

"Why did you cast him out?"

"I could no longer tolerate his cruelty and sloth," Jack said. "What threats, Chastity?"

"He demanded that I meet him tonight in the field where the Lady in Red moans on nights o' the full moon," I said, "or he shall tell the congregation about us."

Jack laughed again. "The congregation would ne'er give credence to his account, dearest."

"Nay, you're amiss," I cried. "Obadiah will believe Matt and the Reverend will believe Obadiah, for I have not lain with my husband since the loss of our babe. And I am with child."

Chapter Sixteen

Monday afternoon

Davy stood up and reached for the ceiling. Then he touched his toes with his fingertips and shook like a wet collie. Then he sat down again.

"I've got a crick in my back," he said.

"Mayhap it's time we stopped."

"Mayhap?"

My cheeks baked. "Maybe we should stop."

"Why? Are you still feeling voyeur-ish?"

"No. I feel . . . sad."

"Aw. Don't. Chastity Barker found her one true love and—"

"I'm not sure that's the case, Davy. Chastity says Jack never talked of love. But he expressed his love by . . ." I glanced over at my parrot. "By humping her in the loft. It sounds as if Jack simply wanted a piece of—"

"Ruttish, pox-marked malt-worm," Mercy squawked, flapping her wings.

"Hush, Mercy. What do you think, Davy? You're a guy. You should be able to read between the lines."

"You have too many Jim-memories, Syd. Did Jim ever talk of love?"

"Of course he did. Don't look at me like that. Okay, he equivocated by playing songs by The Ice Man whenever we . . . um . . ."

"Humped?"

"Yes. That was the closest Jim ever came to saying 'I love you.' But we were in lust, not love. You can justify lots of . . .

134

sins . . . when you're in lust."

"And you think Chastity was in lust?"

"No. Not Chastity. Jack."

Before Davy could reply, Chasdick leapt to his paws, barked, then cowered underneath the computer desk. Miraculously, he didn't ruffle Annie's fur or mangle Davy's feet.

The toad-knocker *thwacked* impatiently.

"There's a 'Closed' sign in the window." To my ears, the reluctance in my voice sounded loud and clear. Tommy Murphy always says that business is like a bicycle; when it isn't moving forward at a good speed, it wobbles.

Davy glanced at his watch. "Damn, it's Rosie."

"Rosie who?"

"Rose from Vegas. Maurice's wife. Maurice's ex. Maurice sobered up."

"And had the marriage annulled?"

"In a way. Turns out, he's already married. Two and a half kids. He gave Rose a sizable payoff, *very* sizable, but she'd quit her job. She honestly believed she'd play a senator's wife. Did I tell you that Maurice was a sleazy politician?"

"Sleazy politician is redundant. Is his name even Maurice?"

"Nope. I'd better get the door, Syd."

"Wait. What's Rose doing here?"

"She's here because I'm here. After picking her up at the airport yesterday, I deposited her at the White Hart Bed and Breakfast."

"You're in lust, Davy. I can see it in your eyes."

"Do you want to meet Rose before she takes me to lunch?"

"Is she literate?" I asked sarcastically.

"Define literate."

"Hillary Clinton. Barbara Walters. Chastity Barker."

"Yes."

"Yes, she's literate? Or yes, Hillary, Barbara, and Chastity are literate?"

"Yes, *Rose* is literate. She has a small drinking problem, that's all. You'll like her, Syd. She's a stripper with a degree in chemistry."

Chapter Seventeen

Monday afternoon

Together, Davy and I answered the door.

A black limousine squatted at the curb. A chauffeur stood next to the limousine, polishing its fender with his uniformed butt.

I remembered telling my brother that Rose had to be drop-dead gorgeous.

What an understatement.

Her blonde hair made Farrah's Charlie's-Angels-coiffure look benign. Her eyes hinted that Paul Newman's sperm had found Betty Boop's egg. Under a blue silk dress, her breasts were unfettered and the narrow portion of her body between the thorax and hips would have induced Margaret Mitchell to re-calculate the size of Scarlett O'Hara's corseted seventeen-inch waist.

Yet, Rose possessed a waif-ish, almost virginal quality, and I could understand why The Senator had purchased Davy's lodestone.

A *small* drinking habit was an understatement, too.

She stood swaying on the doorstep, a Stolichnaya vodka bottle in one hand.

Slung across her shoulders was what I hoped was a fake fur coat.

"Davy, wizard mine," she said, breathing alcoholic fumes into my face.

"I'm Sydney. Wearing Davy's clothes," I added, just in case.

"I'm Rosie, as in O'Donnell, only tha's not my las' name."

"What is your last name?"

"Had one. Maurice's. Lost it." Her big blue eyes welled up with tears as she fumbled through her pockets and pulled out a pair of tortoise-shell glasses. Peering through the lenses, she squealed, "Davy!" then took a slug from the vodka bottle. "Davy, where's my las' name?"

"I'm sorry, Syd," my brother said under his breath. "She's not coping very well with the divorce."

"Give me a break," I whispered. "She was married to The Senator for three minutes."

"Three nights."

"Two nights. One night she puked on the lodestone and passed out."

"That doesn't mean she wasn't married. If you were married to a man who was already married, wouldn't you drink?"

"Davy, she consummated her wedding vows in your hotel room."

I realized the volume of our voices had risen when Rose said, "Weddin' vows. Awesome. Elvis sang 'Viva Viagra.' "

" 'Viva Las Vegas,' " I said.

"Yeah, that too."

"Rosie," Davy said, "let's go back to the B&B."

"He promised I could schmooze all the Bushes," she said, and it took me a moment to realize she meant George, George, Barbara, Laura, and the rest of the clan.

Rose peered at me. "You're the sistah-witch, right? Make me a spell, Witchie. Davy, tell'er to make me a spell."

I didn't say: *Poof, you're a spell.*

Instead, I said, "A degree in chemistry, Davy?"

Rose said, "Ummm . . . tha's a nice perfume, Witch."

While she sniffed at my neck pulse, I calculated her budget. "It's called New Mown Hay and it's only two-hundred-and-seventy-five dollars per ounce."

"Ring around the Rosie."

"Wha's that?" Shoving her way past Davy and me, Rose squinted at the banister. "Oooh," she said, "a parakeet."

Before I could tell her to put her glasses back on, my parrot squawked, *"David, David, bo bavid, banana fanna—"*

"Mercy, hush," I said.

"Mercy, shut up," Davy said.

"Mercy," Rose said as she spun around, dropped the Stoli bottle, closed her eyes, and slumped against my brother.

"Ring around the Rosie, all fall down," Mercy squawked.

"Who belongs to that limousine, Sydney?" Aunt Lillian scampered down the path, toward the wide-open front door. Her skirts swayed and her bloomers teased. Following in her wake was John. Henry. Elway. Kissinger.

Chapter Eighteen

Monday afternoon

Five Harry Potters sat on five endangered animals.

Aunt Lillian had ordered our Harry mugs: three dozen for the shop, a half dozen for our kitchen. My friend Nina had given me the endangered-animal placemats, a birthday present.

Unwilling to hurt Aunt Lillian's feelings, John, Davy, Harlan-the-Chauffeur, and I sipped scalded milk. Aunt Lillian, who loves the taste of corn syrup, sugar, albumen, and mucilaginous root, kept adding marshmallows to her hot chocolate.

Half-raw cookie dough, shaped like cats, dogs, parrots, and horses topped a china plate. Except for Aunt Lillian, no one had touched the cookies.

"Presumably, the cats, dogs, and parrots are Annie, Chasdick, and Mercy," I said, "but why the horse?"

"Reb Ashmare," Aunt Lillian said, her expression smug.

"Excuse me?"

"I bought a mare, Sydney. That's what I meant by errands, why I needed John to drive me. She's lovely. Mostly gray, a little dappled, with the prettiest rump you've ever—"

"You bought a horse and named it Reb Ashmare?" My question was rhetorical, yet I couldn't stop my gaze from probing the kitchen, as if she'd hidden the animal inside our broom closet. "Did you ride it home?"

"Of course not, Sydney. I can't ride."

"Then why did you buy . . . oh, I get it. Reb Ashmare. Rebecca Ashe. Anne, Mercy, and Chastity's mother."

140

"Exactly." Aunt Lillian beamed. "I saw a classified ad in the paper, and somehow I knew—"

"That the horse possessed the soul of Rebecca Ashe." I glanced over at John, who struggled to contain his laughter, then a grinning Davy, then Harlan, busy drowning marshmallows.

"I wanted to keep the family together," Aunt Lillian said. "The nice man who owned Reb recommended another nice man who boards horses. Once the horse trailer transfers Reb to Black Forest, we can take Annie, Chastity—"

"Chasdick."

"And Mercy to visit her."

Davy excused himself to check on Rose, who snoozed inside the guest bedroom. John had carried her upstairs as if she weighed nothing, and I had contributed my Denver Broncos wastebasket, now fitted with a clean plastic liner.

Aunt Lillian had invited Harlan inside, after saying he'd "freeze his balls off."

Outside, winter had decided to pay Colorado a surprise, return visit. An icy wind whistled through my backyard gazebo and cumulus clouds cumulated. No doubt, snow would swirl by nightfall.

The gloomy sky reflected my mood. "How much did you pay for the horse, Aunt Lillian?"

"Mare, Sydney, and she was within my price range. I raided Noah and used some money from the stuffed-critter fund."

I pictured Aunt Lillian working endless hours stitching our stuffed animals. Still, I couldn't stop myself from asking, "How much did the *mare* trailer cost?"

"Nothing. I'm borrowing it and I have AAA."

"AAA won't pay for towing a trailer."

"Yes, they will. After Luke talks to them."

"Please don't start asking Cool Hand for favors, Aunt Lillian."

Harlan, who'd been earnestly scrutinizing his endangered owl placemat, looked up.

John said, "Cool Hand? Cool Hand Luke?"

"Yes," I said. "What did you remember, John?"

"Just the name. I don't know why and I can't see a face to go with it."

"After he had your driver's license amended, Davy might have mentioned Cool Hand," I said, disappointed. "And you'd better start saving some money for Tempest," I told Aunt Lillian.

Beneath her fan of silver ringlets, my aunt's ears perked, and I could have bitten my tongue. "Rebecca had a fourth daughter, Tempest," I mumbled. "It was in her journal. If you decide to adopt a mouse or hamster, please ask me first."

"There's no Tempest Ashe on our family tree, Sydney."

"Maybe she died young."

"She'd be listed in our family Bible, regardless."

"I forgot about the family Bible. Where is it?"

"Oliver has it."

"Of course. Why am I not surprised? He probably auctioned it off on eBay."

"No, Sydney. He steals names."

John said, "Steals names?"

"For his book characters." Snatching up an Annie-cookie, Aunt Lillian ate its tail. "Sydney, I wish you'd . . . what's Xanthia's word? Oh, yes, chill out."

I gave up, chilled out, and turned toward Harlan. If I hadn't been caught between the past and present, rattled by Chastity (who, in her own words, was morally corrupt) and Rosie-all-fall-down and Reb Ashmare, I might not have asked my stupid question. "Have you always wanted to be a chauffeur, Harlan?"

"No, ma'am." His well-manicured hands clutched imaginary reins. "I wanted to be a jockey."

"Oh, good. You can ride my aunt's new horse." I heard the sarcasm in my voice and shot Aunt Lillian a look of contrition. "What happened, Harlan? You grew too tall?"

"No, ma'am. Unlucky. A woman got raped, almost killed, and she gave my description to a sketch artist. I didn't have an alibi, went to the movies alone, *Grease* with that Kotter kid. The movie complex was near the rape scene."

"But surely that's not enough—"

"The woman described her assailant as over six feet. I'm six-one. She said he had a bald head and a couple of tattoos. I shave my head."

Shedding his chauffeur's jacket, Harlan rolled up his shirt sleeves, revealing an I-heart-Lola on one arm, a Black Panthers' salute on the other.

I stared at the raised-fist tattoo. "She remembered the Panthers' salute?"

"No. She remembered the heart. She got confused during the line-up, seeing so many black faces and all, but they asked us to say something that had been said during the rape and she picked me. Then, in court, she was positive. To make a long story short, while I was wasting away in prison, someone told me about Cool Hand. I must have sent him a hundred letters before he paid me a visit. Thanks to Cool Hand and his lawyer, my DNA was tested and—"

"They let you go."

"Let me go!" Wearing a pair of bikini panties and a whole lot of bare skin, Rose entered the kitchen, preceded by Annie and Mercy.

Davy, his cheeks maraschino-cherry-red, followed Rose.

He tried to hold her back, but she yanked her arm free from his grasp.

Annie undulated toward John and vaulted into his lap.

"Ta-ta, Sydney." Mercy flapped her way to her cage and sat on her swing. Spying Harlan and John, she squawked, *"Noddy, rump-fed clotpole. Maggot-pie."*

Rose staggered to the table. "Oooh, a White Russian," she said. Before anyone could stop her, she took a few gulps from Harlan's mug. Then her face contorted.

Davy managed to pilot her to the sink before she spit up burnt milk, melted marshmallows, and a whole lot of Stolichnaya. Like a ballet dancer, her feet arched and un-arched as she moaned the chorus from "Witch Doctor."

I thought she might all-fall-down again.

Instead, she made an about-face. Still somewhat drunk, staring at John, she said, "I know you."

Chapter Nineteen

Monday afternoon

Although John's face remained passive, indifferent, I could sense his intensity as he said, "Who am I?"

"Clint Black."

Aunt Lillian, Davy, and Harlan just stared while I said, "Clint Black? The country-western singer?"

Rose squinted at John. "No, no, not Clint Black. Keith Snyder."

Totally nonplused, I said, "Who's Keith Snyder?"

"A musician." John's voice sounded foggy, as if he'd just recalled the title of an elusive book or movie. "Keith has long hair and looks like the face I see in the mirror every morning, but I'm not Keith."

"How do you know, John? You play the guitar and—"

"He's younger, Sydney, and he writes books. I don't think I could write a book if my life depended on it."

"Sure you could. You made up that terrific story about the yellow dog and the white rabbits."

He gave me a let's-get-real look, then turned to Harlan. "I suffer from memory glitches."

"Don't we all?" Harlan said, and I knew he was thinking of the woman who had put him behind bars.

Davy said, "Where did you leave your glasses, Rosie?"

She patted her mostly-naked body as if searching for pockets. I had a horrible feeling she'd frisk her panties, but she merely shrugged.

Harlan rose from his chair. As if dressing a doll, he shoved her arms inside his chauffeur's jacket. At the same time, Davy said, "You probably dropped the damn glasses when you—"

"Swooned," Aunt Lillian said, rising. "I'll look for them."

"I'll look." John placed Annie on the floor. "Why don't you make some coffee, Aunt Lillian?"

"Good idea." She walked toward the counter canisters, and I could hear her muttering something about how automatic coffee makers didn't burn water.

As John left the kitchen, I steered Rose to his chair. She seemed dazed. "He looks like Keith, I swear he looks like Keith," she mumbled. "I di'nt make it up."

"Of course you didn't," I said, soothingly. "It's just that you can't see very well without your glasses."

"Los' my contacts when I los' my name."

"Where did you meet Keith?" I asked, hoping she'd shelve the bigamous senator.

"Vegas. Lounge act. He signed his name on my cocktail napkin. Have it somewhere, purse maybe. Don't feel good, Witch. Tum-tum."

As she hugged her tum-tum, Aunt Lillian said, "Maybe you should go down to the shop, Sydney. Fetch Davy's girl-friend a healing amulet."

Our most popular healing amulet is fashioned from a peeled clove of garlic, a pinch of eucalyptus, a pinch of cinnamon, two pinches of sage, and a pinch of saffron. Sewn up—by Aunt Lillian—inside a blue cloth, we anoint our all-purpose remedy with sandalwood oil.

I knew Aunt Lillian wouldn't ask "Davy's girlfriend" for money, so I said, "Maybe you should lie down again, Rosie."

"Maybe she should wait for her glasses." Davy's voice sounded impersonal, cold, and I had a feeling his Vegas virgin would soon be history.

As if on cue, John entered the kitchen. In one hand he carried tortoise shell frames. "They got stepped on," he said, exposing the shattered lenses.

I studied John, trying to gauge his sincerity. Had he stepped on the glasses himself, not wanting Rose to recognize him? Was that remotely possible?

Suddenly I remembered that, thanks to Cool Hand, The Newts had played Las Vegas. A lounge act in a big-name hotel. Gusta Lowenfeld's gossip column had touted their success.

"Rosie," I said, "did you ever meet a singer by the name of Clive Newton?"

"Clive. Newton. Yeah. We hooked up at the MGM." Attempting a wink, she managed to curl half her lip. "Clive looks jus' like Keith Snyder."

I pointed at John. "But you said *he* looks like—"

"An' you know what, Witch?"

"What?"

"Clive was awesome, like that pink bunny rabbit in those TV 'mercials. He just kept goin' an goin'."

She gave me a Scarlett-after-a-night-with-Rhett smile. Then she pushed John's mug toward a salt shaker, lowered her face to the table, and rested her cheek against an endangered tiger. "Oooh," she said, "a striped pussycat."

Annie hissed and Mercy squawked, *"Membretoon gipsyfilly."*

Chastity Barker's Journal

September, 1692

I thought Jack would be craven, benumbed by the censure that is sure to befall us, for he is more God-fearing than I. Instead, he picked me up in his arms, whirled me around the loft, then placed my befuddled head and breathless body across a drift of hay.

Whereupon, he divested me of my red velvet gown.

My head still reeled. Jack kissed me. My husband does not kiss me. Perchance it is the reason his seed never took root. The congregation might not concur, but I believe kisses are fodder for all and sundry, assuming one desires growth. Not that I would kiss a cow. Or turkey. Or swine. Mayhap a shoat, but a barrow? 'Tis clear God looks with favour upon the barrow, as He does all animals, though I sometimes wonder if He extols castigation. But at no time would I deem one of my husband's barrows worthy of a kiss.

Shedding his outer garments, clothed in nothing more than his body linen, Jack reached for the bottom of my chemise. As he drew the smock over my head, I must confess that two of Herrick's lines sailed through my consciousness—

A sweet disorder in the dress

Kindles in clothes a wantonness

—and, momentarily, I regretted the donning of my red gown.

My heart's pit-a-pat thundered in my ears as Jack's finger delved (I dare not say where, though none but I shall ever read this), smoothing the way for more exquisite delights. Every bone in my body fluxed and—oh lud, there is someone at my door.

★ ★ ★ ★ ★

'Tis long past eventide as I take pen in hand.

'Twas my sister Mercy, with her small son Sammy, who knocked at my door. Entering, Mercy gave me greeting, then said, "Nay, Sammy, do not bite Uncle Obadiah's hound, for he will bite you back."

Rising from my chair, I knelt and said, "Give Auntie a kiss."

Sammy regarded me solemnly. "Naw, Aunt," he said, "kiss Scatch."

Old Scratch did not protest, merely licked Sammy's face. Soon the dog and the small boy were asleep, entangled.

"Now we can talk," Mercy said. Sitting at the kitchen table, she glanced around. "Why have you not begun to prepare the evening meal?"

I felt my face flush. "Obadiah shoots the cat so often, no food will settle in his belly," I said.

Mercy said, "Where did you hear that turn of phrase? Shoots the cat?"

"From Obadiah's favourite servant," I replied. "He is called Trump, after the card game. Trump pleases my husband, so he can say anything he pleases. Before Obadiah fell ill, I asked him to dismiss Trump, and wanting to please me, he assented. But when I lost our babe, he reneged."

"Fall ill?" Mercy's brow furrowed. "Do you mean to tell me that Obadiah still vomits from drunkenness, despite my incantations and Anne's amulet?"

I tiptoed toward the bedroom door and pulled it open. A nasty smell emanated, just before Obadiah said, "Come closer, wife."

As I timidly advanced, he screamed, "Whore! Gipsyfilly!" His bald head and shaven face were so pink, he looked like a fat old baby. "Laced muffin!" he shouted. "Cock lane wench!"

149

Backing away, I shut the door on his next profanity.

Little Sammy stirred but did not wake, praise God.

"That scurvy, stinking ferret," Mercy cried, as I sank onto a stool near the fire. "What right has he to brand you with those names?"

"He is besotted with grog," I replied, "which I think Trump fetches. Obadiah believes I have been unfaithful. 'Tis the reason I sent for you."

"You shall bide with me until your slapsauce husband comes to his senses," Mercy said. "Or drinks himself to death."

"Nay," I said. "I need a different favour, one that might grant me the time to ponder my situation and make a decision, for I am with child."

"But that's splendid," Mercy said. "Undoubtedly, Obadiah will recover with haste when he hears about the babe."

"The child is not his."

Falling back against the slats of her chair, she said, "Jack Grayson."

I felt my eyes widen. "You are verily a witch."

"Nay. 'Twas not difficult for me to guess the true meaning of the glances you did share with Jack during our Reverend's sermons."

"Does Anne know?"

"I think not," she replied. "Nor anyone else."

"Except Obadiah," I said, bitterly. "Even though his 'rheumatics' keeps him to home, absent from sermons. On my oath, Mercy, 'twas not deliberate. Jack found me weeping in the loft and merely sought to comfort me. This afternoon, when I told him of the babe, he was joyful."

"But not shamed," Mercy said. "Or repentant. Men always weasel their way out from under distressing situations,

Chastity. Remember Mum and Mr. Ratcliffe?"

"Praise God, Mum evaded his advances."

"Only after he had his way with her. Can you not count, girl? Tempest is, in truth, the get of Mr. Ratcliffe."

I opened my mouth to rebuke my sister. Then, silently, counted. Tempest had not been born nine months after the storm at sea, but nine months after our departure from Bury St. Edmonds. "Our father has forgiven Mum," I said.

"Aye, though he will not allow Tempest to be writ in the family Bible. But 'twas not Mum's sin, Chastity, and our father is a freethinker. Your Jack is more devout. He might even say you bewitched him."

"Jack would ne'er do that. You vilify him, Mercy."

She shrugged then said, "Why did you send for me?"

"I need a spell," I said, "not unlike the spider spell Mum put on Mr. Ratcliffe."

"For Obadiah?"

"Nay. Matthew Grayson." Tears coursed down my cheeks as I told my sister of Matt's threats.

"Chastity, my incantations are curative," she said. "I cannot beseech spiders to attack."

"Penned in my journal are all the charms I can remember, from Aunt Prudence and Mum. A charm to recall the dead in the name of love. A charm to dispel a state of melancholy. A charm to assuage anger. Even a charm to keep a cat from straying."

"Grimalkin, grimalkin, feasted in my kitchen, there shall thou stay, nor from it care to stray." Mercy smiled. " 'Tis the first charm I ever learned." Her smile faded as she said, "Please, Chastity, do not ask me to cause harm to a living soul."

"There is no spider conjuration in my journal," I said, "nor do I wish you to cause bodily harm. You shall not maim or kill Matt, merely frighten him."

Chapter Twenty

Monday afternoon

Looking up from the journal, I said, "What's a barrow?"

Davy just stared at me.

"Chastity wrote about shoats and barrows," I said. "A shoat is a young hog, so a barrow must be an old hog. Right?"

"A barrow is a male hog, castrated before sexual maturity."

"Stop cracking your knuckles, Davy, and how do you know that?"

"I've used 'barrow's blood.' For one of my wizard spells. Barrow sounds much more authentic than hog or sow. I've also used 'warthog's blood.' My clients are duly impressed because it reminds them of warts and toads. Toads have warts. And people always remember the story where a wizard turns a prince into a toad."

"Are you saying you've slaughtered a hog?"

"No. For my spells I use the blood from a pork roast. Before cooking."

"A witch, not a wizard, cast the spell that turned a prince into a *frog*, Davy, and for some reason I thought Chastity meant wheelbarrow."

"Wheelbarrow?"

"Yes. Which syllable didn't you understand? I thought she said she wouldn't kiss a wheelbarrow."

"Syd, are you upset about something?"

"Of course not. Why should I be upset? We have a house guest who may or may not be an amnesiac. Your house guest is perpetually drunk . . . in fact, she'd give Obadiah Barker a run for his money. She's also blind as a bat, and Chastity wants her sister to kill Matt Grayson."

"First of all, Chastity doesn't want Mercy to kill Matt. Second, Rosie will be deposited at the White Hart as soon as she wakes up. And what do you mean by 'may or may not be an amnesiac?' "

"Suppose your Rose doesn't wake up until tomorrow morning? Where will John and Harlan sleep?"

"With you," Davy snapped, his patience wearing thin.

I felt my lips twitch in the semblance of a smile. "I can't possibly handle both of them. Neither can my bed. Harlan's six-one. John's at least that tall."

"Harlan can sleep anywhere, but you're in lust with John." Davy winked. "I can see it in your eyes."

"I don't sleep with married men."

"Who says John's married?"

"Who says he isn't?"

"He doesn't wear a wedding band."

"Give me a break, Davy. What about The Senator?"

"*Chasdick sheds,*" Mercy squawked, and I felt my face flush as I recalled, in detail, the dropped clown-pants and aborted seduction inside my bedroom. If Aunt Lillian hadn't knocked on my bedroom door, I might have slept with—

"*Matt sheds lice,*" Mercy squawked, flapping her wings.

Davy said, "Matt?"

I stared at my agitated parrot, perched atop the sewing machine. "She's been listening to us decipher, Davy, but I don't know where 'lice' came from."

"She said lies, not lice."

"Matt sheds lies?"

"*Matt, Matt, bo batt, banana fanna—*"

"Hush, Mercy," Davy and I said together.

"*Jack be nimble, Jack be quick.*"

"I'm putting her in the kitchen," I told Davy. "Want anything?"

"A Coke. You're the one who reads out loud but my throat feels parched."

"Okay, I'll be right back. Don't cheat and read the journal without me."

"Don't cheat, don't cheat. Ollie, Ollie, oxen-free."

Toting Mercy through the shop, I heard a subtle sound. My fractious parrot sensed freedom, mainly because my fingers had turned outward in a startled gesture of supplication. Flapping her wings, she flew toward the ceiling fan.

I heard the sound again, a little louder than the rustle of wind-blown leaves.

"Is there someone in here?"

Dumb question. Would a sneaky intruder stand up and introduce himself?

Maybe the shop had mice.

No. Annie prowled. A mouse wouldn't dare raid Annie's domain.

My mind raced. By now an armed burglar would have made his presence known, threatened me with a gun, knife, or chainsaw. Why hadn't Chasdick barked and/or cowered under the computer desk? The intruder had to be a family member.

Or John Elway Henry Kissinger, supposedly investigating employment opportunities at Nina's.

"John, is that you?"

Silence.

I might be in lust with John, but I hadn't deleted him from my who-killed-Clive-Newton list. Should I scream for Davy?

If John was the intruder, he'd overpower me before Davy could rise from his chair. Harlan, supposedly gassing up his limousine, could trounce me too. Harlan had spent umpteen years in prison. For rape. I felt the color drain from my face.

"Harlan?"

Silence.

Broken by Mercy. *"Picklock. Cutpurse. Folly-fallen footpad."*

The person who crouched behind my counter stood up, sneezed, then said, "Don't you ever dust, Sydney?"

"Jessica?"

My brother's wife brushed at her blue cashmere sweater. "I can recommend a good cleaning service," she said. "Or maybe my maid has a few hours—"

"What are you doing here?"

"Snooping. Obviously." Placing a sheaf of hand-printed spells on the countertop, she walked toward me.

"But how did you get inside? The front door was locked and the only other entrance is through the sun porch where Davy and I were deciphering Chastity Barker's journal."

Jessica discovered a dustbunny, burrowing, perhaps even reproducing, amidst the twill weaves that patterned her tweedy slacks.

"Jessica, answer me!"

"Oliver has a key."

"For emergencies."

"This is an emergency. Do you mind if I sit down?"

"Yes. Why were you snooping?"

"If I wanted you to know, I wouldn't have snooped."

"Okay." I reached for the counter phone. "I'm calling Oliver."

"You don't have the number," she said, her voice sullen. "We changed it first thing this morning, and it's unlisted. Yogi's still with us, sick as a dog. You wouldn't believe the weird calls he gets. Some were even phan . . . uh, phantasmagoric."

155

"That's an Oliver word, and dollars to doughnuts he didn't change his cell phone number."

"Please don't call Oliver." Like a chastised (Chastity would say chidden) child, Jessica dug at the floor with a leather shoe that cost more than my toothache charm. "I wanted to borrow a spell, that's all."

Tears blurred her eyes. Damn. If her tears were genuine, I had encountered more weeping women in the last four days than the last four years. First, Veronica Whitney Sanderson. Then, Rosie-all-fall-down. Now, Jessica Whitney St. Charles.

Even Chastity Barker, dead for three hundred years, had cried.

No way were Jessica's tears real. Conjuring up tears is easier than listening to the wind. "During Xanthia's party you said you didn't believe in my spells."

"No, Sydney. I said Oliver didn't believe in your spells."

"Semantics. How did you get the key?"

"While Oliver showered, I took it off his key chain."

Ingrid Bergman in *Notorious*, Jessica's favorite Alfred Hitchcock movie. "When did you steal it?"

"I didn't steal it. I borrowed it."

"Semantics again. When did you borrow the damn key?"

"What's the difference? I'm going home now."

"If you step one foot out that door, I swear I'll call Oliver."

"You're overreacting, Sydney."

"You scared me to death, Jessica. There's a killer running loose and—"

"What's going on in here?" Davy entered the shop from the sun porch.

I said, "Jessica was playing cat burglar."

She said, "Sydney has been beastly," and her eyes teared up again.

Naturally, soft-hearted Davy reacted soft-heartedly. "Sit down, Jessica. Here, I'll help you. Syd, do you have a hanky?"

"Dozens," I said. "Gee, I think they're all in the laundry hamper."

"A cat burglar," Davy said, ignoring my sarcasm, "enters and leaves without attracting attention. Clearly, Jessica attracted your attention."

"Semantics," I said, and heard the hiss in my voice. "She was planning to steal a spell."

"What spell?"

"I don't know. Ask her."

"I can't." Davy's face reddened. "She's crying."

"She's not crying. Okay, I'll ask. Even though my guess is, the spell has something to do with Yogi Demon."

"Wrong." Jessica clutched Davy's hand. "I wanted to make Oliver love me."

She began to sob violently, and this time I could tell she wasn't faking it because she sounded like a barrow. Correction: a sow.

Davy extracted his hand. He said, "I'll get her some water," and hurdled his way upstairs. Watching him leave the room, Jessica emitted yet another series of blubbering, pig-like snorts.

No one in their right mind would sound like that on purpose.

"Oliver . . . and my sister . . . slept together," she said between snorts.

I didn't say: *I know.* Still angry, I didn't say: *I'm sorry.* "If you wanted a spell," I said, "why didn't you simply ask?"

She stopped sobbing, thank God. "You and your brothers are thick as thieves. You'd have laughed. At me."

Somehow, her explanation didn't ring true. I wouldn't have laughed. Davy wouldn't have laughed. And Oliver would have shrugged off one of my spells as insignificant. Or, as he might say, exiguous.

How long had Jessica carried Oliver's key around? Had she snooped before today? Suppose she'd left the door unlocked? If yes, anybody could have tinkered with Xanthia's birthday present, even before the party. Or had Jessica tinkered?

She wasn't strong enough or gutsy enough to have killed and cut up Clive Newton, but she, along with everyone else, knew about Clive's missing body parts. Using ex-wife Carol as a corpse-source, Oliver studied dead body parts; research for his books. Could Jessica have visited Carol on some pretext, "borrowed" an ear, and effected the CD-ear substitution? Why would she do that? Because she didn't get along with Xanthia? No. She couldn't be that insensitive. How about an Oliver-threat? Cheat again, you snake, and say goodbye to your face.

Where had she been sitting during the party? Next to Oliver, who sat next to his daughter. So she could have reached across his body and snatched up the box before Xanthia looked inside. She had to know that Oliver would deliver the ear to his old precinct.

Testing her, I said, "Did Oliver find fingerprints on the ear?"

Her face scrunched, as if she sucked a lemon. "What ear?"

Then she must have remembered Gusta Lowenfeld's party-shriek because, still looking baffled, she said, "The ear from Mr. Potato Head?"

Either Jessica was a great actress or an accomplished liar; essentially the same thing, I guess. "Never mind, it's just a plot detail Oliver and I brainstormed together for his new suspense novel," I improvised. "Is he home? Writing?"

"No. He's at a book signing. In Denver."

Damn. I needed to talk to my big brother. Not because he and I were as thick as thieves, but because I was now in the thick of Clive Newton's homicide.

Had the "birthday ear" been Clive's ear? Had Veronica been killed before her cremation? What evidence had the cops found and/or developed?

On *Law & Order*, Aunt Lillian's favorite TV show, it takes twenty-eight minutes to capture and Mirandize the killer . . . shortly before the third commercial.

Unfortunately, real life didn't take routine commercial breaks.

"When will Oliver be back?" I asked my snoopy sister-in-law.

She looked as if she'd sob-snort again. But she merely shrugged and said, "I'll pay whatever you ask, Sydney, for a love spell that works."

"My spells don't come with a money-back guarantee, Jessica."

"Fair enough." Rising from her chair, she walked over to the window.

Ducking behind the counter, I wondered if she wanted the love spell for her wayward husband or Yogi Demon. I'm not seriously superstitious, yet I didn't want to sell Jessica the same charm I'd sold her dead sister.

Undecided, I heard her say, "Damn, it's snowing."

That worked for me.

Maybe it would even work for her.

I snatched up a piece of red velvet cloth and a pair of scissors, then handed her both. "Cut this into the shape of a heart, as wide as your hand. Go outside and stand where the snowflakes float down freely. Hold the heart on your palm and say: 'Star crystal, silver stone, I warm thee now to blood and rain, nor shalt thou turn to ice again.'"

"Star crystal, silver . . ."

"Stone."

"Stone. I warn thee—"

"*Warm* thee."

"*Warm* thee now to . . . uh . . ."

"Blood."

"To blood and rain, nor shalt thou turn to ice again."

"Repeat it, Jessica, all the way through."

She did. "Is that the whole spell, Sydney?"

"No. When the velvet is topped with snow, come inside and breathe on the flakes until they melt. Then fold the cloth into a triangle. I'll pin it with this." I fished a golden pin from behind my counter and placed it near the phone. "You must chant the incantation every day."

"Every day," she echoed.

"While wearing sexy underwear," I said. Although that wasn't part of the charm, I figured it couldn't hurt.

Aunt Lillian walked into the shop.

Bunny slippers sheathed her feet. She'd been napping. Her silver ringlets were mussed, her eyelids at half-mast. Her gaze touched upon Jessica, cautiously cutting a heart. When my aunt didn't react, I realized she was still ninety percent asleep.

"Damn," Jessica said, "I messed up. Do you have some more red velvet, Sydney?"

Retrieving another piece of cloth, I handed it to her. Then I said, "What's wrong, Aunt Lillian?"

"Knock at door," she mumbled. "Gloves."

As she sleep-walked back up the stairs, I opened the door.

Sure enough, it was snowing. Big soppy flakes, perfect for Jessica's Charm to Warm the Affections of Another. Sure enough, a glove-clad fist rapped at the door.

Terey Lowenfeld stood on the threshold. I wondered why

she hadn't used the toad knocker, then saw that it was frozen solid.

Brushing Terey aside, almost knocking her over, Jessica pranced to the middle of the yard and raised her red-velvet palm. Snow fell on her blue cashmere sweater as she said, "Star crystal, silver stone, I warn thee now—"

"*Warm*," I shouted.

"Star crystal, silver stone, I *warm* thee now to blood and rain, nor shalt thou turn to ice again."

Despite the fact that Terey was bundled inside a pink padded jacket and blue jeans, she reminded me of a tall, skinny bird, a blonde flamingo. Except flamingos appear delicate, almost frail. Terey wasn't frail. She couldn't have weighed more than a hundred-ten pounds, and yet I'd seen her arm-wrestle men who looked like Venice Beach lumberjacks. "It's all in the wrist," she had once told me, after beating a man who bore a striking resemblance to Arnold Schwarzenegger.

Handing me a plastic-wrapped mock-up of the *Manitou Falls Monthly*, she said, "Ma wants you to proof your ad before the paper comes out."

Though evening, four-thirtyish, it could have been noon or daybreak. White cobwebs suffused the sky, as if Mother Nature and Mother Spider had crocheted a gossamer throw blanket. Tinseled snowflakes shrouded houses and trees; the quintessential Christmas card. Should Peter Cottontail peremptorily herald Easter by hopping down the bunny trail, he'd be camouflaged.

Terey's breath formed Siberian smoke. "You look half frozen," I told her. "How about a cup of coffee or hot chocolate?"

Jessica brushed past us again, huffing on her palm.

Terey said, "Maybe some other time."

"Sydney, the gold pin!" Jessica shouted from inside the shop.

As I gave Terey an embarrassed shrug, she said, "Are you casting a spell?"

"You could say that. Listen, sweetie, anytime you want one, a spell or an amulet, I wouldn't charge you anything. You always pick up my ads and—"

"Why would I want a spell, Sydney? I have my health. And a boyfriend."

"That's great, Terey. Who's the lucky man?"

"Paulie. Friday, when we had him for supper, he asked me to go steady."

Once again, an image of Gusta and Terey feasting on Paulie the Pimple flashed across my mind. And wasn't going steady, especially at age twenty-eight, a tad time warp-ish? I remembered a song from some musical—*going steady, steady, steady for good.*

Terey looked unhappy, so I said, "Is there a problem? Maybe I can help."

"No one can help," she said. "Paulie's mother's the problem. She doesn't know about me. He won't tell her. He's thirty-five years old and . . ."

"Mary Lou spoils him," I said; an understatement.

"It's more than spoiled, Sydney. It's obsessive. If Paulie scrapes his knee, she wants to put a splint on his leg. She irons his clothes, even his underwear. She visits his apartment every day. To clean, she says. But I think she's nosing around for a girlfriend. Or condoms. Paulie just laughs. He says she'd kill for him."

I pictured Mary Lou riding her bike, her wicker Toto-basket (behind the seat rather than on the handlebars) bulging with copies of *The Manitou Falls Monthly*. She delivered Gusta's free newspaper to stores and restaurants every

month, and she'd cuss any kid—or adult, for that matter—
who got in her way.

Paulie had gotten in Clive's way (or Clive's face) and been
fired. Had Mary Lou DiNardo killed Clive? No. Clive had
been kidnapped, and I couldn't see Mary Lou tying him up,
stuffing a gag in his mouth, propping him on her handlebars,
then pedaling madly toward Black Forest. Even if my *Wizard
of Oz* image was accurate and she could pedal her way across
the sky, she'd have to submit a flight plan. After all, the Air
Force Academy and Colorado Springs airport weren't far
from Black Forest, and one never knew when the next plane
would take off. Mary Lou owned a car. But, just like Aunt
Lillian, she rarely drove and—

"Sydney, I've got to go. And you're shivering."

"I really want to give you a present, Terey. How about a
going-steady gift? When you have a few minutes, choose
something from the shop."

"Damn it, Sydney, the snow's all melted!" Jessica
yelled.

"You'd better finish your spell." Terey gestured toward
the *Monthly* with her glove. "If your ad's not A-O.K., call my
mother."

"I'm sure it's fine, Terey, and I like your hair."

"I cut it Saturday morning, for Xanthia's party. Ma says I
look bald, but my hair has no curl and I used to have to pin it
up all the time. Headache City."

"It looks terrific, sweetie, very *à la mode*."

"Thanks, Sydney. Bye."

As I turned to walk inside, I remembered the name of the
going-steady-for-good musical. *Bye Bye Birdie*.

Jessica nearly spun me around as she dashed outside and
ran to the middle of the lawn. "I'm going to kill you, Sydney,"
she said, her voice filled with frustration.

Terey stopped short, turned, stared at Jessica, then stared at me.

I gave Terey a shrug and a smile. If I had a nickel for every time I've heard my sister-in-law say, "I'm going to kill you, Oliver," I could probably put a down payment on a cashmere sweater.

Raising her red-velvet-clad palm in an ersatz Black Panther salute, Jessica repeated the incantation, and this time I didn't tell her that "warn" was "warm."

Chapter Twenty-one

Monday evening

"Ta-ta, Sydney."

I glanced up at my parrot, still perched on the ceiling fan, then tossed Gusta's *Manitou Falls Monthly* toward the cash register.

After running upstairs and exchanging my wet T-shirt for a green Davy-turtleneck, I ran back downstairs and pinned Jessica's heart.

"How much would it cost," she said, "for another spell? Something to say or do should Oliver decide he wants to mess around again?"

Why did I keep getting the impression she meant Yogi Demon, not Oliver? "There's a charm for Recalling the Faithless, Jessica, but it's very expensive."

She reached behind Lucinda Lizard and retrieved a tweedy suit jacket that matched her slacks. Putting on the jacket, she cocked her head like a bird, a canary, Tweety in tweed. "Okay, Sydney, chant the charm." She glanced at her diamond-studded wristwatch. "Please hurry. My sweater feels icky and I can't leave Yogi alone for too long. If I'm not there, he forgets to take his medicine."

"Doesn't your laid-up Newt have a concert in a few days?"

"Yes. That's why he needs his meds. Chant the charm, please."

"*You* have to chant it."

"When?"

"When/if Oliver decides to be unfaithful."

She shook her head, spraying me with droplets from her

limp blonde hair. "I meant, does it require a blizzard?" Her voice oozed with sarcasm. "Or a rainy day? Or a full moon? Or midnight?"

"Yes." A smile creased my face at her expression. "Lock yourself in a room when the clock strikes midnight. Light a black candle. Take the white wing feather of a dove or pigeon and dip it in some pungent scented oil. Let the feather's tip burn in the candle flame and chant: 'Thy flight be stayed. Thy wing be bound. This cloud casts thee. To the ground.' Dip the feather into the oil again, then break it into small pieces and fold the pieces up in silver paper. Bind the charm with black thread and bury it near your doorstep. When it calls Oliver back, the same oil must be touched to his brow and palms so he doesn't leave again. But you can't tell him the reason for the anointment, lest its power be diminished, so think about ordering a *Playboy* video. Learn how to give a massage. Wear sexy underwear."

As I paused for breath, she said, "Where do I find a dove's wing?"

"That's why the charm is so expensive. I'll give you the wing, thread, silver paper, candle, and oil. Rue or wintergreen, your choice. The spell is printed on a small scrap of parchment."

When she heard the price, her face paled, but she merely reached into her jacket pocket and pulled out some crumpled hundred dollar bills.

"This should cover both spells," she said.

"You've paid too much, Jessica."

She shrugged. "Keep it, Sydney. Hire a cleaning service."

"Fine."

"If you tell Oliver—"

"I won't tell Oliver, and as you can see, I'm not laughing."

Why the heck would I laugh? Her crinkled currency would

round out next month's mortgage payment, and the charms were harmless.

If Jessica believed in them, they might even work.

Unless Oliver tripped over Rosie-all-fall-down.

Speak of the devil.

Jessica had barely shut the door behind her when Rose entered the shop. Her lips looked kiss-swollen. *Damn it, Davy,* I thought. *Why do you succumb so easily? And couldn't you have waited until you escorted her back to the B&B?*

Looking unfocused, she said, "Yo, Witch."

"The name is Sydney, and do you really have a degree in chemistry?"

She ran her hands over her blue silk dress, lingering at its low-cut bodice. Then, with an almost imperceptible shrug, she let her shoulder strap drop to the middle of her arm, revealing the top half of one perfectly-formed breast. She'd obviously bathed. Her skin glowed from an herbal cream and smelled of my favorite perfume. Every so often, I take a handful of rose buds, place them in a silver goblet, and pour one dram of rose oil over them. The buds soak for a week. When added to a bath, they induce peace, harmony, and love vibrations. Mentally, I tallied Rosie's tab—assuming she still wanted a few ounces of New Mown Hay.

"I have a degree in physical chemistry," she said.

"You went to a striptease school," I guessed.

"Yeah. Graduated first in my class. Remember the movie, *Gypsy*?"

"Natalie Wood. Rosalind Russell. Everything's coming up roses."

"You gotta have a gimmick, Witch. Mine's purity. Oh, I don't pretend to be modest when I take my clothes off, like Natalie did, but without my glasses or contacts my eyes look—"

"Out of focus. Innocent. Virginal."

"*Virginal,*" Mercy squawked. "*Jack and Jill went up the hill, to fetch a pail of water. Jill fell down and broke her membretoon.*"

"Yeah, innocent," Rose said, after a startled glance at the fan. "What's a membretoon?"

Undoubtedly, my parrot had picked up the word from Chastity's journal. I wouldn't have known what membretoon meant, either, had I not read the journal. "It's a name women used for their . . . privates . . . a long time ago," I told Rose. "As early as the seventeenth century. It's a swear word, but I think it sounds much better than the words we use today. Don't you?"

"Yeah, for sure. Anyhoo, Witch, I don't wear my glasses when I strip."

"Did you have your glasses on when you met Clive Newton?"

I could hear the sarcasm in my voice. Apparently she couldn't because her expression never changed. "No," she said, "But I wore them when Clive took me home with him. Maybe that's one of the reasons he dumped me."

"Clive took you to Colorado then dumped you?"

"Yeah. We binged for a week, some killer weed, mostly booze, but he couldn't hold his liquor. Turned mean." Her hand formed a fist. "Then his girlfriend told him to get rid of me. Clive called her Mother Theresa and made fun of her, but I guess, deep down, he loved her. Anyhoo, that's how I met Cool Hand. He paid my way back to Vegas and got me Harlan."

"Harlan," I repeated, stunned.

"To drive me. Cool Hand owns a fleet of limousines."

"Harlan drove you back to Vegas in one of Cool Hand's limousines?"

"No. I flew to Vegas. Harlan drove me here, to your house. Cool Hand said Harlan's at my beck and call."

"Are you at Cool Hand's beck and call?"

This time she caught my sarcasm, but she merely shook her head. "That's the funny thing, Witch. Cool Hand didn't want anything from me. Not even when he got me Harlan so I could come see Davy. 'Enjoy,' he said."

"Did I hear my name?" Davy walked through the archway, into the shop.

He had bathed, too, and smelled of Tuberose. Also called Mistress of the Night, Tuberose is an aphrodisiac. While it promotes peace and aids in psychic powers, men wear it to attract women. Not surprisingly, it's the only Lilly's Apothecary oil Oliver has ever embraced. Enthusiastically.

"I wish Rose would remember *my* name, Davy," I said. "How would you like to be called 'Wizard' all the time?"

For some reason, I felt cranky. Maybe because I didn't like hearing about Clive's mean streak. Maybe because no one had mentioned a girlfriend. Not one newspaper. Not one TV reporter. Not even Gusta Lowenfeld.

"Do you remember the name of Clive's girlfriend, Rosie?"

"No, Witch. I never met her. When she called and said she was coming over, Clive got scared. And mad. He smacked me around, as if everything was my fault. The man who worked with the horses carried me to the stables. But I was so out of it, I can't remember much, not even what he looked like. He was black, I think. Or Mexican." She shrugged. "My eyes were swollen, from Clive, and I didn't have my glasses. The man wore a cowboy hat and he put medicine, something gooey, on the cuts from Clive's ring."

Davy looked as if he wanted to kill Clive Newton all over again.

A thought occurred. "Rosie, was it Clive's house or someone else's house?"

"Clive's. At least, that's what *he* said. Funny thing is there were pictures of a bleached blonde and an old man, but only one picture of Clive. With The Newts. But it must have been his house, Witch. He knew where everything was, and when Yogi came over, they both changed into white shorts and played tennis."

"Did they change into bathing suits and swim in a pool?"

"No. It was too cold."

"Was the house in Black Forest?"

"That sounds familiar. Cool Hand would know. His limo drove us there. Not Harlan. Another chauffeur."

Davy said, "What's the big deal, Syd?"

"The stables, tennis court, and pool sound like Veronica Whitney Sanderson's estate. So do the pictures of a blonde and an old man."

"And your point is?"

"Rose said Clive 'got scared.' Suppose the house belonged to Veronica, his drop-dead gorgeous manager? She was ten, maybe twelve years older, but she could have been the mad girlfriend. She could have threatened to drop The Newts, trash Clive's career. He hadn't hit superstar status . . . that didn't really happen until *after* he died . . . and don't forget, Clive got killed in Black Forest. Maybe Veronica and/or the man who worked with the horses killed him."

"Maybe Yogi Demon killed him. Maybe the butler killed him. Maybe a fanatical fan killed him. Clive was abducted after a concert and—"

"His body was found a few days later in Black Forest."

"That doesn't prove anything."

"It could prove the killer lived in Black Forest. Otherwise, why dump the body there?"

"Stop it!" Face bleached of color, Rose leaned against the counter. "You're making me sick, talkin' 'bout Clive as if he was John Lemmon."

"John Lennon," I said.

"I need a drink," she said. "There's a Stoli bottle inside the limo."

"Sorry, Rosie," Davy said. "Harlan's gassing up the limousine."

"Witch, would you pour me a drink? Please? I need one bad."

"No, you don't," Davy said. "Tell you what. We won't wait for Harlan. I'll drive you to Nina's or the Loop-de-Loop. I'm hungry and you must be starving."

"Damn you, I need a drink!"

"Who needs a drink?" Oliver walked through the archway, into the shop. He wore a black overcoat, dotted with snow, and his gloved hands strangled the necks of two champagne bottles. His gaze undressed Rose, not that she wore many layers. Then he gave a construction worker's whistle. Hefting the bottles like a couple of dumbbells, he said, "This is your lucky day, beauteous lady."

"It's night," Davy said, "and my lady needs food, not booze."

"This isn't booze, David. It's Dom Perignon."

Quickly, I stepped between my brothers. "Davy, why don't you get your lady's coat? Oliver, go home. Share the champagne with your *wife*."

"I want to share it with you, Syd."

"Why?"

"My agent phoned."

"How did your agent get your unlisted number?"

"What? Oh. Yogi. Did Jess call?"

"No. She stopped by." I suddenly realized that Oliver

couldn't give Yogi a nickname. What would he call him? Yo?

"My agent phoned the bookstore." Oliver preened like a rooster. "He said *Cop a Plea* is number one on the *Times* bestseller list. The list won't come out until next week, but—"

"Sweetie, that's terrific," I said sincerely.

"And he negotiated a new contract."

Ever the braggart, Oliver mentioned a sum that would have paid off my mortgage and still left enough pocket change for the late Veronica Whitney Sanderson's estate. In other words, unless my brother divorced Jessica, he was flush. Very.

Davy returned with Rosie's coat, but the fur could have been roadkill. Oliver was, after all, a champagne roadhouse, road-worthy, and worth a pretty penny. Visions of lush Russian ermines danced in her head as she sidled up to him and said, "Let's toast your success, Mister . . ."

"St. Charles. O. T. St. Charles. Best-selling author of *Cop-out*, *Copperhead*, *Coprophiliac*, and *Cop a Plea*."

You couldn't fault my brother for low self-esteem. "And husband to Jessica Whitney St. Charles," I said, hoping the charms I'd sold Jessica would work.

Both Oliver and Rose ignored me. Oliver had taken off his gloves and was popping the cork on a champagne bottle. Rose watched him, fascinated, as if she'd never seen a cork popped before.

Davy extended his hand, dropped the fur coat, turned, and left the room.

I heard the front door slam.

The cork-pop (not the slam) had awakened Aunt Lillian. She bounded down the staircase, bloomers flashing, and entered the shop.

The front door opened.

Momentarily, John and Harlan stood framed by the archway.

"Rank, onion-eyed pignut," Mercy squawked. *"Maggot-pie."*

Face half-hidden by a couple of brown sacks, John surveyed the shop. "I'll put these groceries away," he said.

Harlan said, "The limousine's all gassed up, Miss Rose."

She said, "I won't be needing you. Right, O. T.?"

Oliver had the grace to look embarrassed. "My new book is on the *Times* bestseller list, number one," he told Aunt Lillian.

"That's nice. Cork that bottle of spirits and take it home. Davy's girlfriend doesn't need a drink and your wife is waiting for you."

Rose's face turned ugly. "Hold the phone, you old bitch. O. T. here was—"

"Out," I said. "Get out!" Scooping her coat off the floor, I flung it at her. "No one calls my aunt a bitch."

Rose caught the coat, then grabbed the open champagne bottle and clutched it against her breast. "Harlan, we're leaving," she said. "O. T., I'm staying at a bed and breakfast. It has a heart in its name."

"Harlan, sit down and take the chill off your bones." Aunt Lillian glared at Rose. "You, missy, can wait in the car."

"Don't be stu . . . ridiculous. It's cold in the car and Harlan works for *me*."

"Harlan works for Cool Hand," I said, still seething.

"I'll drive Miss Rose to the White Hart." Harlan smiled at Aunt Lillian. "The limousine has a heater. It'll take the chill off my bones."

Impulsively, I said, "Why don't you come back and join us for supper?"

"Thanks, but my wife Lola's waiting for me."

"Should you need it, we have an herb called Ylang-Ylang. It helps soothe the problems of married life." Picturing his

I-heart-Lola, in all likelihood tattooed when Travolta was a Kotter kid, I figured Ylang-Ylang was one sale I'd never ring up, at least not to Harlan. I should have given a pinch or three to Jessica, however, along with her dove's feather and rue oil.

After Harlan shut the door, there was dead silence. I could have broken it by inviting Oliver to supper, but I wasn't feeling very charitable toward him. Also, I hoped Davy would return soon and didn't want another War of the Roses. Or, in this case, War of the Rose. Finally, Oliver said, "I guess I'll drive home now, share my news with Jess. Good thing I have snow tires."

"I'll help John put the groceries away," Aunt Lillian said.

Her curt statement sounded like expulsion, and Oliver knew it. With all the dignity he could muster, he snatched up his gloves and strode through the archway. His parting words, perhaps to appease Aunt Lillian, perhaps to mollify his own wounded pride, were: "I'll phone you from home and let you hear for yourself how Jess takes the news. I'm sure *she'll* be excited."

Speaking of news, I had to proof my *Manitou Falls Monthly* ad.

Damn, I hadn't asked Oliver about the birthday ear, Clive-clues, or Veronica Whitney Sanderson's combustion. On the other hand, my questions might have sounded a tad boorish, taking into account Rose's femme fatale performance and Oliver's drool-lipped feedback.

Should Oliver really phone from home, I'd ask him about the ear, although I doubted he'd tell me anything. The police probably wanted to keep the ear under wraps. That way, if they cornered a suspect and he mentioned a gift-wrapped ear, the interrogation cop could say, "Aha! Gotcha!"

Aunt Lillian bounded up the stairs and John walked into the shop, a mug of what smelled like coffee in his hands.

"This is for you, Sydney," he said.

Chasdick shadowed John's heels and Annie undulated around his ankles. Two of my pets had given John their seals of approval (Mercy didn't count; she hated all men), so why was I quibbling over his marital status?

With that thought, I took the coffee mug from his hands, placed it on the table, and—with a sigh—buried my face against his green, too-tight, hand-me-down, The-Dells-inspired IF IT AIN'T ONE THING IT'S ANOTHER tee.

John stroked my snow-dampened curls. Then he tilted my chin and thumbed the curve of my cheekbone.

Still pressed against his body, I felt growth beneath his jeans.

In my pocket was the love talisman. Behind my ears were several drops of New Mown Hay oil.

His lips found but didn't capture mine. Tentatively, he took my kisses. As his lips explored with caution, I began to writhe in his arms, my lips burning, my tongue sliding past his teeth in a search for more response.

I let my tongue probe deeper, finding his tongue, touching, teasing, seeking to initiate a dance, frustrated because we were out of step.

Giving me back my mouth, he said, "Counter."

"On top of the counter?"

"No Sydney." His voice was tender. "Behind the counter."

"Right. Privacy. Jessica's hiding place. Good idea," I murmured, as we two-stepped across the room.

Once we were safely ensconced behind the counter, John's tongue danced with mine in a primitive, savage tempo that sent fluttering, pulsating messages to my belly.

The romance writers would have said, his lips plundered my mouth, and I was more than ready to sink to the floor, dustbunnies be damned. In fact, had my parrot not intervened, there would have been what Aunt Lillian likes to call "coital fadeout, dot-dot-dot."

Soaring from the fan, Mercy landed on my shoulder. Crest quivering, she squawked, *"For they're hangin' men an' women there for wearin' 'o the green."*

John stepped back as if he'd been slapped. He stared at my green turtleneck, then down at his green T-shirt. "Please explain," he said.

"I'm not sure. My guess is, she heard 'The Wearin' of the Green' from Jim, my old boyfriend. He's Irish."

Mercy's kibitzing had cooled John's hot blood. "You'd better drink your coffee, Sydney," he said, "before it turns ice-cold."

If a parrot can smirk, Mercy smirked. Then she flew back to the ceiling fan.

My lips still tingled as I reached for the *Manitou Falls Monthly* and pulled it from its plastic wrap.

Before I could spread it out, I saw the headline: DEAD SINGER ATTENDS BIRTHDAY PARTY.

Chastity Barker's Journal
September, 1692

Before his leave-taking, Jack counseled that I propose by God's grace to reflect more often upon the assurance of everlasting happiness through our Lord. I might also reflect upon the perils of vanity and worldly felicity, Jack said, his voice as sober as the judges who rule at the witch trials. Though I sometimes fear that Jack is a shade pietistic—dare I say hypocritical?—I did resolve to follow his advice.

After reciting her own incantation, rather than one from my journal, Mercy roused Sammy and set out for home. Whereupon I meditated, absolving myself through His grace, finding a small measure of peace.

Then Trump returned, shattering my serenity.

He tugged his forelock in an unexpected but much appreciated gesture of servility, and bid me prepare Obadiah's evening meal, though 'twas exceedingly late for a sumptuous repast. One should not go to bed on a full stomach. If one does, one might suffer the evil spirits that possess people while they sleep.

I, myself, have ne'er suffered nightmares. Indigestion, however, frequently visits me in their stead, should I gratify my nocturnal hunger with nanny goat cheese, pease porridge, and the like.

Sometimes I dream I am chasing rabbits.

Trump then insisted that Obadiah clothe himself and walk about.

Docile where Trump is concerned, Obadiah acquiesced.

"Trump says Governor Winthrop is walking again,"

Obadiah stated, donning his greatcoat. " 'Tis bad luck to those who see him, Chastity, so do not leave the house, lest he appears."

John Winthrop died forty-three years ago, yet I have no doubt he walks when the moon is full. Mayhap he conjoins the Lady in Red.

Trump eased himself through the doorway whilst Obadiah said, "I have been short-tempered of late and ignored your needs, wife." Then, with a sneer, he said, "I shall remedy that situation upon my return."

My heart sank, but I managed to control the tremor in my voice whilst blessing my husband.

As I write this, I weep. I should not have wed in haste. I could not know that Jack would be widowed. Nevertheless, I should have bided my time, for I saw pity in my sister's eyes.

I do not wish to be an object of pity.

Mercy would have recited an incantation to ward off my husband's bestiality, had I but asked.

The moon hangs high in the sky. My servant, Sally, has come and gone. Roused from her sleep by Trump, Sally grudgingly helped me lay out my husband's repast.

As we placed a cold duck on a platter, I said, "What think you of Trump?"

"He is given to sorcery, Mistress," Sally said. "He ha' a black dog."

" 'To whom he speaks in a strange language,' " I cited, then yawned.

"Aye, Mistress," she said, "but did ye know the dog answers him?"

"Should you talk to Old Scratch there, he will answer you." Kneeling by my hound, chafing the inside of his ears with my fingertips, I said, "Is the moon out tonight?" Old

Scratch whined deep in his throat, then uttered a disappointed yip-yip when I stopped rubbing.

Sally scowled. "Last Sabbath day, a cow died where Trump was seen to walk his dog," she said, "an' when Ketzia Van Rijn did mistrust him by reason o' her cat dyin' an' came to accuse him, he denied her words wi' a foul oath. Ketzia swears there's a mole on his arse, Mistress, shaped like a cloven hoof."

"Ketzia's cat died of old age," I said. "My sister tried to revive the wretched creature, but 'twas no use. And how can Ketzia know that Trump has a mole on his arse? Did he drop his breeches in her presence?"

"Hold thy tongue," Sally cried. "Ketzia Van Rijn is a gentlewoman."

"Then how," I asked, "did she come to see a cloven hoof on Trump's bare arse?"

"Oi know not, Mistress, but oi believes her, as does others. Me mum says oi should seek out a new situation, so herewith ye ha' me notice. Heard tell Jack Grayson ha' need o' daily help, so I'll leave on the morrow, be it all roight wi' ye."

I tried to still the loud beat of my heart. Only this afternoon Jack had talked of leaving Salem and I had dissuaded him. When had Sally heard of his need for servants? With her overripe form, heart-shaped face, pink-patched cheeks, and yellow curls, Sally could fulfill many needs. 'Twas fortunate, indeed, that Jack possessed a spiritual nature and strength of character, unlike his brother Matt.

" 'Tis not all right," I said. "Tomorrow is Sabbath eve. My husband has recovered from his affliction and shall require his usual fare."

"Then ye, Mistress, shall ha' to cook it," she said with a disobedient sniff. "In truth, Master Obadiah no longer pleases me."

When I questioned such an odd statement, she nodded toward the bedroom. Then her face and neck turned quite ruddy. "Oi thought ye knew," she said, "believed ye grateful."

"Grateful? For bedding my husband? Why on earth would I be grateful?"

"It did keep the turdy-gut meacock away from you."

"I guess I should be grateful," I whispered. Louder, I said, "Did Obadiah pay you well?"

"Aye, Mistress."

"I'll give you my silver candlesticks if you stay another fortnight?"

"Naw, Mistress, but oi'll stay through the Sabbath."

" 'Tis a bargain, Sally."

As the girl set out bread and butter, my mind raced. I've ne'er tested my skills, thinking I had none, but now I'm older, wiser. Long ago my great-aunt Prudence recited a charm that requires three thorns of noble length from a hawthorn tree, oil of civet, and the heart of a fowl. At the same time, Aunt Pru issued a warning. The spell, she said, was terribly potent and should be used sparingly, if at all.

Aunt Pru's caveat is the reason why I remember every word.

When performed with its incantation, 'tis a Charm to Work Revenge.

Chapter Twenty-two

Monday night

Squinting at my brother, I said, "I think I need glasses."

"Syd, sweetheart, your teeth may be crooked and your hearing selective, but your vision is twenty-twenty. Please keep reading."

"I can't. My eyes hurt."

"Would they hurt less if you typed?"

"I'm a lousy typist, Davy, and you'd never be able to decipher Chastity's squiggles. Or her spelling. For example, she puts an 'e' at the end of 'gown.' She spells vanity v-a-n-i-t-y-e and crucify c-r-u-c-i-f-i-e."

"When did she say crucify?"

"When she wrote about meditating. I did the best I could with Sally, Davy, but Chastity writes Sally's dialogue in some kind of syntax. A Cockney accent would be my guess. Without apostrophes."

"So far, the dialogue makes perfect sense."

"Wait until she quotes Trump." I heaved a deep sigh. "Sorry, I'm cranky."

"And I'm Dopey."

"What?"

"You said you were Cranky. I'm not Bashful or Sleepy or any of the other three dwarfs, so that leaves—"

"Dwarf number seven is Grumpy, not Cranky. Why are you Dopey?"

"Rose." Davy cracked his knuckles. "I think she uses people, Syd."

No shit, Sherlock! "Obviously, she used you for sex, Davy.

Your wizard's income is too iffy. She's sniffing after Oliver because of his new book contract, and she probably connected with Clive Newton because of his . . . connections."

"Do you think she killed him?"

"Not unless she had an accomplice. I've seen pictures of Clive. He wasn't exactly Stallone, but he could 'Rambo' a Rose."

"Thank God your friend Lynn's no Rose."

"True. But all women have thorns. May I suggest you handle her gently?"

After bolting from the house, Davy had bumped into my pretty neighbor, Lynn Whitacre. Literally. By the time he helped her up, brushed the snow from her clothes, offered Baron the Boxer a chin scratch, and shoveled her walk, they'd renewed their friendship.

Davy had seen Lynn at Xanthia's birthday party, but he'd spent quality time with her during the restoration of my house. I had sensed a physical and mental chemistry between them. Had my little brother not wanted to quit Manitou Falls immediately, if not sooner, a relationship might have developed.

This evening, snowed in, unable to drive to the Loop-de-Loop and wait tables, Lynn had accepted Davy's dinner invitation. Right now, upstairs in the kitchen, she chatted with Aunt Lillian.

Inside the guest bedroom, John read one of Oliver's cop books. At the same time, he listened to Paul Simon's "Graceland" on Davy's portable CD player.

"Just call me Al," I sang, my voice one octave higher than Paul's.

Chasdick started to howl, but Annie, situated between his paws, cut him off with a green-eyed glare.

Davy said, "Why are you so cranky, Al?"

"Because the phone lines are down. You saw Gusta's article, Davy. Where did she get her information? Who was her reliable source? And who thought up that cutesy headline?"

"My guess would be Terey. She's inventive, always has been, even in high school."

"Dead singer attends birthday party . . . damn, I still can't believe it."

"Dead singer," Mercy squawked from the sewing machine. *"Malt-worm."*

Up until now, my parrot had been silent, as if she understood that any kind of interruption would lead to her eviction.

"Please tell me how Gusta knew about the ear, Davy."

"She saw it."

"She glimpsed it. She thought it was part of a Mr. Potato Head. Just before I blacked out, I shut the box. John saw my face and grabbed the box. It didn't hit the floor, open up, spill—"

"Maybe Gusta sensed the ear was Clive's, rang up Oliver, and promised him free advertising if he gave her the scoop."

"Oliver doesn't need free advertising, especially in the *Manitou Falls Monthly*. His publisher advertises in *People*, the *New York Times*, *Romantic Times*, *Publishers Weekly*—"

"Romantic times. Jack and Jill went up the hill."

"Hush, Mercy. Let's assume Gusta figured out the ear was Clive's. Xanthia's party was yesterday, today Oliver had his book signing in Denver, and first thing this morning his phone was assigned an unlisted number. So it stands to reason that if Gusta wanted to validate her information, she'd call me."

"You're not a cop."

"Neither is Oliver. Not anymore."

"Come on, Syd, he's the next best thing to a cop."

"How did Gusta know the ear included a gecko earring?

Even I didn't see that. It must have been hidden beneath the ear." Standing up, I pressed my nose against a window pane. "Gusta always seems so scatterbrained," I said, my breath clouding the glass. "But that could be a ruse."

"A ruse for what?"

"Snooping."

"Speaking of snooping, how did you pacify Jessica?"

"I sold her a Charm to Warm the Affections of Another."

"That spell needs snow. You lucked out."

"I think I subconsciously conjured up the snow. Wish I could un-conjure it." Turning away from the window, I walked over to my brother, still seated in front of the computer desk. "Then I sold her a Charm to Recall the Unfaithful."

"How many black candles?"

"One."

"I sell my clients five. At ten dollars apiece."

"Supposedly, it only takes one."

"Do you have a webpage, Syd?"

"No. Do you?"

"Sure. Wizard-Inc-dot-biz." He grinned. "I list all my spells and charge a thousand dollars for a Charm to Defy Death, just in case a draft from an open window hits the five black candles." Snapping his fingers, he made a *whoosh* sound. "My website has a link to hex insurance."

"You're teasing, Davy, but I believe it was a human draft that inflamed Veronica Whitney Sanderson."

"You're kidding. You're not kidding. Who'd want Jessica's sister dead?"

"I don't know. Maybe the same person who killed Clive Newton. Veronica could have been Clive's mysterious girlfriend. She could have been pissed over Rose and helped someone kill Clive. That same someone could have killed Veronica . . . because she knew too much."

"And you've been reading too many Oliver books."

"Okay, here's another theory. This one is really off the wall. Suppose John, your new bud, my object of lust, is Rosie's man who trains horses?"

"Now you *are* kidding."

"No, I'm not. Rosie thought she recognized John."

"Without her glasses, Rosie wouldn't recognize Elvis, not even if he drove a pink Caddy, wore blue suede shoes, and carried Obadiah Barker's hound dog."

"Rosie said the trainer could have been Mexican. John looks Indian."

"He looks more Irish than Indian, and wouldn't she remember blue eyes?"

"Not necessarily. Her eyes were swollen shut."

"Half shut."

"Hear me out, Davy. John remembered the white stallion that gallops round the football field when the Broncos score. And the blonde who rides him. John also remembered Marilyn Monroe's beauty mark. Veronica has . . . had a mole."

"Did Veronica own a white stallion?"

"I don't know, but I plan to tour her Black Forest estate when we visit Aunt Lillian's reincarnated acquisition, Reb Ashmare. First, I'll pay Gusta Lowenfeld a call, in person, assuming the damn snow ever stops falling."

"According to Lynn, who heard it on the news, tomorrow will be warm and sunny. Snow plows will have cleared the streets, and I'm going with you."

"To Veronica's estate?"

"No. Gusta's house."

"Davy, that's a great idea."

He blinked, surprised and suspicious. "What's a great idea?"

"We'll split up. You can take Miss Gusta."

He shook his head. "I'll take the estate, ask John to go with me."

"That's a dumb idea. Suppose he's the murderer?"

"Do you honestly believe John killed Clive Newton?" When I didn't answer, Davy said, "Just for grins, where did he hide the body parts?"

"Somewhere on Veronica's estate, maybe the stables. He could have driven there the night she was killed or the day before Xanthia's party."

"To pick up the ear and substitute it for the CD? No way, Syd!"

"He hid his identity by playing Bozo the Clown. Why would he do that?"

"Friday night, at dinner, you said you wanted to hire a magician but spent too much on groceries."

As I contemplated my brother's rationale, another thought occurred. "When I asked Rose about Clive's girlfriend, you said Yogi Demon or the butler could have killed Clive. You were being flippant, Davy, but Yogi has the strongest motive. Except he's the most obvious suspect. And, according to Oliver, the most obvious suspect is never the killer."

"Besides, Yogi wasn't anywhere near the party."

"But Jessica was."

"Surely you jest."

"She knew about the CD, and it's the only reason I can come up with for planting the ear at the party rather than mailing it to a member of The Newts."

"You've lost me, Syd."

"Shock value. An Oliver-warning. Cheat on me again and lose a body part."

"If Jessica's in cahoots with Yogi, why would she care if

Oliver strays? And why would Yogi send body parts to his own group?"

"Publicity. Every time it happens there's national news coverage."

Walking back to my chair, I thought: Davy and I *should* split up. That way, I can put Yogi on my agenda. After Gusta and Yogi . . . and Oliver if he's home . . . I'll visit John's motel, ask the desk clerk about Mary "Goldilocks" Smith.

"A better motive is revenge," Davy said. "An ex-manager, a songwriter who feels he's been ripped off, a singer who was dropped from the group."

"How do you know a singer was dropped from the group?"

"Terey. She said Veronica cut The Newts down to five, but they started with eight. She said Paulie wasn't the only person 'downsized.' "

"Did she happen to know the names of the dropped singers?"

"I didn't ask. We were making small talk at Xanthia's party."

"By now the police would have questioned a disgruntled Newt."

"Well, it doesn't help to brood or nitpick. We don't have enough information to make a judgment call, and in less than an hour I've got to cook a rose-petal meatloaf. Why don't we forget about Clive Newton's murder and—"

"Decipher Chastity's journal?"

"Yes. How do your eyes feel?"

"Confused."

Chastity Barker's Journal

September, 1692

My great-aunt Prudence and my sister Anne believe that one can be reborn as an animal whilst numerous folk believe that witches can turn themselves into animals. 'Tis called shape-shifting.

There are tales of werewolves, men who change into wolves inasmuch as a spell was cast upon them. Or they willingly don a wolf-pelt, along with a girdle of human skin, when the moon waxes full.

I believe the devil can don the skin and horns of a beast, but shape-shifting is against the divine laws of nature and those who fancy themselves to be wolves are deluded by the devil.

Ketzia Van Rijn swears she saw Trump turn himself into a black bitch and rut with his dog. The magistrates, however, did not give much credence to her account. Yet when Abigail Williams spoke of the man in black, sometimes in his own likeness, sometimes in the likeness of a red dog, they took her tattles to heart.

'Tis late afternoon and my hand shakes so badly I fear my ink will blotch. Yet, much as I dread it, I must pen an accurate account.

Trump and Obadiah did not return last night.

Having fallen asleep whilst writing in my journal, a commotion outside the door woke me. Glancing toward the window, I encountered staves of barbed sunlight. The cold duck reeked and the butter smelled rancid and, praise God, my first impulse was to hide my journal.

Rising to my feet and stumbling across the room, I managed to pry loose the fireplace stone, forfeiting two fingernails in the achievement. I had barely thrust my journal inside the hollow hole and replaced the stone, when I heard the sound of a door scraping against the floor.

Ketzia Van Rijn stepped into my house. "Hemel, Goodvife Barker," she said. "Your cornfield. Scarecrow. Lice."

Ten or twelve goose-necked goodwives stood in the yard. Whilst their feet did not move, their elbows flapped in an effort to avoid the press of overly zealous neighbours. They looked like ruffled crows, all atwitter, thronged together on a single tree branch. Ketzia Van Rijn, alone, appeared steadfast, allowing that she gave me a glare of pure hatred, as malignant as a serpent's.

"Did you say lice or locusts?" I asked her. "How could lice invade my field? A louse needs a warm-blooded animal to feed upon."

"You vill come to the field, see vat you have done," she said. Turning, she faced the other women. "Shoo! Scat! Vy don't you go home?"

The goodwives parted to let Ketzia and me through, but followed along behind us. I shivered at the eerie silence, broken only by the stomp of footsteps and the rustle of wind-whipped leaves.

Wishing I had not been awakened so abruptly, unable to think with a clear head, I pictured my sister Mercy stepping outside the house to recite the incantation meant to frighten Matt Grayson—but I did not hear her words. Afraid of bugs, most especially moths and bees, I have ne'er penned a spell that includes insects, the reason why my daybook does not cite my mum's spider charm, and I wondered if Mercy had conjured up lice. Lice were not hurtful, but 'twould be a bother, especially in cold weather when bathing is difficult, if not impossible.

I soon saw the cornfield, occupied by several men, most of whom stood in front of a scarecrow. Fear rose in my throat, though I knew not why. As I approached, the men watched, but none offered a greeting. Not even Obadiah, who sat motionless on the ground, mayhap fifty feet from the other men. Obadiah looked shrunken, as if hewn from a block of wood, whilst Trump, normally of short stature, seemed to loom above him. My steps lagged, my legs turned to water, and I might have slumped to the ground had Ketzia not encircled my waist.

"You vill not svoon," she said, her thumb and first finger pinching my abdomen.

With a yowl of pain, I tore myself free from her grasp. As I walked hurriedly forward, I recognized numerous folk. The Reverend Deodat Lawson. Magistrate John Hathorne. Thomas Danford, deputy-governor of the colony, who oft acts as presiding magistrate at the witch trials. Yosef Solom. Tobias Birdwell. My nearest neighbour, Rueben Cavin, who fixed his malevolent stare upon me. Once again, fear rose in my throat. What had I done? How had I sinned?

Halting, my gaze shifted to the scarecrow.

Who was, in truth, the corpse of a man.

Bound to a crosspiece, neck anchored by a cut rope, his tongue lolled from the black hole that had once been his mouth.

Though I stood a short distance away, I could ascertain that his face was overlaid with blisters and warts.

"Lice," Ketzia said, observing the direction of my gaze. "They sucked the blood and juices from his face. Ven his body grew cold, they disengaged, fell, and died. There are dead lice everyvere."

"Dead lice everywhere," I repeated, dazed.

She nodded toward the scarecrow. "Lice are not vat killed him," she said. "A vitch-curse killed him."

Swallowing the bitter bile that rose in my throat, I managed to say, "Who is he?"

"Jack Grayson," Ketzia stated.

Words of denial were heavy stones that never made it past my lips, plunging, instead, to the pit of my stomach.

As my vision dimmed and the field began to revolve in ever-widening circles, I heard a man say, "Begging your pardon, Miss Van Rijn, but 'tis not Jack Grayson. 'Tis his brother, Matt."

Chapter Twenty-three

Monday night

I felt a hand tap my shoulder, and whirled about.

John stood behind me. "Sydney," he said, "you look—"

"Awful," Davy finished. "Your face is as green as Mary Lou Dinardo's."

"Sometimes, when I'm deciphering, I feel as if I'm there. I was in that cornfield, Davy. With Chastity. I couldn't understand every word . . . her hand *was* shaking badly, *was* making ink-blotches . . . but the dead lice and the tongue lolling from a black hole were more than enough."

If I looked green, John looked ghost-white.

"Oh, God." I placed the journal on the computer table. "I'm sorry, John. I forgot about your suspenders."

"Suspenders?"

"The motel. Your brush with death. Didn't you just have a memory flash?"

"No. Yes. A friend. Dead. His mouth looked like a black hole. A black hole with teeth. He was smiling. But his eyes didn't smile."

Rising and moving away from the computer, Davy said, "Do you remember the name of your friend?"

John shook his head. "Maybe I saw his face in a movie. Or a newspaper photo."

John still looked as if he might throw up. No. He looked worse than that, as if he'd suddenly become infected with a highly contagious Stephen-King flu. "There's a charm in the shop," I said, "to Win Healing from the Sun."

Instinctively, we all glanced at the window wall. Snow still swirled. The sky was a weird color, more gray than black, and the teensy flakes looked like the static on an out-of-whack TV screen.

Davy reached over to mouse the computer's save-icon. "We're finished for today," he said.

Annie stood and stretched. Chasdick gave what sounded like a disappointed *whoof.* Mercy squawked, *"Hand and hand, on the edge of the field, they danced by the light of the moon."*

"The edge of the *sand,* you silly parrot." Turning to John, I said, "That was Xanthia's favorite nursery rhyme. *The Owl and the Pussy-Cat.*"

"John," Davy said, "tomorrow I plan to tour Veronica Whitney Sanderson's estate. Do you know who she is? Was?"

"Yes. Aunt Lillian told me about the fire. Why do you want to tour her estate?"

"Sydney thinks she was murdered by the same person who killed rock star Clive Newton. I'm supposed to look for clues. Do you want to come with me?"

"Veronica bought one of my spells the night she died," I explained. "Maybe the spell had something to do with the fire." *And her death,* I thought. "Veronica was Clive's manager, possibly his girlfriend."

"Aunt Lillian wants to visit her new mare," Davy said, "assuming the weather clears up. Syd has other plans, so—"

"You could man the shop." Purposefully, I interrupted Davy, still unsure about my brother's safety should John accompany him. "I'd pay you a decent hourly wage."

"If you don't mind, Sydney, I'd rather go with Davy."

"I don't mind. It's off-season and business is always slow on a Tuesday."

Following Davy and John upstairs, my steps lagged.

Maybe it was my imagination, or my reaction to the last journal entry, but I could almost swear that when I mentioned the fire and Veronica and Clive, John's initial reaction had been a glare as malevolent as the glares Ketzia Van Rijn and Rueben Caven had bestowed upon Chastity Barker.

Chapter Twenty-four

Tuesday morning

In food terms, Augusta Lowenfeld resembled a puffed pastry. Or a soufflé.

Having out-scooped legit newsmen, visions of journalistic Pulitzers danced in her head. Her eyes looked like just-washed crystal. Her cheeks reminded me of John's Bozo the Clown. Pressed powder, liquid eye liner, and violet eye shadow accentuated her "laugh" lines. The eyebrows that dominated her forehead had been plucked. Her fake lashes favored centipedes. A newly-appended beauty mark led one's gaze to blood-red lips, and she'd stuck two pretentious pencils through hair that had been bleached banana-peel-yellow, then tortured into a beehive.

Like Gloria Swanson, Gusta was ready for her close-up.

Excluding the three pink plastic flamingos that fiercely guarded the front yard, Gusta's cottage was picturesque. Or, as John might say, "quaint." A pocket-sized living room, eat-in kitchen, and fairly-large bathroom filled the downstairs. Upstairs, two bedrooms nestled beneath a pinnacled roof.

I couldn't get over Gusta's make-over, and remembered telling Davy that her scatterbrained persona could be a ruse. Now, re-evaluating, I decided the ruse had become the persona.

On May 22, 1976, Barry Manilow's "Tryin' to Get the Feeling Again" hit the charts at number one and Gusta's husband joined a flying circus. Some people say he nose-dived his plane into a mountain on purpose. Some say he's still flying, free as a bird. Be that as it may, before he hit the wild blue yonder, he compensated Gusta with the cottage. Plus, an annual stipend.

On June 22, 1976, as a portable radio belted out Paul Simon's "Fifty Ways to Leave Your Lover," Gusta donned widow's weeds. Eventually, she moderated her weeds to include black pedal-pushers.

Gusta is very Catholic. Since she didn't have her husband's death certificate in hand, she'd never remarried. Terey was her only child, but I'm fairly certain she wanted more kids so that she could dominate *them,* order *them* about. Despite her religious convictions, she'd be first in line to clone her daughter, and if she could, she'd give Immaculate Conception a try. Most people considered Gusta a harmless gossip, but my father would have recognized a kindred spirit.

During the fifteen minutes she allotted me, her phone never stopped ringing. Her gossip sheet wouldn't be out for a couple of days, had, in fact, not even gone to press. But the merchants who'd proofed their ads had seen the front page. And despite yesterday's downed phone lines, the news had spread far and wide, from Manitou Falls to Denver. Then, evidently, to the left and right coasts.

"Excuse me, Sydney, long distance!" she kept saying.

After three attempts to question her, I'd gotten as far as "Mrs. Lowenfeld, how did," so I decided to eavesdrop on her next phone conversation.

Gusta had been "tipped off" by a member of Yogi Demon's fan club,

(*her reliable source?*)

so Sunday night she paid a visit to the police precinct,

(*translation: she wanted to snoop*)

where she told the "nice officer" at the desk that she needed to "tinkle." The bathroom was down the hall and the officer didn't leave his post. The police, as always, were keeping Manitou

Falls "safe from looters and rapists and drunk drivers," so the hallway was empty. Trained as a reporter practically from birth,

(*one correspondence course, never completed*)

she noticed a box on a table, inside a dimly-lit room,

(*translation: dark until she flicked the light switch*)

and the scrap of paper, still taped to the box, "caught her eye." Witches and cauldrons, gift-wrap from Lilly's Apothecary. Having attended the birthday party at Lilly's Apothecary, she'd seen the ear inside the box. But she believed it a gag gift, like those candles that won't go out. Someone had once given her a cake with candles that never go out, even if you blow and blow,

(*someone had goofed; Gusta's face was a mask of hatred*)

and although she could take a joke, the candles were mean.

She knew from her "reliable source" that the ear was a real ear, but was it Clive Newton's ear?

Only one way to find out.

Due to "freedom of the press," she could investigate the box's contents and not get in trouble, which she wouldn't have gotten into anyway because there was no one in the room.

Yes, the headline was a grabber. Her sister, Terey,

(*Sister? Who the heck was Gusta talking to? CNN?*)

had thought it up. Could Mr. Geraldo stay on the line, please, or call back? Gusta had another "reliable source" in her office.

Placing the phone's receiver on the counter, sitting across from me at the table, she said, "Do you know how Clive's ear ended up in Xanthia's present?"

I'd come to question *her,* dammit, and her "office" was a kitchen. Before I could jump-start my mouth, Terey entered from the back door.

"Ma, there's a TV van out front," she said.

Gusta responded by cloning herself into one of the ruffled

crows Chastity's journal had mentioned.

Every portion of her body quivered with anticipatory enthusiasm.

Until she said, "Comb your hair, Teresa! Or, even better, put a hat on!"

"Why?"

"What do you mean, why? The TV cameras are here and you look like a skinny porcupine! Frankly, I don't know how Paul puts up with it!"

"The TV reporters don't want me." Terey's expression turned rebellious. "And it doesn't matter how you look, as long as you can satisfy your man. You couldn't satisfy yours, Mother, but I happen to have some experience in that department. Does the word 'blow' mean anything to you?"

"Teresa Margaret!"

"Besides," Terey said, expressionless again, "Paulie likes the way I look."

"He does not! I distinctly heard him say he likes girls with long hair, just before you went and cut it as short as what's-her-face, the actress who practically shaved her head for *G. I. Jane*, the one who cries all the time!"

"Ma, we have a guest. Could we talk about my hair later? Would you like a cup of coffee, Sydney?"

"Maybe another time."

Terey smiled at my response, having never taken me up on my frequent beverage offers.

"Guest?" Gusta's brow beetled. "Oh, Sydney St. Charles!"

I waited for her *as-I-live-and-breathe,* but she merely said, "Sydney's not a guest! She's a reliable source!"

"Ma, the TV reporters are waiting."

Gusta stood up, straightened her too-tight black skirt and sweater, adjusted her hair-pencils, sucked in her gut, and headed for the front door.

Terey laughed. I couldn't remember the last time Terey had laughed. Her girlish gurgle startled me and, for some reason, made me feel uncomfortable.

Maybe it was my thing about clowns.

My father had once flown the whole family to New York, ostensibly for a job interview. After telling the staid personnel manager that we practiced nudism, Nicholas insisted we visit Coney Island. To this day, I can picture the Fat Lady who towered above the Fun House. She wore a polka-dot dress and she laughed. The sound of her laughter scared me to death, but Nicholas grabbed my hand and pulled me through the Fun House. He said no kid of his would be a yellow-bellied coward (his drunken words), and he made me ride the roller coaster, then the parachute jump. After I'd tossed my cookies twice, my mother conjured up a windy rainstorm, turbulent enough to close down the rides.

Terey said, "What's the matter, Sydney?"

"Huh? Oh. Nothing." I wiped the memory-sweat from my brow with the sleeve of Davy's long-sleeved, navy-blue turtle-neck. "Terey, do you happen to know the name of the person who 'tipped off' your mom? The 'reliable source' who told her about Clive's ear?"

"No. She got a phone call." Terey's finger and thumb fiddled with her Arthur Miller High School graduation ring. "I was at the movies with Paulie."

"Did your mom recognize the tipster's voice?"

"She said it was so muffled, she couldn't even tell if it was male or female."

"Muffled by a handkerchief?"

"I guess." Terey looked at her watch. "Sydney, I hate to be rude, but I've got to call the printer. Ma wants the paper out a day early."

"No problem, sweetie. If it's okay, I'll leave by the back door."

"Sure. Let me collar the dog first. Her bark's worse than her bite, but she'll jump up on you and her paws are muddy."

"You have a dog?"

"No. I've got a yard. Molly is Paulie's dog. He named her for Molly Ringwald. But he's so busy, he hardly has time for me, much less a dog."

"What's Paulie doing now? Last I heard, he was working at a Burger King."

"He's working for The Newts," she said, as two black cats slunk into the kitchen. "Yogi Demon hired him."

"You mean re-hired." The cats hissed at me. "Didn't Clive fire him?"

She shook her head. "Paulie was downsized. But The Newts have become so famous, they've been able to hire more staff."

Opening the door, she walked into the yard, leaned against a crude, wooden storage shed, and whistled through her fingers.

Molly looked friendly enough, more congenial than the cats. An Irish terrier with a wiry, brick-red coat, she chuffed at the hand I extended, smelled Chasdick (and Annie), gave a happy *whoof,* and wagged her tail.

I said goodbye to Terey (and Molly), then exited through a side gate.

As I walked toward my Honda, my mind digested Gusta's phone conversation, especially the part about her visit to the cop-shop.

The Manitou Falls police department employed six cops, not including the "nice officer" who manned the front desk.

On a Sunday night, three kept Manitou Falls safe from "looters and rapists and drunk drivers." The three off-duty cops would have attended church services or taken their families out for dinner or visited a local bar, where one can down a few brews and watch the Avalanche skate against a rival hockey team. At least, that's what Oliver used to do.

Had Oliver left the birthday box in plain view?

Only one way to find out.

Chapter Twenty-five

Tuesday afternoon

My brother and his third wife live on top of a hill.

Actually, they own the hill.

Which is why their "street" isn't named for a Salem Reverend.

Instead, Oliver named the hill.

Not surprisingly, he calls it OLIVER'S TWIST.

Our local post office has a motto, paraphrased from the inscription inside a New York City post office: "Neither snow nor heat nor gloom of night nor Oliver's Twist stays these couriers from the swift completion of their appointed rounds."

The curves, zigzags, and loops aren't difficult to navigate, if one has a stick shift and/or power steering. However, occasionally, dead trees block the road. So do deer. In fact, multiple DEER CROSSING signs rupture the spectacular vista.

Today, my enemy was mud.

The sun had turned snow to slush, and slushy mud sucked at my tires.

The sucky din of slime-absorbing rubber made me feel peevish, so I turned on the radio. And, for the first time, really listened to the words of a Newt song.

As I was going to Jordan wood,
There was the water and there it stood.
So shall thy love stay in thy heart,
Ne're shall we part, ne're shall we part,
Even if we should die . . .

Ersatz Romeo and Juliet, I thought. No wonder Yogi's lyrics appealed to kids. Hopefully, the lyrics didn't inspire teen suicide pacts.

Against incantations of false prophets,
Against the black laws of paganism,
Against spells of women, smiths, and druids,
Against all knowledge that is forbidden the human soul . . .

Holy smoke, the Horseman's Word! Aunt Lillian had once told me that blacksmiths were believed to possess strange powers. Many were blood-charmers, some could heal diseases, and some were possessed of the Horseman's Word, a chant to gain control over horses.

Then, of course, she taught me the chant.

Yogi Demon sang the Horseman's Word as a chorus to "Fuary, Gary, Nary," The Newts' most popular song and the title of their latest CD.

Another Lillian-memory kicked in, one that should have smacked me in the face when I bought Xanthia's birthday gift. Centuries ago, a mad dog's bite could be cured by writing "Rebus Rubus Epitepscum" on a piece of paper and giving it to the bitten person, who'd eat it in bread. But a similar charm consisted of writing the words "Fuary, Gary, Nary" three times on a piece of cheese, varying the words each time, then giving the cheese to the mad dog.

What did Yogi's song lyrics mean?

I didn't have a clue.

Before the next refrain could begin, a deer stepped into the road.

Leaning back in my seat, I clutched the steering wheel for dear life, hit the brake pedal with both feet, and heard my car grind to a halt.

Whereupon, the engine died.

"Damn it, Bambi," I shouted. "God should have given you a roadrunner's beep-beep. Roadrunners don't need it and deer do."

"Bambi" flicked his ears. Bounding toward the bushes, he saluted me with his flag-tail.

If Aunt Lillian comes back as an animal, she'll come back as a doe.

With that thought, I shifted into first gear.

Somehow, my shaky fingers managed to turn the ignition key, but by the time my Honda revved up again, The Newts' song had been sung. Instead of enigmatic lyrics, a weatherman predicted warmer temperatures and more sunshine.

Which meant more mud.

Turning off the radio, I concentrated on the road.

Chapter Twenty-six

Tuesday afternoon

Had he lived, Nicholas Nickleby St. Charles III would have moved into his eldest son's digs.

Its façade reminded me of an illustration I'd seen for Nathaniel Hawthorne's *The House of The Seven Gables.*

Except Oliver's house sported five gables, their shingled roofs painted green, because, as a kid, Jessica had loved *Anne of Green Gables* books.

So had I, the one bond Jessica and I shared. Only she preferred the grown-up, married Anne, while I preferred—and, in fact, identified with—Montgomery's feisty, freckle-faced orphan.

As my Honda crested Oliver's Twist, I hoped Yogi Demon hadn't vacated Green Gables yet. Apart from my other questions, I wanted to ask him about the lyrics to "Fuary, Gary, Nary."

I parked next to a white, late-model Mercedes. Had Oliver had already spent the first five percent of his newly-negotiated book advance?

There were no other cars, assuming one can call a Mercedes a mere car, but the house boasted a five-car garage; one substantial parking space per gable.

Walking down a fired-clay-tile path toward the front door, I stopped briefly to admire a sea-blue sky. Milky clouds. Tangerine sun. Mountain peaks, sparkly with snow. Breathtaking view. *Oliver's Twist* by Walt Whitman. Or Bing Crosby.

And yet, it felt wrong. I felt wrong. Or, as Chastity Barker would say, fear rose in my throat.

Like Chastity, Jessica had servants. A maid. A part-time cook. A gardener—in Oliver-speak, "landscaper"—and someone who shoveled or mowed or simply hauled away the trash. Usually, Green Gables hummed with activity.

But today it looked unoccupied, quiet as a . . . well, tomb.

I felt as if I'd stepped into a Boris Karloff movie.

If a mad scientist opened the door, I'd turn tail.

The doorbell played the first five syllables of "Food Glorious Food," from the Oscar-winning musical, *Oliver*.

A scientist opened the door, but she wasn't mad.

"Did you forget something?" Carol Rodriguez St. Charles said with a smile, just before she saw me. "Sydney. Hi. What are you doing here?"

"I came to see Yogi. Yogi Demon. And my brother."

Oliver's ex-wife looked disheveled, but in an attractive way. Her cheeks were flushed. Her hair fluffed around her face. Her beige silk blouse, buttoned wrongly, revealed the deep cleft between her breasts. Her straight skirt didn't hang straight, and . . . she wasn't wearing pantyhose. I'd never seen Carol without pantyhose. She even wore them under designer jeans and shorts.

"You just missed Yogi," she said. "He left fifteen, maybe twenty minutes ago. Went back to the apartment he shares with another Newt."

"What are *you* doing here?" I asked, startled into rudeness by Carol's missing pantyhose.

"Luncheon appointment. With Jessica. We've become friends. Good friends. We like to vent. Over Oliver."

Had I been on a jury, listening to her testify, I'd have sworn she committed perjury. But which choppy sentence was the lie? Her luncheon appointment? The fact that she and Jessica had become friends? Good friends?

"Sometimes we vent by e-mail," she continued. "Yesterday Jessica invited me for lunch. Today. Noon. I got here early. Around eleven-thirty. Oliver looked scared. Very pale. He jumped in his car, said he was a best-selling mystery author and could damn well find a missing person. Then he—"

"Missing person? Jessica or Yogi?"

"Jessica. I just told you. Yogi left—"

"How long has she been missing?"

"Since last night." Carol's hand brushed at her hair and the sun captured her imitation Denver Broncos Superbowl ring, garnished with diamond chips. "This morning the police searched the grounds. And the Twist."

I glanced at my watch; one-forty. "Carol, may I come in?"

"Of course. Sorry. I'm still half asleep. Oliver asked me to stay by the phone, just in case Jessica called. I made myself comfortable . . ." she pointed to her bare feet ". . . then drank a glass of wine, actually a couple of glasses, and nodded off."

"Could you have slept through the phone?"

"No. I sat on the couch, next to the phone. I would have heard it ring."

"It's ringing now." Brushing past Carol, I raced into the family room, snatched up the receiver, and said hello.

"Did she call?"

"Oliver, it's Sydney. Where are you?"

"At the precinct. Did Jess call?"

"No." A thought occurred. "Where were you last night?"

"At home. At first. Then I went for a drive."

"In a snowstorm?"

"I've got snow tires."

Suspicions confirmed, I said, "Rose."

"Wrong. I didn't spend the night with Rosie."

"Jeez, Oliver, you're a lousy liar. How'd you know her nickname's Rosie?"

"Because, when she met me at the door to her room, she

told me to call her Rosie. Rosie O'Donnell. She said that wasn't her real last name, that she'd lost her last name, just before she took a swig of champagne, finishing the bottle. Then she hugged her stomach, puked on my galoshes, and passed out cold."

"Little Rosie has a big problem."

"So do I." Oliver paused to swallow something; maybe coffee, maybe guilt. "Jess is missing."

"Yes, I know. Maybe she finally wised up. Maybe you'll have to split your generous book advance. Or your new Mercedes."

"The new Mercedes is Carol's and Jess didn't walk out on me."

"Really, Oliver!"

"You don't understand, Syd. She didn't take a suitcase or clothes or her purse. She left her wallet, cell phone, and credit cards."

"She paid for her spells with cash. Maybe she stashes cash."

"What spells?"

Should I add to Oliver's guilt? "She bought a charm to make you love her. And one to keep you from straying."

Silence. Then, "Obviously, the straying-spell didn't work."

"Obviously, she didn't cast it. Did the servants see anything?"

"No. But they leave around four."

"What about Jessica's car?"

"That's the first thing I checked. It's in the garage."

"Maybe someone picked her up."

"In a snowstorm?"

"Maybe the someone who picked her up had snow tires."

"Very funny. I'm crazed with worry and you're—"

"Oliver, where was Yogi when Jessica disappeared?"

"Gone. Helping Tiffany celebrate her birthday. Remember Tiffany?"

"Of course. The magenta-haired child who had a yen for Yogi. I wonder if she used my suppository love potion."

"She did. Yogi came back, said Tiff had, you know, diarrhea."

"Don't tell me Yogi's car has snow tires, too."

"No. But cabs do. We met at the door. Shared a nightcap. He told me about Tiff, you know, guy stuff. Then we went to bed."

"And?"

"I got . . . I felt . . . stirred."

Stirred but not shaken. I wanted to shake my brother, would have if we'd been face-to-face. "You got horny, Oliver. There's no other word for it."

"Okay, horny. So I went to Jess's room and crept into her bed. She wasn't there."

"No kidding. Did you search for her?"

"No, not then. She could have been anywhere. Upstairs, downstairs, five freaking gables, and I was exhausted."

"Exhausted *and* horny. You poor man."

"I can live without the sarcasm. Is Carol there?"

"Yes. Do you mind if I fix myself a sandwich? I skipped lunch."

"How can you eat at a time like this?"

"What makes you think something bad happened to Jessica?"

"Veronica."

"What the bloody hell has Veronica got to do with anything? Jessica found out about you and her sister weeks ago."

"Veronica was strangled, Syd, before the fire. Maybe the same person came after Jess."

Veronica had been murdered. My conjecture had been correct. There was no satisfaction in the thought. "Why would the same person come after Jessica?"

209

"Because I write mysteries."

"Excuse me?"

"Leverage. Extortion. Blackmail. I'm an ex-cop and a best-selling mystery author."

"Are you saying that, should you discover the identity of the killer, he'll use Jessica as his trump card? To shut you up? Are you insane? Or have you been watching too many Mel Gibson movies? Maybe you suffer from rectal-cranial inversion. Maybe I should give *you* a suppository."

"Put Carol on the phone," Oliver said, his voice petulant.

Furious, I thrust the receiver at my ex-sister-in-law, then stomped into a huge kitchen that could have operated as the cookery for a small hotel. Or a dude ranch.

Framed paintings, prints, and photographs of horses dominated the walls. A polished horse harness, with bells, functioned as a piece of sculpture (Jessica had once told me she paid a mere $5,000 for it). Wooden canisters read: OATS, HAY, and GRAIN. Miniature, exquisitely-carved carousel horses stood on top of ceramic counter tiles. A local artist, commissioned by Jessica, had kilned black, white, and brown horse-head tiles, creating a unique, original pattern.

Oliver's enormous ego and asinine hypothesis had killed my appetite, but I wanted to check out Jessica's refrigerator.

Multiple magnets pressed coupons, grocery lists, business cards, recipes, and other assorted minutiae against the Frigidaire's stainless steel surface.

No magnetized message for Oliver. Or anyone else. Hope died.

I just stood there, wondering what to do next, when a wall photo I'd never noticed before drew my gaze . . .

Jessica's sister Veronica, her jodhpur-clad rump glued to the saddle that graced a white stallion.

Chastity Barker's Journal
October, 1692

Yesterday Obadiah lost his hearing, speech, and sight.

As he moaned and writhed in agony, Trump and my neighbour, Rueben Cavin, carried him from the cornfield. Fearing he might do himself an injury, they roped him to his bed.

At noontide I changed his befouled bedding whilst I cursed Trump, who slept in the woodshed, and Sally, who refused to venture near my flailing husband—or his soiled sheets. At twilight I spooned broth between Obadiah's lips, though he did spit most of it back at me.

By nightfall he had subsided into a lengthy slumber.

Today he has regained the use of his eyes, ears, and diction, but seems to have lost his memory. He has no recollection of our conjugality, calls me Sarah, and believes I am the sister who drowned when he was but eight years of age. Over and over, he implores me to stay away from water. Earlier, he seized a fold in my gown and followed me about the kitchen, begging "Sarah" for gingerbread and gull's eggs. When I feigned giving him what he asked for, he pretended to eat it. As I write, he sits across the table from me. He shows no interest in my journal. Instead, he sings verses from "The Man in the Moon." I have sent Sally for my sister.

'Tis the morrow, the first day of October. I tried to pen my journal last night, but felt so heart-sick I knew 'twould be useless.

Yesterday, when Mercy arrived, her cheeks were as red as

her hair. The wind had blown off her bonnet and clusters of loose curls spilled down her back and bosom. In one hand she carried a knapsack.

"Sally rode pillion," she said, "and Pyewacket did not care for that. Sally squirms like a newt."

Sally then entered, her hands molding her buttocks. "Me bum hurts, Mistress," she said.

"Hush, you worthless wench," Mercy said. "Chastity, send the girl to the stables."

"Go to the stables, Sally," I said, as always somewhat cowed by my servant's temperament. "Take my sister's horse and rub him down."

"Oi won't," she said. "The horse'll boite me, him havin' sech big teeth."

For the first time in my life, I felt rage overcome fear. "Do as I say, trollop," I screeched, "or I'll haul you before the magistrate. For whoring. Do not set one foot inside this house until I send Trump for Pyewacket."

"Trump be gone," she said. "Him an 'is black beast o' a dog."

"Gone? Where did he go?"

Sally shrugged. Still molding her buttocks with both hands, she stomped outside and warily eyed Pyewacket whilst I shut the door.

As if he had waited for the comely servant to leave, Obadiah sang, "The man in the moon came down too soon and asked the way to Norwich."

Setting her knapsack on the floor by the window, Mercy said, "How long has he been like this?"

"Since cock crow. But yesterday he could neither see, hear, nor speak."

"He went by the south and burnt his mouth," Obadiah sang, "with eating of cold pease porridge."

As I gazed upon a pot of boiled chicken, I knew my expression revealed a guilty anguish. Sure enough, Mercy said, "Where is the hawthorn branch?"

"Out by the pig sty." Tears brimmed. "I could not bear to look at it."

"And the chicken heart?"

"Old Scratch ate it."

"Sarah," Obadiah said, "kindly serve me some cold pease porridge."

"He deems me his sister who drowned when he was a boy." Tears overflowed. "When I cited Aunt Pru's revenge charm, I did not know it would spawn the loss of memory or turn my husband into a child."

"What thought you?" Mercy asked, her voice reproachful.

"I did not think at all. I steeped the thorns in oil of civet. I seethed the heart in vinegar, boiled it over the fire, and put it into the oil with the thorns. At the last stroke of midnight, I plunged three thorns into the heart and chanted the incantation. 'This shames the deed, this blames the hand, this blights the heart.' I did not have three black candles, nor did I wrap the heart in a scrap of cloth and bury it where weeds flourish. On my oath, I believed the spell would not work."

" 'Tis no excuse," Mercy said. "The conjuration could have been lessened and a weaker form of revenge worked on Obadiah, had you maintained the heart in the oil in which it was steeped."

Having heard his name, Obadiah sang, "The world is full of care, much like unto a bubble. Women and care, and care and women, and women and care and trouble."

"He condemns me," I cried. "Though he knows not why."

"Oh fiddle," Mercy said. " 'Tis naught but a foolish ditty. My Toby has oft sung it to me." She heaved a deep sigh. "Let us help your husband to his bed."

As we flung Obadiah's arms around our shoulders, he said, "I saw the Lady in Red, Sarah. She was on her knees and she moaned something awful."

Between the two of us, my sister and I managed to get him into bed. Then, retrieving her knapsack, Mercy placed it on the kitchen table.

"Mayhap 'twas the Lady in Red, not your curse, that led to Obadiah's situation," she said. Rummaging through the knapsack, she pulled out a mortar and pestle. "Suppose Obadiah truly believed he saw the Lady in Red? His attempt to shriek would choke in his throat. His body would tremble and twist. Swaying backwards, he'd fall to the ground, and after a short time appear to be in a swoon."

" 'Tis how I found him," I said, "in the field."

"Soon after he would writhe, as if in mortal agony."

"He did so," I said. "Trump and Rueben Cavin roped him to his bed."

"Should he refuse to eat, his death would be a matter of days."

"I spooned broth down his throat, but he spit it back at me. Mayhap he'll eat porridge."

"Nay," she said. " 'Tis not in keeping with the effects of his fear."

"Then all is lost."

"Nay," she said again. "We shall chance another charm."

"Mayhap Matt Grayson saw the Red Lady. Mayhap he died from dread."

"And having dropped dead, he tied himself to a cross-piece?" Mercy sniffed. "Do not talk rubbish, Chastity. 'Tis lucky for you that Matt was murdered. Toby told me Ketzia Van Rijn accused you of witchcraft, until they cut Matt down and found the grievous knife wounds in his back. Then Ketzia said you'd made a pact with the devil and 'twas one of his vassals that stabbed Matt. John Hawthorn and Thomas Danforth did not take Ketzia's accusations to heart. But if I were you, I'd watch my back where she is concerned."

"Why does she hate me?" I asked.

"Because you are plump and comely whilst she is thin as a nail," Mercy said. "And because she set her sights on Jack Grayson, once he became widowed."

"As did every lass in Salem." I heard the sinful pride in my voice.

"That must stop at once," Mercy said, her voice stern. "If discovered, excommunication would be the least of your problems."

Wanting to change the subject, I said, "How fares our dearest sister?"

"John says Anne fares well," Mercy replied. "She asked for a hearing before the judges, but I know not what she plans to say."

Chapter Twenty-seven

Tuesday night

The phone rang, startling me.

I dropped the journal, picked it up, and carefully flipped through its pages, trying to find Chastity's last line . . . not an easy task. Though her pages were numbered, all her entries ran together.

Davy waited impatiently.

Aunt Lillian entered the sun porch. Her gaze touched upon Annie, Mercy, and Chasdick, just before she said, "You have a phone call, Sydney. It's Xanthia."

"Has she heard anything—"

"About Jessica? No. Use the kitchen extension. I made lemonade for you and Davy. And some 'sandwitches.' Tonight, at dinner, you ate like a bird."

"Like a bird," Mercy parroted, and I could have sworn Annie grinned.

As I left the porch and entered the apothecary, I heard Aunt Lillian say, "Bring me up to date, Davy. What happened after Chastity saw Matt dead in her cornfield?"

Taking the stairs two at a time, I walked into the kitchen, picked up the receiver, said hello to Xanthia, and asked about Hamilton.

"She's fine, Aunt Syd. She loves brooms, just like her namesake."

I could hear the smile in Xanthia's voice.

"Aunt Syd," she continued, "would you do me a big favor?"

"Sure, as long as it's not illegal or fattening."

"I still have two tickets for The Newts. The whole school knows Natasha, Ashley, and Megan are my best friends, so that's okay. But I can't give the tickets to somebody else. Everybody wants to go. No matter who got picked, I'd get into trouble. So I told everybody I gave the tickets to my aunt and her boyfriend."

"Boyfriend?"

"Bozo the Clown."

"Sweetie, his name's John, and he's not my boyfriend."

"Daddy says he is. Daddy says you're 'romantically automated' and Bozo undresses you with his eyes. Megan, what did Daddy call it? Megan's staying over tonight. Oh, yeah. Daddy said Bozo has 'introspective pornographic moments.' "

"And your dad has swine empathy."

"What does that mean?"

He's a male chauvinist pig. "Nothing. It wasn't very nice and I shouldn't be mean to your dad, especially when he's tearing his hair out over Jessica."

Xanthia giggled. "Sorry," she said. "I shouldn't laugh. It's just that Daddy doesn't have much hair. Will you take the tickets, Aunt Syd? Please?"

"I'll have to ask John."

Speak of the devil.

Entering the kitchen, John sidled up to my side. "Ask me what?"

"Can I call you back, Xanthia?"

John wore faded jeans, no shirt. Putting his arms around me, he nuzzled my neck and the romance authors would have said my legs turned to pudding.

"The tickets are for opening night, this Thursday," Xanthia said.

As John slid his hand beneath my tee, my breath caught in my throat.

"This Thursday?" I managed. "That's the day after to-morrow."

John's hand moved lower, his fingers caressing, until he reached the waistband of my jeans. I sucked in my stomach, giving him easier access, and leaned back against the bulk of his body.

"Please say yes, Aunt Syd. I really want you to come."

As John's fingers found the slit in my borrowed boxers, I heard the echo of Xanthia's last six words.

"Hold on," I said. "John's here. In the kitchen. I'll ask him."

Placing the receiver on the counter, I pulled his hand from my jeans, then turned and faced him. My whole body was sending feverish signals to my brain, and the romance writers would have said . . . hell, I didn't know what the romance writers would have said. I only knew what Oliver would have said. He would have said I was romantically automated.

"Let's go to your bedroom," John urged, "where we won't be interrupted."

"We can't. Xanthia's on the phone. She has two extra tickets for The Newts concert. She wants us to escort her. And her three friends."

"Tell her no." He began to pull my tee over my head.

Stepping backwards, I patted down the shirt. "It wouldn't be a date or anything. We'd sort of chaperone."

"Okay. Tell her yes. Hurry."

I suddenly realized I wore Davy's jeans, the pair I'd worn to the birthday party, the pair with the love talisman in its pocket.

"Are you sure, John?"

"Yes, I'm sure."

"I mean, are you sure about the concert?"

"Yes. Tell Xanthia yes, then hang up."

I gave up. Leaning against John again, feeling his hand snake around my waist again, I reached for the receiver. "John says yes, Xanthia. I'll call you tomorrow, make arrangements to meet and—"

"Would you bring the talisman that'll help me lose weight?"

"Absolutely. I'll bring talismans for all your friends."

"Megan, Aunt Syd says she'll give you a magic talisman like the one I told you about, the one with the moon. Which one do you want?"

This time John paid tribute to my breasts. Reaching beneath my shirt again, unsnapping my bra, he ran his palm across my nipples, back and forth, back and—

"Megan says she wants a talisman for intelligence, Aunt Syd, but she's got to be kidding. She's the smartest girl in the whole school. What, Megan? Okay, I'll ask. She says she's going to California next month and she wants to know if you have a talisman for earthquakes. To keep them away."

I stifled a moan. "Tell her yes."

"She wants to know what it says. Here, I'll put Megan on."

" 'Now earth be fixed, and dare not quake, that I and mine, may sleep and wake.' Xanthia, sweetie, I really have to—"

"It's Megan Graham, Miss St. Charles. I'm supposed to tell you what Ashley and Natasha want. Natasha's easy. Money. She's always broke."

"Okay. There's a talisman To Gain Wealth."

John thrust his hand between my legs and gently squeezed.

"Ashley is very pretty but she hates her glasses," Megan said. "Do you have a talisman that'll let Ashley see without her glasses?"

"Maybe. If not, I'll think one up. Please say goodbye to Xanthia for me."

As I returned the receiver to its cradle, John pressed his lips against my ear.

"Bedroom, Syd," he said, then flicked his tongue.

The wet warmth traveled from my ear to my belly, and I would have melted like the Wizard-of-Oz witch, had Aunt Lillian not walked into the kitchen.

"Sydney," she said, "what's taking you so long?"

My body faced the counter and John's body hid most of me. Quick as a wink, I hooked my bra. No way would Aunt Lillian find me unfettered, bra dangling, twice in one week.

"Xanthia wanted to chat," I replied, stepping away from my human shield. "She invited John and me to a concert. The Newts. This Thursday."

"I hope you said yes, dear. You've been looking wan lately. Stressed. And tonight you look downright sweaty. Have you got a fever?"

"No. Honest. I'm okay, just worried about Jessica."

"Oliver made his bed. Now he can lie in it."

"Then you don't believe Jessica was kidnapped?"

"Not for a moment. There's been no ransom note, no phone call. If Jerry was on the case, it would have been solved by now."

My aunt has a thing for Jerry Orbach. Every night, without fail, he visits her bedroom via *Law & Order* reruns.

"Jerry memorizes a script," I said.

"Do you want me to take Davy his lemonade?"

"I'll take it, Aunt Lillian. He's anxious to get back to Chastity's journal." I shot John an apologetic look.

"Good. I'm watching a video, *The Caveman's Valentine*. Samuel L. Jackson can warm my sheets anytime. And the special effects are splendid."

As Lillian left the kitchen, I opened the refrigerator and reached for the lemonade pitcher—knowing that if John reached for me again, I'd be lost.

He didn't. Sitting at the kitchen table, he said, "I'm sorry."

"For what?"

"I don't know what came over me. I have no right to start a relationship with anyone, especially you, when I might be involved."

"Involved in what?"

He gave me a strange look. "Involved with someone else."

"Why 'especially' me?"

"Because every time I see you I want to make love to you. You're such a tasty little morsel. Strong yet vulnerable. Beautiful, smart—"

"Knock it off, John. I'm not beautiful. For one thing, I need to lose fifteen or twenty pounds."

Fifteen or twenty pounds . . .

Fifteen or twenty . . .

I remembered Carol's did-you-forget-something? If Yogi had left the house fifteen (or twenty) minutes before my arrival, he would have been driving south on the Interstate by the time Oliver's doorbell chimed, "Food, Glorious Food."

Why would Carol ask if he'd forgotten something, her voice all purry, unless he'd left ten (or five) minutes before she answered the door?

But wouldn't he have passed me on the Twist?

Not necessarily. I'd chanced a shortcut, figuring the road was rougher but would be embedded with leaves rather than gooey mud.

"Don't be silly," John said. "You're the perfect size. I wouldn't want someone who was all skin and bones."

My mind was still on Yogi. And Carol. Her disheveled ap-

221

pearance. The missing pantyhose. What did Yogi Demon (nee Yogi Berra Brustein) have that made every woman crave him? A magic wand?

"I'm serious, Syd," John said. "You turn me on. You have 'curvature.' You're a goddess. An enchantress. A Muse. Venus and Calliope."

And there's a love talisman in my pocket, I thought. *Not only that, but last Sunday I chanted a love incantation that Aunt Lillian says works like a charm. I even added "so-mote-it-be."*

Bothered by John's flowery flattery, feeling a change of subject was in order, I said, "You visited Reb Ashmare today, right?"

"Yes. She's a lovely mare, and she got along well with Annie, Mercy, and Chasdick. Aunt Lillian kept saying, 'See? My hunch was spot-on.' Then she talked the stable owner into giving her a riding lesson."

"While she rode, did you and Davy tour Veronica's estate?"

"Yes and no. We couldn't get close to the house. Until they sort things out, it's considered a crime scene. But we explored the woods. And the pastures."

"Did you find anything suspicious looking?"

"No."

"Did you remember anything?"

"Yes."

"You did? What?"

"A stampede. Several horses were running, their hooves pounding . . ."

"And?"

"A duck pond looked familiar."

"Exactly what did you picture when you looked at the duck pond? Quickly, John, without thinking."

"Nice try, Sydney, but I'd rather not talk about this until I can sort it all out in my mind."

"Fair enough. Did you see Veronica's white stallion?"

"How'd you know she had a white stallion?"

"There's a photo in Jessica's kitchen. Veronica riding a white—"

"Sydney, I really don't want to discuss this. Ask your brother."

"I'm asking you. Davy keeps saying 'later.' He's more involved with Chastity Barker's journal than—"

"Okay, let me put it this way. I *won't* talk about this."

"Why not?"

"Because it's none of your business." He pounded his fist on the table, then splayed his fingers. "I'm sorry. I've taken advantage of your incredible hospitality and I'm nothing but trouble. I'll leave first thing tomorrow morning."

"No. Please. I don't want you to leave, not until we solve your . . . identity crisis. And you'd break Aunt Lillian's heart."

"What about your heart?"

Looking down at my sneakers, I heard John rise from his chair. His index finger lifted my chin. His lips claimed mine. As I opened my mouth, his tongue darted inside. His hands molded my back, and I felt my breasts flatten against the hard expanse of his chest. Overwhelmed by the taste of him, by the sensation of his tongue as it leapt to dance with mine, I twined my right leg around his left leg and tried to press myself closer. His fingers touched my brow, my cheek, my chin, and my throat, moving lightly as they explored and caressed. And still his tongue danced in a savage yet somehow languid tempo that sent pulsating messages to the rest of my body. I shut my eyes and a whimper rose in my throat.

"Bedroom," John whispered for the third . . . or was it the fourth? . . . time.

I didn't want to move, didn't want to open my eyes, lest the dream be lost.

Despite the loud beat of my heart, I heard the sound of flapping wings. Reluctantly, I raised my heavy eyelids.

"Ta-ta, Sydney." Landing on top of her cage, Mercy squawked, *"John, John, bo bon, reeky, rump-fed maggot-pie."*

"Syd, what's taking you so long?" Davy yelled, his feet stomping up the stairs.

Chastity Barker's Journal

October, 1692

Anne is at liberty, freed of all charges.

Her ploy was daring and I laud her courage.

Owing to Mercy's Charm to Nourish the Wits, my husband is considerably improved. However, he oft lapses into the madness that claimed him three weeks ago. I dare not stray too far from home, thus Mercy did give forth Anne's account.

Upon facing the judges, Anne said she was a healer, not a sorceress.

One of the judges said, "Anne Kittridge, what evil spirits have you familiarity with?"

Anne replied, "None."

"Have you contact with the devil?"

"No."

"Why did you sink the boat?"

"I did not."

"Who do you employ to do your evil?"

"I employ nobody."

"What creature do you employ?"

"No creature. I am falsely accused."

'Twas fortunate the afflicted girls were absent, for Anne swore on a Bible that she had never tormented the children. Then she recited the Lord's Prayer to prove she was not, nor ever had been, Satan's pawn. Following her recitation, she wept.

'Tis believed a witch cannot say the Lord's Prayer. 'Tis likewise believed that, having rejected Christian charity, a witch cannot weep.

Anne reminded Judge Johnson that she had treated his goodwife's illness with honey and powdered turmeric, not witchcraft. Due to Anne's curative skills, Charlene Johnson was now as fat as a parturient cow.

"And twice as lazy," the judge said, inviting laughter.

All of the judges then conferred and shortly thereafter came to a decision. Abigail Williams had seen someone other than Anne Kittridge.

God be praised.

I have not written in my journal lo these many days. Trump and Sally are gone and there is much work to do. As the moon waxes full again, Obadiah chafes and frets and grows faint-hearted. He talks of the Lady in Red as if she were in the flesh. For good measure, he speaks of the Man in the Moon. I am beginning to think the Lady in Red and the Man in the Moon killed Matt. Could they have wielded a spectral knife?

I did not tell Jack about Obadiah's Red Lady and Moon Man, fearing he might believe me mad.

Despite Mercy's counsel, I met Jack in the loft. I told myself that he might have devised a ploy to forestall my condemnation. Vowing to remain chaste, I donned the gown I wear when slaughtering shoats and barrows. My red velvet gown makes me feel wanton, I know not why. Mayhap 'tis the touch of the fabric, not unlike the skins that gird the evolving antlers of deer.

My drab, patched gown did not deter Jack. With a laugh, he stripped it from my body. He stroked my belly, where his child thrives, and—God forgive me—I did surrender to his touch.

After we had finished, he suggested that I travel to Connecticut and visit my mum. That way, Jack said, I could give birth to our child and no one would be the wiser. The flaw in his scheme, I said, was that Obadiah would surely know the babe was not his upon my return.

Jack thought that over. Then he said that he and Ketzia would raise the child and pretend it was a foundling.

When I questioned such an odd statement, he said he had pledged himself to Ketzia, taking the place of his slain brother. He said that with her dower he could purchase more acreage.

Furious, I tried to scratch his face. But my fingernails are blunt, not sharp like talons, and I am no bird. Nor am I a sharp-clawed cat. Jack easily held me off. I tried to bite his fingers. If, after death, I could re-emerge in a newborn form, I'd want to be a dog. I'd want to be a dog so that I could bite Jack's fingers.

Nay. I'd gnaw his throat.

I told him this and he laughed. He then chastised my behaviour and said that should I accuse him of lewd morals, he would swear I had bewitched him.

I am not a witch.

I weep.

'Tis much later and I have stolen a few precious moments to pen my thoughts.

Earlier, having dried my tears and donned my warmest cloak, I stepped outside and walked toward the woodpile.

My neighbour, Rueben Cavin, last filled the wood box. He stopped by on a matter of business, having stated many times that he wished to purchase a portion of Obadiah's land. Holding back tears, I said that my husband was indisposed and Trump was gone.

Rueben then chopped wood, cleaned the pig sty and coop, mucked the stalls, and would accept no coin for his labour—naught but some cold potato soup and a pinch of tobacco.

'Twas during the lighting of his pipe that I, of a sudden, began to weep. Rueben did not touch me, merely listened. I finished my mournful tale by confessing that I was with child. He said he would help as best he could. He told me to be brave, then bid me good-night. The stars in all their splendor had been out that night, but Rueben's goodness shone brighter than any star.

I heaved a grateful sigh at the remembrance and walked toward the woodpile again. Hefting the heavy ax, I began to stagger and might have fallen had not Trump caught me and set me back on my feet.

"Where on earth did you come from?" Dropping the ax, I tossed him my cloak, for the little man was naked as a frog.

He appeared to be half-starved and frozen unto death. His hair had been shaven and his aggrieved face looked like an organ grinder's monkey. Ignoring my query, donning the cloak, he said, "Be the Marster cured?"

"He is somewhat recovered," I replied. "But as the moon grows full, he frets and wrings his hands as if washing them free of—"

BLOOD, I thought. "You saw," I said. "You saw Matt Grayson. You saw the man who killed him. You saw Obadiah kill him."

"Nay, Mistress," Trump said. "Oi seen nothin'."

"If you saw nothing, why did you flee?"

" 'Cause 'twould be me wot gets the blame fer the doin' in o' Grayson."

I felt my eyes narrow. "Where were you when Matt was slain?"

"On the side o' the cornfield," he said. "Oi takes a bog behind some trees, Mistress, an when oi comes back the Marster were gone."

"Where did he go?"

Trump shrugged. "When next oi sets me eyes on the Marster, he be grovelin' on the ground an frothin' at the mouth. Oi gets him into cover, Mistress, but when oi sets out fer help, he starts crawlin' at the scarecrow an yellin' how he seen the dead Red Lady what moans on noights o' the full moon. 'Tis where he stayed 'til ye found him."

"Why did you not go for help when he became sluggish?"

"He bade me wait by his side."

"But he was out of his wits."

Trump's jaw jutted. "He bade me wait."

"What a brave and loyal servant you are, Trump. In truth, I have sorely misjudged you." Herding him toward the door, I said, "Let us go inside, where you shall tell me what happened to your hair."

Chapter Twenty-eight
Tuesday night

"I'll bet you anything Obadiah killed Matthew," I said, rubbing my eyes. As predicted, Trump's dialogue had been difficult to decipher.

"You're on," Davy said.

"What do you mean, I'm on?"

"It's a bet." He cracked his knuckles. "Trump took a dump, leaving Obadiah alone. When Trump found him, Obadiah was loony-tunes."

"Right. Exactly my point. While Trump was dumping . . . bogging . . . Obadiah could have—"

"Where's the knife?"

"What knife?"

"The knife used to stab Matt Grayson."

"Obadiah threw it away? Buried it? Ate it? How should I know?"

"Okay, sweetheart." Davy stood up. "That's enough deciphering."

"No. Please. I want to find out what happened to Trump's hair."

"You're in no mood to squint at squiggles, Syd, and I want to see Lynn." He glanced at his watch. "It's almost midnight. Her restaurant closes at eleven, so she should be home soon."

"John started at eleven. He's washing dishes at Nina's. The graveyard shift."

"Get some sleep, Syd. You're exhausted. First thing tomorrow morning, we'll pick up where we left off."

"I'm not exhausted. My eyes are tired, that's all."

"Bull, sweetheart. Your eyes look like a raccoon's. I saw some jars of Kyphi in the shop. That'll help you sleep."

Kyphi is an ancient Egyptian blend, a heavenly incense. Its aroma lulls one to sleep, reduces anxieties, and brightens dreams.

On the night of a new moon, Aunt Lillian tosses half a handful of raisins into an earthenware bowl. She steeps the raisins in white wine for three nights, then adds equal parts of Juniper, Sweet Sedge Root, Acacia, and Henna. The next day, as the sun sets, she grinds Peppermint, Bay Laurel, Cinnamon, Orris, Calamus, and Gum Mastic, until the herbs are the consistency of a powder. Then I mix together one tablespoon of myrrh and one tablespoon of honey, add it to the drained raisins and herbs, work in the powdered herbs, spread it out on a wooden board, let it dry uncovered, and pack it into jars.

We may be dreadful cooks, but we're gourmet incense chefs.

Kyphi is one of our most popular offerings, and I hated to "waste" it on me. Inside my dresser drawer, along with my New Mown Hay oil and Weight Winners gift certificate, I'd stashed an audiotape of waves lapping against the shore.

Tonight, I'd try the tape.

As I followed Davy from the sun porch, an even better idea occurred.

Or, as Chastity might say, befell.

Oliver had left behind his unopened Dom Perignon. Rose had appropriated the first bottle (and upchucked its contents all over Oliver's galoshes), but Aunt Lillian had unceremoniously placed the second bottle under the counter.

Tommy Murphy's *tap-tap-tap* came through loud and clear.

"One sip won't hurt me," I whispered, as Davy gave me an

Elvish grin and headed for the front door. "A sip or two will relax me, help me sleep."

Tap-tap-tap.

"Shut up, Tommy. I'm not Nicholas."

Tap-tap-tap.

"Okay, I didn't eat much supper, but three sips won't make me drunk."

Very slowly, keeping the sound to a minimum, I popped the bottle's cork, then sat in the chair that had cradled the rump of the snort-sobbing Jessica.

Whom, Aunt Lillian believed, had taken a powder.

If she had, where had she gone? Oliver, with all his cop contacts, couldn't find her. Maybe, having killed her sister in a fit of angry passion, she'd stuck around long enough to hear the verdict: murder, rather than divine providence. Maybe, unwilling to risk discovery, she'd left her I.D. at home.

Oliver's champagne didn't pack a particularly powerful wallop, and no bubbles escaped through my nose.

By the fourth or fifth sip, I saw Tommy Murphy dancing on the counter top.

He wore his Gene-Kelly slant-brimmed hat. His butt was nicely sculpted by his *American in Paris/Brigadoon* slacks, the ones that expose an inch of white sock. His striped tee (from *Anchor's Aweigh*) revealed bulging arm muscles.

Except for the scowl on his face, he looked yummy.

"Don't worry," I told the scowl. "I'm not planning to puke all over your tap shoes. What do you think? Should we try and solve Jessica's disappearance? Chastity's dilemma? Or Clive Newton's murder?"

"Go home, go home, go home with bonny Jean," Tommy sang.

"You're a big help, pal. I need logic and you sing a song from *Brigadoon*. Whoa. I get it. Maybe Clive wasn't abducted from the concert. Maybe, like Elvis, he left the building and went home with Veronica. Or the mysterious girlfriend, assuming she's not Veronica."

"Go home, go home."

"Yes, I know. Go home. Wait a sec, Tommy. Do you mean Obadiah Barker? Wow, that's a good question. Why didn't Obadiah go home? Because . . . because he planned to kill Matt. Somehow, he found out about Matt's threat to tell the congregation about Chastity and Jack. Obadiah wouldn't want to play the cuckold. That's why he mentioned the ghost of John Winthrop, so Chastity would stay inside."

"Come to me, bend to me."

"Come to me, bend to me? Another song from *Brigadoon*. Oh my God, the Lady in Red!"

Sipping from the champagne bottle, I pictured Obadiah's Red Lady.

Bending. Coming. On top of Matt . . .

Wearing Chastity's red velvet gown.

If I had deciphered the journal correctly, Chastity only wore it when she and Jack made love. So, when she wasn't making love to Jack, she'd have hidden it.

Where?

In the hayloft.

Aside from Chastity, who'd have access to the gown?

Trump.

But the thought of Trump stealing a red velvet gown made no sense.

Sally.

It had to be Sally.

She'd stolen or borrowed the gown, then met Matt in the field where the two of them . . . had Matt been Obadiah's Man in the Moon?

Damn. The champagne bottle was half empty and my

muzzy mind kept hopping like a hare.

First, the image of Sally on top of Matt.

Bending. Coming. Moaning.

Obadiah had spied the Red Lady, heard her moan, and become paralyzed with fear, unable to stand up, much less kill Matt.

So who killed Matt?

Chastity's journal would, eventually, name the killer.

At least I hoped it would.

"Tommy," I said, "forget about Obadiah and concentrate on Jessica."

"Good morning, good mor-ning, it's great to stay up late."

"Tommy, please stop singing Gene Kelly songs."

"Good morning, good mor-ning, we talked the whole night through."

"True, but we need to talk about Jess—"

"What a glor-ee-ous fee—"

"Tommy, please focus."

"I'm read-ee for love."

"Tommy!"

The tap-dancing figure on top of my counter vanished.

"Tommy," I cried, "don't go."

A new voice, a real voice said, "Tommy who?"

"John? Is that you?"

"Yup, it's me. What's wrong, honey? Are you okay?"

"No. I'm not okay." As the room began to swirl, I heaved a deep sigh. "John, come to me, bend to me."

Through the swirls, I saw him bend. "Sling your arm around my shoulders," he said. "First, drop that damn champagne bottle."

I felt myself lifted into the air.

"John," I said, "I'm ready for love."

Chapter Twenty-nine
Wednesday morning

Opening my eyes, I reached for John.

He wasn't there, nor could I smell his scent—a combination of soap suds (from Nina's) and Davy's sandalwood aftershave.

Clothed in bra and boxer shorts, I glanced at the bedside clock—five-forty a.m.—then tiptoed toward the guest room.

A dawning sun lanced the undraped window. John slept nude, on his stomach. He looked like an octopus, with four rather than eight appendages. His top sheet and blanket graced the floor. His spread-out arms and legs seemed to embrace the bottom sheet, and I took a moment to admire his chiseled butt.

On the second bed, Davy slept restlessly, wound tightly inside a blanket, as if he were a caterpillar about to butterfly himself awake.

I was turning to leave when I saw a camera on top of the bureau, half-buried by a neatly folded pile of T-shirts. Tiptoeing toward the bureau, I snatched up the camera, my camera, then escaped into the hallway.

The roll of film was missing. Why was I not surprised?

Walking toward the bathroom, camera in hand, I strove to put last night's puzzle pieces together.

John had swept me up in his arms and carried me to my bedroom.

I remembered him taking off my sneakers, jeans, and tee, stroking my face with his index finger, prying my lips apart with his tongue. He had sucked my breasts through the cotton fabric of my bra, and I could vaguely recall his fingers searching for the slit in my boxers, finding it, then teasing . . . teasing . . . until I moaned . . . and continued moaning . . . just like the Lady in Red.

Biting my lower lip, I tried to remember more, but my mind blanked. The only thing I knew for sure was that we hadn't . . . finished . . . at least not together. If I had been a virgin, I'd still be a virgin.

Could the removal of my love-talisman-jeans have subdued John's ardor? But what about the love incantation? The so-mote-it-be? The bathtub ducky?

And why was I suddenly giving credence to magic I didn't believe in?

Surprisingly, no harpoons spiked my skull. No hammers pounded my head, and my belly seemed stable.

I've been tipsy (my high school prom, my parents' wake) but I've never suffered from overt drunkenness. Tommy Murphy's *tap-tap-tap* usually halts any drinking spree. And while I probably have my father's alcoholic genes, a long time ago Tommy warned me that Nicholas wanted to be mentioned in "Booze Who."

Xanthia's party didn't count. Granted, I'd consumed a potent Grasshopper, but Clive's ear, rather than hard liquor, had inspired both my blackout and subsequent wastebasket episode.

So why wasn't I experiencing a champagne hangover?

I'd only slept three and a half hours. Maybe the hangover would come later. Maybe I should try some hair of the dog.

No. That would *really* put me in the same league as Nicholas. And Rose.

Since the Apothecary didn't open until ten, I'd take a

quick shower, get dressed, then drive to the motel where John had been strangled.

Yesterday, after my unproductive visits to Gusta and Green Gables, after making my way back down Oliver's Twist (and braking repeatedly for mud-slick downhill curves), I'd ditched my motel-jaunt scheme.

Now seemed the perfect opportunity.

Aunt Lillian doesn't believe in aspirin, but I washed down three with instant coffee, just in case a hangover hung around.

One turn of the ignition key and my Honda purred. Tommy Murphy always says: "When you're thirsty, it's too late to think about digging a well," so I paid a visit to my mechanic every time my engine knocked—*paid* being the operative word.

If I were a real witch, I'd conjure up an auto mechanic who looked like Mel Gibson; someone who'd adore and desire me. Of course, he'd comp my repairs.

Thankful that I didn't live in 1692 Salem, I sped to the motel, tires rather than hooves humming, and backed into a slot near the registration office.

To the left of its entrance, directly under a *USA Today* logo, a newspaper kiosk bulged with Gusta's *Manitou Falls Monthly*. Her DEAD SINGER ATTENDS BIRTHDAY PARTY headline loomed twice as large as when I'd seen it last, and the free *Monthly* wasn't free anymore.

The desk clerk wore a faded Denver Broncos sweatshirt, Levis that exposed one third of his underpants, a nose earring, a lip earring, and a Marine haircut. In one hand he held an old, used paperback. *Salem's Lot.*

Trying to sound authoritative, I asked if he'd been on duty last Thursday.

Baring a tongue earring, he said maybe.

I asked if he remembered a man with a guitar, long hair, and a beaded headband.

He said maybe.

Had Aunt Lillian been with me, she'd have played *Law & Order*'s Jerry Orbach; threatened warrants and motel closure. Somehow, I didn't think I could pull it off, so I resorted to the oldest trick in the book . . . pretended to cry.

The embarrassed clerk said, "Hey . . . hey . . . don't do that."

"My sister-in-law's missing," I said with a pseudo-sob.

"And she stayed here?"

Using his favorite comeback, I said, "Maybe."

His coffee-colored eyes constricted. "Why'd ya ask about the man with the guitar?"

This time, I couldn't say: "Maybe." I couldn't say: "Because he got bopped over the head and strangled with his suspenders" either. For all I knew, the clerk might pick up a phone and call the cops.

Probing my brain for a good story line, I said, "My sister-in-law, Janet, stole some money from her boss. By the time she hit your motel, she regretted the impulse, so she phoned her boyfriend, the man with the guitar. But when he got here, her luggage and car were gone and . . . and the shower curtain had been ripped from its hooks."

"Man, that's cool," the clerk said, as he put a Cafe Utopia brochure between the pages of his paperback, then placed the book on top of a three-legged stool.

The Cafe Utopia is, arguably, the best restaurant in town. A sign above its front façade reads: PEACE . . . LOVE . . . AND GOOD FOOD. One could quibble about the peace (on most nights there's live music), but the food is to die for.

"My family doesn't want the police in on this," I said, "because of the stolen money. So I'm hoping you can tell me what name Janet used, maybe even help me search her room. If we find her," I added, inspired, "there's a reward."

"Do you happen to know her room number?"

While I told him the room number, he checked the ledger.

"Can't read the freaking name," he muttered, shoving the ledger at me.

I could. Because it was the same scribbled signature I'd seen on a check last Friday, when Veronica bought my toothache spell and love charm.

Unfortunately, Veronica was much too dead to resolve John's strangulation.

"What's your name?" I asked the clerk.

"Manny Glick."

"Did you tell the man with the guitar that a 'Mary Smith' paid for the room?"

"Yeah."

"Why?"

"He tried to bulldoze me." Manny made a fist, then splayed his fingers. "Ya wanna see Janet's room?"

"Yes, please."

As I followed Manny down a narrow sidewalk, rimmed by structures that resembled miniature Swiss chalets, I pictured a slum landlord wearing lederhosen.

The path was uneven. After stumbling twice, I looked down at the ground.

And saw a white dove's feather. What a lucky break. Feathers from a dove are hard to find and Jessica's had been the last of my supply.

I'd still have to call Aunt Lillian's feather distributor, but at least I could put it off for a couple of weeks. I hadn't lied when I told Jessica my dove-wing-charms were expensive; most people liked to try my cheaper spells first.

I picked up the dove's feather, put it in my jacket pocket, walked a few more feet, then entered the motel room where John had been strangled.

Except for the carpet, dotted with cigarette burns, its interior wasn't as run-down as its exterior. For starters, the walls weren't chipped. A double bed with what looked like a firm mattress (the better to strangle you on, my dear) dominated the small room. An unvarnished, four-drawer bureau, a hinged shelf with the same brochures found inside the registration office, and a TV—chained to a metal stand—filled in the rest of the space. Correction: on top of the TV was a VCR. Next to the VCR were X-rated videotapes. A coin slot, attached to the bed's headboard, promised mattress vibrations.

Somehow, I couldn't picture Veronica in this room. Her slinky white gown had to have cost more than all the furniture put together, even if you threw in the slightly askew, framed caricature of a cowboy roping a buxom blonde.

The blonde promised vibrations, too.

Speaking of blondes . . .

I walked into the bathroom and glanced down at the floor, hoping to find more bobby pins. My thought was: *DNA, just in case.* Just in case what? Maybe I should stick to my *Psycho* script, the one I'd used inside the registration office. Janet Leigh had shredded something—money?—and flushed it down the toilet. While Manny watched, I checked the toilet bowl, then the towel rack, sink, and tub.

"The maid must've re-hung the shower curtain," Manny said.

Feeling claustrophobic, I returned to the room.

Unless there was some kind of evidence inside the Bible that shared shelf space with the brochures, this trip to the motel was yet another unproductive adventure.

Just for grins, I decided to look under the bed . . .

Where John had found his guitar.

Kneeling, I swept my hand along the carpet . . .

And encountered something sharp.

A gold gecko earring.

Still on my knees, staring at the gecko, I sneezed.

Dustbunnies were breeding under the bed. If Jessica could see them, she'd never complain about my dusty shop again.

If Jessica could see them . . .

Call it woman's intuition, call it a hunch, call it divine intervention.

Or call it the dove's feather I'd found on the path outside the motel.

"Manny," I said, rising to my feet, "how many rooms are occupied?"

"Five. Last night was a slow night. You should see this place when there's a high school prom."

"Could I look inside all the rooms?"

"You've got to be kidding."

"Please? We could pretend I'm a detective or something."

I remembered his Stephen King book, *Salem's Lot.* The TV movie had been one of Aunt Lillian's favorites and I can't even count the number of times she's rented the video.

"Or," I said, handing Manny a twenty-dollar bill, "we could search for vampires."

He laughed. "Okay," he said, pocketing the twenty. "Vampires."

The first room was unoccupied. I checked the bathroom. Empty.

My knock on the second door was answered by a man in rumpled pajamas. Still half asleep, he let me search his room.

"D'ya think that guy's a vampire?" Manny said in a stage whisper, as we stepped outside again.

"Nope. The sun would have killed him when he answered the door."

My repetitive knocks on the third door brought no response.

Manny whipped out his keys. "What are you looking for?"

"I told you," I said, walking toward the bathroom. "Vampires."

"I'll bet you're looking for Janet. Right?"

"Yes. Only her name's not Janet." Sagging against the bathroom door, momentarily immobilized, I stared at the bound woman in the tub.

Her eyes were closed, her mouth covered by duct tape.

"Who paid for this room?" I blurted.

"No one." Manny gazed, goggle-eyed, at the tub. "Someone must have jimmied the lock. Do you think Janet's alive? She don't look alive."

"Call 911, Manny. Then call the Manitou Falls police station and tell them to give this address to Oliver. Can you remember that?"

"Yeah. Oliver." He sounded dazed. "When was the last time the maid cleaned this freaking can?"

"Manny, focus!"

Kneeling by the tub, I laid my first two fingers against Jessica's neck and prayed for a pulse.

Chastity Barker's Journal

October, 1692

Had I not wasted my tears on Jack, Trump's tale would have made me weep.

Arriving at a village some distance from Salem, bedding down in a wood, he built a fire. Then he unwittingly stepped on a smoldering ember, burned his foot, and dared not continue his journey. Whilst his dog nabbed rabbits, Trump caught fish from a nearby river.

One day he caught the fancy of a Landlord's wife.

She persuaded her husband to hire Trump as a hostler at his inn, and she gave Trump 'comfort' inside the stable.

I must admit I cringed when Trump touched on the stable and hayloft, though he did not cite intimate details.

Alas, the Landlord learned of his wife's nightly visits to the loft. Rather than play the cuckold, he accused Trump of being Satan's tool and preferred a charge of sorcery. He said that Trump had a familiar, a black dog with whom he could converse. He said that ever since Trump's arrival, many disasters had occurred. When asked to enumerate the disasters, he said that three shoats had died and the cordwainer's shoe shop had burned to the ground. Before he could further prove his charges, his young daughter fell into fits, screaming that "the hostler" had bewitched her.

Seized, stripped, shaven, and searched, a mole was found on Trump's arse. A red spot on his neck—from a flea bite—and a scar that blemished his injured foot were displayed. Though the scar's letter could not be deciphered, it was clear that Satan had forged the brand.

To silence any naysayers, the Landlord insisted the towns-folk bind and fling Trump into the river. If he sank, mayhap drowned, he was guiltless. If he floated, he was blameworthy. Trump floated.

Aunt Pru had once told Anne, Mercy, and me that King Henry abolished the water ordeal in 1219, but he could not abolish the popular faith in its efficacy.

Trump was then dragged to the inn's cellar and chained to a post.

When I asked how he escaped, he said the Landlord's wife unchained him. Whereupon, she led him to a trap door, hidden behind several crates.

With tears coursing down his face, Trump told how the townsfolk built a pyre of faggots, purposing to burn his dog. But someone, mayhap someone who felt timorous over the torments of fire, had stabbed Dog to the heart, first. The minister read an exorcism over Dog's ashes and recited a fine prayer, Trump said, ending his tale of woe.

I told him that my sister's bitch had recently whelped and when the pups were old enough he could choose one for his very own. Though I suspect the offering gave him scant solace, he thanked me. I asked if he could sew. When he answered in the affirmative, I suggested he forage my husband's wardrobe. He thanked me anew. But first, he said, he would 'tidy the Marster's bedroom' and chop some wood.

I am certain my sigh of relief could be heard in Boston.

'Tis night and I fear I am too tired to write coherently, but I'll try.

This afternoon, whilst Trump tidied Obadiah's bedroom, a knock sounded. After placing my journal inside the cavity behind the fireplace stone, I opened the door. Whereupon, I blessed Mercy, Sammy, and Anne's son, Johnny, then threw my arms around Anne's neck.

"Nay, poppet, you strangle me," she said with a laugh. "And I have barely escaped the hangman's noose."

Releasing Anne, I looked at Mercy. "Before I disremember," I said, "I promised Trump a pup from Pandora's litter."

Mercy blinked. "When did that knotty-pated malt-worm return?"

"A short while ago," I said, as Trump emerged from the bedroom. "And I must confess that I misjudged his worth."

Trump's breeches were secured by one of the ropes that had bound Obadiah to his bed. A brown wool jacket, not yet buttoned, fell below his knees. A second man could easily fit inside the garments, I thought, biting my lip in an effort to keep my burbling laughter at bay.

Anne lips twitched as she said, "God bless you, Trump."

"Bless ye, Goodwife Kittridge," he muttered, fumbling at his buttons. "The Marster sleeps, Mistress, an oi 'spects it'll be a goodly toime 'til he wakes. The Marster thinks oi be his papa, so I gives him the draught ye put nigh his bed."

"He has worsened if he thinks you his father, who expired ten years ago." I glanced toward the window. "Earlier, I saw some juncoes. Mayhap you might take the boys outside." I gave Johnny and Sammy a smile. "Do you want to look for snowbirds with Trump?"

"Aye, Auntie," Johnny said.

"Aye, Auntie," Sammy said. "Scatch come too?"

"Old Scratch might chase the birds," I said. "Dogs and birds do not get along."

"Oi needs t' split logs fer the wood box," Trump said with a wink. "Will ye help wi' the kindling, lads?"

After the door had been shut, I scrutinized Anne. Except for the stomach bulge beneath her black gown and white linen apron, she looked thin, well-nigh bony. The gauntness of her milk-white, freckled face made her green eyes appear enormous, and the black felt hat that covered her white cap seemed too heavy for her head. "Take off your hats, my sisters," I said, "and sit at the table. We shall drink tea, and I have prepared a tasty rabbit stew. I did not know I could cook until Sally left me for Jack Grayson."

Mercy raised one eyebrow and opened her mouth to speak, but Anne said, "John, bless his heart, feeds me day and night. I cannot tolerate another crumb, poppet, having just consumed a noontide meal that would have sated Goliath and his many Philistines. Hot tea, however, sounds lovely."

"Whilst I pour, dearest Anne, pray tell me how you cozened the judges. Mercy has recounted the tale, but I wish to hear it from your lips." When Anne had finished, I said, "How did you manage to weep? Witches cannot weep. 'Tis one reason I believe I am not a witch."

"If she tries very hard, poppet, a witch can weep. 'Tis like a specter who can move a tangible object, though the specter himself is not physical. If you believe in witchcraft, it works. If someone other than you believes, 'twould be even more favourable." She peered at me. "Your eyes imply you've shed tears."

" 'Tis rumoured that Jack Grayson pledged himself to Ketzia Van Rijn," Mercy said, "and now Chastity says her worthless wench of a servant left her for Jack."

Anne's face looked bemused. "What mean you, poppet?"

Walking to the bedroom door, I opened it a crack. Though fretful, Obadiah slept on his back. His wheezes and snores were followed by soft sneezes, as if he'd plugged his nose with snuff.

I then related Trump's tale of woe, followed by my own. "My misery seems of less import than Trump's," I said, "and

I'm shamed that I wept at the loss of a lying cur whilst Trump did lose his dog."

"The meaningful matter to consider is your babe," Anne said. "If Obadiah cannot remember when his father passed, he'll not recall the last time you and he conjoined."

Such a simple solution. About to cover my sister's face with grateful kisses, I heard Mercy say, "Obadiah might not recall his last conjoining, but Jack will."

"Surely Jack will not admit his lapse of morals," I said, "for he would be severely chidden by the congregation."

"If your babe is a boy," Mercy said, "Jack will devise a scheme to seize his son. Given the temper of the times, he'll say you bewitched him."

I looked at Anne. "What think you?"

"I think we must prove to the congregation that Jack is a liar and a sinner. I think your servant, Sally, was the Lady in Red and Jack was Obadiah's Man in the Moon. I think Jack killed his brother."

My mouth opened and closed. Finally, I said, "How could Sally be the Lady in Red?"

"Did not Mercy give you a red velvet gown and did you not wear it when you engaged Jack?"

I could only nod.

"Mayhap you were spied upon by Sally," Anne said. "Though bedridden, Obadiah knew about you and Jack. Sally whored with Obadiah, so she might have tattled before she pilfered your gown."

"Chastity," Mercy said, "go to the loft and see if the red gown is still hidden there."

Chapter Thirty

Wednesday night

Placing my index finger between the journal's pages, I walked over to the computer desk and drank from Davy's glass of iced tea.

"Damn," I said. "It's hard to believe I'm so thirsty."

"Half a bottle of champagne will do that to you."

"How'd you know I drank champagne?"

"You left the bottle in the shop, on the floor by the chair. I got rid of it before Aunt Lillian could find it. She doesn't approve of 'spirits' and she has enough on her mind."

"Thanks, Davy." Reaching into my jeans pocket, I pulled out my lighter and the cigarettes I hide beneath Lucinda Lizard. Mercy watched my every move. I had a feeling she was about to squawk: *Just say no,* so I made an about-face, lit a stale Camel, and blew smoke rings through an open, unscreened, sun porch window.

In the sky, a hunter's moon grew fuller by the moment. Tomorrow night its perfect orb would shine down, like an orange eyeball, on Yogi Demon's concert.

Gazing out through a closed window, Davy stood nearby.

"Aunt Lillian feels guilty and she shouldn't," I told his reflection. "I didn't believe Jessica was kidnapped, either. Did you?"

His reflection grimaced. "No. But you found her, Syd. That makes up for—"

"Finding Jessica was serendipitous, Davy. And speaking of guilt, I really should be at the hospital with Oliver, Aunt Lillian, and Carol."

"You had to drive Xanthia—"

"To her friend Megan's house. Yes, I know. But I should have gone back."

"Oliver will call if there's any change."

"At least she's alive, Davy. As Chastity would say, 'God be praised.' "

Staring at the backyard gazebo, I pieced together the tidbits I'd overheard at the precinct. The police hadn't found the kidnapper's fingerprints. The snowstorm had killed any footprints or tire prints. The motel occupants hadn't seen or heard a car. Neither had Manny Glick, who'd spent Monday night huddled next to a space heater. All Manny knew, for sure, was that no one had registered for the room. And since no one had registered, the maid hadn't "cleaned the can."

Hopefully, when Jessica woke up, she'd give the police a description of her kidnapper.

I'd given Oliver a twig of rowan, twined with several dozen yards of red thread, and told him to place it in Jessica's hospital window. I had to accept it would protect her, if only to mitigate my culpability. Had I explored the motel yesterday, after my visit to Green Gables, I might have found her sooner, assuming the leftover snow had melted enough to expose the feather.

Oliver hadn't quibbled over the charm. In fact, the only time he'd displayed emotion was when Gusta, shadowed by Terey, sailed down the hospital corridor. Furious, he'd told both women to get their butts out of his sight.

Terey looked chagrined but Gusta's jaw jutted like a bulldog.

"There's a little thing called freedom of the press," she told Oliver, then saw me. "Sydney St. Charles, as I live and breathe! They say you found the body!"

"I found Jessica, not 'the body,' " I said, trying to keep my temper in check.

Oliver said, "There's a little thing called obstruction of justice, Mrs. Lowenfeld."

"How am I obstructing justice? I just want to ask a few ques—"

"For starters, you blithely strolled into a police precinct, asked to use their bathroom, then picked a goddamn lock."

"I did not!"

"As a good Catholic, would you say that under oath?"

"So I picked a lock! So what? Any other reporter would have done the same thing!"

"Reporter? You're a goddamn gossip and snoop—"

"Does your mother know you swear like that?"

"And you left your fingerprints all over the box."

"Don't be silly. Sydney touched the box and so did Bozo the Clown."

"They didn't touch the ear, Mrs. Lowenfeld, and that's tampering with evidence." Oliver nodded toward a uniform, stationed at Jessica's door. "If this woman doesn't leave in thirty seconds, arrest her."

"Ma," Terey said, "let's go."

But Gusta was too far gone, her smokestack blown. "If you arrest me, you'll have to arrest my daughter!" she screeched. "Teresa's the one who taught me how to pick locks. She learned it from that Stephen King book. The movie starred Kathy what's her name . . . the motel . . . Bates!"

"Ma, I'm leaving." A red-faced Terey looked at me. "Is it okay if I phone you later, Sydney? Maybe you could answer my mom's questions."

"Sure," I said, admiring her shrewdness. She knew I'd hang up on Gusta.

Bringing my attention back to Davy, I tiddly-winked my half-smoked Camel through the open window while Mercy squawked, *"Waste not, want not."*

"My concentration's gone," I said. "I keep waiting for Oliver to call."

"That's why we should continue deciphering, Syd. Chastity will keep your mind off Jessica."

Before I could reply, the phone rang. It sounded more metallic than usual.

"Please let it be good news," I prayed under my breath, as I dashed into the shop, made a beeline for the counter, and snatched up the receiver.

"Sydney, it's Terey."

"Sweetie, could we play question/answer another time? I'm waiting for Oliver to call."

"How's Jessica?"

"Still unconscious," I said, as Mercy perched on the ceiling fan, Chasdick sprawled at my feet, and Annie rubbed against Davy's ankles.

"The only time we ever met," Terey said, "was when she stood in the middle of your lawn and made that death threat, but I'm praying for her recovery. So's Ma. On our way home, Ma stopped at a church and lit some candles."

"Thank you and thank your . . . what death threat?"

"Jessica said she was going to kill you."

"When did she say that?"

"Monday. In the snow. She said 'Sydney, I'm going to kill you.'"

"She said it out of frustration, Terey. It didn't mean anything. You and I were chatting . . . about Paulie, I think . . . and Jessica wanted the rest of her spell cast." As Davy silently mouthed: *hang up,* I said, "I've got to hang up now."

"Could you answer a couple of questions, just so I can shut my mom up?"

"Make them quick."

"How'd you know Jessica was at the motel?"

"A hunch. Or put it down to me being a witch."

Aunt Lillian would like that answer, I thought.

"Did the police find any clues, Sydney? Fingerprints? Maybe something the kidnapper dropped and left behind? You know what I mean."

"If they found anything incriminating, they didn't tell me."

My gaze settled on a wall poster: PREJUDICE IS A LAZY MAN'S WAY OF THINKING. The poster, hand-printed by Aunt Lillian, had been her response to a nasty episode of witch-bashing by Colorado's Christian Coalition.

"Terey," I said, "why on earth would you teach your mom how to pick a lock?"

"After she locked herself out of our house for the hundredth time, I gave her a teensy screwdriver and showed her how to use it. I'll get off the phone now, Sydney. Thanks for answering Ma's questions. She's been bugging me."

"That's okay. Bye."

As I hung up, Davy said, "Do you want to get back to the journal?"

"Yes. Maybe you're right. Maybe Chastity will take my mind off Jessica."

"Lynn won't be home for another hour. She plans to bring us some Loop-de-Loop tacos."

"If I eat Loop-de-Loop tacos before I go to bed, I'll have Chastity's 'evil spirits that possess people while they sleep.' "

"What makes you think you'll sleep?" He nodded toward the phone, then eyed the lighter-bulge in my jeans pocket. "Damn, I'm dying for a cigarette."

"Have one of mine."

"No, thanks. Lynn wants me to quit."

"So that's why you stopped mooching. Davy, are you in love with Lynn?"

"I cooked her a rose-petal-catnip meatloaf, didn't I?"

"But what happens when your wanderlust kicks in? I really like Lynn and I wouldn't want to see her hurt."

"If we decipher more journals, I'll stick around. I can still play wizard, and Lynn and Baron can come with me should I get an urge to hit the road."

"Is that fair to Lynn? Leaving at the drop of a hat?"

"Ask her."

"What if she gets pregnant or something?"

"Or something?"

"I mean, without your . . . scams . . . you don't earn a living."

"And you don't have a webpage," he snapped.

"Okay. I'm sorry. It's just, for a moment there, you sounded like Matt Grayson."

"No, Syd. If I sounded like anyone, I sounded like Jack Grayson."

"Do you think he killed his brother?"

Davy shrugged. "They were twins. Maybe somebody killed Matt, thinking he was Jack."

That concept had never occurred to me, even though it made sense.

In the dark, Jack's scars wouldn't be so obvious.

But what about the full moon?

"What about the full moon, Davy? Jack and Matt might have looked alike, but Jack's face was badly scarred, and the moon would have beamed down—"

"Matt was knifed in the back. Suppose the killer hid behind some sort of rise or hill and caught a mere glimpse of Matt's face? Suppose clouds hid part of the moon? Suppose the killer stabbed Matt by mistake?"

"Because he thought Matt was Jack?" I shook my head. "On the surface, Matt was the sleazy brother. Who'd want Jack dead?"

"Jack and Sal went up the hill," Mercy squawked.

"Obadiah," Davy said. "He knew about Chastity's loft liaisons. Or maybe Obadiah told the 'brave and loyal' Trump to kill Jack."

"Jack fell down and broke Sal's membretoon."

"I can't believe Trump would kill anyone, Davy, and you said Obadiah didn't have a knife on him. Let's take this step-by-step, logically. Sally, wearing Chastity's red dress and moaning, crouched on top of Matt. Obadiah was scared stiff . . . you might even say psyched out . . . because he thought Sally was the Lady in Red, and why are you staring at Mercy as if she just said something profound?"

Davy shifted his gaze from the ceiling fan to me. "Suppose Anne was right? Suppose Sally was on top of *Jack,* not Matt?"

"But Matt got himself killed."

"Hear me out, Syd. In those days men would have worn identical clothing. Black cloak, hat, and boots. Black or brown jacket and breeches. Let's say Jack and Sally 'conjoined.' They were so engrossed, they didn't even notice Obadiah, slumped in a heap, quiet as a mouse. But someone saw Jack and Sally, and thought Jack was Matt. Sally hitched up her panties . . . well, I guess they didn't wear *panties* in those days . . . hitched up her petticoats and went home. Jack disappeared into the trees, to pee . . ." Davy grinned. "Or something. Then Matt came strolling along, hoping to meet Chastity. The killer, thinking Matt had just 'conjoined' with Sally, stabbed Matt in the back."

Chasdick, on his feet, chuffed into my hand. "Good dog," I said distractedly. "You've lost me, Davy."

"Little Bo Peep, she lost her sheep. Boil-brained looby."

"Jack made it with Sally," Davy said, ignoring Mercy. "The killer thought Jack was Matt. Jealous, she killed Matt."

"She? She, who?"

"Ketzia."

I realized my mouth gaped open, shut it, then opened it again to speak. "But Ketzia told Chastity the lice-ridden scarecrow was Jack. Why would she do that if she knew it was Matt?"

"To throw the scent off her trail."

"According to Chastity, Ketzia was skinny as a crane. She wouldn't have the strength to tie Matt to a crosspiece."

"And here I thought you believed women were as strong as men."

"In mind, Davy, not body."

"Well, sweetheart, that's where Jack comes in. Somehow, Ketzia bribed him. Maybe with her money. Jack's a greedy bastard. He's also pious and hypocritical, so he'd never admit he conjoined with Sally. Or maybe Ketzia told Jack she'd pin the dirty deed on him."

"But she tried to pin the dirty deed on Chastity. Why would Jack let her do that when Chastity's pregnant with his baby? Conceivably, if you'll excuse the pun, his son."

"They didn't hang pregnant women. But my guess is, Jack didn't know what Ketzia planned to do."

"Neither do you. Hell, you don't even know if she witnessed whatever went on between Sally and Matt . . . or Sally and Jack."

Davy grinned again, a dead giveaway.

"You rat. You told me that way-out-in-left-field theory so I'd forget about Jessica . . ." I paused, then said, "We could read the last few journal pages."

Davy shook his head. "I won't even do crossword puzzles if the answers are upside down. You can sneak a peek if you want to, Syd. Just don't tell me who—"

"No. You're right. It's more fun playing along. Anyway, the journal isn't a *book*-book. Maybe the mystery was never solved."

"Is *my* theory really so far-fetched? Sally and Jack?"

"Yes. No." Walking toward the sun porch, I had a sudden thought. "You were at the hospital when Gusta made her entrance, Davy. Did you happen to hear her verbal explosion?"

He shook his head. "I didn't listen all that closely. Oliver sounded pissed, but he looked as if he might burst into tears. I wanted to keep a shoulder handy, just in case. Why?"

"Gusta said something about Oliver arresting Terey because she showed Gusta how to pick a lock. Gusta said Terey learned how to pick a lock from 'that Stephen King book.' She meant *Misery*. I've read it. Twice. The *Misery* character picks a lock with a bobby pin. Terey told me, on the phone, that she showed her mother how to pick a lock with a 'teensy screwdriver.' Why would she lie?"

"Come on, Syd. Bobby pin, screwdriver, what's the difference?"

"What if Gusta didn't use a screwdriver? What if she used one of Terey's bobby pins? The cop-shop is at least a hundred years old, so it might have those old-fashioned keyholes, easy to pick. I was looking for blonde bobby pins, just before I had my Jessica revelation, and—"

"Terey's hair is short. Porcupine quills. Why would she need bobby pins?"

"She cut her hair last Saturday, Davy. It was longer than John's when he got himself strangled."

Chastity Barker's Journal
October, 1692

It has been three days since Anne and Mercy called on me. The moon begins to grow round as a spinning wheel. Whilst it does, Obadiah's spirit weakens. If only he could bring to mind what happened in the cornfield, but I fear Death may claim his wasted body before the moon doth reach its zenith.

I gave Anne and Mercy articles of clothing from his wardrobe—a white band and a buff boot. Anne promised she'd recite a Charm to Drive Away Evil, which requires a dark night, moonless and cloudy. Mercy, whose medicinal skills are more powerful than Anne's, vowed she'd cast a Charm to Rid the Mind of an Affliction.

After my sisters and nephews departed, I retrieved my journal and thumbed the pages until I found Aunt Pru's incantations. Remembering what Anne had said about a witch being able to weep, I resolved to cast a spell of my own—a Charm to Transpose Death Into Life—used once before, by Mercy.

In the dark of a summer's night, she had gathered three long strands of ivy from where they trailed upon the ground. Lighting a candle, she twined the vines into a wreath to fit upon my head. Then, in her mortar, she crushed white limestone to a fine powder and dusted my hands and face. Whilst I screamed, bested by belly cramps, Mercy recited Aunt Pru's incantation.

The Charm had been fruitful. Arresting my miscarriage, Mercy brought my babe back to life. Then, unbinding the strands of ivy, she'd set their cut ends in water, leaving them so for two weeks. When the time had passed, she planted the ivies at the foot of my oak tree. Whereupon, she besprinkled the powdered limestone about the oak and recited Aunt Pru's second incantation.

When watered and cared for, the charmed vines retain a strength as the oak's, but I fear I did not faithfully attend to that chore. On my oath, I shall ne'er forgive my indifference, for I suffered a miscarriage one month later.

The vines now thrive. Even a slugabed cannot kill ivy, and the autumn rains quenched their thirst. Perchance I could make up for the loss of my babe by redeeming my husband's life.

Upon ascertaining that a portion of Mercy's crushed limestone had been safely preserved, I picked three strands of ivy and twined them into a wreath. Setting the wreath aside, I returned to my journal and found Aunt Pru's Charm to Win the Moon's Aid for a Secret Purpose.

Anne had once given me a small piece of uncoloured glass, secured inside a leather bag inscribed with the Moon's phases. She then told me to tie the bag to a thong and wear it round my neck during those days and nights between the crescent and full moon. By doing so, the glass would procure my secret wish.

Here, I must confess that I wore the Charm to win Jack's regard, though he did chide me for what he called my irreverent folly. After our first liaison, I wrapped the bag in a black cloth and hid it away.

Three days ago, following my sisters' departure, I reached into the hole where I keep my daybook, retrieved the bag, and tied it round Obadiah's neck—praying he would not only be cured but remember the events of last month. Then I chanted the incantation: "Crescent be full. And crystal fill. Thus my eye. And thus my will. *Fiat voluntas abdita.*"

I sang the words and told Obadiah to repeat them. He followed my lead, since that is all he does. He sings. He sings about the moon until I want to scream. Praise God, Trump attends to his more intimate needs.

Now, each night, Obadiah echoes my wish, making it his. Like a trained parrot he says: "I wish to regain my memory and my health."

Unfortunately, a Higher Power has decreed that my husband shall not recover his vigor, nor repossess his memory.

Here I must confess that I would in no way be distressed if the secret of Matt's death lingered, unsolved till Doomsday. However, once again, Ketzia doth spread her malicious rumours.

In truth, I have no right to escape to the hayloft, eschewing Obadiah and his endless singing. And yet, if I hear one more verse of "The Man in The Moon" I fear I shall lose my mind. And I need to be alone, in order to ponder recent events.

No one has postulated a source for either the lice or Matt's grievous knife wounds. Thus, Ketzia keeps insisting that witchcraft was at the heart of the matter and she denounces me by using Obadiah's strange illness as an affirmation.

"The poor man vitnessed his vife's dalliance vit Matt," Ketzia told several goodwives, one of whom told Mercy. My sister then penned an account and gave it to her husband, Toby. Who, in all haste, delivered it to me. "Matt vould have nothing to do vit the flax-vench, so she set lice upon him," Ketzia further stated. "And, vit the devil's help, she killed my Matt and bevitched her own husband."

Aware of Ketzia's imputations, furious that Anne had talked her way out of being hanged, the "stricken" girls fell into fits. All merely followed Abigail Williams' example, as she writhed and screamed and choked and said that I pinched and smothered her. Then the wicked girl swore that I, not

Anne, had whored with Tituba's white-haired man.

'Tis by the goodness of God and my neighbour, Rueben Cavin, that I have not been gaoled. Shamed that he had believed Ketzia's talk of witchcraft before he and the other men cut Matt down from the crosspiece, Rueben disavowed all conjectures and persuaded others to do the same. He even wrote letters to Cotton Mather and the Privy Council, pleading for "a halt to the committing of any more that shall be accused."

Should the court's proceedings be suspended, the hunt for witches will not stop, and a letter to the Throne is a futile gesture since the dispatch will not arrive until far too late to be of use. Still, once again, I value my neighbour's act of kindness, and, at the same time, wonder why my hands shake and my heartbeat quickens every time he addresses me.

Tall as a tree, Rueben's body seems hewn from granite. Topped by a thatch of flaxen hair, his face possesses intense blue eyes and a nose that the devil himself might have tweaked in passing. But 'tis his lips that oft draw my gaze. Full and tempting, I have the oddest feeling that, should I taste his breath, I'll ne'er go hungry again.

Ten months younger than I, he looks older. His mother and father died during an outbreak of cholera, and 'tis rumoured he'd have wed a cousin had she not expired during her voyage to the New World. Diligent and devout, he influences magistrates and ministers.

Oh lud, I must make ready to leave. This morning Rueben brought me bacon that needs smoking and several fish that need scaling, and I nearly swooned when his hand mistakenly touched my bod—

I must ride for the magistrate. But first I must start at the beginning. Pray God, my nib does not break.

Earlier, whilst up in the loft, I heard a sound below, and barely had time to hide my daybook before Jack ascended the ladder.

"Your head is in the clouds, dearest," he said. "Are you thinking of me?"

My heart pounded, but 'twas from fear not desire. "Do not call me dearest," I said.

With a laugh, he hoisted himself up onto the loft floor. "I have decided to lay with you one last time, dearest," he said, "before I chain myself to the heron."

Except for his scars, he looked and sounded like his brother Matt. With an effort, I slackened my tense body and assumed a coy expression. "Do you wish me to don my red gown?" I asked, lowering my lashes so that he could not see the hatred in my eyes. "My gown is here, hidden behind some bales of hay."

"Nay, dearest," he said, " 'tis not."

"Aye, Jack. The gown has not been worn past your last visit. Thus, it must be here."

" 'Tis not necessary to change gowns is all I meant, since I'll soon disrobe you." He laughed again, but this time he twittered, as if he were on edge. "Come, give us a kiss."

The quest for my gown had turned up naught, and Jack's prevarication sounded as false as his promises. No longer concealing my contempt, I said, " 'Twill be a cold day in Hell before my lips travel anywhere near your lying, thieving mouth."

Whey-faced, Jack slapped me.

To my utter astonishment, I slapped him back.

His scars stood out in stark relief as he tore my band and bodice, then shoved me to the straw. "We shall see whether 'tis Heaven or Hell," he spat. "If you do not please me," he threatened, "it shall be Hell."

"Bully for you, Jack," I taunted. " 'Tis a sad day, indeed, when the mighty Jack Grayson feels he must rape an unwilling goodwife."

" 'Twill not be rape," he said. "On my oath, you shall enjoy it."

"When I fight you," I said, "take care you do not harm your son."

My words stopped him, though his eyes gleamed with rage and lust. "Nay, Chastity," he said. "You've prayed for a healthy babe. No matter what I do, you'll not endanger my son."

I lost my breath at the truth of his reply. Then, remembering Mum and Mr. Ratcliffe, I thrust my knee into the softness of his groin.

With a painful squeal, Jack fell backwards.

I crawled toward the ladder. As I did, I felt a flutter in my belly.

Jack grasped my ankle and pulled me away from the ladder.

"Nay, Jack, desist," I cried, "for I am riding my belly and it hurts."

"Do not play the liar with me, Chastity," he raged.

" 'Tis you who lie, Jack," I said, covering my face with my hands.

I managed to gain my knees again, just before I vomited.

Jack said, "Chastity, stop it."

I placed my hands across my mouth until I felt compelled to vomit anew. "Mercy," I moaned.

"You'll get no mercy from me," he growled, "if you've miscarried."

"Please fetch my sister Mercy, Jack. 'Tis the only way to snatch our babe from the jaws of death." I gave another moan, shut my eyes, heard him descend the ladder, and waited until I harked the clatter of hooves.

Then I climbed down the ladder, straightened my gown as best I could, and strolled toward the house. In one hand, I clutched the three unbroken stalks of straw with which I'd gagged myself.

'Twas the belly-flutter that had given rise to my scheme. My babe's first kick, a signal that it was alive and well. "I did not play the liar, Jack," I murmured, "for I never said 'twas a miscarriage."

Walking inside the house, I saw that the door to the bedroom stood open. Odd, I thought. Trump usually shut and barred the door when he did not sit with Obadiah. I had asked Trump to deliver a note to Rueben, thanking him for the bacon and fish. Mayhap Trump had left in haste.

Feeling weak from my enforced vomiting, I downed a glass of cider. Then I took a deep breath and entered the bedroom.

Obadiah wasn't singing, praise God. He slept on his back, but why did he not wheeze and snore?

Because blood spurted from his nose.

Advancing toward the bed, I saw a pillow on the floor. Picking it up, I saw blood on its cloth. I felt my eyes widen as I looked from the pillow to my husband. Whilst I had been fending off Jack, someone had smothered Obadiah.

Chapter Thirty-one

Wednesday night

"That's it," I said, looking up from the journal.

Davy cracked his knuckles. "What do you mean, that's it?"

"There is no more. Those are Chastity's last words."

"You've got to be kidding."

"I'm not kidding. Look for yourself."

"I believe you, Syd. It's just—"

"Davy, I told you at Xanthia's party that the journal was missing a bunch of pages."

"But I thought you meant the beginning. The pages that are missing between June and September."

Feeling sad and angry and cheated, I said, "Someone ripped the last few pages out. See?" I held up the journal. "We never should have started this crazy project."

"Calm down, sweetheart."

"Don't tell me to calm down. Chastity was probably re-accused of witchcraft and hanged. End of story."

"They didn't hang pregnant women."

"Okay, Davy, what do *you* think happened?"

"Let's assume Ketzia killed Obadiah while Jack was in the loft with Chastity."

"There you go again. Let's assume. Let's suppose. Ketzia killed Matt. Ketzia killed Obadiah." With a shaky hand, I placed the journal on the computer desk. "Why couldn't Trump have killed Obadiah?"

"You said you didn't think Trump could kill anyone. And, just for grins, what would be his motive?"

"Putting the 'Marster' out of his misery. Obadiah was

about to starve to death, not a pretty way to die. And Trump knew it. He almost starved to death."

Davy snorted. "Talk about a trumped-up theory."

"How about Sally? *Let's suppose* she really did 'conjoin' with Jack. Should Obadiah regain his memory, she'd be in big trouble. Or how about Jack, before he hit the loft? He wouldn't want Obadiah to remember, either. Damn it, Davy, how about Rueben?"

"Rueben? Rueben Cavin? Where did that come from?"

"He was falling in love with Chastity. If she suddenly became widowed—"

"Chastity was falling in love with him. He was being neighborly."

"Chastity falls in love rather easily, don't you think?"

"Are you talking about you or Chastity?"

"Low blow."

"Sorry."

"No, you're right. I'm not saying I'm in love with John, Davy, but I've got Chastity's symptoms. Shaky hands, thumpy heart, the urge to taste John's lips instead of food, even the feeling I'd 'swoon' should John touch my breasts."

"Chastity said body, not breasts."

"No, Davy, bodice. She nearly swooned when Rueben touched her bodice. John has already unhooked my bra. Twice."

"John's terrific, Syd. And, in my opinion, he's very fond of you."

"He's not fond of me. He's charmed. I'm charming. John put me to bed last night. But once he took off your jeans, the magic was gone, the spell over."

"What spell?"

"A love talisman . . . in my . . . your pocket."

"And that's why you think John stopped? Because he took off your jeans?"

"*Your* jeans."

"Syd, he told me about last night, some of last night. He said he wanted to make love to you."

"Sure he did. Before he took off the jeans."

"Forget the jeans. Since when do you believe in talismans? John wanted to make love to you, but you were toasted. He said there were rules—"

"Oh, great. An amnesiac who suddenly remembers rules." I heaved a deep sigh. "Don't listen to me, Davy. I'm stressed out over Jessica. And the journal."

"We can't do anything about Jessica, but maybe we can find the journal's missing pages."

"How?"

"For starters, where do you keep the other journals?"

"Aunt Lillian stores them in the attic. She let me shelve this one because I'd read a few notations and—"

"Where in the attic?"

"There's a box, a carton."

Rising from his chair, Davy tucked an errant curl behind my ear. "Where's the carton, sweetheart? And do you remember what it says on the outside?"

"I don't know where it is, and I think it says 'Charms and Potions.' So do a dozen other cart—"

"Who put the box in the attic? Aunt Lillian?"

"No." I pictured moving day. Davy had already left for parts unknown, but just like the reconstruction of my house, people came to help. "Carol carried the boxes, Davy. Oliver had a book signing so Carol was the brawniest person there. Jim was busy getting drunk and Bambi couldn't lift a teacup. Carol toted two or three boxes at a time and—"

"Didn't you do an inventory, Syd? Afterwards?"

"I've only seen the attic once, Davy, when Aunt Lillian and I toured the house, before we bought it."

"Why?"

"I could say I'm claustrophobic. But the truth is, Aunt Lillian keeps her icky spider webs up there."

Davy chortled. "How many enemies has she bound lately?"

"None that I know of. If she found and bound one, she'd most likely chant a fertility charm."

"Don't tell Lynn about the spider webs."

"Lynn?"

"When she gets here, we'll look for the missing pages. You can wait for Oliver's phone call. If we're lucky, Lynn and I will find the pages inside the carton with the other journals. If not, we'll look in all the boxes."

"Davy, that's insane. Maybe Chastity simply stopped writing. If she was jailed, she wouldn't take her journal with her. It's too incriminating. She'd have given it to one of her sisters, who passed it on to the next generation."

Chasdick chuffed, Annie mewed, Mercy squawked, *"Little Jack Horner sat in the corner,"* and Davy said, "Do you have a better idea?"

"Yes. Forget about the journal. Chalk it up to a fun experience. Speaking of chalk, I'm getting low on powdered limestone."

"And just whom do you plan to transpose from death to life?"

"Don't be silly. I use the crushed chalk for lots of things. But if I ever needed to . . . transpose . . . there's ivy growing round my oak."

Davy looked at me, his eyes as serious as I'd ever seen them. "Listen, Syd," he said. "I know I'm not a real wizard, and I know my spells are, for the most part, scams. But I've a gut-feeling Chastity's missing pages are here, in this house. Call it the same gut-feeling you had when you thought Jessica was locked inside a motel room."

As if on cue, the phone rang.

Chapter Thirty-two

Thursday night

I stepped onto the bath mat, tossed Aunt Lillian's yellow ducky back into the tub, and listened to the ducky squeal. It sounded ticked-off. But I didn't know if its indignant squeaks came from hitting the side of the tub or from the words tattooed across its behind.

Steam from my shower shrouded the bathroom. Feeling as if I'd been cast in a Jack the Ripper docudrama, I lavishly anointed my body with Rose Petal perfume and wondered what one wore to a Newts concert.

Aside from a newt.

Come to think of it, I still had the gecko earring I'd found inside John's motel room. Was a gecko a newt?

I draped myself in a bath towel, pulled a Webster's from the hall bookshelf, and looked up gecko: *Any of numerous small harmless chiefly nocturnal insectivorous lizards.*

As an ersatz witch, I already knew that a newt was a salamander, so I looked up salamander: *Any of numerous amphibians superficially resembling lizards.*

Okay . . . a gecko was a lizard and a newt resembled a lizard. So why hadn't The Newts called themselves The Geckos? They were nocturnal. And, according to Xanthia, they were vegetarians. Did vegetarians eat insects?

They'd named themselves after their leader, of course. Clive Newton.

Usually, I wasn't so dense. But tonight I felt giddy and footloose. Because tonight I had a date with John.

Unless he canceled at the last minute.

He had worked the day shift at Nina's. Any moment now I expected him to call and tell me he'd have to work the night shift. John felt "safe" at the diner. Very few people ever saw the dishwasher. The cooks and servers hadn't recognized him and Nina gave him as many hours as he wanted (and paid him under the table). He had even painted her office for ten dollars an hour, tax free.

Maybe, in his other life, he'd been a workaholic.

Yesterday, on our way to her friend Megan's house, Xanthia had given me the two concert tickets. Despite his sleazy technique, sleeping with Veronica, Oliver had "done good." The seats were for the second row and he'd arranged a brief backstage visit before the show began. Xanthia had wanted to meet Yogi when he stayed at Green Gables. Carol had said the sick singer might be contagious, so once again Oliver strove for "progeny popularity." Only this time he'd swapped "hospitality for dispensation."

If John chickened out, I'd hand the concert tickets over to Davy and Lynn, assuming they came home in time. They'd spent the day with Lynn's parents, confirming my impression that Davy was seriously serious. Last night they had searched the attic until an exhausted Lynn called it quits. They hadn't found Aunt Lillian's spider webs. Nor had they found the missing journal pages. But Davy had a "gut-feeling" they were getting close.

I'd spent the morning and afternoon at the hospital, along with Aunt Lillian. As she knitted a twelve-foot scarf, I tried to read Oliver's new book.

The strident peal that had interrupted Davy last night had been a solicitation call for, of all things, a free chiropractic exam. Wishing I could relieve tension by cracking my own bones, I said no thanks.

Then, as Davy and Lynn munched Loop-de-Loop tacos,

Oliver had, at long last, phoned.

Jessica would recover, he said. She had awakened, briefly, to tell the police she'd driven home, straight from my house, and parked her car in the garage. Someone had sneaked up from behind, covering her nose and mouth with a gloved hand. Just before she fainted, she managed to retrieve the dove's feather from her jacket pocket, hoping its "magic" would save her. When she woke up, the feather was gone and she found herself bound and gagged. She waited for her kidnapper to come back or for somebody to find her. Then, trying to wriggle free from her bonds, she'd passed out again. And she'd peed her pants, more than once.

Physically, Jessica had sustained some nasty bruises, a chipped front tooth, and a broken arm. She suffered from dehydration and frostbite. The cops surmised that she'd been locked inside a car trunk for several hours during the blizzard.

Mentally, she couldn't quite comprehend what had happened. She didn't know why the kidnapper had picked her. She fretted over peeing her pants. And she kept insisting that she needed to cast a spell, Oliver said, his voice accusatory.

Jessica would stay in the hospital a few more days. She ran a fever but complained about being cold. The doctor wanted to monitor her frostbite. A psychologist would work with what Oliver called her "mental instability."

First thing this morning, at the hospital, I asked him how Jessica was feeling, and his reply lit my fuse.

"Thank God I have insurance," he whined. "Publishers don't buy policies for their authors, not even their bestselling authors."

"The kidnapper picked your wife," I retorted, "because you bragged about your lucrative book contract. How many people did you tell, Oliver? A hundred? A thousand?"

"Don't be ridiculous, Syd. There was no ransom call."

"That's because you changed your phone number," I said, turning away before my lit fuse could score an irreversible explosion.

I hadn't spoken to Jessica. Heavily sedated, she slept most of the day away and the hospital only allowed two visitors at a time. Oliver and Aunt Lillian had both offered to let me go in their stead, but I declined.

My irrational fear of hospitals is even greater than my irrational fear of clowns. My parents had been airlifted to a hospital. I had visited both, in their rooms, then never saw them again until they were ashes. And while I know, rationally, that the doctors didn't kill Nicholas and my mom, I couldn't help feeling that a Charm to Transpose Death Into Life might have worked just as well.

Speaking of clowns . . . if John didn't get home soon, I could kiss the concert goodbye. Maybe, despite spider webs and claustrophobia, I'd comb the attic for the missing journal pages. Davy's "gut feeling" had hooked me.

Entering my bedroom, I saw a flower-decorated shopping bag on my pillow.

Slowly, cautiously, I walked toward the bed.

What if the bag contained another Clive appendage?

I heard my ragged breath.

Reaching into the bag, I pulled out a white-fleece sweater and a pair of jeans with embroidered salamanders on the pockets. Then, a pair of black satin panties.

A flower-decorated card that matched the bag read: "Roses are red, violets are blue, I spent my first wages on presents for you. Soldiers wear khaki, sailors wear navy, take off those boxers, and give them to Davy. Love, John."

My first thought was: *Rueben Cavin.*

Rueben had given Chastity bacon and fish while my hewn-from-granite, intensely-blue-eyed beau had given me undies, but the principle was the same.

I tried to remember the last time I'd received such an inti-mate gift, and could only come up with Oliver's Weight Win-ners diet club certificate.

Flushed and elated, smiling like a Cheshire Cat, I retraced my steps. At the same time, I wondered why Mercy hadn't greeted her favorite maggot pie. Maybe she had, while I showered. Maybe, like me, she'd grown accustomed to his face. Maybe Annie and Chasdick had told my potty-mouthed parrot that John wasn't such a bad guy.

So . . . who was the bad guy who'd killed Clive and Ve-ronica?

Did my eavesdropping parrot know? Hard to tell, since she hated all men.

And one woman.

I remembered Mercy's "membretoon gipsyfilly." Mercy had squawked the obscenity during Xanthia's birthday party, just before the front door slammed. I had been answering Aunt Lillian's tap on my bedroom door, so I couldn't see whom she'd squawked it at. She'd also squawked it at Rose, inside the kitchen. Later, I'd told Rose that membretoon was a name women used for their "privates." From Obadiah's accusation, directed at Chastity, I knew that gipsyfilly was a name men used for women who either flirted or whored around.

Rose did both, but she hadn't been at the birthday party.

Who else slept around? If my suspicions were correct, Jessica had been sleeping with Yogi. Had Carol slept with Yogi? Since her divorce from Oliver, she'd undergone at least two torrid affairs and I couldn't forget the missing pantyhose.

Aunt Lillian, *Law & Order* addict, would say, "Circum-stantial, Sydney."

Susan Partridge, the bank teller, slept around. According to Nina, Susan flirted and picked up partners inside the diner.

Nina even joked that Susan should pay her a pimp's percentage.

Had Susan left the house during Mercy's membretoon-squawk?

I tried to remember Aunt Lillian's conversation, after she entered my bedroom. I had asked her who was watching the kids. Nina, she'd said, because Carol had an emergency at the morgue and Jessica wanted to go home. Jessica had left with Terey Lowenfeld.

But Susan, Carol, Jessica, and Terey had no reason to kill Clive or Veronica.

Granted, Mercy didn't like Jessica, but had my parrot seen her substituting an ear for the CD? Was that why Mercy had squawked her obscenity?

I remembered telling Davy that Jessica might have been in cahoots with Yogi. So, logically, Yogi was the "bad guy."

Circumstantial, Sydney!

Still draped in my towel, standing at the doorway, I extended my head like Spielberg's ET. "John? Are you home?"

No answer, but he had to be here. The flowered bag hadn't been on my pillow before I showered. Maybe he'd furtively slipped in and out of the house.

Which reminded me. Aunt Lillian wanted me to change our locks. The key to our house hadn't turned up in Jessica's jacket or pants pockets. Her car key had been found, along with paraphernalia from my charms, but there'd been no Lilly's Apothecary key.

"John," I called again, "where are you? I want to thank you for—"

"I'm here, Sydney." The guest room door opened. "Sorry. I conked out. And you're welcome. The clothes are nothing, compared to your generosity." He yawned. "Give me twenty minutes to bathe and throw some clean jeans on. Okay?"

"No problem. We're meeting the kids early, before the

ΑΒ

concert, but we have an hour, maybe more."

"Want to join me in the shower?"

"Been there, done that," I said, and felt my cheeks bake. "I mean, I've already bathed."

Shutting the door on his dimpled laughter, I returned to the bed and sorted through his presents.

My new, skin-tight jeans slid nicely over the butter-slick panties and the thigh-length sweater sought to hide my chunky hips.

When Davy was ten-ish, he double-dared me to pierce my ears. Nicholas threatened dire consequences, but I did it anyway; one of the few times I've stood up to my father. Then, having validated my mettle, I rarely wore earrings, and I had never, in my whole life, worn one earring.

I found a barrette, snagged the unruly curls on the left side of my face, and slid the gecko's pointy stud through my left earlobe. On the right side, curls tumbled to my shoulder, hiding my naked right ear.

I'm not sure why I wore the earring. Maybe I wanted to challenge Yogi and The Newts, assuming I could get close enough. Someone had lost an earring inside John's motel room. Since John wouldn't have owned a signature gecko, that someone had to be a Newt.

Gusta's "dead singer attends birthday party" article had included three photos. Clive Newton alive, Clive's funeral, and an album cover.

With a magnifying glass I had scrutinized the musicians. Clive grinning. Yogi looking somber. A freckle-faced kid who flaunted drumsticks. An expressionless kid who could have been a *Night of the Living Dead* co-star. The fifth Newt, cherubic and bald-headed, was a dead ringer for Cuba Gooding.

All wore gecko earrings, identical to the gecko I'd found under the bed.

God knows how many fans could have duplicated the earring. But its design was intricate, and my gecko had two tiny jade eyes, one black, one green.

Again, I felt slow-witted. Veronica had signed the motel's register. Veronica had managed The Newts. Veronica could have sported a signature gecko.

I heard John singing in the shower; a Joe Tex song; "Charlie Brown Got Expelled." John had a great voice, distinctive and powerful, loud enough to penetrate both the bathroom door and my bedroom door.

Suddenly, an off the wall, out in left field, far-fetched thought invaded what was left of my mind.

John had remembered a blonde woman riding a white stallion.

John had been strangled inside Veronica's motel room.

Rose had said John looked familiar.

John played the guitar and sang like a pro.

Had John been a Newt?

I recalled what Terey had told Davy at Xanthia's party. The bit about the dropped singers.

Before Clive's murder, before the group's incredible success, before their manager had selected the final fab five, there had been three other Newts.

Was John one of them?

Why would Veronica have dropped John? Because he was too old?

What about Yogi? Yogi wasn't exactly moppet material.

Had Veronica killed John's bid for stardom?

If yes, he had the perfect motive for killing her.

To my mind, one big, un-hypothetical question needed an answer.

Why had John and Veronica shared a sleazy motel room?

Chapter Thirty-three

Thursday night

John sat in the passenger seat since, unlike Aunt Lillian, I wouldn't let him drive with a Henry Kissinger license.

Slamming on my brakes at the Salem Street pedestrian crosswalk, I watched Mary Lou DiNardo maneuver her bike across the street. At the same time, I wondered how I'd broach my big question.

Maybe I'd simply tell John that Veronica had signed the motel register, then wait for his reaction. What if he had no reaction?

I heard Tommy Murphy's *tap-tap-tap*. Was he trying to tell me not to open that particular can of worms? Or did he mean I should enjoy the concert, enjoy my first date in nine months, and play question/answer later?

Mary Lou had one of those stretchy-net shopping bags slung across her arm. A loaf of Italian bread tickled her armpit as her swollen feet pounded the pavement. I stuck my head out the car window. "Congratulations, Mrs. DiNardo."

"For what?"

"Paulie's engagement."

"She's not Italian," Mary Lou said with a derisive snort.

"What difference does that make? Anyway, Terey's Catholic. Well, half Catholic. I'm not sure what her father was. Is."

"Terry who?"

"Terey Lowenfeld."

"Paulie ain't engaged to her. He's engaged to Martina

Brustein, a Jewess. She lives up in Woodland Park and she writes dirty books."

"Dirty books?"

"Them books with half-nekkid men on the covers."

Aunt Lillian calls your half-naked men stud-muffins, I thought, *and dollars to doughnuts, Martina's full name is Martina Navratilova Brustein, just like her brother's real name is Yogi Berra Brustein. No wonder Paulie got his old job back.*

Aloud, I said, "Do you mean romance novels, Mrs. DiNardo?"

"I mean dirty books, Missy. She erupted my Paulie."

"Erupted? Oh, you mean corrupted."

"Don't tell me what I mean, you . . . you witch!"

While Mary Lou cussed me out, I wondered why Terey had told me that she and Paulie were engaged. A figment of her imagination? Or had Paulie "pledged" himself to more than one woman?

Come to think of it, Terey never actually said that she and Paulie were engaged. She said they were going steady. What did going steady mean? Engaged to be engaged?

Funny how present-day events were beginning to sound more and more like Chastity's journal. Ketzia Van Rijn had pledged herself to a couple of men, even though one of them had turned up dead. Paulie's face was scarred by acne while Jack's face had been scarred by an accident. And—

"The old lady made it to the curb," John said, nudging my ribs.

My ribs responded. If it hadn't been for Xanthia, I'd have pulled into the Arthur Miller High School parking lot and ravaged John's beautiful body.

Maybe the same game plan had occurred to Veronica the night she rented a sleazy motel room. But then what the hell had happened between the ravaging and the suspender strangulation?

I played Davy's "suppose." Suppose a sated (and I had no doubt she'd be sated) Veronica had left for home? Suppose someone lurked outside the motel room? Suppose John knew the someone who lurked? Otherwise, how could he be caught unaware?

Cutting into my suppositions, John said, "How about parking the car, Sydney? I'd love to inspect your new panties."

"I'd love to let you, John, but we can't disappoint Xanthia. And her mother would kill me if we reneged. Carol told me at the hospital that the only reason she allowed Xanthia to attend the concert was because there'd be adult supervision." Although my gaze encompassed the road, I felt John tense. "What did you just remember?"

"A rock concert," he said. "Loud screams. Kids trampled." Perspiration dotted his face and his whole body shook.

"You remembered a concert where kids stampeded?" My question was rhetorical, but all at once I recalled the horse-stampede comment he'd made when I had asked about his visit to Veronica's estate. Plus, the I-think-I-had-a-sister statement inside the kitchen. "John . . . did your sister get trampled?"

"Stomped. My fault." His voice sounded foggy.

"How could it be your fault? Things like that happen. Rock concerts. Soccer matches." I wanted to pull over to the side of the road, but Mary Lou had left us barely enough time to meet Xanthia and her friends. "People get separated and—"

"We weren't separated. I wasn't there."

"If you weren't there, it couldn't possibly be your fault."

"I was responsible."

"Why, John? Did you plan to attend?"

Sweat streamed from his face. "Yes. No. I can't remember."

"Maybe you don't want to remember. Maybe that's why you've been trying to avoid recognition. Somebody might identify you and you'd have to relive the memory. You should see a doctor. Or a hypnotist. The shop's done really well this month. I can lend you enough money to—"

"No. Thank you, Sydney, but no."

"Why, damn it?"

"I've seen a doctor. Nina insisted. She knows about—"

"What did he, or she, say?"

"He said my memory loss could have been caused by a concussion or by a 'psychiatric illness.' "

"I could have told you that."

"He said something might trigger my memory. A shock."

"And how did he suggest we shock you? Shout 'boo?' "

John didn't crack a smile. "He said my memory could be prodded by a humdrum event . . . like a TV show."

"That's all he said?" I tried not to sound disappointed.

"He wanted me to take tests. Hospital."

"Obviously, you refused. What else?"

"I asked him about hypnosis. He said it could be dangerous and the results were almost always negligible."

"Why don't you drop by a police precinct, John? They might have your fingerprints on file. While that wouldn't cure your amnesia, at least you'd know who you are."

"Cops. Hate 'em. Useless. Can't control a damn thing."

He's talking about the concert stampede, I thought.

As John lapsed into silence, I heard Tommy Murphy loud and clear. This time he didn't regale me with Gene Kelly songs. This time he reminded me that I knew the words to the same incantation Mercy Birdwell had vowed to recite, hoping to cure Obadiah Barker. A Charm to Rid the Mind of an Affliction:

The dark be lightened
The harsh be softened
The rank be sweetened
By the power of the knife
And by the power of the water.

All I had to do was gather a quart of water from a spring and pour it into a large bowl, set within a darkened chamber. Candlelight. Silver knife. Write John's name upon the water's surface with the knife and . . . whoa. I didn't know John's real name. Writing John Elway might cure John Elway, assuming he had an affliction, but it wouldn't cure my John.

Speaking of charms, was there a Charm to Find a Parking Space?

Aunt Lillian's fertility charm might work, but I didn't have an egg.

How about visualization?

"John," I said, "visualize a parking space."

"Huh?"

"Never mind. There's a space. Except it's awfully small. Help me out here, pal. I need a rune . . . a short chant that rhymes. A spell that'll make my Honda fit."

"Sydney, your car won't fit, rune or no rune."

"Please try."

John humored me. "Honda shrink, so we may drink, of song and glee, we've paid our fee."

"So mote it be."

Chapter Thirty-four

Thursday night

The parking space fit like a glove. Literally.

Walking toward the back of the theatre, I had a sudden thought. If John hadn't been there when his sister got trampled, how could he have heard kids screaming? Had video cameras recorded the traumatic event?

Kids had been trampled at a Who concert in Cincinnati and a Guns-n-Roses concert in Toronto. I tried to remember if there'd been a recent newscast about a deadly stampede but came up empty.

Carol greeted me at the stage door entrance.

Upon spying John (without his Bozo makeup), she sprang into bird-dog mode. She dropped ten years. Her eyes brightened. Her lashes grew longer and thicker. Her mouth moistened. Her cheeks flushed an attractive pink, her nose seemed to quiver, and her breasts attacked her blouse buttons.

Pinned to her collar were a cluster of pansies.

Eros is said to have released his arrow, and where it fell pansies stemmed in bright colors. I had once told Carol that pansies heal the wounds of past mistakes and generate a new beginning in one's love life. "Choose yellow if you want an intellectual man," I had said, "blue if you're seeking a simple but true man, purple for passion."

Tonight, Carol wore purple.

John wasn't unappreciative. Or unaffected. He drew closer to the pansies. Carol's breasts practically punctured his chest. Undaunted, he said, "Nice to see you again," and kissed her on both flushed cheeks.

Watching Carol flirt, I felt ninety percent certain she'd slept with Yogi. But what I didn't know was when the affair had begun. Before or after Clive's murder?

"You look different," she purred, her manicured fingers stroking John's face. "A red clown's nose doesn't do you justice. Neither do baggy pants."

"I should get out more," John murmured, as I seethed.

Having never staked a permanent claim on John, I had no right to seethe. Trying to temper my temper, I turned, walked away, and bumped smack-dab into Rosie-all-fall-down.

Who clung to Harlan the Chauffeur.

"Witch," Rose squealed, staring at me through her new glasses. "What're ya doin' here?"

"I've got tickets to the concert," I replied, too startled to say I just happened to be in the neighborhood.

"Me, too. Cool Hand got 'em for Harley."

Harley? "I thought you'd be back in Vegas by now, Rosie." *Or the Betty Ford Clinic.*

"No, Witch, I'm in l-o-v-e-love." She squeezed Harlan's biceps.

"What happened to Lola?" I blurted.

"She divorced Harley when he was in jail, di'nt she, Harley? An ya wanna hear a co-inky-dink, Witch? After the divorce, Lola married Clive's father."

"Clive Newton's father?"

"Yeah. Clive was Lola's kid."

"Rosie, shut up."

"Shut up yourself, Harley. Witch here ain't no gossip. She can't be in her line of work. She's a doctor, sort of, so what we say is priv'leged infa'mation."

Harlan looked as if he wanted to land an uppercut across Rosie's gorgeous chin, and I wondered why she'd hooked up with him. Granted, he made an okay income driving for Cool

Hand. Granted, she had money from The Senator. But Harlan had to be at least thirty years older. Maybe that was the attraction. Maybe Rosie "conjoined" for fun or profit but fell in l-o-v-e-love with father figures. And I had to admit that Harlan was what Chastity would call "comely" or "pleasing to the eye."

"Why did you lie?" I asked him. "About Lola?"

"Habit," he replied. "Cool Hand says women trust married drivers."

That sounded fishy, but it was really none of my business.

What concerned me was Rosie's revelation about Lola being Clive's mom. Could Harlan have fumed over the divorce, fermented in jail, then taken out his frustration on Lola's son?

But why mail Clive's body parts to The Newts? That made no sense. And Harlan hadn't been anywhere near Xanthia's birthday party.

Speaking of The Newts and Xanthia . . .

I said goodbye to Harlan and Rosie-all-fall-down, then returned to Carol, who was scowling at her watch. "Damn," she said, "I have an appointment and I'm running late. Sydney, would you round up the girls? And would you drive them home after the concert? Xanthia's throwing a pajama party. I'm not sure when I'll get home from my . . . appointment . . . so Aunt Lillian promised to chaperone."

John's eyes looked glazed. I knew that expression. Pansies or no pansies, my ex-sister-in-law had lapsed into one of her maggot stories.

"Sure, Carol," I said. "Have fun." *And try not to talk too much.*

Beckoning to Xanthia, I pulled the talismans out of my handbag. At the same time, I realized I hadn't told John about the backstage visit. "John, Oliver arranged for Xanthia,

Megan, Ashley, and Natasha to visit The Newts backstage, before the performance. I'm not sure we're on his list, so we'll have to explain—"

"If you don't mind, Sydney, I'd rather take my seat and wait for the show to start."

"Okay," I said, wondering if he'd skip out on me.

He grasped me by the shoulders and pulled me up against him. My breasts didn't even come close to denting his chest. Staring into my eyes, he said, "Did I tell you how beautiful you look in that sweater?"

All I could think to say was, "I don't plan to get toasted tonight."

"Good." He kissed me on the lips, then turned and walked away.

Reaching my side, Xanthia said, "Where's Bozo going?"

"Inside, sweetie, and his name's John. There's this woman who calls me 'Witch' all the time. I hate it, and I imagine John would hate being called 'Bozo.' "

There were appreciative squeals when I gave the girls their talismans.

Delayed by the guard with the roster, we made it backstage in time to see The Newts saunter down a long corridor, then stop and form a football huddle.

"Pre-performance prayer," Megan told me.

"For luck," Xanthia added.

"So nothing will go wrong," Natasha said.

Ashley was trying to see without her glasses.

"I couldn't find a talisman for perfect vision," I told her. "So you have a talisman to walk in harmony with the earth, which is much, much better. Besides, you look adorable in glasses. Like Jamie Lee Curtis."

"Jamie Lee Curtis wears glasses?"

"She sure does. Lots of movie stars wear them. Newscasters, too. Diane Sawyer wears glasses."

My ears strained to hear The Newts' prayer, but all I caught was: "God begins with us in affliction, which is the greater argument to us of His love."

You can't have a rainbow without some rain, I thought, then wondered whether Clive or Yogi had started the backstage tradition.

My charges stood perfectly still, awed, cheerleader contortions forgotten.

Finally, The Newts clapped once, hugged each other, then headed for the stage.

"We'd better find our seats," I said, not even sensing Xanthia's fury.

White-faced, she ran toward the musicians. "My daddy said we could meet you," she yelled. "My daddy's O. T. St. Charles, best-selling author, and he's been on the *Today Good Morning America* show, and your manager, Veronica, was my stepmother's sister."

"Veronica?" One of The Newts stopped dead in his tracks.

White hair covered his ears and fell past his shoulders. Clothed all in black, he wore a Pilgrim-ish jacket and breeches, cloth rather than wool. His feet were clad in boots. Under his arms he carried two black cats. They looked like the cats I'd seen in Terey's kitchen, except they weren't hissing. Were they tranquilized?

Yogi Demon said, "How well do you know Veronica?"

"Her whole name is . . . was Veronica Whitney Sanderson," Xanthia replied, her teeth clenched, her cheeks as red as poppies. "But my daddy nicknamed her Ronnie 'cause they were such good friends."

"Yeah, I'll bet they were," said another member of the group, the freckle-faced drummer.

"Shut up, Chas." Yogi turned toward a shadowy figure

who wore headphones. "Hold these cats, DiNardo."

Stepping out from the shadows, Paulie scurried to the singer's side. Just like his mother, he'd slung something across one arm: a black, silk-lined cloak. Surprised, I saw that his face had cleared up. A few acne scars remained, but no suppurated pimples marred his forehead, cheeks, and chin. What magic had he used? Sex? Clearasil? Or had he suddenly escaped puberty at age thirty-five?

Having rid himself of the cats, Yogi faced my niece again. "What's your name, sweetheart?"

"Xanthia St. Charles. My daddy calls me Xanthie."

"Xanthia. Right. Your dad's Oliver. Why don't you introduce me to your friends, Xanthia?"

"Really?" Her teeth unclenched and she gave him a brilliant smile. "Okay. Sure. Thanks."

"My pleasure. Your father was very nice to me when I had the flu. So was your mom."

"Stepmom," Xanthia said, walking toward me. "Did you hear she was kidnapped?"

"I knew she was missing, but didn't hear she'd been kidnapped."

"My Aunt Syd found her. Inside a motel room. This is my Aunt Syd."

I had thought the singer un-charismatic. How wrong can you get?

Up close he radiated a sexual tension that was almost tangible. His dark eyes were mesmerizing, and I had a sudden urge to shed my jeans and sweater. Now I knew how Elvis fans felt. And the fitful Salem girls.

Guys wouldn't get it. Guys would look at Yogi and wonder what all the fuss was about. Guys would think: *Big deal. I have a penis, he has a penis. I'm taller. My arms are stronger, my chest broader, and the white hair makes him look old. Even his clothes are weird.*

But Aunt Lillian would swoon. Women of any age would swoon. Yogi had a magic wand all right, only it wasn't between his legs. His whole body was a royal scepter.

He kissed my knuckles. I didn't swoon, just melted. "Thanks, Aunt Syd," he said. "Jessica is good people. She took fantastic care of me."

"I guess Tiffany is good people too," I said, throwing caution to the wind. "And Carol. And, of course, Veronica."

His black eyes sparked. But then he smiled, ruining the effect. Like mine, his teeth should have been braced. One hand snaked out. Tenderly, he finger-combed the unruly curls behind my left ear. By the time I realized my barrette hadn't held my curls back, he was staring at the golden gecko.

I repeated his tender gesture with both hands, finger-combing his hair behind his ears.

No signature earring!

Xanthia thrust Natasha, Megan, and Ashley in front of me. "These are my best friends," she said. "We all brought pictures. Of you. Would you autograph them, Yogi? Please?"

"Sure, sweetheart."

I waited until he'd scribbled his name four times.

Then, stepping between Megan and Ashley, I fingered my left earlobe.

"You were staring at my earring," I said. "Does it belong to you?"

"Lost mine," he managed, sounding like John when he tried to remember something.

"You'll never guess where I found this one, Yogi. Under the bed, inside a sleazy motel room."

Chapter Thirty-five

Thursday night

It took forever to get into the theatre. Security guards stood at all entrances. They searched every pocket, every knapsack, every boot and shoe, every purse.

Inside my handbag was a golden candle stump. A gold-colored cord had been tied in a bow around the candle. Aunt Lillian's Charm to Attract Powerful Light Into the Home.

For one week Aunt Lillian would cleanse the house by trailing a gold cord behind her as she walked through each room. Then she'd place sunflowers on tables and counter tops, shelves and window sills. Each night she'd burn a golden candle, notched equally in seven places. While the candle burned, we'd focus on attracting happiness and luck, drawing the optimism of a sunny day into our house.

At the end of the week, Aunt Lillian would tie the cord around the candle's stump and I'd carry it in my handbag for another week.

The spell is best performed in late July or early August, when the sun is at its zenith. After moving into our house, we had enacted the spell every single year without fail. A beaming Aunt Lillian always swore the apothecary looked sunnier, brighter, and more welcoming, but on rainy days I couldn't detect a difference.

My forgotten candle stump from last August gave the door-guard pause. Maybe he thought I'd use the cord to strangle one of The Newts. After scrutinizing me from head to toe, he snapped my purse shut, handed it over, and gestured for me to enter. My guess is that a chunky-hipped, thirty-five-year-old woman didn't pose much of a threat, and I wondered what his reaction might have been had he known that most Manitou Falls taxpayers considered me a bona-fide witch.

Next, I bumped into Terey Lowenfeld, who'd undergone an incredible transformation. Not only was her hair the same magenta shade as the potty-mouthed teen, Tiffany, but Terey wore a nose earring.

As I stared at her earring, she stared at mine. Then, together, we both said, "Nice earring."

I said, "What did your mother say?"

She said, "Where'd you get it?"

I said, "Found it."

She said, "Ma nearly fainted dead away, but Paulie really likes my hair. And my nose-ring."

The perfect cue line . . .

Assuming I wanted to ask her about Paulie and Martina Brustein.

No. I didn't. Despite the magenta porcupine quills, Terey looked beautiful. She wore white carpenter's jeans and a red, bulky, cable-knit sweater that flattered her too-thin figure. Her smallish blue eyes, enhanced by purple eyeshadow, glistened with excitement.

I said, "Did Paulie give you a ticket?"

"No," she said. "Yogi. First row. Because of my cats. I loaned him my cats. Two cats, two tickets."

"Who did you bring? Your mother?"

"Are you kidding? I brought Susan Partridge. She's already seated, but I need to tinkle."

Terey waved goodbye to me and my four giggly companions, then headed toward the restrooms. When she sheds her mother for good, I thought, maybe she'll say "pee" instead of "tinkle."

"C'mon, Aunt Syd, hurry," Xanthia said, as she and her friends nudged me forward; a flock of sheep herding a dog.

Moonlighting as an usher, Manny Glick showed us to our seats. The motel clerk wore a THE NEWTS tee and jeans that showed his underpants, and I almost dropped my teeth when Xanthia, watching Manny walk back up the aisle, said, "He's cute."

John hadn't skipped out on me. As he stood up to let the girls slither past his long legs, I thought: *Yogi makes my brain melt, John makes my bones liquefy.*

I saw that Ashley, happy in her glasses, had developed an instant crush on my handsome amnesiac. Ordinarily the least aggressive of Xanthia's friends, she stubbornly insisted on sitting next to John, provoking an argument with Xanthia, who felt that *she* should sit next to John. After all, Ashley wouldn't even *be* here if it weren't for Oliver. Nor would anyone have met Yogi Demon.

John settled the argument by saying he'd sit between Ashley and Xanthia, but he didn't want the two girls jumping up and down, stomping on his toes.

Xanthia thought that over, then graciously said that Ashley could sit next to John since she weighed less and wouldn't hurt his toes. Thanks to Aunt Syd's talisman, by this time next year she'd weigh less too, Xanthia added.

John didn't tell her he admired "curvature," but the disappointed look he gave me made me feel uncomfortable—and apologetic—so I turned away and glanced around.

Oh lud, I thought, using Chastity, Anne, and Mercy's appellation. Not counting Terey Lowenfeld and Susan Partridge, John and I were the only adults in the first five rows, and I surmised that by the time the concert ended I'd be deaf.

Purple Buddha, a Denver group, opened the show. They were good, very good, and had often entertained at the Cafe Utopia, but you could sense the tension in the audience. The kids wanted The Newts.

And finally got them, shrouded in smoke.

Audience reaction could be likened to *The Gladiators*. Instead of Russell Crowe, Yogi Demon stomped to the middle of the stage. Instead of tigers, there were cats. But just like the sound of spectators watching a fight to the death, a roar began, then built, until it was as solid as a wall, impenetrable and unbroken.

I wondered if Xanthia, Megan, Natasha, and Ashley would pass out from lack of breath. Surely they'd have to breathe, eventually. I glanced at John, hoping to share a smile and a shrug. His face looked deathly pale and he kept swallowing, as if he needed to vomit. Should I suggest we leave? Impossible. Even though I sat next to him, my voice would never carry. I prodded him with my elbow. Tried to pantomime: *Do you want to leave?* by slicing the air around my neck with a finger, then pointing toward the exit. A wasted effort. He didn't move a muscle.

On the stage, Yogi just stood there, his arms full of black fur and paws and claws. A black, silk-lined cloak garnished his shoulders and billowed out behind his back.

While I realized, rationally, that some sort of wind machine blew the smoke and cloak, the effect was spectacular, and so dramatic it took *my* breath away. Yogi Demon looked as if he'd just come from another time, another world, the bowels of Hell. Had I really met this man backstage? Had I really told him about finding the gecko earring? Had I really been so stupid?

From the stage, thunder sounded and bolts of lightning flashed. Holding the cats by the scruffs of their necks, Yogi thrust them forward. Was he planning to indulge in some sort of sacrificial hocus-pocus? If he was, I'd leap up onto the stage and—

The audience hushed.

I'd never seen anything like it. One moment bedlam, the next silence.

Placing the cats on tufted cushions, Yogi announced that The Newts would sing a new song, dedicated to their late manager.

Surprising me, they sang the words from my straying-cat charm.

"Grimalkin, grimalkin, feasted in my kitchen," they sang, each syllable punctuated by cymbal clashes. "There shalt thou stay, nor from it care to stray."

"Veronica, ronica, feasted on my essence," Yogi sang, solo. "There shalt she stay, nor from it care to stray."

The Newts and Yogi repeated all four lines ad nauseam, occasionally adding a six-line chorus:

"John Stewart
Once a schoolmaster
Kept three bumblebees
Under a stone
And fed them with drops
Of blood from his fingers."

As The Newts began their umpteenth "grimalkin-grimalkin," I glanced around, trying to determine if anyone else thought the lyrics sounded bush-league. Then I reminded myself that the Beatles' "I Want to Hold Your Hand" had been repetitious. And not majorly poetic.

I'd only heard . . . half heard . . . one Newts song. On the car radio. "Fuary, Gary, Nary." But that song had been lyrical, unforgettable, destined to become a Golden Oldie.

Actually, the schoolmaster-bumblebee chorus wasn't bad. Except it sounded as if it belonged in another song. Even its music was out of sync. No cymbals. No discordant guitar strums.

Maybe the loss of their manager had screwed up the nuts and bolts in The Newts' song-writing mechanism. Every group, I imagined, had a loser every now and then, and this song was definitely a loser.

Veronica was feasting on Yogi's soul again when he sensed a restlessness in his audience. Aha! The un-lyrical lyrics hadn't been a figment of my imagination. Signaling the other Newts with a hand gesture, Yogi brought the song to an untimely, about-time halt, and immediately launched into "Fuary, Gary, Nary."

The audience emitted its Gladiator-roar. Rising from their seats, some kids swayed left and right. A few sang along with The Newts, but most convulsed, as if they were having fits, as if they attended a Salem witch trial, as if Yogi Demon was, in truth, Tituba Indian's white-haired black man.

Kids from the first row were on the floor, on their backs, flailing about like turtles. Strange to see Susan Partridge, my bank-teller-with-an-attitude, playing turtle. Terey sat on her heels. Her throat arched, her mouth formed an O-shape, and she reminded me of Chastity's Lady in Red. Or a howling wolf. I couldn't hear Terey's moan, but I could see it.

Drawing my gaze away, I stared at the aisle, where kids were performing a weird version of Chubby Checker's "The Twist." I shot a glance toward my charges. All four were singing and swaying, not contorting, thank God.

More smoke enveloped the stage. A huge movie screen unfolded. An American flag filled the screen. Then, in quick succession, flags from other countries. I'm fairly certain The Newts wanted that rapid-fire effect, but to me it felt as if a slide-show operator had taken one too many hits of speed, and the *blink-flag-blink-flag* did nothing for my Coney-Island-roller-coaster stomach.

I caught British Stripes and a red Canadian Maple Leaf before the screen became a total blur. Finally, a skull and crossbones stayed put.

"Fuary, Gary, Nary" continued, with an emphasis on the Horseman's Chant.

The audience roar had become one continuous groan. Kids shed their shirts, unsnapped their bras. Several girls rode shoulders, and a few began to faint. When they did, they were passed overhead, like beach balls, to the back of the theatre. It was Salem without the ministers and magistrates. Woodstock without the mud.

Or drugs. Pockets and purses had been searched thoroughly. Not many drugs could have gotten past the guards. Yogi Demon was tonight's drug.

Just as I was debating how I'd get Xanthia and her friends out of the theatre, or into the lobby for a breath-break, Yogi and The Newts finished singing "Fuary, Gary, Nary."

Normality prevailed.

The fainters miraculously revived.

Kids put their bras and shirts back on.

Kids sat.

Kids applauded.

Many still filled the aisles, but Susan, Terey, and the other contortionists from the first row were standing and brushing themselves off—as if nothing had happened.

Maybe nothing had.

Perspiration dotted my brow, but Xanthia, Ashley, Natasha, and Megan were chatting away, as if they'd just received a new homework assignment.

The third Newts song was a ballad. It sounded familiar. I felt John move. Brushing past my knees, he said, "Sorry, Sydney, gotta go."

Chapter Thirty-six

Thursday night

I told Xanthia and her friends I'd be right back.

Then, stepping on multiple toes, I wended my way to the aisle.

John had vanished, a lost shape among dozens of other shapes. I spied Harlan, plunging through the aisle-kids. Just like Mary Lou's shopping bag and Paulie's Yogi-cloak, Rose was draped over Harlan's arm. Arms.

I spotted John. At least the man looked like John from the back. Long hair, dark blue polo shirt, and faded, butt-tight jeans. "John, wait up!"

The man turned, his teeth very white in his dark beard. Damn!

Lacking Harlan's chutzpah—and size—I couldn't move forward. Maybe a rune would work, except I didn't have time to compose a rune. I pictured Ashley's walk-in-harmony-with-the-earth talisman. Figuring an aisle was part of the earth, I chanted, *"Cor terrae, cor meum,"* several times.

And, somehow, made my way through the aisle-kids.

Entering the lobby, I saw Rose, seated on a backless bench. Her knees were at right angles, her face between her legs. Manny Glick towered above her, his hand frantically gesturing toward the restrooms. Harlan was nowhere in sight.

John stood in front of the T-shirt concession stand. He looked like a mime. His face was on the brink of mime-white, and his hands were stiff, palms facing me. He didn't move his body, just his hands, as if he'd suddenly become trapped behind an imaginary, wall-size pane of glass.

Without thinking, I placed my body in front of his hands and instinctively shivered when his palms grazed my fleece-clad breasts.

He blinked. "Sydney?"

"Let's go outside."

He didn't move.

"I'm not kidding, John . . . or whatever your name is. Outside, please, now."

I turned, walked toward an exit, and felt him follow me.

Cold, fresh air slapped my face. Hopefully, the impudent nip would have the same effect on my handsome amnesiac.

Whom, I surmised, wasn't an amnesiac any more.

His legs bent as if his weight couldn't support him, a vein throbbed in his forehead, and his face now had a greenish, Mary Lou DiNardo tinge.

I said, "Do you want to throw up?"

He gave me the ghost of a smile. "No, thank you. Besides," he added, "there aren't any Denver Broncos wastebaskets handy."

"Do you feel like talking?"

"What if I said no?"

"I'm sure I could conjure up a spell to make you talk."

"I'm sure you could," he said, moving closer.

"For starters, why were The Newts singing the same ballad you sang at Xanthia's birthday party?"

"Because I wrote it for them. For us."

"You were a Newt."

It wasn't really a question, but he said, "Yes."

"You played the guitar."

"Right."

"And your real name is?"

"John."

"Listen, pal. I've had enough bull—"

"John Black Wolf Fitzgerald. Clive called me John Suspenders. My sister's name was Nalin. It's an Apache name. My great-great-grandmother was Apache." He swallowed. "Before they hit it big, The Newts were hired to open for another rock group. I was backstage. The tickets had been oversold. I'd given my sister and her friends tickets. They got caught in the crush." He swallowed again. "After Nalin died, I quit The Newts."

His eyes conveyed his anguish. I wanted to stroke him, comfort him, but he had the look of a familiar stranger, so I simply said, "I'm sorry about Nalin."

"Thanks. That's why I didn't go to the police, why I tried to avoid Oliver and wore the clown makeup, why I stole your camera. I felt deep down inside that I'd killed somebody."

He stared above my head, not as high as the sky, and the complex contours of his face reminded me of Michelangelo's David. Then, expressionless, as if he were reciting someone else's story, he told me about Friday morning.

His first thought, the first word that came to mind when he opened his eyes, was headache. The second was splitting. He had a splitting headache. Blood stained the pillow case, suspenders had been wrapped around his throat, and aside from the fact that he could barely swallow, he craved water. He couldn't remember what had happened to him, or his name, but he latched on to words. He knew words. His throat felt bone-dry, dry as dust, dry as a stick, dry as a mummy, dry as a biscuit . . . words became his anchor.

He loosened the suspenders around his neck and struggled to sit up.

How could he not know his name?

First things first. Water. Stumbling into the bathroom, he filled a water glass to the brim, drank greedily, heaved, then refilled the glass and drank again, slowly, sipping rather than gulping. With a shaky hand, he placed the glass on the sink and caught his reflection in the mirror. He didn't look like anyone he knew, even though he smiled wryly at the realization that he didn't know anyone. And all he could remember, possibly from his childhood, was an Indian warrior's song. He stepped into the shower. "My horse be swift in flight," he sang, his voice raspy. "Even like a bird. My horse be swift in flight. Bear me now in safety. Far from the enemy's arrows. And you shall be rewarded. With streamer and ribbons red."

Drying off, he wrapped a towel around his waist. Then, stepping toward the toilet, his foot encountered a bobby pin. He picked it up and put it next to the water glass. Finally, he returned to the room and looked around, trying to find some clue to his identity.

He saw an empty bottle; printed on its label: Johnny Walker Black. Johnny sounded familiar. So did Black. Was his name Johnny Black? He almost smiled again. He didn't think he'd been named for a bottle of scotch.

No clothes. No wallet. He walked to the door. Saw a beaded headband on the threadbare carpet. Just outside the door, blood. His headband? His blood? Or had he killed someone, dumped the body, then returned to the motel room?

"It was your blood," I interjected, "from your head wound."

True, but the killed-someone part felt right. His legs threatened to give out, so he made his way to the bed. Stubbed his toe on something. A guitar case.

The rest I knew, John told me, ruffling my curls.

"I can remember everything now," he said, his voice filled with relief, his face no longer expressionless. "All the way back to the day my mother was supposed to pick me up from a horseback riding lesson. She went shopping and couldn't find her car in the parking lot. I was only four years old. It grew late, cold, dark, and I calmed my fears by singing 'Winnie the Pooh.' I think that's when I started writing my own songs, in my head. We had a summer place, on the Cape, with a pool. But Nalin preferred to cool off in the duck pond. We named all the ducks. Donald and Daisy, of course, and Froot and Loop. We called the smallest, prettiest, loudest duck Ritz Quacker . . ."

Suddenly silent, he looked as if The Newts' giant stage-screen had unfolded before his eyes. Only instead of flags, he saw his life projected, scene by scene, frame by frame.

"I play the piano, Sydney," he said, eventually. "They considered me a child prodigy. I can remember the afternoon I lost my virginity . . . to a neighbor whom I considered very, very old. She was thirty."

"As long as it's confession time, once or twice I thought you killed Clive." I looked down at my sandals. "You wrote 'Fuary, Gary, Nary,' didn't you?"

"Yes. But Clive never sang it like Yogi does. Clive sounded spiritual. 'Fuary, Gary, Nary' is meant to be . . . otherworldly."

"Where did you learn the words to the Horseman's Chant?"

"I researched witchcraft for my dissertation. Graduate school. UCLA. History major."

I looked up at his face. "You're from California?"

"Yes."

"I thought you said you were from the Cape."

"No, Sydney, I said we had a vacation cottage there."

I stared into his dark blue eyes. "If you're from California, why aren't you a Raiders fan? Why did you choose John Elway instead of a Raiders quarterback?"

A part of me realized that my question was stupid, but my

nerves were still raw. From Yogi's performance. From John's *memorable* reaction. I felt as if I'd nicked myself while shaving my legs, then poured lemon juice over the cuts.

To his credit, John treated my question seriously. "My mother and father are divorced," he said. "Mom's from Colorado. She's a fanatical Broncos fan. After the divorce, she moved back to Colorado. I was visiting her, and my sister, when I hooked up with Clive. I'd give anything if I hadn't met him."

"Because of Nalin? Her death isn't your fault, damn it. You had nothing to do with the stampede that killed your sister. Would you feel better if I tied you up and threw you into Veronica's duck pond? If you float, you're blameworthy. If you sink and drown, you're guiltless. We can invite Davy to go with us, try it tomorrow. I've got a gold cord in my purse, perfect for the water test."

"That's what Veronica said." Once again, John gave me the ghost of a smile. "The part about me having nothing to do with the stampede."

"Veronica . . . tell me about Thursday night."

"Veronica begged me to meet her at the Café Utopia. She sounded so agitated, I said yes. The café was crowded, loud. She suggested we find the nearest motel room. Just to talk. Don't look at me like that, Sydney. Veronica had a thing for Yogi."

"And?"

"She offered me a cool million, up front, to rejoin The Newts and write their songs."

"I can understand why. 'Grimalkin' is Amateur City. Wait a minute. The schoolmaster-bumblebee chorus. That's yours, isn't it?"

"Yes. Taken from a song I never finished."

"Veronica offered you a million dollars to finish it?"

"Actually, she offered me even more when I turned down the million. She wanted enough songs to fill a CD. Then we'd renegotiate my contract. Naturally, I'd get a hefty percentage from CD sales and concerts. Yogi was at the meeting, too. He's no fool. Without good songs a group'll fizzle, no matter how many special effects they throw at the audience. And my music's difficult to duplicate."

"That's true. I imagine it would be like trying to clone Elton John or Billy Joel. Okay, who strangled you?"

He shrugged his broad shoulders. "I don't know."

I began pacing. "Let's take it from the beginning. Who was at the meeting?"

"Veronica and Yogi and Paul."

I stopped pacing. "Paulie DiNardo?"

"He prefers Paul. Yogi brought him to the restaurant because he's engaged to Martina, Yogi's sister. Yogi asked Veronica if she'd re-hire Paul."

"And she said?"

"Before she could say anything, I reminded her that Paul's a thief. He'll steal anything that's not nailed down. I caught him stealing my guitar picks. Who in their right mind steals guitar picks? When he tried to steal my music sheets, my songs, Clive fired him. Paul denied my accusations, but Yogi told him to shut up. Veronica said she'd think it over. Paul left and we adjourned to the motel."

"Paulie's always been a liar and a thief. That's how he made it through high school. I assume he was angry when he left the restaurant."

"Understatement."

"So he could have hung around, fuming, outside the motel."

"I suppose."

Davy's favorite word. *Suppose.* "Why did you put your guitar under the bed?"

"Habit. When I stay at motels or hotels, I slide my guitar case under the bed. Just in case a maid has sticky fingers. Maids rarely clean under the bed, at least not until you check out. I had my guitar with me because Veronica asked me to bring it," John said, anticipating my next question. "Maybe she thought I'd compose a new song on the spot. Veronica could be . . . persuasive."

"Did she and Yogi leave the motel at the same time?"

"No. Veronica's thing for Yogi wasn't reciprocal. Veronica drove off alone, Yogi retrieved a bottle of Johnny Walker Black from his limousine. Then he—"

"Limousine? One of Cool Hand's limousines?"

John nodded. "After Clive was killed, Cool Hand insisted The Newts ride around in his limousines. His drivers are trained as bodyguards."

But Yogi didn't use a limousine the night Jessica disappeared, I thought. He used a cab. Maybe he didn't want Cool Hand, or anyone else, to know about Tiffany. He told Oliver because . . . because why? Because they were pals and he was toasted.

"Did Harlan drive Yogi last Thursday?" I asked John. "Do you know who I'm talking about?"

"Yes. Rosie's chauffeur. But I don't know who drove Yogi's limousine. We all had separate cars."

"Were you with The Newts when they played Vegas?"

"No. Why?"

"Rosie recognized you."

"She didn't recognize me, Sydney. She thought I was Clint Black."

"What happened after Yogi retrieved the scotch from his limousine?"

"We shared a couple of drinks while he tried to talk me into accepting Veronica's offer. I finally used her Paul-excuse, said I'd think about it. After Yogi left, I drank more scotch, finished the bottle. Veronica had brought back memories of my sister, and I wanted to drink myself into oblivion."

"Obviously, you succeeded. Do you remember opening the door?"

"No. I was very drunk."

I fisted one hand. "You opened the door, probably stepped outside," I said, holding up my thumb. "Someone hit you on the head, dragged you inside, put you on the bed, then strangled you with your suspenders." My first finger joined my thumb. "The last thing you thought about was Nalin, so when you woke up you wanted to bury the memory." My thumb and fingers formed a W. "You've been hiding." My third finger fused with the other two, forcing my pinkie to integrate. "So the killer probably doesn't even know you're alive."

"But I am, Sydney." He grabbed my hand and twirled me round and round, as if we were on a dance floor rather than the front lawn of the Pikes Peak Center. "I'm alive and I'm me. I can't even begin to tell you how great that feels."

John kissed me, and my bones melted, liquefied, or in Chastity's words, fluxed. Somehow, I managed to pull away and whisper, "You're not married, are you? How about engaged?"

"No and no. Divorced. My wife didn't like . . ."

"Didn't like what?"

"My father has money, Sydney, a fortune. But I wanted to make it on my own and my wife thought Dad should subsidize me. Us."

"Do you have any children?"

"A daughter. Sammy. Samantha. She's five. My ex-wife is Haitian. I wrote the dog-rabbit story for Sammy."

"One of the sisters in the journal I'm deciphering has a son named Sammy." *Which has nothing to do with anything,* I thought, *except my biological clock is ticking and I'm jealous.* "John, why did you glare at me when I mentioned Veronica and the fire?"

"I glared at you?"

"Yes. Monday night, on the porch, just before Davy cooked dinner."

"It wasn't a glare, Sydney. I was trying to remember and forget, both at the same time. The dead face I saw . . . the face in my head . . . was Clive's face. The cops showed me pictures . . ." John swallowed.

"Speaking of pictures," I said, "did you really picture the Broncos cheerleader when you chose your name? Or did you picture Veronica?"

"I'm not sure. Probably both. I've been to Veronica's estate, ridden her horses. What difference does it make?"

"None," I said.

I didn't ask him why Veronica needed a love spell to charm Yogi Demon, who apparently "conjoined" at the drop of a hat, because something else occurred to me. Veronica had bought my spell to lure a devil, not necessarily a Demon, and Mercy's "screw Yogi Demon" squawk could have meant *fire* Yogi Demon.

Maybe Veronica bought the spell to lure John, whose songs had devilish lyrics. If Yogi had known, he could have killed Veronica to protect his star status.

John was looking at me expectantly. "Veronica was so beautiful," I said.

"So are you." Tenderly, just like Yogi, John finger-combed my curls behind my ears—and saw the gecko. "Where did you get that earring?"

"I found it in your motel room. It must have dropped out of Yogi's ear."

"I've got a bone to pick with Yogi Berra Brustein."

"What bone?" I wished John would kiss me again.

"Using my song, my words, as part of that grimalkin piece of dreck."

"Why don't we go home, John? You said something about checking out my new panties."

"We can't, Sydney. You have to drive the girls to Xanthia's house. Did you forget?"

I nodded, and felt my curls fall forward, hiding my golden gecko.

No. Yogi's golden gecko. Which could have fallen out of his ear when he hefted an unconscious John up onto the bed.

Should I share my suspicions with John? If he picked a bone with Yogi and Yogi believed John dead . . .

Suddenly, my mental hypothesis sounded dumb. Yogi already had superstar status. He'd been on the cover of *Rolling Stone*, for God's sake. Even if he'd killed Clive to become the lead Newt, even if he'd mailed Clive's fingers and toes for the publicity, he'd achieved his goal. He could step away from the group and still attract groupies. Strangling John and Veronica would be . . . superfluous.

I saw Manny Glick and Rosie-all-fall-down, zigzagging toward a monster motorcycle. Manny walked, Rose staggered. He stopped to explore her cleavage and, momentarily, I thought they might "conjoin." All Manny had to do was push his jeans down another couple of inches. But Rose stumbled backwards, lifted the bottom of her dress, and withdrew a silver flask from beneath her garter belt. Her new glasses were missing. So was Harlan.

"Sydney, the girls are waiting," John said.

"Right. The girls. How could I forget the girls?" I summoned a grin. "You've got your memory back, John, while I seem to have lost mine."

As it turned out, my flippant remark was prophetic.

Chapter Thirty-seven

Thursday night

By the time I returned to my seat, loudspeakers were booming.

Yogi Demon, it seemed, had left the building.

All the same, his audience stayed put—hoping for an encore.

"The Newts don't have any more songs in their repertoire," Megan said perceptively.

"Let's get out of here," I said, "before the rush begins. Everyone chant, *'Cor terrae, cor meum'* and run like hell."

Chanting and laughing, we ran like hell, until we reached the car.

"Wow," Megan said. "How the heck did you get into that parking space?"

Panting, I leaned against my Honda and stared at the Pikes Peak Center, now regurgitating children of all ages.

Xanthia looked around. "Where's John, Aunt Syd?"

"I made him disappear, then couldn't bring him back."

"Seriously."

"What makes you think I'm not serious?"

"You always say you're not a witch."

"John had to find his car. He left it parked miles away, outside a motel."

One of the things I like about kids in general, my niece in particular, is that they'll essentially take an adult's words at face value. Probably too much TV. Xanthia didn't ask why or when John had parked his car. She simply devised a mental script: PARK CAR MILES FROM CONCERT. ATTEND CONCERT.

Come to think of it, I hadn't asked John how he'd start his car, assuming he hadn't locked it. His keys had been stolen, along with his clothes and wallet.

Maybe he could jump-start a car. Maybe he kept one of those magnetized key-boxes under the fender. Maybe he'd get home before I did.

That thought made my body toasty rather than toasted.

I drove the girls to Carol's house, watched them enter, then sped toward Reverend Hale Avenue.

Davy's convertible squatted across the street, in front of Lynn's quaint bungalow, but no car squatted at my curb, and I wondered if John had encountered problems finding and starting his car. Or had he picked bones with Yogi?

"Aunt Lillian, I'm home," I said, walking inside and locking the front door.

A light shone from the kitchen and something smelled burnt. "You would have loved the concert, Aunt Lillian. It was very loud. Thanks to Oliver, Xanthia and her friends met Yogi Demon. And you'll never guess what happened."

Planning to tell her about John, I climbed the staircase, two steps at a time, then entered the kitchen—empty except for Mercy, Annie, and Chasdick.

Lord, I really *had* lost my memory.

Aunt Lillian was chaperoning Xanthia's pajama party.

The burnt smell . . . oven cleaner.

"Ta-ta, Sydney."

"Ta-ta yourself, you silly parrot. What's on the fridge? A message from Aunt Lillian?"

Chasdick woofed.

I read the magnetized message, short and sweet: CALL THE 24-HOUR LOCKSMITH.

Not bloody likely, I thought with a smile. Murphy's Law

said the locksmith would knock on my door as soon as John and I "conjoined."

The new locks and keys could wait until tomorrow.

While waiting for John, I'd brew a cup of coffee and read Oliver's new book. Or, even better, I'd throw some clay on my potter's wheel. My hands felt like shaping something, preferably John, but clay would do for now.

That meant I'd have to change my clothes.

I retrieved my cutoffs from the laundry hamper. John liked me in cutoffs.

The heavy-handed scissors-trim exposed my new panties.

Panties or cutoffs? With a sigh, I threw the shorts back into the hamper and donned my Davy-jeans. Fishing the love talisman out of the pocket, I stared at the charm's inscription, then tossed the talisman on top of my bureau. At the same time, Tommy Murphy's *tap-tap-tap* sounded loud and clear.

"Hush, Tommy. You know the rules. John wants me and I want him."

"Waiting for my dearie," Tommy sang, though he didn't materialize.

"That's a Cyd Cherise song," I reminded him, "not a Gene Kelly song."

"Syd St. Charles song," Tommy said.

"Right." I stroked the soft fleece of my new sweater. Then, because I really had no choice, I exchanged it for an ancient black tee, worn (with pride) when I weighed fifteen or twenty pounds less. Frank Zappa rode my belly-button.

I could have raided Davy's T-shirt pile. Was I trying to flaunt my chunky hips on purpose? Did I want to evaluate John's "curvature" remark? Did I feel, deep down inside, that John Elway Henry Kissinger Black Wolf Fitzgerald was just another Jack or Matt Gray—

"Pox-marked foot-licker."

With a flurry of wings, Mercy flew into my bedroom and landed on my hops cauldron. *"Humpty Dumpty sat on the wall,"* she squawked.

Annie, hissing and meowing, clawed her way up my jeans.

"Ouch! Ouch! What do you think you're doing, you crazy cat?"

Reaching for Annie, my peripheral vision caught Chasdick. He shook all over, as if he'd just stepped out of the water.

Chasdick, more than Annie or Mercy, set off the alarms in my head.

Tommy Murphy tap-tapped frantically, as if he were Sammy Davis Jr. rather than Gene Kelly, and my perceptions captured the rhythm of his tap shoes.

Call the 24-hour locksmith.

Oliver's emergency key.

Whomever had kidnapped Jessica now owned the key.

Mercy squawked. Annie clawed. Chasdick quaked, and I was all alone.

Suddenly, the lights went out.

Chapter Thirty-eight

Thursday night

Moonlight shone through the glass doors that led to my balcony.

Downstairs it would be dark, which meant that the person who'd turned off my electricity probably carried a flashlight.

Whomever he or she was, he or she made no attempt to keep his or her movements quiet. Was the intruder looking for something to steal? Money?

My Honda crouched in the driveway. Obviously, I was home.

He or she wanted to steal *me*.

Kidnap me.

Just like Jessica.

Had the kidnapper cut the phone lines?

My bedroom didn't have an extension. Feeling my way down the hall, I entered the kitchen. All my senses were working overtime, at double their usual capacity, and I choked on the smell of Aunt Lillian's oven cleaner. Moonlight pierced the window here, too, but the moon's glow looked weak, dull, faded. Bleached lemon rather than crayon-orange. A twenty-five-watt bulb, compared to fluorescence.

The phone had no dial tone. Big surprise.

Although I could barely see it, Aunt Lillian's magnetized message branded itself in my brain. I should have followed her advice, called the locksmith, told him it was an emergency, asked him to hustle.

Shoulda/coulda. Too late now. And where the heck was John?

My gaze touched upon my handbag, where I'd left it, on the kitchen counter.

I opened the handbag, pulled out the candle stub, fumbled around in the what-not drawer for a pack of matches, and heard footsteps on the staircase.

For the second time in one night, I played Spielberg's ET . . . and saw a flashlight's wavering circle climb the stairs.

But the person who held the flashlight was less than a shadowy shape.

It had to be Yogi. I remembered Jessica saying that Oliver had given Yogi my address so that he could sing happy birthday to Xanthia. Not only had I worn Yogi's gecko earring, but I'd shown it to him, flaunted it, made my stupid remark about the sleazy motel.

And yet . . . why would Yogi strangle John? That made no sense, especially since he needed John to write more songs. Yogi had been inside the motel room, stayed to drink scotch. His earring could have simply fallen out of his earlobe.

I tiptoed to the head of the stairs and flattened myself against the wall. Whereupon, several things filtered through my brain. First, I had truly lost my memory. Or rather, my mind. Candle and matches? Why hadn't I grabbed a knife? Why hadn't I stood on my bedroom balcony and screamed my head off? Where the hell was John?

Holding my breath, I stiffened my fingers. The flashlight came into view. Then a hand and an arm. Without taking time to think, I karate-chopped.

The flashlight went flying. So did I. As I brushed past the kidnapper and literally flew down the stairs, I smelled Clearasil.

Paulie DiNardo's face might have un-pimpled, but he hadn't given up his magic potion. I heard him utter a continuous stream of profanities as he searched, on hands and knees, for the flashlight.

To this day, I don't know why I didn't hit the landing and fling open the front door. Maybe because the darkness hit me like an eclipse. Maybe I figured I'd have to fumble at the lock. Maybe I simply panicked.

Stone-blind, I groped my way toward the apothecary counter. Behind the counter were scissors; the same sharp, pointy scissors Jessica had used to cut out her heart. I needed light. My cigarette lighter was underneath Lucinda Lizard, too far away. Placing the candle stub on the counter, I lit a match. Its brief flicker didn't make a dent in the stygian hell that Aunt Lillian swore looked sunny, bright, and welcoming. Of course, that was during daylight hours.

"Okay, Aunt Lillian," I said, lighting another match and stepping behind the counter. "Let's see if we can bring the optimism of a sunny day into the shop."

I held flame to wick.

Then, for good measure, I recited a Charm to Win Immortality From the Sun. "Scarab of sun. Dark death is done. Gold life begins. So mote it be."

Problem was, if the charm worked at all, it wouldn't work without a beetle, a beetle with a metallic luster and hue, preferable a Japanese beet—

The room lit up.

Stunned, I dropped the candle. Its flame went out, but the room stayed bright and sunny.

And welcoming. Paulie stood at the entrance, blocking my escape to the front door, had I even remembered there *was* a front door.

He didn't seem surprised by the light. Maybe he thought I controlled an auxiliary power plant. But then, just like The Newts' Grimalkin song, Paulie's scheme was Amateur City—

lucky for me. He could have sneaked inside, crept upstairs, and caught me unaware. Like Jessica.

Maybe he hadn't kidnapped Jessica.

Had he killed Clive?

No. Paulie wasn't smart enough. He'd have been caught before he made it back to his car.

Stepping out from behind the counter, clutching the scissors, I said, "What do you want, Paulie?"

"Why can't you mind your own business, Sydney?" Furious, he spit the words. "Why do you have to poke around in things that don't concern you?"

"What the hell are you talking about?"

"You always have to rock the boat, don't you? Why did you wear Yogi's earring backstage? Why did you tell him you found it in the motel room? I stole the earring before his meeting with Veronica. Eventually, Yogi would have put two and two—"

"Paulie, I want you to leave. Right now. A friend of mine will be here any minute."

"John Suspenders? I don't think so."

"What did you do to John?"

Paulie smiled. "I killed him." Paulie scowled. "Again."

My heart stopped, just before I screamed, "Liar!"

Paulie's second smile looked smug. "I peeked through the stage manager's hole, behind the curtains. You can only make out the first few rows and I didn't think I'd see you, but I did. John Suspenders stood up and talked to some girls. Coulda knocked me over with a feather, him being dead and all. He came backstage, after the concert. 'Yogi Demon has left the building' is bullshit, and John knew it. We used to say it for Clive, too."

"You're a damn liar. I don't believe you. How did you kill him?" Heart now racing, I tried to keep my voice calm. If I gave in to hysteria, I'd be on the floor, convulsing like the concert turtles.

"With this." Paulie brandished a knife. Its blade had been cleaned on a towel or rag or shirt, but the apothecary's extraordinary illumination, brighter than normal light, seemed to accentuate rusty specks of blood.

My mind whirled. I pictured Matt Grayson, knifed in the back and tied to a crosspiece. I remembered Chastity's reaction when she thought the lice-riddled scarecrow was Jack, her feeling that she'd swallowed rocks. My reaction was a tad different. Roaring like a wounded bull, I charged the sleazy matador.

My excess fifteen or twenty pounds gave me a weight advantage. Plus, Paulie hadn't expected me to attack. Off balance, he dropped his knife and fell backwards, and the next thing I knew I was on my knees, my scissors less than an inch from his throat.

The smell of his Clearasil almost overwhelmed me. Almost, but not quite. However, the arms that wrapped themselves around my upper body succeeded where the smell had failed.

"Drop the scissors, Sydney," a voice huffed in my ear.

A familiar voice.

Chapter Thirty-nine

Thursday night

"Damn it, Paulie," Terey Lowenfeld said. "Can't you do anything right?"

"I killed John Suspenders, didn't I?"

"Not quite. Even as we speak, John Black Wolf Fitzgerald is at the hospital. An ambulance practically delivered him to Jessica Whitney St. Charles, whose room, I might add, is only one floor away from John's."

"That's impossible. I knifed him in the back."

"You stabbed him. How many times have I told you that stabbing doesn't always work? In any case, you hit his arm. The back of his arm. And his shoulder."

"So sue me. I aimed for the back of his back. He looked dead."

"He looked dead last time. You're such a screw-up, Paulie. You dropped the earring . . . I didn't even know about the earring . . . and you lost my bobby pin."

"So sue me. I had to take a dump. It fell out of my pocket when I pulled my pants down. And for your information, smarty-pants, I never used the bobby pin to jimmy the lock. John answered the door. This time I didn't do anything wrong. John looked dead, I swear to God. There was blood all over the place. I washed up backstage and changed my clothes and—"

"What did you do with the bloody clothes?"

"Dumpster. Behind Nina's."

Stunned into speechlessness, I'd listened to Terey and Paulie bicker. But my relief at John's resurrection finally unhinged my mouth.

"Terey," I said, "I thought we were friends."

"We are friends, Sydney. That's why I didn't want to be here, why I waited for Paulie in the car. But then I saw the lights in the shop go on, and figured he'd screwed up again."

"I didn't screw up," Paulie protested. "I did what you said to do. Killed the electricity and phone and jimmied the porch lock so it would look like a robbery."

My mind raced. Paulie hadn't climbed the stairs right off the bat because he'd been too busy killing the phone and electricity, fiddling with the sun porch lock. Terey had entered the apothecary from the porch, catching me off guard.

Rubbing my arms, sore from Terey's grip, I tried to devise an escape plan. Paulie had retrieved his knife, but he didn't scare me; Terey did.

As if to belie my last thought, Paulie lunged toward me, his right arm aloft, his knife aimed at my chest.

Terey stood directly behind me, not that it mattered. My legs had turned to concrete and I couldn't have moved if my life depended on it.

At that last thought, I laughed. To my ears, it sounded hysterical, but Paulie stopped short. "Are you laughing at me, Sydney?" he asked, his face a mask of fury. I continued laughing, couldn't stop, which only fueled his rage.

When he lunged again, Mercy intercepted him, her wings flapping in his face. His left arm swatted her out of his way.

It was the funniest thing I'd ever seen.

Annie vaulted onto Paulie's back, and I'm fairly certain her sharp claws did some major damage before he bucked her off.

Hugging my aching ribs, cracking up, I doubled over.

"Damn you, Sydney, stop laughing!" Paulie lunged for the third time.

Chasdick, fearsome and fearless, weighing one hundred

pounds, twenty pounds less than Paulie, pawed him to the floor. Teeth and gums exposed in a macabre grin, Chasdick went for Paulie's jugular vein.

"No!" Terey screamed.

"Chasdick, no!" Laughter gone, adrenaline pumping, I grabbed my Lab's collar and pulled him off Paulie, who preferred to be called Paul, who now lay very still.

His chest didn't rise and fall. His face had a bluish cast. His eyes were open, the irises half under the lids. Unwilling, or unable, to dip my hand in neck blood, I knelt and felt for a wrist pulse. Nothing. Nada. Not one throb. Briefly, I thought about CPR.

Rolling to my feet like a seasick sailor, I shook my head. "Terey, I'm sorry. No. That's not true. Paulie tried to kill John. And me." I shivered, delayed reaction.

Annie jumped up on the counter. With one delicate paw, she washed her whiskers. Mercy flew to the ceiling fan. *"All the king's horses and all the king's men,"* she squawked. Except for the blood that stained his muzzle, Chasdick looked like he'd looked when he performed for John. Gleefully, he plopped himself down by the armchair.

"Sydney," Terey said, "you've got to do something."

"What can I do? Paulie's dead."

"You once promised me any spell in the shop. Please, please bring him back to life."

"I can't do that, Terey, even if I wanted to. There's no spell . . ."

Actually, there was. Aunt Pru's Charm to Transpose Death Into Life, handed down from generation to generation.

Forget it. I stumbled toward the phone, then remembered that the phone was as dead as Paulie the Pimple DiNardo.

"Sydney," Terey pleaded, "I'll pay anything, do anything."

"Why do you want him back? He's engaged to another woman."

"No, no, that's a ploy, so he could get rehired by The Newts. He doesn't love Martina Brustein. He loves me."

As if to prove her last three words, she waved her hand in my face, and I saw a ton of string wound around her Arthur Miller High School graduation ring. No. Not her ring. Paulie's ring. The same ring that had bruised John's forehead the first time Paulie killed him.

"Why do you love Paulie?" I asked.

"Because he needs me. He'd be lost without me. Haven't you ever wanted to be needed?"

Fleetingly, a Jim-image blinded me like a camera's flash. "Yes," I said.

"Every relationship I've ever had has failed, Sydney. I can't be my mother all over again."

"Okay, Terey. I'll bring Paulie back on one condition."

"Anything."

"While I cast the spell, you tell me about Clive and Veronica."

"Tell you what?"

"How and why you killed them. It had to be you. Paulie's too dumb. I thought maybe Yogi was the murderer, but John said Veronica had a 'thing' for Yogi. If he wanted Clive out of the picture, he'd have charmed the pants off her, talked her into firing Clive. Last Saturday, while we were at the bank, I saw a padded envelope in your briefcase. You planned to mail another Clive appendage. Instead, you substituted Clive's ear for the CD. You chose my present because it was so easy to rewrap. My gift-wrapping skills are almost as bad as my cooking skills. You lucked out. A CD is small, flat. It's probably on the bookshelf, wedged between Charlaine Harris and Alice Hoffman. I don't know why you planted the ear, Terey, but if you want me to cast the spell you'd better 'fess up."

She ran her fingers through her magenta quills. Then she stopped, as if she'd just discovered that her hair wasn't long any more. She looked at Paulie. She looked at me. Her face seemed to shrivel. She shrugged, just the merest lift of her shoulders, but it was the most pathetic gesture I'd ever seen.

"Deal," she said. "What can I do to help?"

"Go outside to my oak tree and pick three long strands of ivy."

"You won't leave, will you?" She looked toward the sun porch.

"No. I promise."

Truthfully, I'd considered leaving. But curiosity consumed me, and my gut-feeling said Terey wouldn't hurt me.

The same gut-feeling that said I couldn't resurrect Paulie.

"I can't promise the spell will work, Terey." Despite her shriveled face and shrug of defeat, I envisioned the hidden strength inside her flamingo-body. "And if it doesn't, you've got to promise not to get mad."

She didn't respond. "Strands of ivy, strands of ivy," she muttered, racing across the shop toward the front door.

I didn't like being alone with Paulie. He looked so . . . dead. Momentarily, I considered vomiting. But I didn't want to reveal any kind of weakness in front of Annie, Mercy, and Chasdick. They had been so brave. They had come to my rescue at the risk of being injured. Or killed.

Instead of focusing on Paulie, I focused on the charm's ingredients. I needed a full-boogie candle, not a stub, preferably a green candle. My chalk supply was low, but would have to do. Chastity's journal or Davy's typed pages would include the words to the charm. I'd never memorized it, figuring I'd never use it.

The moon, my ally, shone through the sun porch windows.

Journal or typed pages? The journal looked more authentic.

As I returned to the shop, so did Terey, her arms full of ivy.

"I couldn't remember how many strands," she said, holding back tears.

I pulled a jar of powdered chalk from the shelf. At the same time I thought: *It won't take long to bind a wreath.*

"I'm glad you brought extra," I told Terey. "Sit on the floor. No, not next to Paulie. Over by the stuffed lizard. Start braiding ivy, three strands at a time."

Retrieving a candle-filled carton from my wall cabinet, I placed it by her feet. "When you finish the ivy, find a green candle. Green works best."

I sat in the armchair, journal in hand. "Okay, Terey, let's begin. Who killed Clive and why?"

"I killed Clive. Because he ditched me."

"Ditched you? Oh my God, you're the girlfriend. The mysterious girlfriend."

"Is that so hard to believe?"

"No. It's just . . . well, you're so much older than Clive. Not that age matters." I held up the journal. "Chastity Barker . . . the woman who wrote this journal . . . is older than the man she loves. His name is Rueben and he gives her bacon and fish and . . ." *Stop babbling, Sydney.*

"I was Clive's first," Terey said. "He couldn't get enough of me. I realized he'd stray once he started to get famous, but he always came back. To me. I hate to brag, Sydney, but no other woman could satisfy him like I could. Then he and The Newts went to Vegas and he found someone who was almost up to my speed. I told him to get rid of her."

"He did get rid of her, after beating her to a bloody pulp."

"You know about The Rose?"

"Yes. She said Clive called his girlfriend Mother Theresa. It flew right past me. I never caught it."

"His big joke, ha-ha. He got rid of Rose, but then he got rid of me. He didn't want to be shackled. Can you imagine? 'Shackled.' What a stupid word."

"When did Paulie enter the picture?"

"Clive told me how much Paulie hated him, how Paulie blamed Clive for his downsizing. I took a chance, asked Paulie to help me."

"Help you kill Clive?"

She nodded. "I'm strong enough, but I thought I'd chicken out. Of course, I rewarded Paulie well. At thirty-five, he hadn't experienced much in the way of sex, and I'm very good. It comes naturally, somehow."

"Membretoon gipsyfilly."

"If Ma had been half as good," Terey continued, ignoring Mercy, "my daddy would have stuck around."

"Where did you keep Clive's, um, body parts?"

"In my backyard. The storage shed. No one ever goes in there. Molly nosed around, but the smell of formaldehyde put her off."

"Why did you send Clive's fingers and toes to The Newts?"

"That was Paulie's idea. He thought the cops would pin the murder on one of the members who'd been dropped from the group."

"And the ear?"

"I wanted Ma to get the scoop, print the story first. The *Monthly* has been losing money hand over fist. But Ma thought it was an ear from Mr. Potato Head, so I used a pay phone, put some tissues over the mouthpiece and gave her the 'Clive tip.' Shouldn't we hurry, Sydney? Or does time matter?"

"A few more minutes won't hurt. Why did you kill Veronica?" I watched Terey put down one braided ivy and pick up three new strands. "You have to answer me or I won't cast the spell. Why did you kill Veronica?"

"I didn't."

"Paulie killed her?"

"No."

"Who, then? Yogi?"

"Yes."

"No, he didn't. You're lying. Okay, I'm leaving."

"Wait, Sydney, please. Mary Lou killed Veronica."

"Mary Lou DiNardo? Paulie's mother? You've got to be kidding." I peered at her face. "You're not kidding."

"At a meeting, last Thursday night, Veronica said she'd think about rehiring Paulie. He told his mother. She paid Veronica a visit Friday night, asked her if she'd made up her mind, yes or no? She said no."

"Mary Lou's too old. She doesn't have enough strength—"

"Veronica was out of it, weak as a kitten. She'd taken a prescription drug, some kind of major-league painkiller. Mary Lou said Veronica said she had a toothache."

So much for my toothache charm. If I couldn't cure a toothache, how could I bring a dead person back to life?

"But Paulie had an ace up his sleeve," I said. "Martina."

"Mary Lou didn't know about Martina. Paulie hadn't told her. Because Martina's Jewish. When he finally told her, last Sunday, she wasn't happy."

"She wouldn't be happy with you, either."

"I'm Catholic."

"Half Catholic."

"I've braided all the ivies, Sydney."

"Open the carton and look for a green candle. Why did you kidnap Jessica?"

"Paulie needed money. He said we'd fly to Vegas and get married."

Her declaration sounded uncertain, and once again I remembered the song from *Bye Bye Birdie*—going steady, steady, steady for good.

"We hid Jessica inside the same motel where Paulie strangled John because the locks were so easy to jimmy," she continued in an angry-whiney voice. "We weren't going to ask for much, maybe five thousand, but your brother changed his phone number. By the time we'd changed our game plan, you'd found Jessica."

"Damn it, Terey, she almost died."

"So what? Jessica got what she deserved. What goes around comes around."

"Excuse me?"

"Sydney, you're the only woman who's ever been truly kind to me. You're my best friend. So when Jessica threatened to kill you—"

"I told you. On the phone. She didn't threaten to kill me."

"It sounded like a threat. You're too nice to know the difference."

"People don't go around killing people," I said, then realized how ridiculous that sounded. "If I'm so 'truly kind,' how could you allow Paulie to kill me?"

"I figured Davy would bring you back to life."

"Davy?"

"When we were in high school he took me to the movies. On our way home we came across a dog who'd been run over. Poor thing looked like roadkill. Davy chanted something. The dog got up, licked Davy's hand, and limped away."

I remembered Davy's words: "I know I'm not a real wizard, and I know my spells are, for the most part, scams."

For the most part. Apparently, Davy hadn't scammed the dog.

What incantation had he used? Not the Transpose Death Into Life charm. That charm required a candle, and one didn't tote candles to the movies.

"Sydney, there's only one green candle. Do you need more than one?"

"No. One's enough. I hope you understand, Terey. If I resurrect Paulie, he'll have to go to the hospital. And I'll have to turn you over to the police."

"Mary Lou, too?"

"Mary Lou, too," I said, thinking I sounded like the bubbled, bubbly Billie Burke, the good witch of Oz, when she told Dorothy: *Toto too.*

"I don't care," Terey said. "Just one favor. Let me call Ma, first, so she can have the scoop."

"Sure." I stood up and retrieved a candle holder from a shelf near the Harry Potter mugs. "Put the green candle in this, then bring me one of the braided ivies."

Ivy in hand, I formed a wreath. Trying not to breathe, I placed it on Paulie's dead head.

"Here's the book, Sydney."

"Thanks." I put the journal on the counter, picked up the pack of matches, and lit the green candle.

Then, trying not to breathe again, I sprinkled powdered chalk on Paulie. The chalk matched the color of his waxy face.

"Hurry, Sydney."

"There's no hurry, Terey. Relax. It'll either work or it won't."

"It'll work. I know it'll work. Just like the dog."

I remembered Anne's advice to Chastity. *If you believe in witchcraft, it works. If someone other than you believes, 'twould be even more favorable.*

Maybe Terey's certainty would make up for my lack of faith.

"White of bone," I chanted, reading from the journal. "Dark of shade. Of dust and night. Death is made. Death thy self. Death thy peer. What I hold. I do not fear. Thus bone to flesh. And shade to leaf. Death my dear. I give thee life."

I turned the page. The next incantation was for the ivies planted round the oak, but I figured it couldn't hurt. "Bone be flesh. Shade be leaf. As death is thine. It bears thee life." Then, just for good measure, I added, "So mote it be."

If possible, Paulie looked even more dead than before.

Someone should close his eyes, I thought, but I'm not touching him.

I swiveled toward Terey. "I'm sorry, sweetie. I tried. Honest."

Chasdick woofed, Annie mewed, Mercy squawked, *"Fawning, flap-skinned hedge-pig,"* and Terey said, "Look!"

I looked.

Paulie blinked.

Then he moaned.

I knew my mouth gaped open, and shut it so hard my teeth clicked.

Maybe Paulie hadn't really been dead; a wrist pulse isn't as accurate as a neck pulse. Maybe the spell truly worked. But if it worked, why hadn't Chastity brought Obadiah back to life? Maybe she had. Maybe the missing journal pages revealed the transposition. Maybe, maybe, maybe.

Spell or no spell, if Paulie didn't get help soon he'd die all over again.

Somehow, I managed to strip off my too-tight T-shirt. Goodbye Frank Zappa.

"Terey," I said, "use this to try and staunch Paulie's blood. I'm going across the street to a neighbor's house.

Davy's there. He can help while I call 911. Okay?"

"Okay. Please hurry."

I didn't trust Chasdick, who looked unbelievably pleased with himself. For all I knew, he'd attack again, once he realized Paulie wasn't dead any more.

"Chasdick, come," I said, snapping my fingers. He didn't move. "Chastity, come," I said, giving in to Aunt Lillian's ancestor-claim.

My Lab followed at my heels as, dressed in bra and jeans, I ran across the street and knocked on Lynn Whitacre's door.

Chapter Forty

Monday morning

I sat up in bed and watched John get dressed. Awkwardly donning a pair of jeans, he sang "Bloody Fingers," composed during his hospital stay.

John Stewart,
Once a schoolmaster,
Kept three bumblebees
Under a stone
And fed them with drops
Of blood from his fingers.

Agnes Waterfield
Of Hatfield Peveril
Owned a cat
With white spots on its fur;
The cat told Agnes
To call it Satan
And feed it with drops
Of blood from her fingers.

Nanny Morgan
Of Much Wenlock,
Murdered in eighteen fifty-seven,
Had a whole box full
Of toads in her closet . . .

I was so relieved to hear John singing. Overcoming my irrational fear of hospitals, I'd spent last Friday in his room, my rump glued to his hospital bed. Most of the time he slept, drugged to the max, so I finally read my brother's new book. And could understand why it hit the bestseller list. Too bad, in real life, Oliver didn't have a clue.

Saturday John and I watched the Colorado Rockies play the Dodgers on his overhead hospital TV. Sunday we did the *New York Times* crossword puzzle (in ink). Nina joined us, toting goodies, and I regained the five pounds I'd lost worrying about John.

After his discharge from the hospital, early this morning, he had visited his mother. Then, me.

"Why don't you let me help you get dressed?" I said, watching him try to button a crisp white shirt. "You're clumsier than a one-armed paper hanger."

He gave me a smile to die for. "That's because I can only use one arm, you silly girl. And until my other arm heals, I've got to learn to fend for myself."

I pulled my knees, then the bed sheet, up to my chin. "You're not bad for a one-armed 'conjoiner.' "

"That's because I had help."

"No, you didn't. The love talisman is over there." I pointed to my bureau.

"Sydney, all I can say is . . . you're wonderful."

Actually, John had been wonderful. I never would have believed that a man lying on his back, one arm in a sling, could do so many wonderful things with one hand, four fingers, and a thumb.

My cheeks baked at the remembrance; time to change the subject. "I don't know if you've heard, John, but Paulie's been upgraded to 'serious' rather than 'critical.' "

My gaze touched upon the *Manitou Falls Monthly*, balanced precariously on top of my antique hops cauldron. Gusta had put out a Special Edition. The headline read: WOLF ATTACKS BOY THAT KILLED CLIVE NEWTON.

"Gusta's headlines piss me off," I said. "Paulie hasn't been a 'boy' for twenty years. Grammatically, 'that' should have been 'who.' And Terey was the one that/who killed Clive."

I didn't mention the wolf. The cops had wanted to impound Chasdick, but Aunt Lillian swore up and down that a wolf had come out of nowhere and savagely attacked Paulie. Terey, for whatever reason, corroborated her story. Paulie, of course, couldn't talk.

My feeling was that the cops believed the imaginary wolf my "familiar" and didn't want to pursue the matter any further.

Terey had been jailed. Whereupon, Gusta hired the Manitou Falls attorney who was older than God. He planned to submit an insanity plea. Mary Lou and Paulie DiNardo were on their own, although it was rumored that Mary Lou had called Cool Hand.

"I wonder what he said."

"Who?" John walked over to my bed.

"Cool Hand. Sorry . . . thinking out loud. Mary Lou supposedly called him."

"No, Sydney. She called Martina Brustein. Mary Lou said something about Martina finding her 'a good Jew lawyer.' Martina slammed the receiver down."

"It's hard to believe Mary Lou killed Veronica, although Terey did say Paulie said his mother would kill for him."

"Mary Lou's fairly strong, Sydney. Biking develops muscles. Even drugged out, Veronica could have fought back, maybe even trounced the old woman, but I'm sure she didn't consider Mary Lou a threat. Veronica was totally caught off guard."

"Just like you, when Paulie attacked you at the motel. And

backstage. How'd you hear about Mary Lou and Martina? From Yogi?"

"Yup. He came to visit me in the hospital." Sitting on the bed, John began to stroke my knees.

For the first time in my life, I realized that knees were an erogenous zone. "Did Yogi beg you to write songs for The Newts?"

"Not at first. By the way, they're changing their name to 'Yogi Demon and The Newts.' Eventually, he begged. Said he couldn't offer me a million dollars, but if they won a Grammy he'd give it to me."

"And you said?"

"I said yes. It's never been about money, Sydney. I couldn't care less about the money. It's always been Nalin."

"What made you change your mind?"

"You did."

"Me?"

"I can deal with Nalin now, thanks to you."

"But I didn't say anything noteworthy."

"It was your reference to the duck pond and the water test. When you said I'd float if I was guilty, drown if I was blameless, I realized I couldn't just mourn and put Nalin's death behind me. I had to blame somebody. So I blamed me. And, indirectly, The Newts."

"I hope you don't think you could have prevented your father's stroke."

"No. It was inevitable. He's a workaholic. My mother tried to find me, even went to the police. If I had turned myself in, I would have heard sooner."

"Woulda/coulda doesn't fly, John."

Briefly, I thought about all the mistakes I'd made in my life. I still wasn't sure I believed in witchcraft, but I couldn't explain the golden candle or Paulie's resurrection, and I knew that, in the future, I'd have more respect for white magic.

"I've got to be there for Dad," John said. "And I miss my daughter. I'll come back as soon as I can, I promise."

"If you don't, I'll put a spell on you."

"What kind of spell?"

Before I could reply, I heard a woman scream.

The sound came from above my head.

"We found them," Davy yelled at the top of his lungs. "Lynn found the missing pages."

"I did not," Lynn shouted. "Mercy found them."

"Bring them to the kitchen," I shouted back. "Do you have time for a cup of coffee, John?"

"Sure." Giving my knees one last pat, he rose from the bed and walked over to the suitcase he'd retrieved from his mom's house. With one hand, he zipped it open and rummaged through its contents. "This is for you," he said, tossing me a shirt.

"Thanks, John, but I finally did my laundry."

"It's a keepsake."

I gazed down at the tee. Green. White lettering: THE NEWTS.

What goes around comes around. I had watched John. Now he watched me. Flinging aside the sheet, I found the floor with my toes, donned a bra and my new/old Newts tee, then retrieved my cutoffs from a bureau drawer.

John's eyes were warm, appreciative. He'd been totally sincere about my curvature and I thought: *Forget the excess fifteen (or twenty) pounds; I like me the way I am. Maybe I'll line Mercy's cage with my Weight Winners gift certificate.*

Entering the kitchen, I said, "Where did you find the pages, Davy?"

"It was Lynn's idea," he replied. "We carried Mercy up

into the attic and she made a beeline . . . well, I guess she made a parrot line . . . for her old bird cage. She was squawking that Jack Horner nursery rhyme, you know, stuck in his thumb and pulled out a plum."

"Slow down, Davy. Breathe."

"I can't, Syd. I'm too excited. Mercy seemed to know that someone had lined her old cage with pages from Chastity's journal."

"Oliver's ditzy bride, Bambi, lined Mercy's cage. During the reconstruction of—"

"I'll never understand why Oliver hooked up with Bambi. She has no respect for books. I'm not even sure she can read."

I didn't mention Davy's brief addiction to Rosie-all-fall-down. "Nina gave us a brand new cage, a housewarming gift. Carol toted the old cage up to the attic. Mercy couldn't have known that the journal pages lined her old bird cage, Davy. She simply remembered her old cage."

"For they're hangin' men and women there for wearin' o' the green," my parrot squawked from her perch.

It took me a minute. "You don't like my Newts shirt? Silly bird. Oh, look. Now she's preening in front of her mirror, taking full credit for finding the pages. Wake up and smell the coffee, Mercy. It was a lucky accident."

Aunt Lillian, who brewed coffee, gave a derisive snort. Then she said, "Are all the pages there?"

"I don't know." Davy thrust the pages at me. "Are they, Syd?"

I squinted at the yellowing paper, filled with squiggles. "Chastity didn't take chapter breaks, but she numbered every page. The first two, following Obadiah's strangulation, are indecipherable. As far as I can tell, the rest seem okay. Let's cheat, Davy. Call Oliver and ask him to look inside the family Bible. It would have the name of Chastity's baby. And her new name, if she remarried."

"But as soon as John leaves, we'll decipher—"

"I'll call." Quivering like a bird dog, Aunt Lillian headed for the phone. She said hello to my brother, made her request, waited, thanked him, then hung up. "Chastity had a girl . . . Rebecca."

"Did she ever become Chastity Cavin?"

"If she did, it's not in the Bible."

"Damn," I said, as Davy gave me a smug look.

"I think Chastity's daughter kept a journal," Aunt Lillian said. "But I don't remember her married name. Or maybe it was Chastity's daughter's daughter."

"I don't have time for that coffee after all." John scowled at the clock. "Aunt Lillian, I'll send you an e-mail as soon as I hit California."

"E-mail?" Davy and I said together.

Aunt Lillian beamed. "John bought me a computer. My e-mail name is Lillith. She was a woman of the night, you know."

John bent down, kissed her cheek, then hugged Lynn and Davy.

"I'll walk you to the door." I grasped John's hand. Descending stairs, I said, "You do realize that Aunt Lillian will try and e-mail all our dead ancestors."

"Yup."

"You devil."

Opening the front door, I gave John a mouth-to-mouth-resuscitation kiss. I still didn't know if I was in love with him, or in lust with him, but the kiss would have to keep until he returned.

Unfortunately, I had no spell to bring *him* back.

"Sydney," he said, "are you crying?"

"No," I sobbed, as tears blurred my eyes. "Witches can't weep."

Chastity Barker's Journal

October, 1692

This morning I listened to the wind. I lay down in the midst of tall trees, closed my eyes, and felt the earth support my body. Wind voices began to whisper—"Chastity Barker, Chastity Barker." They soughed through the leaves. Matters may go wrongly, they sighed, but everyone I held dear would, in the end, be unharmed.

'Twas Anne who charted our course. She insisted her 'poppet' stay to home, but darkness no longer frightens me. In truth, the only thing that frightens me is Rueben Cavin. Or rather, my feelings for Rueben. 'Tis not seemly to lose one's heart so quickly, even though I now comprehend that Jack was a passing fancy whilst Rueben is forever.

I know he loves me. This time I am not mistaken. As soon as we are pledged, we shall scandalize the congregation by joining together in wedlock. I reject the fundamental waiting period. I shall not play the hypocrite, nor shall I unduly mourn my dead husband, who treated me with cruelty and neglect. If necessary, I shall ask Rueben to sell our land and we shall move elsewhere—though I pray it does not come to that.

In all haste, I now pen the scheme Anne dreamed up.

Shortly before eventide, Mercy told several goodwives that Trump had been sighted near the field where Matt Grayson was slain.

Mercy said that Trump's black beast of a dog had witnessed Matt's murder. Since the dog and Trump oft conversed, Trump now knew who Matt's killer was, and he wanted Widow Barker to meet him in the field where the Lady in Red moans on nights o' the full moon.

Tonight there would be a full moon, Mercy stated. But 'twas rumoured that John Winthrop walked, mayhap hand-in-hand with the Lady in Red. Therefore, Chastity Barker dared not leave her house.

As Anne surmised, the goodwives spread Mercy's tale throughout the village. One goodwife even told it back to Mercy.

No one knows that Trump fled from a charge of sorcery, or that his black dog died. During Obadiah's funeral, Trump stayed hidden, up in the loft. He grieves for Obadiah, but does so in the manner of a dog who displays distress at the loss of a master, unmindful of his master's brutal nature.

All being well, Mercy's tale shall reach the ears of the man who killed Matt—Anne still believes 'tis Jack—and he shall impose upon the cornfield.

Anne and Mercy's goodmen, John and Toby, lay in wait, along with Jonathan Corwin, one of the magistrates.

Trump, the bait, left an hour ago.

After tonight, I do not know if I shall ever pen my thoughts again. The wind assured me that everyone I held dear would be unharmed.

But the wind did not say that I would be unharmed.

Salem Village

31 October, 1692

Chastity heard a board creak.

The sound came from the bedroom.

Obadiah's disembodied soul?

She almost laughed out loud. If her dead husband's spirit haunted her, surely he would bypass the worn-out board.

'Twas verily a mortal stalker. She felt her eyes widen with dread. Then she stiffened her shoulders and lifted her chin.

Fear was a familiar cloak, but she had vowed to modify her vestments.

She snuffed out all her candles. Moonlight, however, shone through the window, shadowing the room. She eyed the heavy musket above the fireplace. She had never fired a musket, nor did she think she could, though she had oft seen Obadiah pull back the matchlock and sprinkle powder in the flashpan. Grasping a keen-edged knife, she flattened herself against the wall, next to the bedroom door.

The door inched open. She saw a boot and breeches, just before the door blocked her view.

She heard the stomp of boots. Then, as if he were surprised by the sight of an empty room, the hunter's footsteps slowed and stopped near the table.

Chastity toed the door shut.

Despite the dim, shadowy moonlight, she recognized the tall man who possessed rough-hewn features and a nose that the devil might have tweaked in passing.

"Lud, Rueben," she said, walking forward and placing her knife on the table. "You scared me unto death. Why did you

338

not enter through the front door?"

"I was told Mercy's tale, Chastity, and hoped you would be alone."

She smiled. "Until one is wed, 'tis not seemly to climb through a bedroom window. Did you wish to surprise me?"

"Nay. Kill you."

She continued smiling, of a certainty she'd misunderstood his words.

When he did not clarify, her smile faded and all she could say was, "Why?"

"I want your land."

"But should we wed, my land will be yours."

"Did you believe we would wed? What a dunce you are, Chastity. 'Tis the respect of the congregation I crave, as well as land. You are much too outspoken, my dear, and would surely hold me back."

"What mean you, Rueben? Back from what?"

"I wish to become Governor some day. You are fit for bedding, my dear, but I need a wife who is more well-bred. A wife with a dowry."

"Ketzia Van Rijn," Chastity gasped.

"Aye."

"But she pledged herself to Jack Grayson."

Rueben shook his head. "Jack is on his way to the cornfield. My guess is that a magistrate lies in wait. Jack plans to meet up with Trump, who does not know the name of Matt's killer. If he knew, he would have told you."

"Trump asked to meet me in the field where the Red Lady moans."

"You forget, Chastity. You sent Trump to me. On foot. After I received your letter, I rode across my fields and tied my horse to your oak tree."

"*Belle sainte vierge*, you killed Obadiah. Why, Rueben, why?"

"Are you hard of hearing, my dear? I want your land. Sick as he appeared to be, Obadiah would not gainsay my request. In truth, he would not stop singing."

Before she could think twice, Chastity threw herself at Rueben, raised her arm, and sent a violent, resounding smack across his face.

Off-balance, surprised by her assault, he fell backward.

With her fingernails, she scraped her knife from the table.

Sinking to her knees, she secured the blade against his throat.

Arms wrapped themselves around her upper body. "Drop the knife," a voice said in her ear. "If you vant to breathe, you vill do as I say."

Chastity flung her knife at the nearest wall.

All the same, thin, strong arms squeezed until spots began to obscure her vision. She prayed to keep her wits, but knew her prayers were in vain. Wits required breath. Barely mindful that she was in a room, much less her room, she felt herself dragged up from the floor and slammed, hard, onto a chair. She tried to sit straight but could only sprawl. Slowly, inch by painful inch, she slid from the chair to the floor again.

"Ve do not have much time," she heard Ketzia tell Rueben. "Jack is dead. Ve vill talk of that later. The men vill stop to collect Mercy Birdwell and Anne Kittridge, but then they vill come here."

Chastity felt less dizzy. Somehow, she managed to sit up and lean her back against a table leg.

Rueben retrieved the knife and tested its blade against his thumb. He smiled, and Chastity thought she had never seen anything so evil in her life.

"Trump hones a knife well," he said.

"Nay," Ketzia said. "Nay, Rueben, not the knife. Ve vill carry her to the spring and drown her. 'Twas a mistake, stabbing Matt. I vant this death to appear unforeseen."

"I would not be suspect."

"But I vould. I've not hidden my disregard for the vench." An expression of contempt shaded her face. "If you had not stopped her from being hanged as a vitch, ve vould not be in this situation."

"She is with child, Ketzia, and would not be hanged until after she whelped. I could not wait months for my land."

"Nay, Rueben, she is plump. Are thee with child, Chastity?"

How to answer? Would Ketzia treat her more gently if she said aye? The best answer, Chastity decided, was no answer. Shutting her eyes, she groaned.

"Are thee with child?" Ketzia repeated.

"Why did you kill Matt?" Chastity countered, blinking open her eyes.

"He pledged himself to me, then lay with the servant girl." She glared at Rueben, as if to remind him that perfidy meant death. "Jack helped me rope his brother to the crosspiece. 'Tis the reason he wanted to confront Trump."

And you ne're asked Jack why he was in the field, Chastity thought. Strange how one can deceive oneself. Of a certainty, Jack had lain with Sally, and Chastity now saw Rueben for what he truly was. Strong on the outside, weak on the inside.

"Then Jack lay with you," Ketzia continued. "He played me for a fool."

And you played him for an accomplice, Chastity thought, then sent him to his death.

She ached for what might have been, had Jack not been corruptible.

Stroking her belly, she said, " 'Tis Jack's babe. He planned to raise it as a foundling, after you and he wed."

She did not say she had foiled his rape scheme and would

have foiled that scheme, too.

Uncertainty flickered in Ketzia's eyes. Killing a woman did not bother her overmuch. A woman with child, however, seemed to give her pause.

"Had I known about the babe I vould not have caused you pain," she said, helping Chastity rise. "You have my promise that your death vill be quick and painless."

Even Rueben looked bemused at her declaration.

Chastity did not respond. As she tried to devise a means of escape, Rueben hooked an arm about her waist and guided her toward the door.

He opened the door and pushed her outside. She thought she heard voices in the distance, but mayhap 'twas the wind.

Apparently, Ketzia heard the same sound. "Ve must hurry," she said.

The words had barely left her mouth before a huge shape lunged itself at Rueben. Teeth and gums exposed in a macabre grin, Old Scratch went for Rueben's throat.

Chastity had oft seen her hound worry a bone till Doomsday, so a mere throat did not present much of a challenge.

Rueben, on the ground, tried to free himself from the dog's deadly grip.

Ketzia just stood there, as if she were Lot's wife, as if God had turned her into a pillar of salt.

Old Scratch finally moved away, still growling low in his throat.

Rueben's chest did not rise and fall. His open eyes stared at the moon as Anne and Mercy and their goodmen crested a small rise. When Anne and Mercy saw that something appeared amiss, they increased their pace.

Ketzia spared one look at Rueben before she grasped her skirts and ran.

As though a giant hand had shaken her awake, Ketzia spared one look at Rueben before she grasped her skirts and ran.

" 'Twas Ketzia who killed Matt," Chastity told her sisters. "She and Rueben schemed to drown me. Stop her before she gets away."

"Nay, she shall not escape," Mercy said, then murmured some words under her breath.

Chastity did not hear her sister's incantation, but Ketzia stopped as if struck by lightning.

As Chastity drew nigh, she saw Ketzia lean against the oak tree.

The moon shone. No clouds marred its brilliance. Ketzia began to vomit. Pieces of brass, bodkins, egg-shells, bones, and other objects gushed from her mouth. Finally, after one last violent heave, she brought up a row of pins neatly stuck in blue paper.

"If you try to flee again," Chastity said, "I shall summon lice and spiders."

Chastity Barker's Journal
31 October, 1692

Everyone has departed, even Trump, who helped transport Rueben Cavin to the cornfield. There, he shall lie beside Jack Grayson, killed by a bolt of lightning. One bolt, Trump said, before the sky calmed anew. Mayhap the shade of Matt Grayson managed the deadly deed.

I must confess that, briefly, I did think about bringing Rueben back to life—if only to test my skills. I would have attempted the Charm when I found Obadiah dead, but before I could light a candle I heard the clatter of hooves. Jack, believing his babe in mortal danger, had returned with Mercy. Thus, I could not recite the Charm, nor could Mercy. Mayhap, in the end, 'twas more charitable that way. Having lost his wits, Obadiah did not want to live.

I do not know what will become of Ketzia Van Rijn. Mad as a March hare, she sat near the oak and toyed with one of the bodkins she had vomited. When Magistrate Corwin arrived, along with a number of inquisitive goodmen and goodwives, Ketzia could do naught but babble.

As she did, Anne caught my gaze, crossed her second finger over her first finger, then held up five fingers.

Mercy, who had watched Anne, nodded her head.

Anne's gesture meant that on the morrow, at cock crow, we would come together in our secret cave. There, we would practice witchcraft.